As Singer clutched his wound, blood oozed between his fingers

"Key's in the ignition," he gritted through his teeth.

Mack Bolan slipped under the car and crawled to the other side. He reached the driver's door without exposing himself to enemy fire and snagged the keys.

In one quick move he sprinted to the trunk and opened the lid, then heaved out the footlocker, slamming it down between him and the fence. He pushed it around, flipped the lock and grabbed the Desert Eagle, crouching as a bullet chewed through the trunk lid and cracked the rear window.

Then, looking north along the fence, the Executioner spotted a tall, broad-shouldered man standing on a small rise, staring at the hard site, interested, but above it all. He was also a perfect target.

Bolan sighted well to the left of the big man and pumped a round into a patch of weeds. The guy looked down at the ground with disdain.

Then, with a small salute, the Trained Wolf turned and slowly walked into the fog.

Accolades for America's greatest hero Mack Bolan

DON PENDLETON's

MACK BOLAN.

DEATH'S HEAD

A GOLD EAGLE BOOK FROM

WORLDWIDE.

TORONTO • NEW YORK • LONDON
AMSTERDAM • PARIS • SYDNEY • HAMBURG
STOCKHOLM • ATHENS • TOKYO • MILAN
MADRID • WARSAW • BUDAPEST • AUCKLAND

First edition April 1994

ISBN 0-373-61435-7

Special thanks and acknowledgment to
Roland Green for his contribution to this work.

DEATH'S HEAD

Printed in U.S.A.

Stand your ground, men. Don't fire unless fired upon. But if they mean to have a war, let it begin here.

—Captain Jonas Parker, to the minutemen on Lexington Green as the redcoats deployed, April 19, 1775

When you're forced to strike a blow in your own defense, don't waste time on feeling guilty. All guilt does is make you an easier target for the next person who comes after you.

—Mack Bolan

PROLOGUE

Thuringia, Eastern Germany
April 1945

The tunnels had wound deep into the hills for centuries. Some were natural caves. Most were old silver workings, going back to the Middle Ages. All were drier than usual, which was important for the storage of most of what the Polish and Czech slave laborers had been loading into the tunnels for two weeks.

"We ought to have stainless-steel barrels for the Compound 58," Helmut Kuhn remembered saying. "Even minor leakage could endanger German soldiers." The general director had merely shaken his head, and now Kuhn knew why. Even a year earlier in the spring of 1944, the Reich had been running out of stainless steel.

Kuhn felt a queasiness that the wartime breakfast of ersatz coffee, bread and jam couldn't explain. The general director had lied to him about that. Could they also have lied to him about how the gas was tested? They said condemned criminals, but now he wondered.

A handcart rumbled by, with five barrels of Compound 58 and assorted ammunition boxes roughly lashed to it. Six laborers pushed, six more pulled. The laborers' clothes were sweat-darkened, ragged and baggy, and not only because they'd been cut that way.

The men inside were half-starved. A thousand calories a day was their ration, if they were lucky.

The handcart rolled past Kuhn, then turned into the Blue Tunnel. "Halt!" Kuhn shouted. The man in charge of the handcart crew stared at him.

"Halt!" Kuhn shouted again, then tried to remember what little Polish he knew. "The load must be divided. The boxes go down the Yellow Tunnel. The barrels go down the Blue."

The man frowned. He didn't look any smarter than the rest of his breed of ass-lickers. How to explain the danger of mixing Compound 58 barrels and ammunition without giving away state secrets? These fools probably didn't care if the gas contaminated the Werewolves' stored weapons or not.

A Waffen-SS *Schar fuhrer* came hurrying along the tunnel. "What are these pigs doing!" he screamed. "Sabotage? We've a dozen more loads on the way, and the Russians are almost in artillery range!"

He unslung his machine gun, stepped back against the wall and aimed it. "I count three, and you pigs are back to work or I shoot."

"God Almighty!" Kuhn muttered. A round could easily pierce a weak spot in one of those barrels, and every one of them had to have a few. Then there would be Compound 58 all over the tunnel, and nothing living in it.

Dr. Helmut Kuhn was even more analytical than a chemist had to be. He had once quarreled with his wife, Gerda, over the amount of time he took to choose the color of his socks. He had lost some of his faith in that sort of analysis in the past few years, as Germany slid into the abyss.

The SS man, however, was one of those hard cases who thought the scientist had his head in the clouds. He paid for that mistake in the next moment, as Kuhn calmly reached over and snatched the weapon from his hands.

The sling caught on the back of the man's helmet, but only tipped it over his eyes. He lashed out blindly with one hand, going for his P-38 side arm with the other. The fist hit only empty air, and by the time the other hand reached the pistol Kuhn had the machine gun aimed and ready.

"You idiot!" he snapped at the SS man. "That's fuel for the Werewolves! Do you want them to die because you've set it—"

The guard spewed curses at everything but kept his pistol pointed away from both Kuhn and the barrels. Then he swung it toward something the chemist couldn't see. As Kuhn turned, he saw one of the slave laborers cautiously sidling along the wall, back toward the entrance.

"No, my friend," the SS man said, almost affectionately. Then he shot the laborer in the head. Everyone, even the crew chief, froze during the moment it took the man to fall.

Without any analysis at all, Kuhn concluded that the time had come to consider the danger to others.

The laborer sprawled on the rock floor, blood puddling around his head. The sergeant stepped toward him, holstering the P-38, so complete was his contempt for the rest of the work crew.

The moment the SS man's gray-clad back was turned, Kuhn raised the machine gun to miss both the barrels and the work party, then squeezed the trigger. Ten 9 mm rounds stitched the sergeant messily from the back of his head to his waist, flinging him forward on top of his victim. His feet kicked briefly, then jailer's and prisoner's blood mingled on the rock floor.

"Run!" Kuhn said, pointing toward the tunnel entrance. He thought he shouted, but he suspected it came out a croak. The laborers heard him, at least, and started hurrying away.

The chemist looked up and down the tunnel. Luck had been with him. He'd given way to his impulse in a bend of the tunnel hidden from both ends. Quickly he dropped the machine gun on top of the bodies. It wouldn't fool anybody for long into believing the two men had shot each other. It also wouldn't need to.

Not wanting to be completely unarmed, he retrieved the SS sergeant's P-38 and stuffed it into the waistband of his trousers under his uniform tunic. Then Kuhn hurried for the open air on the heels of the laborers. As he ran he started shouting, "Gas! Gas! Clear the mine! Gas alert!"

As a way of getting everybody's attention, it was a complete success. It also succeeded in getting everybody moving toward the open air, guards and laborers alike. Nobody stopped to think that the most dangerous gas, methane, was seldom found in silver mines. Everybody was too concerned about getting out of the dark underground before the explosion.

When the explosions did come, they weren't underground. They were four Russian 152 mm shells, a sighting salvo from a long-range battery whose observers had just reached a ridge eight kilometers away where they could spot the camp and the tunnels.

The explosions divided the fleeing men into those who were running even faster, and those who would never run again. Kuhn was one of those still on his feet. He knew he had one more obligation before he let those feet carry him out of the camp and away from the battlefield.

He had to find his son, Erich. He'd promised his wife he'd take care of the boy. He had done so, too, in spite of Erich's occasional defeatist talk, and not just because of his promise. His son would make a fine chemist someday.

Now—where had Erich been, the last time they'd talked? Down by the road, supervising the unloading of whatever was brought by the convoy that had come in the previous night.

Kuhn turned downhill—then was knocked flat, as the next salvo struck. It was aimed at the bridge over the nameless little stream curling around the north end of the village. Being a little overaimed, it landed on the trucks parked at the foot of the hill. Five of the eight still had full loads of ammunition.

The blast wiped out the trucks and everything else over a radius of fifty meters. Shrapnel butchered men farther away than Kuhn, but he was lucky. He'd been knocked down behind the cover of a boulder.

He desperately wanted to stay on the chill, damp ground until his ears stopped ringing and his brain started working. The "sacred soil of the Fatherland" was more comfortable than he'd ever dreamed it could be. Death would be even more comfortable. It wouldn't come to him as easily as it must have to Erich, but it wouldn't be hard, either. All he had to do was lie a little longer, until the Russian tanks came rolling up to the remains of the bridge. . . .

The Soviet observers seemed to be having a bad day. The next salvo was wide, to the left. It struck behind Kuhn, in the tunnel mouth among six handcarts loaded with ammunition.

If Kuhn had been standing, the tongue of flame and shrapnel from the explosion would have mowed him down. Instead he rolled over, curled nearly into a ball and listened to the rumble and crash of falling rock. The blast had found a geological fault somewhere in the mountain.

When Kuhn finally stood, most of the village had collapsed. One blackened circle marked where the trucks had been. Another patch of blackened earth and smoking rock marked the entrance to the mine.

On the far side of the stream, somebody was waving furiously. Kuhn made a rude gesture at him and started up the hill. While looking back, he nearly stumbled over a dead guard, holding a Mauser rifle. Kuhn was tempted to arm himself, then counted the rounds in the man's pockets. A bolt-action rifle with fifteen rounds wasn't worth the trouble to carry, and it was harder to conceal than the pistol.

The best way to desert was to look as if he'd never been in the army in the first place. That meant civilian clothes, to begin with, then a place in the stream of refugees heading west away from the Russians.

With luck, he might even get as far as the spearheads of the Americans, who were a technically sophisticated people. They would know that even if there was no more Germany there were many Germans with useful skills....

Helmut Kuhn took the dead guard's socks, stuffed them in his pocket and began his long walk into the future.

CHAPTER ONE

Southern France
The Present

Mack Bolan crouched behind the stone wall surrounding an olive grove. From the road to the warrior's right came the sound of a light truck laboring up a grade too steep for its weary engine. It was a common sound in that part of France, by day and by night. Farmers hauled everything from calves to empty wine bottles, and smugglers hauled as wide a range of goods, from innocent items such as Spanish leather purses to deadly items such as cocaine and weapons and ammunition for Spain's Basque terrorists.

They called themselves separatists or freedom fighters, but every brand of thug Bolan had ever met had some way of prettying themselves up.

This wasn't the first time the Executioner had chambered a round in his .460 Weatherby rifle for a Basque target. It wasn't even the first time on this mission. Two nights before, he'd picked off the sentries at a Basque training post, then blown up its ammunition dump with well-placed charges of C-4. Some of the Basques had cut and run before Bolan's night vision completely recovered from the explosion. But most had been put down.

That should have been a good start. But there wasn't really anything like a good start to a mission the Executioner shouldn't have been on in the first place.

A FEW DAYS EARLIER Bolan had been briefed and equipped for a mission into Germany. The industries of what had been East Germany were being sold off in what was billed as the largest auction in history. The Mafia was putting in bids for small-arms plants to produce weapons for terrorists, and chemical plants to make designer drugs.

Bolan's first job was to study the intelligence on the bids, both in the Stony Man Farm computers and on the ground in Germany. His second job was to eliminate the most troublesome bidders.

The German intelligence agencies didn't do that kind of work themselves. The national fear of secret-police operations went too deep. With the Mob's infiltration into Russian criminal activities, Germany was trying hard to prevent the same from happening on her soil. If some of the Mafia bidders turned up unexpectedly dead, so much the better.

Then Stony Man Farm received a message from a source too high to be ignored that friendly intelligence agencies wanted Bolan's help while he was in Europe. The target was the Basques, and the "friends" could be English, French, Spanish or all three working together.

"I don't mind doing any of them a favor," Bolan remembered Hal Brognola saying. "Maybe they think we owe them one. If we don't they'll owe us one after this. Fair's fair."

Brognola had been mostly behind a Justice Department desk for the past few years, but he'd been in the field for many years before that. He was as street smart as they came, and knew that both law enforcement and intelligence work depended heavily on both agencies and individuals trading favors. There was nothing in the message that either surprised or bothered him—except one point.

"The problem I have, is how the hell they knew you were on your way to Europe."

Bolan had nodded. The message showed too much explicit knowledge for either of them to doubt that there'd been a leak somewhere.

"Put Aaron on it," the Executioner suggested.

"For starters," was Brognola's reply. Aaron "The Bear" Kurtzman, the wizard of Stony Man's computers, could track any leak in any data-processing system ever invented. He could also penetrate any other system's security, given time.

"Aaron can carry the ball for a few days," the big Fed went on. "Then we'll start going over our human assets. Meanwhile, I don't see any problem with your going ahead with a little work on the Basques. Only make it a fast in-and-out, and try to make it look like the French had a hand in it."

On that point Bolan heartily agreed. Out of dislike for the Spanish or out of political weakness, the French had been easy on Basque terrorists operating out of French territory. If the Basques suddenly lost a few people and started looking over their shoulders for French snipers from the DGSE, it might help more than a few innocents get on with their lives.

Which was, after all, the main reason for the Executioner's career once he'd avenged the deaths of his family, caused, indirectly, by the Mafia. Mack Bolan had given up his chance of a normal life or a peaceful death, to win that chance for hundreds of others who would never know his name or how much they owed him.

THE TRUCK LURCHED into sight. It was the one Bolan was expecting, one of the two that had escaped from the dump site. His Starlite scope confirmed the type—an army-surplus Renault three-quarter tonner with a homemade steel-panel body—the license number, the heavy-duty tires and bumpers and the toolbox on the left front fender.

It also confirmed that there were three people in the cab instead of the two—driver and guard—he'd expected. It was hard to be sure with a night-vision device, but Bolan thought the third person was a woman.

Suddenly the night's mission was a lot more complicated. No straightforward sniping, now. He'd have to immobilize the truck, give the woman a chance to escape, then deal with the terrorists and the cargo.

A round from the Weatherby slammed into the Renault's left front tire. The truck slewed wildly, and a woman's scream pierced the night as the vehicle stopped just short of the ditch on the far side of the road.

Bolan moved his folding-stock Gevarm submachine gun closer, where he could reach it without moving enough to be spotted from the road. He didn't unsling the Weatherby. The truck was well within SMG range, at least for Bolan, but he needed precision and more stopping power than a 9 mm bullet carried. The woman might not run, and more and more criminals and terrorists were showing up with armored vests that could turn .38 or 9 mm rounds at least.

The body armor that could stand up to the Weatherby's massive round hadn't been invented, as far as Bolan knew. Also, at this range the Weatherby carried a nearly one hundred percent chance of a hit with a head shot.

The driver was the first man out. He plunged into the ditch on the near side of the road. Bolan didn't have a chance to get off a shot that wouldn't hit the truck cab. He did see that the man carried an automatic on his belt, a slung subgun and pouches that might hold magazines or grenades.

The combination of weaponry, quick reactions and concealment made him the most dangerous of the three. He would be hard to hit, but he was in a good position to spot Bolan if the Executioner used the Weatherby again.

Also, the bullets could fly both ways, and the terrorist wasn't likely to have any worries about hitting innocents. For Bolan, that ruled out shooting at the truck's gas tank. A miss would just reveal his position. A hit would do the same, and possibly blow up the truck, woman and all.

The warrior could no longer see anyone in the cab. Wasting scarce ammunition on psychological warfare was always risky. Revealing his position was still more so.

Like any good sniper, Bolan had picked several alternate positions commanding the same target. Now he squeezed off a round into the side window. Glass shattered and smashed, and the woman screamed.

She also came into sight again, sprinting through the field beyond the road. She was clawing at her hair as she ran, but anybody moving that fast couldn't be seriously hurt, he knew. A moment later she vanished through a gate in a stone wall that marked the next field, out of sight and out of the line of fire.

Bullets from the ditch spattered the stone wall close to where Bolan had been. They were a good twenty feet wide of where he was now. His new position didn't give him as much cover or concealment, but it did give him a better angle on anybody hiding in the ditch.

The Executioner waited for some sign of movement. When it came, it wasn't from the man in the ditch, but from the terrorist under the truck. The second Basque rolled out from under the vehicle, an automatic in his hand, and squeezed off the rounds.

Flying stone chips stung the Executioner's face. That was too good or too lucky.

Mack Bolan was alive because he could change weapons and tactics as fast as the situation demanded. The Weatherby slid to the ground, and the French Gevarm submachine bucked in his hands as he put half a magazine into the exposed terrorist.

The maneuver revealed his own position, but the demoralizing effect of automatic-weapons' fire slowed the man in the ditch by a few crucial seconds. Bolan was on the move before the next volley of shots struck sparks from the wall.

He worked rapidly along the wall toward an enfilade position on the ditch. It was a gamble: the range would be long for the Gevarm, very long for the Beretta. But if the terrorist moved, he'd lose the cover of the ditch and be an easy target. If he stayed where he was, the Weatherby would put him down.

Again the Basque reacted faster than Bolan expected. He flung himself up out of the ditch, diving over his compatriot's body toward the underside of the truck. The Executioner triggered a burst, heard a high-pitched scream and a torrent of what sounded like Basque curses, then saw the man sprawl under the truck.

His subgun lay under the rear wheels, safely out of his reach, and he hadn't drawn his automatic. That didn't make Bolan relax. These Basques seemed to be of a breed met more and more often among the international terrorist groups—the seasoned professionals, hard to kill and almost impossible to frighten.

Now it was Bolan's turn to use the cover provided by the ditch. He low-crawled along its length until he had a clear view of the rear of the truck. A canvas curtain blocked off his view of the interior. The warrior waited until his eyes recovered their night vision after the glare of the muzzle-flashes, and he studied the curtain.

It wasn't quite as tightly laced as he'd first thought. The bottom eyelets and those a third of the way up either side were empty. The canvas was free to open or close. And was it just the night breeze that made it move gently at the bottom?

Making an easy target of yourself sometimes drew enemy fire and revealed your position. Against these people, it could mean giving them an easy kill.

Bolan slipped a fresh magazine into the subgun and settled down to wait. It would be dawn in another two hours, and somebody might show up then, drawn by the noise of the firefight, or simply roll down the road until they rammed into the back of the Renault.

The waiting turned to anticipation when Bolan saw the truck begin to rock gently. Then to his surprise he heard the cab's right door open with a faint squeal of unoiled hinges. The next sound he heard was a gasping moan from under the truck. The terrorist he'd shot was still alive, in spite of the rounds he'd taken.

More surprises followed. The last man in the truck had been sitting in the back, with the ammunition. He had to have crawled through a hole in the rear of the cab, then out the side that Bolan couldn't cover.

Instead of either running or attacking, he slipped under the truck. Bolan saw a dark shape lying beside the wounded man, who was writhing slowly and moaning almost continuously. Consciousness had returned, and with it, pain.

The Executioner slung the Weatherby and the subgun, then drew the Beretta. The two men were safe from him tonight, unless they made another hostile move. Shooting a wounded or dying man in cold blood wasn't Bolan's style.

The warrior crept up the ditch. As he came opposite the truck, he tossed a pebble under the vehicle and called softly in French, "Do you need help?"

The reply was in Basque and didn't sound friendly.

Bolan kept his head down and called again. "I know first aid. Come out from under the truck and I can help."

He wasn't going to crawl into the cramped space under the truck, where he would have no light to see or room to fight if the Basques were still ready to resist. He also wasn't going to blow up the truck with the two men under it.

A few words that began and ended in groans followed. Then the unwounded terrorist backed out from under the truck—on the side away from Bolan—knelt and began to drag his comrade.

Bolan leapt up and raced around the front end of the truck. The terrorist who was dragging his compatriot had his hands full and would be no danger. The wounded man shouldn't have any fight left in him.

That miscalculation nearly ended Bolan's career. The wounded man had managed to drag his subgun with him in one bloody hand. As he emerged into the open, he rolled half-over, shifted the weapon to his good hand and raised it.

He never completed the movement. The Beretta coughed out a 3-round burst, and the Basque's head shattered, blood spraying on the gravel.

As the terrorist died, his companion launched himself at Bolan. He came so fast that even the Executioner's training and reflexes let him get off only one shot. It could have hit, but it certainly didn't slow the man down.

In the next second the terrorist was all over Bolan, with a vicious-looking knife in each hand. The warrior feinted left and right to keep the blades away from parts of his body not protected by his own Kevlar vest.

Bolan's edge in size and experience gave him the upper hand, but not before the Basque was able to slash the back of the warrior's left hand and nick his chin. Then the big man got the terrorist in a hammerlock, slammed him to the gravel and used nerve pressure until the knives clattered to the ground.

The man wasn't badly hurt; a fluent stream of Basque curses made that plain. Bolan checked the man for bullet wounds and found nothing. Then he collected the knives, pulled the field dressings from his first-aid kit and used them to bind the man's hands and feet tightly. Finally he carried him behind the stone wall and dropped him none too gently at the base of an olive tree. "Consider a new life after tonight," Bolan growled.

In the distance, dogs were barking savagely. The last few rounds had to have awakened a farmer's canine sentries. As the minutes passed, it seemed as though the barking was getting louder, too.

Bolan pulled a clump of C-4 plastique and two fuses from his pack, divided the explosive into two charges and set a time fuse into each. Then he slapped one charge onto a box of grenades in the back of the truck, the other against the gas tank.

Four minutes later, from three fields away, Bolan watched the Basque ammunition truck spew itself in flame and burning debris all over the road.

The barking dogs sounded even louder now, or maybe there were more of them. The explosion would have been heard and seen for miles around, and the truck was still burning. Curious and concerned people would be headed his way, asking questions.

Bolan slung his weapons and started putting distance between himself and the truck. Dawn found him a good six miles away, across broken country where even the most experienced tracker would find it hard to pick up his trail.

He stayed off the roads during the day, eventually returning to the rented Peugeot he'd left at a small hill resort. He followed a zigzag trail to the safehouse in Nantes, where he left the vehicle and his weapons, except the Beretta.

Then he caught a train to Paris, with airline tickets for Berlin in the pocket of his beige sport coat. Now it was time to start the mission that had brought him to Europe. He hoped whoever put him on to this one would be grateful enough to Stony Man Farm to strengthen its position in this post–Cold War world, when all intelligence agencies had to fight to justify their existence. Maybe they would even be grateful enough to help Hal Brognola find the leak in Stony Man security.

Bolan had lived most of his life knowing that other people had cross hairs on him. So had Brognola. But it was possible this security leak might put people in the line of fire who weren't supposed to be there.

Even in the intelligence field, there were innocents. Bolan's obligations to them were the same no matter where they were.

CHAPTER TWO

Berlin

Erich Kuhn stood on the deck of the *Lorelei*, lost in thought. Solitude wasn't Kuhn's usual habit. He was a social creature, even a party animal—"more animal than party," his wife had said just before she left him.

But tonight wasn't a usual night. Tomorrow all the information he had would be in the hands of the people to whom he'd promised it. If the people whose names appeared in the file ever learned who now had it, he would be in danger. But his partying had put him in danger anyway, and the people who would take possession of the file had promised to get him out of it.

If it had just been his father, it might not have mattered so much. Helmut Kuhn had lived long enough to see a great deal and not be shocked by very much of it. Besides, he was born a Berliner, and there was nothing a modern teenager could teach an old Berliner about human folly, vice or whatever you wanted to call it.

His father would have been disappointed, disapproving, but would not have sat in judgment on him. His wife, Liesl, hadn't been so tolerant, nor would his daughter, Trudl, if she ever learned more than a few of the details.

His colleagues would also have something to say. They might not disapprove on moral grounds, but they would say that he'd raised questions about his judgment. A man with questionable judgment, of course, could hardly stay on in a confidential position with a major defense contractor.

Trudl might forgive him for orgies. She would hardly forgive him for not keeping her in tapes for her VCR. So the decision had been fairly simple, and the past year had proved one thing—he still had his skills.

Alone on the *Lorelei*'s bow, Kuhn watched the lights of the Pfaueninsel gliding past. They seemed a little blurred. There would be a fog by morning, possibly even in time to slow his drive home to his apartment.

Blurred was also a good word for his situation, and foggy a good description for his morals. Or at least the morals that had landed him in this situation.

And the people who would get him out of it? What about their morals? He preferred the people he'd been spying for to the people he'd been spying on, but that didn't depend on anyone's morals. It depended on the fact that once the file was in his employers' hands, he could hope again.

Not for much—nothing like getting Liesl back, and anyway she didn't like America. Kuhn would ask to go there, where he might find a new career and could almost certainly count on being safe. His enemies no longer had the resources to do much in the United States, and his friends were very good at covering a man's tracks.

The deck heeled slightly, as the vessel slipped into a turn, and Kuhn heard a change in the note of the diesels below. He held on to the dew-slick railing until the ship finished her turn, then walked toward the portside door in the front of the superstructure.

Being out here alone possibly wasn't the safest thing he could have done on a foggy night. But he couldn't sit looking off into space in the main cabin, not without somebody noticing.

He gripped the door handle, but it wouldn't turn. Locked? But it had been open when he came out. Fear warred with the conviction that there was a logical, even innocent explanation. He decided to settle the argument by trying the starboard door.

If that didn't open, he'd climb the ladder to the bridge deck. Passengers weren't allowed there, or so the signs said, but if nobody saw him nobody would complain. *He* would complain, though, about careless crewmen who forgot to check the fo'c'sle for stray passengers before locking it up.

No, he wouldn't. Complaints meant calling attention to himself. For another twenty-four hours, he had to try to appear inconspicuous. Then, maybe he could complain about locked doors or cold coffee like anyone else. In America, you were even expected to complain.

A deckhand stepped out from under the bridge ladder, withdrew a pistol from his jacket pocket and fired it at Kuhn. The weapon made even less noise than a silenced automatic, but its charge of compressed air was enough to drive the dart into the back of Kuhn's neck.

Kuhn felt a sharp stinging in his neck. He turned, saw a sailor who had to have come out to check the fo'c'sle for passengers and opened his mouth to complain.

But no words came out as he felt his heart race. He tried to call for help, but his vocal cords seemed paralyzed. He tore at his collar; he had to get air somehow. The sailor stepped forward, and Kuhn's last sensation was relief that somebody was going to help him.

The sailor didn't bother feeling for a pulse. If Kuhn wasn't already dead, he would certainly be gone before he hit the water.

In thirty seconds Erich Kuhn was draped over the railing. He was a heavy man, and the sailor had underestimated his weight. But it took only one more heave. The splash was hardly loud enough to be heard above the rumble of the diesels and the gurgle of the wake.

No doubt they would find the body, in time. But by then there'd be no trace of anything except sudden, massive heart failure. The effects of the toxin in the dart would confuse a first-class forensic pathologist even in a fresh corpse.

Best of all, even if the toxin was detected, it would point suspicion in the wrong direction. The Wasp-6 formula was one of the last achievements of the KGB's Third Chief Directorate before the lords of the Lefortovo were buried under the ruins of the Soviet Union. It was barely known in the West.

No one knew who actually had most of the Wasp toxin, or how he had arranged its hijacking during the abortive Soviet coup in August of 1991. The man the assassin served was like the men Erich Kuhn worked for in one important way: he was very good at covering tracks.

"GOOD MORNING, Herr...?"

"Metzger. Peter Metzger." The tall man in front of the Eurocar rental window pushed his passport across the counter.

The clerk studied it in silence. "You're sure you only want a Jetta? We have several BMWs and even a Mercedes 280. Several reservations canceled when their flights were delayed because of the fog."

"Thank you, but I'm on a budget. If I go over it this time, the next time they won't even pay for a Jetta."

As the clerk punched the necessary data into the computer, he wondered who "they" were. If Berlin had still been awash in everybody's intelligence agents, he would have said that the man could easily be a field operative. Something official, anyway, and probably involving violence—the man carried himself like the clerk's old army sergeant.

"Metzger," the clerk said, pushing the envelope with the keys and documents at the tall man. "German ancestors?"

"If you go back far enough, yes. I'm from Massachusetts myself. Technical representative for a machine-tool factory."

"Ah. Going east?"

"Among other places." The man's tone firmly discouraged any more questions.

"I've arranged for our newest Jetta," the clerk said placatingly. "Just six months old and never been out of the Berlin area."

"Thank you." Metzger scooped up the envelope with a sure and swift movement of one large hand. His other held a suitcase, and an overnight bag was slung over one shoulder. The clerk recognized good-quality leather in both, but not the brands.

The fog must have thickened even since the American walked to the counter. When he went out, the clerk saw nothing but gray murk outside.

The man whose passport read "Peter Metzger" didn't see much more. The fog looked ready to close down flights and slow ground traffic to a crawl.

He could live with that, however. Mack Bolan's business in Berlin was important but not necessarily urgent. Certainly it wasn't so urgent that he had to plunge straight into it while fog gave the advantage to enemies who knew the German capital better than he did.

The Jetta was everything the clerk had promised, and newly tuned as well. The warrior dropped his bag on the seat beside him, strapped himself in and backed out of the parking space. He was ready to face an old foe.

For millions of people, the freedom of Eastern Europe and the reunification of Germany had meant new hope. For the Mafia, it meant half a continent of fresh victims.

THE CALL WAS URGENT but the telephone wasn't secure, let alone scrambled. Fortunately the message was short.

"Hello, Lou," the voice at the other end said. "Sylvia's test was negative."

"They're sure?" Hal Brognola asked. "We could be liable if there's even a slight chance—"

"No test's one hundred percent perfect, and you know that," the voice said, sounding like a teacher admonishing a bright pupil who'd talked back in class. Aaron Kurtzman was that close a friend to the big Fed that he could talk to the man in that manner. If anybody who was familiar with his manner listened to a tape of this conversation . . .

If that happened, Brognola reminded himself, Stony Man Farm had a major problem. Electronic leaks would be small potatoes in comparison. In spite of the best efforts of NSA, the CIA, the FBI, the DEA and, for all Brognola knew, the Secret Service, Stony Man Farm's isolation from the rest of the U.S. intelligence establishment remained fairly complete. Which meant its isolation from their leaks *ought* to be the same.

"I do know it, Frank," the big Fed replied. "Thanks for calling, and for the good news." The men said their goodbyes and broke the connection.

Outside the motel in the suburbs of Baltimore, the rain was coming down so hard Brognola could no longer hear the television in the next room. He could well believe the weather reports, which predicted flooded creeks and underpasses all over the area.

Hal Brognola lay back on the piled pillows, kicked his shoes off and poured a very small, very weak bourbon from the bottle in the drawer. That was about as much celebrating as he felt like doing.

"Sylvia" was Stony Man Farm's electronic security. "Negative" meant it hadn't been breached—at least not enough to pick up on anything as critical as Bolan's Germany mission. Aaron Kurtzman had worked eighteen hours a day for nearly a week to come up with that conclusion; Brognola was ready to live with it.

He wasn't so ready to live with the next step: investigation of a human leak. That meant not being able to trust a lot of people who had been friends, some of them for half a lifetime. Questions had to be asked, and a lot of good people would get their noses out of joint.

At least they had some idea of the focus of the leak—Mack Bolan. A logical focus, but one that didn't say much about who was behind it. A lot of people wanted the Executioner's head.

Bolan couldn't help much with the leak. He had to be protected from it, though, at least while he was in Germany. That meant a call to Ludwig. Behind that code name lurked the man who could do a better job of covering tracks—his own or anyone else's—than anybody else in Germany.

Ludwig's real name was Wilhelm Beck, although everybody called him Willi. He was the son of an American father and a German mother, a veteran of the U.S. Army Special Forces and the CIA. Able to pass as either German or American, he'd used his knowledge of Germany and Germans to go free-lance some years earlier. He had made himself indispensable to several major agencies with important coups, and had cooperated with Stony Man Farm more than once.

He might not be indispensable to Mack Bolan—the man took care of himself. But he would be a valuable asset on a mission where the Executioner would need all the help he could get.

CHAPTER THREE

Bolan eased the Jetta to the left around two trucks that had just had a minor fender bender. At least in this fog not even a German was likely to step on the gas.

Visibility had been seventy-five yards when he left the Eurocar rental. Now it was about half that, with spots where you could hardly see the hood ornament of your own car, let alone the bumper of the vehicle ahead.

Bolan kept looking around for signs that he was being tailed, but doubted he'd find any. Somebody with a compact infrared rig could trail him from well beyond visual range.

He reached his turnoff three-quarters of an hour behind schedule. The side road that ran southwest was almost free of traffic, but that didn't tempt the Executioner to speed up. Visibility hadn't improved, and the road was in poor condition.

The Germans were busy getting ready to make Berlin their capital and a great European city once again. Bolan wished them well. He also wished they'd scraped up a few spare marks to pave some of the side roads just the other side of the old border between West Berlin and East Germany. In ten minutes he'd hit fifteen potholes and his overnight case had fallen off the seat. He hoped the Jetta's suspension was coping.

He'd seen buildings in East Berlin that still bore bullet scars from the Russian attack in 1945. Some of the potholes on that road had to have been gouged by Russian T-34s in the same battle.

The odometer told him that he'd covered seventeen kilometers when he began to recognize landmarks from his instructions. Somebody with brains to spare had listed only landmarks close to the road, visible even in the dense fog. Trying to reach a specific point in this weather relying on distant landmarks would have been impossible.

A yellow-striped abandoned railroad bridge was the last landmark. Bolan stopped as instructed fifty meters distant but ignored the next part of his instructions, which told him to go straight in.

The warrior made a wide circle around the bridge, through the grass on the old embankment, up over the roadbed and down the other side. In the States the grass on an embankment like this would have been long enough for a low crawl. Here it had been roughly but closely trimmed, too short to hide anything larger than a cat.

As he slid into the ditch by the road running under the bridge, Bolan knew he'd been right to take precautions. There were two cars at the rendezvous site, parked by a fence that enclosed a patch of ground graded for new construction. That was what he expected.

But a third car was positioned under the bridge. It was a green BMW, and Bolan could see two men inside. Both wore dark raincoats, and hats pulled so low on their brows it was impossible to see their faces. He had the impression that they were rather dark-skinned for Germans, but that was irrelevant. What bothered him was their presence in the area.

Between the road and the construction site was a muddy stretch of earth and turf, bulldozed there when the ground was cleared. The two cars by the fence were on higher ground, with a good view of anyone crawling toward them.

The car under the bridge wasn't so well placed. The piles of earth gave a skilled man routes for getting close to the vehicle. Bolan mentally mapped one, then crept north along the ditch until he was invisible in the fog from any of the cars. Then he low-crawled across the road, and in the shelter of a pile of turf and old roots he drew the Beretta and set it for single-shot. Careful to keep the 93-R clear of the dirt, he began his approach to the car.

He looked up and studied the bridge. From close up, the yellow paint looked weathered and faded, with bare, even rusty spots here and there. No trains had traveled this line for a long time. And no snipers hid among the girders to ambush him.

The warrior took several minutes to cover the last five yards to his planned jumpoff point. It had started to rain, which for some reason, made the men in the BMW more alert. One climbed from the vehicle and began to patrol the immediate area. A bulge in a sagging pocket of his raincoat shouted "gun."

Bolan picked that man as his target. He needed to shift position to shorten the distance, and this time it took ten minutes to move two yards.

His plan was to jump the first man, hold him as a hostage in order to disarm the other, then question them both. He didn't plan to hurt anybody—he didn't know who these people were. But he had to be ready for anything.

Bolan's plan got as far as step one: jumping the first man. He leapt from cover and looped an arm around his target's neck, knocking them both to the ground. A knee pressed against the man's pocket immobilized his gun, and a left to the jaw immobilized him. The Beretta swung toward the second man.

Then the door of the BMW flew open and a third man entered the fray. He launched himself at Bolan, knocking the wind out of the warrior but not the Beretta out of his hand. The man owed his life to Bolan's reflexes. The Executioner saw in time that the man was empty-handed, and didn't shoot him on the spot.

Then a rough voice that still carried authority growled through the fog in German, "Bora, Ismail, Mustafa! Back off!"

The three men obeyed, keeping their empty hands in plain sight.

Bolan didn't completely return the compliment. He kept both hands in sight, but one of them still held the Beretta, with the safety off and a round chambered.

A large man climbed out of one of the two cars parked by the construction fence. In spite of his bulk, he made his way quickly across the rough ground, never setting a foot wrong or losing his balance. He wore a sweater and old Bundeswehr cargo pants, but since both were clean he looked like a male model compared to the wet, mud-smeared Executioner.

"Good afternoon, Herr Metzger. I regret that we ended up surprising you and making you go to such trouble to avoid a trap. I assure you, we weren't allowed the time to communicate with you in advance."

The man's German was good, but something about him hinted to Bolan that he wasn't German, or at least hadn't lived all his life in Germany. Bolan replied in English, which had the added advantage of possibly being secure from the Turks.

"'No time' is one of the oldest excuses in the book. Tell me who you are and what you're doing here, and I might believe it."

The man switched to completely fluent English, with a distinctly American accent.

"They really didn't tell you, did they? Well, here's my authentication code, straight from your boss."

The man reached into one of the capacious pockets of his pants, which certainly held a small automatic, and pulled out a notebook. He tore off the top sheet and handed it to Bolan. The Executioner glanced at it. The codes were readable, and they were also the real thing.

Bolan handed the paper back. He didn't feel quite ready to holster the 93-R.

"Do I have to guess your name, too? Or do you have a code for that?"

"Oh, sorry. Where's my head today? I'm Ludwig, also known as Willi Beck. Surely you've heard of me?"

THE TELEPHONE RANG seven times at the other end of the line before the leather-jacketed man hung up and walked back to his motorcycle. Gunther Wissmann took off his helmet briefly to scratch an itch on his shaved scalp, then strapped it back on.

No answer, and that meant no chance of official authorization. But what the hell. The little ass kisser who hadn't been home might wet himself when he found out Wissmann went off and did the job himself without permission.

His boss wouldn't mind, though, and if he didn't mind, it didn't matter what anybody else said or did. Wissmann would have a big score on his board, and none of the others except maybe Pauli the Pimp would be anywhere near him.

Wissmann's boss called himself Dannemeier, but Wissmann knew better. The tall man with the close-cropped gray hair had been born a lot farther east than the Oder, maybe even east of the Urals.

Which made it all the more remarkable that he was so good to work for. Wissmann had always despised Russians, even in the days when their iron hold on East Germany gave him a good income from smuggling. They were unimaginative, usually didn't have a thing worth stealing and wouldn't blow their noses without three copies of an order from Moscow.

Dannemeier was different, and Wissmann didn't think it was just because he probably had a lot of rank. Rank didn't count much, when many Russian generals had been looking over their shoulders since the failed coup of August 1991. Guts did, and Dannemeier had plenty.

Wissmann unsnapped the flap of the pocket where he carried his Glock 19. First-class equipment all the way was another good thing about working for the Big D. Eighteen rounds was good enough against anything short of an MP-5.

Then he straddled the Hercules and started the motor. The 750 cc engine blatted angrily, then wound up to a high whine as it took him down the side road.

He was going to be sorry to ditch the Hercules after the hit. The motorcycle was an old comrade, but that also meant that it could more easily be traced to him, and the police weren't so stupid they couldn't pick up a trail if one was left.

And Dannemeier wasn't so tolerant that he'd forgive a man for leaving a trail.

CHAPTER FOUR

The Executioner had heard of Willi Beck, a.k.a. Ludwig, but he hadn't expected to be working with the man, and the squared-off face wasn't fixed in his memory.

He also wasn't sure he liked the prospect of working with the man now. Beck had a reputation for taking risks, a "cowboy" type.

But there was no point in being rude. The warrior shoved the Beretta into a pocket and thrust out his own right hand. "Sorry about being slow on the uptake. It's been a busy few days, with jet lag on top of it."

"Since when has headquarters heard of jet lag?" the other asked rhetorically. He seemed to want to continue the charade of Bolan being a machine-tool expert in Germany on legitimate business. It couldn't be fooling the Turks for a minute. In fact it was probably making them more curious about Bolan than they might otherwise have been.

Beck, the Executioner decided, had at least one vice that wasn't listed in his file. He was a frustrated actor, and once he got into a part, getting him out again would be a major task.

Beck turned to his Turks and spoke to them in Turkish, unmistakably giving orders. Two climbed back into their car, one of them the man Bolan had dragged to the ground. He gave the Executioner a dirty look before closing the door.

The third Turk fell in behind Beck and Bolan, just out of hearing if the two men talked quietly.

"I really am here on short notice," Beck said. "It wasn't my idea, either. You saw the codes yourself, so blame Brognola when you get back home."

"Do you have my equipment?" Bolan could improvise an arsenal for nearly anything up to a small war out of what he found in the average-size Western industrial city. He preferred not to scrounge when he'd have need for the long-range shooting capacity of his Weatherby and occasions where the sheer slugging power of the .44 Magnum Desert Eagle would come in handy.

Confidence in his equipment was a good part of any warrior's assets. On this mission, Bolan figured he didn't have any to give away.

"See that car?" Beck replied. He pointed to a dark blue Mercedes, the other car that Bolan had expected. "Your hardware's in the trunk, one of my people's in the back seat and your friendly local CIA rep, Gerry Singer, is at the wheel.

Bolan kept walking in silence. If Beck wanted to chat, he'd tell more than he learned, and that was fine with the Executioner. The Stony Man file on the man known as Ludwig was fairly complete. The Farm didn't work with anybody without being familiar with his or her record.

But there were always things no file could tell you, things you had to learn on the spot facing the man himself. Or listening to him talk, as Bolan was doing now.

Such as the fact that you could easily mistake Beck for a fat man from the way he bulged out his clothes. The bulk actually had to be almost all bone and muscle. The man was too light and sure on his feet, too precise in his movements, to be carrying much flab. It would be easy to write him off as a jolly fat man, useless in a physical confrontation. It was a mistake that might have accounted for some of Beck's kills.

"I'm figuring that somebody tailed the Mercedes. In this fog any turkey with an IR scope could do it."

"I thought the same."

"Good. We've got IR gear in the BMW, so we can clear behind us when we move out. That'll be after you pick up your stuff. Then one of my people takes your Jetta and wanders all over the place until he either picks up a tail or finds a place to spend the night."

"Has he got a radio, if it's the tail?"

"Only the Bundeswehr's best."

Bolan didn't have enough faith in *any* military equipment to be totally reassured by that. At least Beck wasn't leaving his people hung out to dry if they were facing tails with orders to kill.

"What about the rest of us?"

"The Turks and I take you to one of my safehouses, down in Kreuzberg. You look enough like a Turk to fit in there. One of my people drives the Mercedes back into town, drops off Gerry Singer and then does a little wandering, too.

"Again, he'll have a radio, and codes for reaching the Berlin police and the BND. I figure under the circumstances, he's the one the bad guys are most likely to target."

"Unless I'm blown."

"We'll know that if they come after the Jetta. That guy's not top-grade combat material. He's supposed to yell, not fight."

Bolan's expression didn't give anything away, but he was impressed. Maybe Beck deserved a good part of his reputation. The Executioner hadn't fought as long or won as often by ignoring facts.

The German BND combined some of the functions of the FBI, CIA and Secret Service. Logically enough, that made it Stony Man Farm's main—if silent—partner in this mission. If Beck really had those BND connections and knew the skills of his men, his being the Executioner's support on this mission might not be such a bad trade.

Being pulled into the mission so suddenly still seemed to have Beck a little nervous. Bolan wondered if the man was short of assets, or simply having to shift gears from one project to another. It wasn't life or death, anyway.

He wondered how the Farm's team was coming along with its mission. Aaron Kurtzman had the easiest job, sitting in front of a computer monitor sifting through data. From there on things got a lot more complicated very quickly, until it could be that some men Bolan had known or at least worked with for years were going to die.

GUNTHER WISSMANN HIT thicker fog at eighty kilometers an hour and promptly slowed to less than half that speed. He'd pushed through denser fog a lot faster at least once before, but that was when he'd been racing for a bet.

Whatever had happened to little Gertrud, the stakes in that bet? Probably ODed and picked up some cold morning on the Reeperbahn, with the wind from the North Sea making all the decent Hamburg citizens stay inside. They'd said goodbye as he'd said goodbye to most of his girls—no phony promises, just "Thanks for a good time and good luck."

It bothered him a little, though, that he was beginning to wonder what happened to his old girlfriends. That was supposed to be a sign of getting old.

Over the last two kilometers Wissmann was barely able to keep the Hercules upright. The only good thing about the low speed was that if he did go into a skid on the mist-wet concrete, he'd likely enough come through it. The Hercules might not, but he could probably walk the rest of the way as fast as he could ride.

The observer was waiting for him at the gate. He looked about seventeen but was probably twenty and thinking he'd be richer than his unemployed father if this came off. As long as he didn't think about what might really happen to him, he'd be safe, even an easy kill.

"Where's the driver?"

"He took off. Said he had to be where he could block the road if they ran."

"All right."

It wasn't, quite. The man could be useful. He could also be a witness to anything that went wrong. If he stayed too close, he could compromise Gunther to the police. He could also compromise Gunther to Danne-meier, if the skinhead went ahead with his whole plan.

Time enough to worry about that later. Wissmann pulled out his lock picks and went to work on the gate. The young man had the sense to shield his companion with his own body, so that no casual observer could figure out what he was doing.

"Where are they?"

"Beyond the second site. We couldn't get a perfect location on them without coming too close. The ground's higher over there, fog's not so thick. There's an old abandoned railroad bridge that sticks out like a hard-on. Probably somewhere around there, or at least you can observe from it."

The lock clicked open. Wissmann dropped his picks in the same pocket as the Glock 19, using his left hand.

That and the movement of his body to mask the draw was enough to fool the other.

The young man had just time to open his mouth after he saw the Glock. He didn't have time to shout before a 9 mm round drilled into his throat. He tumbled backward, kicking hard enough for Wissmann to risk a second round into the chest.

The custom-made sound-flash suppressor made the compact Glock unreasonably bulky. The fog would do a good enough job of muffling the noise. Gunther hauled the corpse through the gate, locked it behind him, then hauled the body to the equipment park. It was light enough for him to heave into the empty drum of a cement mixer.

That would guarantee nobody's finding it that day, and be a nasty surprise the next. The discovery would probably shut down the site for a week, while the police asked everybody a lot of questions.

Wissmann began a zigzag course through the site, stopping every so often to take cover behind a pile of steel rods or the base of a crane. He'd need to get closer. The extra rounds didn't give the Glock any more range than the next automatic.

He'd need to take out the driver, too. Or did the man have some friends in the network who would think they ought to settle with Wissmann? Dannemeier might not approve, but then they wouldn't tell him, and the boss only *seemed* to know everything and be everywhere at once.

Wissmann decided that he'd improvise on that one. The most important thing was to get that first kill, the man who was known as Gerry Singer. Probably a Jew, or stupid enough to want to be taken for one, and that was reason enough for eliminating him first.

BOLAN'S TRAINING told him to keep his gaze roving in an unsecured area. It had become second nature to the warrior, and had saved his skin on a number of occasions.

He also knew that Beck and the Turks considered that he was their guest, under their protection, and shouldn't have to be on guard himself. Beck was as much German as American by background. Both Germans and Turks took their obligations very seriously.

So seriously, in fact, that they'd be offended if Bolan did anything that hinted they weren't doing their jobs. That could make it even harder to work with them than his earlier confrontation with one of the Turks.

Also, Beck and his people seemed to know their business. They didn't bunch up, and each kept his eyes roving over a different sector of the fog. Beck's driver was out of the car now, and so was Gerry Singer's. Both of them were behind cover, looking in different directions.

Visibility was now about a hundred yards. Bolan decided that his chance of seeing anything before his escorts did was too small to be worth the risk of offending them.

As they climbed up to the cars, Singer scrambled out. He was an ex-Green Beret who looked like a senior accountant until you saw the way he moved. Their common background in Special Forces let him and Beck work together without any conflicts that Stony Man Farm had to settle.

"Any trouble, Peter?" Singer asked Bolan.

"Not so far, except from the weather. Or if you forgot my sample case."

"The fragile stuff's in the trunk, strapped down. The rest is in the back seat."

Bolan opened the Mercedes's back door. There was no reason for unpacking weapons that would need checking before he could use them anyway. But the suitcase in the back seat, with the blacksuit and other gear would at least let him change out of the mud-splotched clothes he wore now.

GUNTHER WISSMANN DIDN'T have to get out his lock picks for the gate to the second construction site. The fence was at the bottom of a slope, and a running jump took him over the top. The second site was merely graded, nothing except a few ditches dug so far. The fence had probably been constructed to keep children, lovers or the odd drug user wandering by from falling into the ditches.

The fence opposite was wire mesh, and close enough to Wissmann's targets. Almost too close, in fact. Standing right up against the barrier, he could practically read the license number on the rear of the Mercedes. At least the fog and the wire mesh together would break up his silhouette, and he didn't want to stretch the Glock beyond its limits.

He might have sixteen rounds, but he wasn't going to have sixteen opportunities to shoot Singer. Not with that many people standing around, even if none of them had a long-range weapon.

Next time he wanted to improvise somebody's death, Wissmann decided he'd have something better than the Glock. It wouldn't be hard to manage, if this one came off.

The assassin decided he'd ask Dannemeier for an MP-5 or a G-3. Or more likely money to find one on the underground market. Dannemeier just might pass off as clean a weapon that could be traced to ensure he could pull a man in after unauthorized use. Or the police could do it, which would leave his hands clean.

Wissmann had looked at Dannemeier's eyes when the man didn't think he was being observed. They were blue, with nothing much Slavic about them, and you could be damned sure they'd witnessed men tortured to death in the Lefortovo or shoved alive into ovens at GRU headquarters.

Wissmann thrust the muzzle of the Glock through the mesh and started sighting in. He saw a big dark man in muddy but good clothing bending into the back seat. Singer stood behind him. Both head and chest were exposed.

He shifted to a two-handed grip and steadied the Glock until the sights came on to Singer's chest. Then he let out a soft breath and gently squeezed the trigger.

THE MERE CRACK of a pistol somewhere close at hand could demand many different responses.

The Executioner was accustomed to those responses. He was already lunging forward as the first bullet passed overhead. The second round creased his back rather than drilling his side because he was half-inside the car. As Singer folded, trying to draw his own Walther, Bolan unlocked the far-side rear door of the Mercedes and rolled on the ground.

By the time he came up with the 93-R in his hand, the whole group had also hit the ground. It said a lot for their discipline that nobody had opened fire before that. Beck had trained them well, it seemed, and the Turks would also be cautious about casualties from friendly fire.

From the time Bolan hit the ground to the moment he finished scanning uphill, he didn't have a target. Not for the Beretta without the shoulder stock, anyway.

"Gerry, how is it?" he called.

"Not...great." It sounded like a chest wound, not the sucking kind that meant either first aid or death in a few minutes, but bad enough.

The Turks started to call to one another in their native language, then Beck joined in. A moment later the sound of at least one submachine gun ripped the fog apart. Bolan watched the bullets strike sparks from the mesh fence, a foot above the ground.

He doubted that the Turks had any more of a target than he did. They were doing the next best thing, warning the shooter that he was outranged. If he broke and ran, he'd have to run into the fog faster than a bullet from an MP-5 could catch him. If he stayed put, he'd be pinned in front while they worked around his flanks.

That way, the fight might take time. Meanwhile Gerry Singer might be dying on the other side of the Mercedes. Bolan crawled under the vehicle, remembering how he'd held his fire when he saw the Basque doing the same thing for his friend.

He doubted the gunman in the fog had the same principles. Or he might not fire out of sheer fright. Even a well-aimed pistol wasn't the greatest weapon for an assassination. Bolan smelled amateur here, or maybe a pro in too much of a hurry, somebody who could be temporarily left to the Turks and Beck, anyway.

Nobody fired at Bolan as he pulled the medical kit out of his baggage. Nobody fired at him while he bent over Singer, injecting morphine, tying a pressure bandage over the wound, immobilizing what looked like a badly shattered collarbone.

Singer looked ghastly but was still alive when Bolan finished. By now the shock of his own bullet crease had worn off. It felt as if somebody had tied a strand of razor wire across his back, and he could feel the blood oozing down his spine.

He flexed back and shoulder muscles, which didn't do anything for the pain but did tell him it was a flesh wound at most. The less unarmed combat he tried in the next few days, the better, but the injury shouldn't affect his shooting.

The wound darted new pain through Bolan as he found the concealment of a bulldozer's trail and joined the firing line. Some of Beck's people were almost out of sight in the fog at either end of the fence. Bolan couldn't see any bodies on either side of the barrier. The gunman hadn't scored again.

Frustration ate at Bolan, sharper than the pain in his back. Risk exposing himself, to get into the trunk and bring the Desert Eagle into action? Not such a big risk, if he could get Beck's men to give covering fire.

But how to get that message across? The gunman had to speak German, he was too likely to speak English, and Bolan didn't speak much Turkish.

No options. He put his mouth to Singer's ear and whispered, "Keys?"

"In the ignition."

Bolan slipped under the car again. Scraping his back on the chassis didn't make it feel better but got him to the far side of the Mercedes. He reached the driver's door without rising too far and snagged the keys from the ignition without more exposure.

There was no way to the rear of the car from underneath. The gas tank was slung too low. Bolan low-crawled as far as he could, then went to a sprinter's stance and burst into the open.

He quickly opened the car trunk, then heaved out the footlocker, slamming it down between him and the fence.

The gunman saw and understood, but he fired too late. Two bullets punched into the footlocker, missing both Bolan and the gas tank. If the couriers had done their job, the locker also held things that wouldn't react too well to bullets.

Bolan heaved the locker around, opened it and grabbed the Desert Eagle, crouching as another bullet chewed through the trunk lid and cracked the rear window.

Then, looking north along the fence, the Executioner saw something that made him wonder if the fog was affecting his vision. A tall, broad-shouldered man with very short blond hair stood on a little rise of ground, staring at the scene. He wore a black windbreaker and gray jogging pants. His feet were hidden in rank grass.

He was looking at the battle rather like a pig farmer watching his stock, interested but far above it all. He was also a perfect target.

The Beretta would do. Bolan sighted well to the left of the big man and pumped a round into a patch of weeds. The guy looked down at the weeds as if they were dog droppings sticking to his shoe. Then he turned and slowly walked into the fog.

It took him longer than Bolan expected to disappear. The Executioner just realized that the fog had to be lifting, when the MP-5 opened up, and several handguns joined in.

THE FOG HID Wissmann's retreat from the fence to one of the ditches. He picked one within handgun range of the fence, so he could hit anyone trying to cut through the wire for a frontal assault.

For the flanks, he had to rely on the fog, the concealment of the ditch and luck. He began to suspect that he'd relied too much on luck when he saw the men begin to spread out the whole length of the fence.

Now the fog would be working both ways. Behind it, they could be through the wire before he knew it. Then they might find a ditch that would give them as much cover as his gave him, and even move the bastard with the subgun onto his flank.

Wissmann knew that there'd be a time when the subgunner would be moving and unable to pin him down from in front. If he picked that moment to run, he'd have a better chance. *If* the Turks forget to leave somebody close to the fence to keep him down.

Those Turks might have no place in a real Germany, but that didn't keep them from being good soldiers. It would be useful for Dannemeier to know that at least one of the enemy bands was using Turkish mercenaries.

From the ditch he watched the big man give first aid to the wounded Jew. A pity. That proved the Jew wasn't dead. Wissmann shifted back and forth along his ditch, trying to get a clear shot at either Singer or the man tending him. Each time his sights were almost aimed the MP-5 opened up.

By the time the big man dragged Singer to cover in front of the Mercedes, Wissmann had a scalp wound and one eye half-blind from sand, which had been kicked up by a 9 mm round. Rage was eating away at his judgment, so he did his best to kill the big man when he saw him trying to get to the trunk, without much caring if he was hit himself in the process.

Wissmann took two hits. One bullet shattered his left arm, the other gouged his ribs. He knew the arm might end up useless and the ribs could puncture a lung if he didn't get care, but it seemed less important now to live than to kill.

As least he hadn't cried out, even when the shock wore off and the wounds started to send daggers of pain through his body. He was fighting and dying like a German soldier, like his grandfather and great-grandfather before him.

Then Wissmann saw him, the one they called the Trained Wolf. He was standing on a little hump of ground, out of pistol range for anybody, almost lost in the fog.

If he had believed in praying, Wissmann would have prayed then for a rifle, or for one of his enemies to think the Trained Wolf was *their* enemy. He was standing out in the open, making no attempt to hide himself, and he certainly looked almost as dangerous as he was. Most people believed that the Trained Wolf could kill with his bare hands. Wissmann had seen him do it twice, one time a woman and slowly.

Then the Trained Wolf looked up, and Wissmann's wounds seemed to grow numb as he felt their eyes meet. In that moment the Trained Wolf learned everything about what the assassin had done this day.

Wissmann screamed in his mind for help, even the smallest diversion. He would have screamed aloud, but he didn't know how near the Turks were. The fog was lifting now, but they might still be within a hundred meters. Giving away his position might—

The Trained Wolf turned his back and walked away into the fog.

The numbness vanished, and the assassin's wounds blazed with new pain, fiercer than before. He groaned, and knowing that the pain was getting the best of him snapped something within his mind. He jumped up and started to run.

BOLAN GAMBLED that the gunman was on the move. If he was, he would be too busy running or dodging other people's bullets to shoot back even if he was in range.

The warrior vaulted to the roof of the Mercedes, using one hand and both legs. The other hand held the Desert Eagle. Bolan's knees and heavy shoes both left dents in the car's roof. He bounced to his feet, spread his feet wide for balance on the mist-slick metal and assumed a Weaver stance.

In that moment he saw the running man. He wore a biker's leathers and was covered with mud, blood and sand. He raced away from the fence, an automatic in his hand and panic in every line of his long-limbed body.

Bolan waited until the man jumped a ditch and had to scrabble for footing. Then he brought up the big .44, aimed and caressed the Eagle's trigger.

The boom of the Desert Eagle was echoed by the MP-5, with a long burst. Pistols cracked from both flanks.

The combined impact of that many hits slammed the fleeing sniper to the ground. His feet drummed briefly on the earth, digging the toes of his boots into the mud. One hand groped for the fallen automatic, then the man lay still.

The Executioner jumped down from the car and joined Beck, who beat him to the fence. He was already working at it with a pair of wire cutters when Bolan joined him.

"Did you see the man off to the right?"

"What man?" Beck answered absently, as he concentrated on a particularly stubborn strand.

Bolan described what he'd seen. By the time he'd finished, Beck had a gap cut in the wire. He slipped the cutters into his cargo pants, took out his Walther and shook his head.

"I didn't see anybody. Are you sure it wasn't one of our own people out of position?"

"Do you have anybody with you like that?"

"No, but Singer might have had backup he didn't tell anybody about."

If Singer was being superconscious about security, he might have brought somebody along. But then the man would have moved in to help, not stood like a vulture hovering over the battlefield waiting to feast on the dead.

"Backup who didn't come in?"

"Who knows?" Again Bolan heard an edge in Beck's voice. It might be just after-battle jitters, but this time the warrior was ready to suspect something more.

It was beginning to be obvious that Beck didn't care about the mystery figure because he had something else on his mind, or even worse, didn't believe Bolan. The Executioner frowned. If his reputation didn't give him even that much credibility with Beck, there were going to be problems.

The problems would multiply if Bolan came right out and accused Beck. Stony Man's contact, Gerry Singer, was going to be out of action for months. Hal Brognola had trusted Beck enough to bring in the man and his people as a backup.

The big Fed would believe the Executioner if he said that Beck was being uncooperative. The problem was, who would take Beck's place?

He'd have to work with Beck and get on with the mission.

THE MAN ON THE HILL hadn't gone as far as Mack Bolan thought. The equipment concealed by his jacket, all except the directional microphone, let him stay back far enough not to be noticed casually.

He listened, and what he heard confirmed what he'd suspected when he saw the man behind the fence. It had been Wissmann, indulging his fondness for unauthorized wet work, as usual, and this time paying the price he had deserved several times over.

This death wouldn't improve discipline as much as an execution would have done. However, Wissmann would no longer be a potential leader for the malcontents. Spreading the rumor among the skinheads that he had been killed by Turks would be useful.

It might not bring the network any recruits, but then there was hardly time or cadre available for training them. Project Gamma was too far along to be abandoned, and using too many resources.

Fortunately it wouldn't matter whether Wissmann's fellow skinheads actually joined a cell. If they were their usual hooligan selves, they would attract a great deal of attention from people who otherwise might come looking for traces of the Gamma Project.

The Trained Wolf shifted his position slightly, to brace his right elbow and steady the microphone a trifle. Most of the opposition team was beyond the wire now, gathered around the body, but they did have security men looking outward. It would be unwise and unnecessary to try to get closer.

Photographs were always useful, but one part of the Trained Wolf that had been trained particularly well was his memory. Anytime in the next year, he would be able to pick the tall dark man out of a crowd or out of the network's secure files.

THE DEAD GUNMAN HAD at least four lethal wounds. Bolan noted that one of them had to be from the Desert Eagle. As well as wounds, something else became obvious when they pulled off the man's helmet. He was a skinhead, well past his teens, but with the shaved scalp, the tattoos, the earrings and the generally scruffy air of the breed.

His pistol, though, was a Glock 19, almost brand-new. Expensive hardware for an amateur, and who else would go on a major hit with just an automatic? There were three other answers, and Bolan didn't like any of them: the man was a professional in a hurry or working outside his charter, the man was a pro sent to imitate an amateur, or the man had known that his target—or targets—would be in handgun range.

Thinking it over, the warrior liked the third answer least of all. It meant the most danger—and one of Bolan's rules of fieldcraft was to keep the closest lookout for your enemy's most dangerous option.

The Turks had finished searching the dead man's clothes. Beck dusted off his hands and turned to the Executioner.

"I think we'd better leave the body here. Unexplained corpses turn up often enough that the police won't push to explain it. If we're caught transporting it, on the other hand . . ."

Bolan nodded. The whole German government probably didn't owe Beck enough to let him go unwatched if they were caught red-handed with the body.

"I'd still like to check the area back where I thought I saw the other man," the Executioner said. "Five minutes?"

Beck shook his head. "I don't say you imagined things. But we've got less than that to be out of here. Mustafa's heard police calls on the radio. Somebody's heard the firefight and been a good German citizen."

Not for the first time, Bolan had the feeling that efficiency was both the greatest virtue and the greatest vice of the Germans.

He decided that mystery man or not, it was time to leave the body to the efficient German police and get Gerry Singer to an efficient German hospital.

"All right. But find somebody absolutely reliable to deliver the heavy gear to the safehouse. If I've been made, I think I should lay a few false trails on the way."

"Your call," Beck said and shook the Executioner's hand. The Turks were already loading Singer, pale and unconscious, into the back of the Mercedes.

Beck had plenty of assets in critical places all over Germany. The problem for Bolan was getting him to use them at the critical times.

CHAPTER FIVE

Bolan changed clothes before he left the scene of the firefight. Any man on foot in the area might have seemed suspicious. A man whose clothes looked as if he'd been crawling in mud was likely to be stopped on the spot. If he had two handguns and a fresh bullet crease across his back, he'd be in jail in short order.

The Executioner had been in countries where being caught with a handgun meant you were arrested, tried and convicted of terrorism the moment the police found the weapon. Since terrorism in those countries was a capital offense, a man who wanted to get out alive had limited choices: go unarmed, shoot it out with the police or avoid the authorities entirely.

Common sense and principles dictated that Bolan choose the third. That wasn't easy in Germany, where there was a plethora of policemen and too many citizens prepared to call them. The next best thing was to make sure that none of the good citizens suspected you of anything.

With the police sirens approaching behind him, Mack Bolan walked off into the thinning fog, to use his fine-tuned skills to avoid both friends and enemies.

"HELLO, Nickel Recycling Corporation."

"Hello, this is Anton. I have to report that our fifth sales agent has failed to meet his quota."

"Permanently failed?"

"We can't hope for any more from him, I believe."

"I will tell the director."

The Trained Wolf nodded and hung up the telephone in the pay booth at the Frohnau S-Bahn station. Colonel Danilov now knew about Wissmann's death. The details could wait for more secure communications, which might take some time. The German police would be exceedingly curious about some things they might normally overlook, once the man's body was found.

Fortunately Berlin had as many gangsters as any other capitalist city, although in that respect the cities of what he still wanted to call the Soviet Union seemed to be catching up with the West. A disgusting and decadent breed, wherever they were, but useful for concealing the tracks of serious professionals. If the Berlin police finally wrote off Wissmann's death as the logical end for a skinhead who made too many enemies, Project Gamma would continue to proceed unhindered.

Meanwhile, there was his own project. He hadn't referred to it, because the man who answered wasn't cleared for such knowledge. Need-to-know for most of the Trained Wolf's projects was limited to Danilov himself, and those men of the team actually assigned to a particular mission.

Like the late Gunther Wissmann, the Trained Wolf had the habit of carrying out missions without checking with his superiors. Unlike Wissmann, he secured their permission in advance to use his initiative—and he always made sure he had enough men and equipment.

BERLIN WASN'T one of the cities Bolan could have crossed blindfolded, but he was an excellent navigator, and Berlin stores were well supplied with detailed street maps.

So by U-Bahn, Berlin's subway, S-Bahn, its commuter rail lines, bus, an occasional taxi and a lot of walking, the Executioner circled Berlin from northwest to southeast. He reached the southeast U-Bahn line about dinnertime, and joined a largely working-class mob scene at a small café for something to eat.

He finally reached the safehouse about ten minutes before the subway shut down for the night. The neighborhood was heavily Turkish, or so the graffiti and posters on the wall suggested. Bolan recognized obscenities in several other languages, however, and the drunks sleeping by the wall cursed in several more when he walked by without giving them a handout.

The safehouse itself was a four-story building that had seen better days, sometime around 1910. Any elegant furnishings that had survived the inflation after World War I must have been looted by the Russians in 1945. The basic building had survived intact, however. It was built so ruggedly that nothing except a direct hit from a heavy bomb could have put it down.

The concierge looked as if she had also been there since about 1910. However, she knew the recognition codes and showed Bolan to his quarters, two shabby but clean rooms on the third floor.

She also knew enough English to grant his request for a safe in the secure area on the second floor. He wasn't sure that she understood his plan to put his own lock on it, and decided it didn't matter. He was more concerned about security than any complaints to Beck.

The warrior was unpacking when the courier arrived, the Turk he recognized as Ismail. The man either spoke no English or pretended not to, but his German and Bolan's were enough for communication.

It also helped that Ismail had brought the rest of Bolan's gear, in the back of a Borgward station wagon whose original color, many paint jobs ago, had been green. Bolan wondered at the reasons for the repaintings, but doubted that he had any need-to-know.

Beck was uncooperative—that didn't prove that he was corrupt or criminal. If being uncooperative was a crime, Bolan knew that the prisons would be overflowing with petty bureaucrats.

By the time Bolan finished assembling and checking his weapons and equipment, it was nearly three o'clock in the morning. But he had one more job. A coded message about the situation had to be sent to Hal Brognola. With a possible security leak, it had to be sent in their personal mission-specific cryptic. No one except Bolan in Europe and Brognola in the United States had the keys to it, and they had them memorized so that no physical trace of the code's existence was left.

The Executioner used the room's stationery, with the letterhead of a defunct East Berlin hotel, to compose the text of a telegram concerning the software for a "smart" turret lathe that Peter Metzger's firm was trying to sell to Germany. He took it down to the concierge's office, found her asleep but quick to wake and laid down a sizable stack of ten-mark notes to see that it got to the telegraph office.

Beck wasn't exactly keeping the lady in luxury; a few little bonuses could be something she would remember if Bolan's life ever depended on her cooperation.

TRUDL KUHN WAS twenty-two and would have attracted attention wearing a potato sack and wooden clogs. Wearing a miniskirt and a well-tailored jacket over a red sweater, she had more attention than she wanted, while trying to make a confidential call to her grandfather.

She finally walked out of the jazz bar's back room and out on the Kurfürstendamm, in search of a public telephone. The first three she found were in use, and by the time she found a fourth it had started to rain.

At least it wasn't a thunderstorm, so she could use the telephone safely. But she had the unpleasant feeling that anybody who might be following her could sneak close to the booth in the rain. She'd also read about eavesdropping devices, too, that could pick up your end of a telephone conversation from outside the booth.

It took three tries to get through to her grandfather's house in Königstein outside Frankfurt am Main, but only two rings to get an answer after that. Unfortunately it was Ilse, the housekeeper.

"He has already gone to bed, Miss Trudl. Or are you forgetting what time it is?"

Trudl hadn't forgotten. She looked at her watch. "I know what time it is, Ilse. But something—I have heard a story about my father. I think Grandfather will want to know."

Ilse couldn't call her employer quickly enough. If there was anything she didn't want to listen to, it was another story about Erich Kuhn's misbehavior. She was quite happy to bother Erich's father, but if *she* didn't have to listen to it, it hadn't happened. Trudl wondered sometimes what her philosophy teacher at the Free University of Berlin would say of Ilse's attitude.

"Hello, Trudl?"

"Grandfather, I think something may have happened to Father."

Her grandfather listened in silence while she told of how she'd been unable to reach him and how nobody had seen him for two days. She had even gone to his apartment, but the concierge hadn't seen him, either. The old woman wouldn't let her in, of course, so she couldn't be sure he wasn't at home but not answering the phone. Still, with all the trouble he had been having since the divorce, she was getting worried.

The silence on the other end of the line lasted so long that Trudl was even more worried before her grandfather answered. He never took that long to answer, unless it was a very complicated question about one of his patents or something where he didn't want to tell the truth.

"Trudl, I know where I can ask a few questions and maybe even find some answers. Give me two days, then call me back, and whatever you hear will be the truth."

The way he spoke turned Trudl's worries into outright fear. Her grandfather didn't speak with that tone about anything except the war or something else as serious. Except that there wasn't anything else as serious. Or there hadn't been, until now.

"Trudl, are you still there?"

"It's pouring rain outside. Where would I go?"

"Home, I hope."

"You're starting to sound like Ilse."

"Ha, perhaps I should marry her, then. She and I are almost the same age to the month, did you know that?"

"You can marry Ilse or not, and if you do I will give you a present."

"Oh?"

"I will *not* have Hedwig sing at the wedding."

Another long silence, and then the welcome sound of her grandfather laughing. "Ilse would be grateful, I am sure." Since most of Hedwig's songs were either shrill, obscene, or both, Trudl wasn't surprised.

"One thing more," Helmut Kuhn added. "I am sure that all of your father's friends know about your being concerned. You don't need to bother them anymore. If they learn anything, I am sure they will tell you. Or if they don't and I find out, they will not like what happens to them."

The line went dead. Trudl saw that the rain was beginning to slacken, and left the telephone booth to hail a taxi. In the back seat, she tucked herself into a corner and watched as the vehicle turned off the Kurfürstendamm onto Uhlandstrasse. Then the familiar sight of the Hotel Egwe told her that she was almost home.

Home, without anything but promises about her father, even from her grandfather. She was being treated like a child, and liked it no better than she had when she was twelve. Her grandfather seemed to be willing to hurt her, to save her father's friends from the embarrassment of telling her that Erich Kuhn had killed himself.

IT WAS THE SAME MAN Bolan had seen in the fog at the construction site. He recognized the face, the crew cut blond hair and the stance.

Except that now the man wasn't wearing a black windbreaker and jogging pants. He wore Russian-pattern camouflage fatigues and carried an AKR submachine gun slung under his left arm. The blue beret of the Russian paratroops was tucked into his belt.

The man turned, lifted the AKR and aimed it at something outside Bolan's field of vision, or maybe something hidden in the fog that seemed to be rolling in again.

The fog blew away and the man vanished. The Executioner reoriented himself carefully, as he always did when he woke up unexpectedly. The Desert Eagle under the next pillow, the cracked ceiling overhead, the green tarnish on the frame of the brass bedstead, the linoleum top of the nightstand...

He went on until he knew how his mind had been working. It wasn't precisely a dream. It was his intuition working overtime, turning a handful of vague impressions into a clear picture.

A clear and not very pleasant picture. The man who'd watched the pistoleer die was an officer of the Spetsnaz, the elite special-operations troops of the former Soviet Union. They had been controlled by the GRU, Soviet Military Intelligence, and nobody in the West was betting that the GRU was out of business.

Which made the man very bad news indeed, but still not worth losing sleep over. Bolan's watch read a quarter to five. Three hours remained before he had to move out.

He turned over, shifted the pillow a few inches and slept again almost at once.

SPETSNAZ OFFICERS assigned to the First Directorate of the GRU had comprehensively documented false identities. On those documents the Trained Wolf was listed as Major Oleg Bytkin.

Personally he thought it should be Colonel Oleg Bytkin. If it hadn't been for Mikhail Gorbachev and all the manure he peddled in place of socialism, it *would* have been Colonel Bytkin.

Oleg Bytkin was sitting in a basement apartment in Berlin with two other Spetsnaz men, planning a mission that might help them all on the road back. Or at least make Germany less of a menace. That wasn't a small gain, when foolish leaders had flushed socialism down the toilet and made its homeland as weak as Cuba.

"Yuri," he said.

The short, deceptively boyish man who used that name—or the nickname the Blade—stopped whetting his knife and grinned.

"Yes?"

"Have you arranged to bring in some Poles?"

"I've been spending money on them as if we had our own printing press, Oleg. But you know how those Poles can drink. I would have to buy the moon to be sure of more than a dozen."

"Oh, well. A dozen will be enough, if the skinheads run into them and the clash is on the American news programs at breakfast the next morning. The fascists beating up on Poles will make more trouble for Germany than their beating up on Turks. Germany didn't kill Turks in the last war, and there are few Turks in America."

He wiped the last sausage grease from his plate with a crust of bread. He could't help noticing that in a Berlin workers' neighborhood you could buy a mass of sausages that a few years ago only the elite could buy in Moscow. It made it harder to believe in the victory of socialism.

That victory would come, though. Danilov had regular reports from home, and it was clear that the Commonwealth was dividing, one nation against another and rich against poor. One day the poor would rise again, and men like Oleg Bytkin would be ready to lead them.

Meanwhile, it was a step toward that day, to organize a mob of shaved-headed German teenagers to beat up Turks and Poles. That was almost harder to stomach than the sausage, but Oleg Bytkin had a good digestion.

"Sasha?" he said to the other man. Sasha was nicknamed the Walrus. He was about the same size and had the same deceptively slow and deliberate way of moving. If he caught up with an enemy, however, that man was doomed.

"You're sure Gunther is dead?"

"Sasha—"

"I'm joking."

"Don't do it again."

"Where's your sense of humor, Oleg?" Yuri said.

"Where is your discipline, both of you?" Oleg shot back.

"I had to hide it during the August Revolution," Sasha said. "Maybe one day I can dig it up and wear it again."

Bytkin gave up. They were a long way from both home and victory, they couldn't quarrel among themselves and maybe Yuri was right. He was being too serious for a man commanding only two officers, who each now commanded only three men. A major commanding a squad!

"Gunther is dead. Take that as certain."

"If we had a few more days—"

"We don't."

"Very well. I'll spread the rumors of Gunther's death. Then I'll spread another rumor, that the first skinhead to lead a really big demonstration will probably be Gunther's successor."

"They'll really fight for leadership over that pack of swine."

"I swear on my mother's grave—"

Bytkin muttered a classic Russian obscenity about Sasha's mother.

The Walrus shrugged. "All right. I only say Gunther ran things too long. Some of the younger ones thought he was too old, and they were as good. They'll push forward. We can get a lot of work out of them while they're pushing, then turn the ones we don't want over to the police and hand-feed the ones we do."

"All right." Bytkin glared. "I hope you know your skinheads better than you know Polish."

Sasha looked wounded. "The old fool was drunk. I said nothing to make a sober man suspect I was a Russian."

"He suspected you just the same." And that was why a man who had survived slave labor in a mine in Thuringia hadn't survived a trip to Silesia to see his grandchildren. Another body, but one they hadn't been able to hide—and every such body was one more trace somebody might use against them.

"The skinheads don't suspect me. Maybe they think I'm a Silesian myself, from the accent of my German, but anything they need to worry about—no."

"Good." Bytkin stretched and yawned. They slept by day and worked mostly by night, but they would need to go on a regular cycle for awhile, starting tonight. "You're calling it a demonstration?"

"Don't worry, Oleg," Yuri said with a nasty twist of his lips. "That's just a fig leaf for the weaklings and police spies. The ones who really want to crack heads and get the women down on the stones will all be ready!"

"Also good."

It *would* work. Maybe not every time, but often enough. Germany would look like a menace again, and who else to defend the world from her but Russia? Who else to lead Russia in that work, but the socialists?

BOLAN SQUINTED through the window of his back room at the movie theater across the street. It was showing a spaghetti Western, dubbed in German and with Turkish subtitles.

The mean streets were everywhere. On them were people you might not want to invite home, but who deserved to live. Then there were the others, the predators. Bolan had long since made the decision that they deserved to die.

He considered tactics as he polished the front lens of the Weatherby's telescopic sight with a soft cloth. Backup from one source—Beck. Intelligence from another—Stony Man Farm.

Cast the intelligence net widely, too. Look up fifty potential troublemakers for every hit he planned. That would take a few days extra, but it would delay the reaction much more.

The Executioner could still put cross hairs on his first target in Berlin before that target knew he was in danger.

That was a satisfying thought for dawn, even dawn in a Berlin slum with the sun trying to creep through a window that hadn't been washed since the building went up.

STONY MAN FARM WAS nine hours behind Berlin. When Bolan was trying to see sunrise, Hal Brognola was ready to shut down for the night.

At least he'd been trying to shut down, when Bolan's cryptic message arrived. The big Fed needed a cup of coffee to kick-start his brain again, but the telegram did the rest of the job of waking him up.

He almost wished it hadn't come until morning. The days were gone when he could be on the streets all day, then leave a clean desk before he went home at night.

One of the men he'd never tried to fool was Striker. Now Bolan was suspicious of Ludwig, and the Executioner's suspicions carried more weight for Brognola than a foot-high stack of documents from most men.

Okay. Striker would for damned sure be digging on his own for a way to work around both the crippled Berlin contact and the unreliable Willi Beck. He didn't need advice, suggestions, his hand held or anyone looking over his shoulder.

What he did need was the use of Stony Man's contact in the BND.

Hal Brognola checked a number, switched his line to the scrambled telephone and started to dial.

CHAPTER SIX

His third morning in the safehouse, Bolan had breakfast at a Turkish-owned café across from the movie theater. The café had mostly Turkish customers, but they were Turks who had been in Germany for twenty or thirty years and whose children had lived all their lives in Germany. They didn't know quite what to make of Bolan, other than that he was probably neither German nor Turkish, but they were polite and not too curious.

Bolan ate the baklava, but drew the line at the sweet Turkish coffee. He drank his black, and while the waiter refilled his cup he opened the *Berliner Tageblatt* and settled down to read.

A lead article and several features inside covered a ceremony that was coming up in Thuringia. The Germans were kicking off a campaign to clean up all the World War II and Cold War arms dumps in what had been East Germany. It would help the environment and repudiate past militarism, so the first job was going to start off with a fancy ceremony. Lots of VIPs would be showing up at an old silver mine in Thuringia, doing all the things that politicians usually do on such occasions.

One feature mentioned that the Green Party was planning a demonstration at the ceremony. The article didn't make clear if they were supporting the idea or protesting inadequate protection for the environment. The Green Party was a strange mixture of common sense and fanaticism; the demonstration could go either way.

About the time he finished the feature, Bolan noticed that his coffee cup was empty and the waiter was nowhere in sight. In fact, the café was nearly empty, and the owner and his wife were busy putting up the shutters.

Bolan was about to ask what was going on, when he got the answer. From outside he heard ugly chanting.

"Germany united must be clean! Germany united must be clean! Germany united must be clean!"

Then a single thundering voice yelled, "Turks, go home!"

Dozens of pairs of heavy boots came thundering down the street outside, before shouts in Turkish and wordless screams rose to drown them out.

Bolan threw some money on the table, made sure that the 93-R was both concealed and within easy access, and ran out into the street.

HELMUT KUHN HUNG UP the telephone and swiveled his chair so that he could look over the Main River. The morning mist was already departing; it would be a fine day.

The study was on the second floor of the big house in Königstein. It had two picture windows, one looking out over the Main, the other looking down the other side of the rise over the rooftops of the town to the S-Bahn station.

How long had it been since he took the railroad to the office regularly? Three years now, and for two years before that it had been mostly keeping up old habits to get over Gerda's death. The staff at company HQ had been kind; they didn't mind his coming and even looking over their shoulders, when they knew how much he missed his wife.

They had more sense than Erich, God help him. Erich had been after him almost before his mother was buried to sell the big house and move into an apartment. At least he hadn't suggested that Helmut move in with him and Liesl, or their divorce would have happened much sooner than it had.

Kuhn remembered how he finally told his son, "I like this house. It's big enough so that all my ghosts can come and live with me."

Erich was quiet after that, at least on the matter of selling the house. Not otherwise—he always found something to fuss about.

The doctor sighed. It wasn't pleasant to have to think that way about any man who was probably dead. It was worse if the man was your only son. Kuhn suspected that this fine day was going to be largely wasted on him.

He walked slowly but with a firm step over to the wall safe. He was in good shape for a man of seventy-eight, except for the arthritis in his knees. It was a good thing it wasn't in his hands, or he might have had to get a less secure safe than this Gleiber Stahlwerke monster with three different locks.

In five minutes he had out on his desk everything he needed: the old Walther P-38 that he had taken from the SS man, with a box of new 9 mm ammunition; the files he hadn't yet acted on, and now probably wouldn't. He had done enough, anyway. He had many people grateful to him, and even some Waffen-SS veterans admitted that he had handled some difficult situations well.

Finally came the deceptively thin envelope he had received yesterday. No doubt his son's enemies would be able to trace it if they thought of him as a possible recipient. But they probably wouldn't, until it was too late.

The one immediate question was, how far should he bring Trudl into this? She might put herself in danger if he didn't, because she would sooner or later ask questions of people her grandfather didn't trust. They might indeed already have her telephone tapped. It was also possible that they knew about how badly she and her father got along and wouldn't expect that she'd be involved.

Still, it would do no harm to warn her. And in case her phone was tapped, he'd do it by way of a message left with her friend Hedwig. That was a very intelligent girl, Hedwig, and she would be fine-looking, too, if she didn't dress so outrageously.

She also didn't like most of the people who could be dangerous to Trudl, as they had probably already been fatal to Erich. She wouldn't give them the time of day, let alone a friend's secrets.

Kuhn picked up the telephone and began to dial. As Hedwig's telephone rang, he pulled his black notebook toward him and opened it to the next number he was going to call.

Matti Förster of the BND had several numbers, depending on the time of day and what sort of business he was on. But he was one of the people who had good reason to be grateful to Helmut Kuhn. If he got a message from him at any of his numbers, he'd call back before the day was done. That wouldn't save Erich, but it might save others.

BOLAN WAS hardly out the door when he began to wish he'd gone out the back way. He was in no immediate danger, but so many people were jammed back on to the sidewalks that he could barely twitch a finger.

He used feet and elbows more firmly than politely to clear a path to the street. About fifty teenagers and young men were marching down the street, wearing biker outfits heavily decorated with studs and chains. Most of them were skinheads, none looked more than twenty-five and all looked in a permanent bad temper with the whole world, not just with Turks.

In fact, they looked like younger versions of the man who'd shot Singer, and apparently killed another young man just before that. Singer's would-be assassin had somebody who was apparently undercover Spetsnaz interested in his fate. What about these people?

Then Bolan had to shove the thought to the back of his mind to keep from being pushed back on the sidewalk by the skinheads. They stopped, formed a circle, unfolded a couple of chairs, then started unfurling banners as some self-appointed leader climbed on the chairs and began a speech.

Some of the banners read, Germany United Must Be Clean. Others read, Guests Don't Work, Germans Must, and Not Your Homeland, Turk.

The speech, as far as Bolan could follow it, was rude, almost to the point of being insulting to the Turks. The man had an accent that made him hard for the warrior to follow, but the German-speaking Turks seemed to be getting the message. So did his followers. They cheered every time he hinted that Turks were lazy, dirty or trying to live off the wages of German women.

Bolan let himself be pushed clear rather than risk being involved in the first of the fights the thugs must be hoping to start. It was a race between the police arriving and the fights starting, and he didn't intend to give the fights any advantage.

His height let him look over the heads of most of the crowd. He saw that the hardware on the biker outfits didn't include any swastikas or other Nazi regalia, and noted that the speaker wasn't using any Nazi slogans. As far as Bolan could see, he didn't need to. Everyone was getting a racial-purity message straight out of Adolf Hitler's speech book, and the Turks didn't like it.

The warrior also picked out a couple of men from the demonstrators who didn't quite look as if they belonged. They were watching the crowd instead of the speaker, for one thing, and for another they looked older and cleaner than the others. They were trying to look young and dirty, but Bolan could tell an act when he saw one.

Then the slogans and the sneers finally got through to one Turk, and he played into the hands of the neo-Nazis. An empty liquor bottle flew out of the crowd, bounced off one of the banner poles and narrowly missed the speaker's shiny head.

The demonstrators suddenly possessed an arsenal. Bolan couldn't see guns, but those biker-jacket pockets seemed to hold a lot of razors, chains, short clubs and brass knuckles. They might still conceal guns, but as long as the guns weren't out Bolan had to keep his own hidden.

As the peaceful demonstration suddenly turned into a riot, the warrior also saw the two odd men backing toward the movie house. Its door was up a flight of four steps, and from there they'd have a good view—and a clear shot at Bolan, if they wanted one.

They might be police, and anyway they hadn't done anything yet. But the Executioner still had a bad feeling about the two ringers.

Then a Turkish woman staggered back against Bolan, trying to get away from a skinhead who was clawing at her blouse. He swung at her face and caught her on the cheek, bringing his arm within Bolan's reach.

The warrior gripped the German's wrist with one hand and his elbow with the other. The man tried to bring up his other hand, and Bolan interfered with this move by driving a knee into his adversary's groin. He doubled up, presenting his jaw, which the Executioner promptly punched. The man went down on his back, and several Turks immediately jumped on him. Bolan rather hoped they wouldn't get into trouble by seriously hurting the man, but had other things on his mind at the moment—two of which were skinheads who came at him from opposite sides.

They weren't quite undisciplined enough to punch each other when Bolan ducked between them, but he was able to jab one hard in the stomach. The motorcycle jacket didn't cushion enough of the blow. The man gagged and fought for breath, as his friend tried to bearhug Bolan.

The Executioner watched a knife sprout in his adversary's right hand, ready to go into his back. He slammed his head up under the man's chin, chopped his hand across the right wrist, then spun him and kidney-punched him. The skinhead would have gone down if the crowd hadn't been too thick to let him fall.

With the borrowed knife, Bolan now faced the man's partly recovered comrade. The skinhead might be a bigot and a bully, but he wasn't a coward. He also had a blade of his own. It snicked out and nearly slashed Bolan's face. The warrior's riposte cut through the heavy leather of the jacket sleeve and into the arm beneath.

At the same time, the Executioner brought one foot around and hooked the man's left leg out from under him. He crashed down, tried to get up, then howled an obscenity as Bolan's foot came down on his knife hand.

The warrior pocketed the second blade and looked around for more opponents. It seemed he'd cleared his immediate area. Between him and the rest of the skinheads was a churning wall of fighting men, with the Turks getting slightly the worst of it in spite of their edge in numbers. Every so often a boy or a man too old for the fighting would stagger back to the women, who had by now put the children indoors and were back out to encourage their men.

Bolan wanted to encourage them to join the children. If somebody was trying to set up a really nasty incident, a bullet into a Turkish woman could do the job too well.

Then he noticed that the two ringers were still on the theater steps, watching one particular part of the fight. A circle of mixed Turks and skinheads was whirling like a dervish. In the middle of it was a short man almost as bald as one of the skinheads, though much older. He wasn't too old to be fast with his hands, though.

One moment he was jabbing a stiffened hand into a skinhead's stomach. The next he was kicking a second in the knee, then chopping the man across the back of the neck as he staggered. Then Turks cut off Bolan's view of the man, but not his view of the two ringers watching.

The view was clear enough for the Executioner to see one of the men reach inside his jacket. Bolan snatched one of the knives from his pocket, snapped up his arm and flung it hilt first over the heads of the fighters in the street.

It didn't hit hard enough to damage, but it knocked the man's hat off. It also drew the men's attention to Bolan. He stared back at them, his own hand inside his windbreaker. The message he sent was simple: if the man went for his gun, he wouldn't live long enough to use it.

The other man put a hand on the first one's arm. His companion glared, then bent to pick up his hat—taking his other hand away from his jacket as he did.

Bolan didn't stop looking at the men until police sirens rose over the uproar of the fight. That uproar quickly faded, as all the skinheads who could struggled free of their opponents and ran. Most of them got free, except for a few already sprawling in the blood-spattered street.

One runner, unlucky or dumb, stopped to pick up a fallen banner. Two Turks caught up with him, and one snatched the banner pole and hit him over the head with it. Then one grabbed him by the arms, the other by the legs. They swung him several times and heaved him through an unshuttered plate-glass window.

Before the last piece of glass tinkled to the street, Bolan was moving out on the heels of the skinheads and covering ground nearly as fast. Protecting the innocent was a matter of principle. It could also be a matter for the police, if he was still around when they arrived— about three minutes, judging from the howl of the sirens.

Police attention on him would be bad enough. Police attention on the safehouse would be a mess. Beck would have a legitimate complaint about the Executioner if the operation had to be closed down. What little cooperation Bolan could expect would fly out the window. He'd have to shift base and weapons, and do it while the two ringers might be circulating a description of him to half his potential targets.

The Executioner covered ground so quickly that he was six blocks from the riot scene before the sirens burbled into silence. By that time the adrenaline high was fading, and his bullet-creased back was protesting at a level just short of outright pain.

Then ahead of him, he noticed someone who must have run even faster. The short bald man was walking along with the deceptive casualness of somebody who was worried about having a tail. With a clear view of the man, Bolan saw that he was no older than the Executioner, in spite of his bald head.

Maybe it was time to make the man's worries come true. The warrior slowed until the man had a chance to open the distance, then settled down with the ease of long practice to keep the man in sight.

It wasn't entirely idle curiosity or a need for something to do until it was safe to return to base. The man had behaved like a professional, on the same side as Bolan, and operating on the same turf. It would help to know if he was a potential ally or just a well-intentioned loose cannon.

COLONEL DANILOV USED his combat knife to slit open the package of literature from Pamyat, the right-wing Russian nationalist organization. It was authentic, printed in Leningrad—the colonel still had to think twice before calling it St. Petersburg—although he personally thought the organization should shoot its German translator.

So be it. The German nationalists he was playing with didn't place much value on literary elegance. Some of them, he suspected, could barely read their own language. But *he* didn't place much value on their intelligence. In their ability to make asses of themselves, yes, but they didn't need intelligence for that. In fact, intelligence would be a positive handicap for their role in Project Gamma.

Danilov heaved the three unopened packages into a corner and started sorting the contents of the opened one. He should have an orderly for this sort of work, also a clerk, a bodyguard and a driver.

He'd had all of them, at a time that now seemed as distant as the reign of the last czar. He'd been a colonel with Soviet Military Intelligence, the justifiably feared and respected GRU.

Now he was trying to cripple Germany with less than forty men, only half of whom could safely stay in these abandoned villages on the fringes of the Thüringer Wald. The rest had a full plate elsewhere in Germany, and none of them could be spared to wait on Nikolai Feodorovich Danilov.

He wondered how Oleg's little Turkish-skinhead battle was getting along. In this valley radio reception was nothing to boast of, unless you used a satellite antenna that could tell the whole world where you were. Or at least a German reconnaissance plane, which would certainly pass the word to the wrong people.

Danilov willed himself not to worry. Worrying brought ulcers, which he didn't need, and not only because if he showed up in any hospital either in Germany or back home in the Commonwealth, questions would be asked. If he developed an ulcer, he would have to give up liquor, and they made that much better in the West than they did at home.

That reminded him that the bottle of Kummel in his desk would go bad if he didn't drink it, and that he'd missed breakfast even if it wasn't time for lunch. He heated some stew in the microwave that ran off the diesel generator in the next house, poured a glass of liquor, and was feeling somewhat better when he'd finished both.

THE BALD MAN SLOWED sharply soon after Bolan began to follow. For a few minutes the Executioner wondered if he'd been spotted and was being played with, or even led into an ambush.

This was an old part of Berlin, with postwar buildings rising on either side along narrow streets. There were hardly any cars, and in fact not many people on the streets at all.

A few groups of young men, mostly East European, seemed to be hanging out on street corners. They gave Bolan hostile looks as he passed, and the warrior realized he'd have to watch his back until he was out of the area.

One of the youths called a greeting, and Bolan had a chance to scope the people behind him. The man a block behind immediately tried to look like part of the nearest group, but it didn't work. They stared at him in a way that would have told a child he was a stranger.

Bolan couldn't stop to be absolutely sure, but the man looked like one of the two professionals he'd seen at the riot scene. In fact, he looked a lot like the one who'd been about to go for a gun.

With an unknown quarry ahead and a known hostile tail, the Executioner realized that things might be about to heat up.

CHAPTER SEVEN

Bolan's tail soon had a companion. The Executioner couldn't identify him, but recognized the behavior. He was part of the same operation.

What about the short bald man? With those looks, he wasn't likely to be undercover Spetsnaz. That only left about two dozen agencies, some of them unfriendly.

For a man who operated mostly in the shadows, Mack Bolan had a remarkably widespread reputation. But most of it was with men who also operated in the shadows, where many of them belonged.

The short man did seem to be looking back from time to time, always in a way that appeared natural. Another professional, certainly. He never looked anywhere near Bolan, and it struck the warrior that he might be watching for other pursuers. Why?

More unanswerable questions.

Bolan decided that there was no way to deal with some bulls other than by grabbing them by the horns. A step at a time, he increased his speed, until he was less than half a block behind the short man.

Then, in the time it took Bolan to blink, his quarry vanished. The warrior swung hard to the right, slipped into a doorway, drew the 93-R and studied the street.

Across the road was an alley—hardly more than a crack—between two buildings, and the warrior detected movement behind yellow-and-blue trash containers. A stone flew out of the alley and landed at his feet. He crouched to pick it up, looking for his tail as he did.

They hadn't seen anything; they were still coming on, slowly, one on each side of the street. A third man was approaching behind them. He had the same look as the others—a hard, fit professional.

Bolan saw that the stone was wrapped in paper, an old candy wrapping, and removed the paper. The scribbled message read: Both of us against men behind? Wave if okay.

That meant he was under observation from the alley. What would happen if he didn't wave. Bolan saw he couldn't leave the doorway now without exposing himself to the tail at dangerously close range.

The message didn't say much. In fact, it didn't say nearly enough. But something else said the rest of what Bolan needed to know.

The bald man fought skinheads attacking innocent Turks. The men tailing Bolan seemed to be working with the skinheads. That was enough to separate friends from enemies, at least long enough to confront the men behind.

The warrior gave the alley the high sign. Another flicker of movement, and the bald man was standing in the street. It was still hard to tell his age, but his face was almost unlined, and he moved with a spring-legged gait that promised good combat reflexes.

In the next moment, the man needed them. The leading tail went for his gun, as he had at the riot. This time the man behind him, the one who'd restrained him, didn't hold back. He, too, was drawing his weapon.

The third man was getting out of the street when the shooting started. Bolan would have liked to pick him off first. He was probably maneuvering for position or going for help.

Rule one of firefights, though: the most dangerous opponent was the first one to draw. Bolan used a chest shot on the guy who pulled his trigger with a dying man's reflexes. The other hardman hit the street almost beside his friend, with the bald man's round in his leg.

The Executioner stepped out of the doorway and looked for the third man. The street was deserted, except for a few heads popping out of windows to see what the noise was. When they saw the bodies, they popped right back in and slammed the windows.

"Let us check their identities," the bald man said. He knelt beside the wounded man and rummaged through his pockets. The man cursed in accented German, but was too weak from loss of blood to resist. Bolan packed and roughly dressed the thigh wound while the bald man was searching. Both finished about the same time. The wounded man might have permanent leg damage, but he wouldn't bleed to death in the streets if help came within a half hour or so.

"Crap!" The bald man held up a plastic card of a kind Bolan recognized.

"Bundesgrenzschutz," Bolan said. The dead man's pockets produced a similar card, and both were carrying the standard H&K 9-S automatics issued to the German Border Guards. "As you said, crap. The BGS doesn't work undercover or hire hotshots like the one I killed. Or if they've started, they may not want to admit it."

It would be hard on his own conscience if he had accidentally killed a law-enforcement officer, but he had serious doubts that the dead man and his colleagues were anything of the kind.

"Maybe," the man said. Then he suddenly kicked the fallen man in the side of the knee and snapped out an obscenity in Russian.

Bolan was ready to stop his new ally if the man assaulted the prisoner again, but it wasn't necessary. The contortions of the man's face from pain and from hearing Russian said everything.

"Russians," the man muttered. He spit, narrowly missing the body. Then he slipped his own automatic into a pocket. Bolan noted that it was an East German-made Makarov—quite serviceable, able to fire standard Western 9 mm ammunition and virtually untraceable, the East German army's arsenal being up for grabs.

"Probably," Bolan agreed. "Maybe Spetsnaz." The man arched his eyebrows in question, and the warrior answered the query briefly, leaving out most of the details that would identify him but making clear his suspicion that undercover Spetsnaz soldiers were operating in Germany.

While he was listening, the bald man took a miniature camera from another pocket and photographed both men and both ID cards. Then he started to reply.

A police siren too close for comfort stopped him almost before he'd begun. "I think we have common goals," he said hastily. "Not just common...turf?"

Bolan nodded.

"Yes, common turf. You should call your chief and have him ask Itzhak Faber about Davidka 978."

The Executioner nodded. Itzhak Faber was a name he recognized, a high-ranking officer in the Mossad, Israel's military intelligence agency. "Davidka 978, right."

"Call fast," the man urged, as he darted into the alley.

TRUDL KUHN WAS TYPING a financial statement on the cabaret's computer when she heard a familiar voice outside the office. She saved the data and stepped out to greet Hedwig Ott.

"Hello, Trudl. Heard anything about your father?"

"No."

"Too bad. Well, anyone who would play games like that—"

"He's still my father, Heddie." *Or he was,* she added silently. "You here on business, or do I get to kick you down the stairs?"

Hedwig laughed. "No. Business, I think. Your grandfather called. Maybe he has news about your father. Anyway, he wants you to call him, as soon as you can, from a public telephone."

"Public?"

"Public. And he sounded like that was very important."

"Maybe it's about my father."

"I hope it all works out for you, my friend."

Trudl crossed her fingers and blew Hedwig's departing back a kiss. The manager came out of the office just in time to see the other woman leave.

"A sad waste of a beautiful woman, that one," he said. "Ah, well, there are consolations. It would be a sadder waste still if you were like her."

Trudl Kuhn decided that the call could wait until lunch. There would be no explanations needed then for going out, since she never ate at the club. The kitchen served food that could only be eaten by people half-drunk on the liquor or half-deafened by the music.

She also decided that she was going to quit her job. She was never going to be promoted to a real assistant manager's position unless she slept with Mark, and she would rather sleep with a pig. The pig wouldn't be so hairy.

Quitting would embarrass her grandfather. He would ask if she planned on living on her inheritance. Also, it would not be as satisfactory as breaking Mark's arm. But that was illegal, which would also embarrass her grandfather.

BOLAN SPENT THE REST of the day killing time. He wanted to see the evening papers' news coverage of the riot before setting up again at the safehouse. As long as his equipment hadn't been caught in a police sweep of the whole neighborhood, he could continue with the mission.

Shifting bases and reducing his backup meant further delay, though, which meant more time for his targets to be warned, move or retaliate.

If they hadn't already started. Rogue agents were a thorn in the side of Western intelligence agencies. Some of them made Willi Beck look disciplined and organized.

Suppose agents from the former Soviet Union were turning rogue now? It wasn't impossible. Hard currency and a free hand would be tempting prizes, if the price of accepting them from say, the Mafia, wasn't a KGB assassin on your trail.

The Spetsnaz would be particularly useful allies for Western criminals. Or at least the ones accustomed to operating undercover would be, and there were several thousand of those, most of them out of work now.

Bolan had encountered Spetsnaz soldiers more than a few times, and had firsthand evidence that the best of them were as good as U.S. Special Forces, which made them people you didn't want working for anyone with a contract on you.

It was quite possible that the mystery men who seemed to be following him around were Spetsnaz, and that the European Dons had made him and were on his trail.

So Bolan systematically made the life of anyone tailing him about as hard as he could for the rest of the day. He got on and off buses, taxis, U-Bahn and S-Bahn trains.

Following a leisurely early dinner on the sixth floor of Ka-De-We, Berlin's biggest department store, he used one of his Peter Metzger credit cards to buy a new suit and accessories. They effectively changed his appearance, and allowed plenty of room for the Beretta, spare magazines and other weapons of war that weren't sold in menswear departments.

Since the new suit was a little fancy for the neighborhood of the safehouse, he also bought a sweater and slacks, and a suitcase to hold the clothes he wasn't wearing. By the time he finished running up the charges, the evening news was on.

The police claimed more credit for breaking up the riot than Bolan thought they deserved. But nobody had been killed, a good many of the skinheads hadn't run fast enough and were going to do time if convicted, and the damage was light. A collection was already being taken up by the Green Party for the benefit of the victims; a photogenic young couple made the pitch for that particular charity.

No mention was made of combat-trained mystery men bashing skinheads, or of strangers who seemed to be egging on the demonstrators. And above all, no mention of Border Guard agents turning up dead less than a mile from the site of the riot.

Which proved that either Bolan was right, and they were fake, or that the government had put the lid on that piece of news while they launched a nationwide manhunt for the cop killers. He would bet on the first—literally betting his life, because he intended to go on with the mission.

Meanwhile, there was a call to make. That cryptic ID, Davidka 978, needed to be followed up. He couldn't get through to Brognola because of gremlins on the transatlantic telephone links, but made sure a message was left for the big Fed with authorized personnel at Stony Man Farm. By then it was getting dark, with promise of another foggy night.

Fog and darkness hid the damage from the riot when Bolan returned to the safehouse. The concierge met him at the door.

"Such a terrible day. Who would have thought Berlin would see a riot like that?" She went on in this vein for a while, then clapped her hand to her head.

"*Gott*, I will forget my name next. A man left a package for you."

"A package?"

"Yes. He told me to test it before he left. I did. It is safe."

Bolan smiled. That the concierge could perform tests for letter bombs proved one thing he'd suspected for some time. Her scatterbrained German grandmother act was exactly that.

The package was a surprisingly heavy cardboard box that contained a Makarov. He wasn't surprised to see that all the serial numbers had been removed, and that the box also held five loaded magazines and another printed note—In case you need a clean gun for your work. I think it is like mine.

Bolan didn't know if Davidka meant the work or the gun was similar, but could sleep on that and a lot of other questions.

"ITZHAK, CAN YOU hear me?"

"Like you were in the same room, Hal. How are things?"

"Do you have all day to listen?"

"No, and you don't have all day to talk." Brognola heard the Mossad officer chuckling. "So in ten words or less, what is it?"

"Davidka 978."

"What?"

"One of our people has a need-to-know about Davidka 978." There was dead silence for a full thirty seconds.

"If your man's in Berlin, I'll admit the need-to-know," Faber finally replied.

This time the silence was Brognola's fault, although it didn't last as long. He decided that the Mossad so far had no quarrel with Stony Man Farm. Other domestic agencies were a different matter, but Stony Man Farm's charter and the Israeli's had never collided.

"I could get the same stuff from the CIA, Itzhak."

"I suppose you could. But at what price? And wouldn't they ask the same question, and wouldn't you trust me to keep the answer quiet more than you would the CIA?"

Brognola held up a hand to stop the torrent of questions, forgetting that his listener was six thousand miles away. "You asked. I'll tell you. Yes. Our man is in Berlin."

"Fine. Knowing you, I know he's there on some business that won't hurt Israel. It might even help if he succeeds. So I'll tell you about Davidka 978, and then you and your man can take it from there. I'll even authorize our man to work with yours if asked."

"Not order him?"

"You authorize this man, Hal. You don't, if you are as smart as you ought to be in this business, give him orders."

CHAPTER EIGHT

Bolan had a twenty-four-hour wait before he got word on the bald-headed man. He spent it dry-firing the Makarov, a weapon he hadn't used recently, and making sure that its magazines and chamber really would take a standard 9 mm parabellum like the Beretta. It was supposed to, but "supposed to" had killed men Bolan thought knew better.

The Makarov didn't feel quite as solid or smooth as a Western weapon of the same vintage, but as a backup gun or an untraceable one it had its uses. Also, if he had to provide a weapon for somebody suddenly involved in the mission, he could give them the Beretta. He could make up for the Makarov's reduced accuracy with his own marksmanship, while the Beretta helped a less skilled partner stay alive.

The arms-disposal ceremony in the Thüringer Wald was getting to be bigger and bigger news. It was crowding the riot off the front page and almost completely off television. Neither the papers nor the TV mentioned any mysterious people, deaths or other incidents in connection with the riot.

Bolan got a clue as to why when he stopped by the local newsstand to pick up the papers. The owner was German but his assistant was Turkish. When the owner was out of hearing, the assistant handed the warrior a bag containing a fifth of whiskey and whispered to him in broken English, "No much—save my sister. You do good."

The local Turks apparently respected their champion's desire to remain anonymous. They probably didn't trust the police. They certainly wouldn't trust the skinheads to leave him alone. They might even think they would need him again.

The telegram from Hal Brognola in mission-specific cryptic came that night. It said that the bald-headed man was an authentic Mossad agent named Zev Ben Shlomo, that he was a sort of floating asset for Mossad operations in Germany, and that he was completely reliable and very good. Bolan had full authority to deal with him as much or as little as might help the mission. The telegram also included a selection of message drops that the Mossad thought were secure no more than twenty-four hours ago.

Bolan decided to leave a message. If nothing else, Zev Ben Shlomo had been operating in Berlin for nearly ten years. He'd have a feel for the territory that the Executioner could draw on.

He also might be something of a loose cannon, maybe even worse than Willi Beck. Anyone who handed over untraceable automatics to people he knew only as allies in a shootout clearly made his own rules.

THE LAST OF THE CRATES came down the hill into the trees, on the shoulders of a thickset middle-aged German. Colonel Danilov counted the boxes now piled beside the mountain track, waiting for the pickup.

The three Germans standing beside the crates looked nervous. Maybe part of it was exhaustion. Nobody went down into any part of the mine linked with the gas cave without chemical protective gear. It was the best from the old Volkswehr stocks, but no protective gear was comfortable for heavy work.

The rest of what was bothering them had to be nerves. Dealing with representatives of Pamyat was one thing. It was a legal political group in the Commonwealth, with its own press, and faithful members. It had the right to send representatives abroad, to deal with other representatives of legal political parties in Germany.

Circulating its anti-Semitic propaganda wasn't so safe. There were German laws about that sort of thing. Danilov personally thought they were silly. Laws against hating Jews were like laws against drinking—nobody could enforce either.

As for paying good money to the Pamyat representatives for weapons and explosives from Volkswehr stocks—that was terrorism. The German laws were very strict in that regard. Everything except the death penalty could strike these men, if anyone was killed by what had started out as a game.

Danilov understood perfectly why they were nervous, but they should also know that he wasn't playing games. But then, Germans had never understood Russians and never would. Russians could do better, particularly if they had spent fifteen years in the German Democratic Republic on an assignment for the GRU that the Stasi never knew about.

If Colonel Danilov hadn't been an atheist, he would have offered up prayers of thanks the day the mobs in East Berlin stormed the Stasi headquarters and looted its files before they could be destroyed. Very few Soviet operations in the GDR survived long after those files reached Western intelligence agencies. Most of the ones not destroyed by the West were shut down by the cowards who now ruled.

The sound of a laboring truck engine rose above the night breeze and the creaking of the pines. Then the faint fireflies of blackout headlights appeared downhill. The truck rattled and banged over the last dozen potholes, then wheezed to a stop.

Danilov decided to part with a little more money to let these idiots buy a better vehicle. He had visions of this one breaking down on the mountain roads back to the Greater Germany Party's headquarters. Oh, wouldn't the police have an exciting night when they opened those crates!

And oh, wouldn't Danilov and his men have an exciting day running for their lives when GSG-9's crack antiterrorist squads parachuted onto their mountain....

The Germans seemed to find new energy with the truck's arrival. The three crates of ammunition and the one crate of grenades and AK-74s seemed to fly into the back of the truck. Then they vanished under a pile of sacks of potatoes and turnips. The driver climbed out, wiped his face with a filthy handkerchief and leaned against the fender while his friends joined the cargo in the back.

Five minutes later the truck was gone, the mountain and the forest were silent and Danilov was alone with Yuri in the middle of the silence.

"Ah, Colonel," the lieutenant said. He was even more nervous than the Germans, and with even more reason. "You have read Oleg—"

"Major Bytkin!"

"Major Bytkin's letter?"

"Yes. It tells me nothing you haven't already told me yourself." That was truer than Yuri would know, until it was too late.

"Thank God." Now it was the Russian who wiped a sweating face.

"Yuri, I hate to ask you to suit up, but I have had too much exposure these past few days, and the circuits for the gas cave need inspecting."

"One of the technicians—"

"Two of them are also at their exposure limit, and one is unavailable for other reasons." Yuri might possibly live long enough to guess those reasons.

"All right. It will take longer to suit and unsuit than to do the checks, though."

"I don't care if it takes all night! Nobody goes close to that poison without gear."

"I serve the Soviet Union."

No, Danilov thought as he watched Yuri head for the dugout where the chemical protective gear was stored. He did not serve the Soviet Union.

He served Nikolai Feodorovich Danilov. *He* served the Soviet Union. At least there were those in the Commonwealth and in what remained of the once-mighty German Group of Forces, who thought he did. They had given him what the capitalists called a "blank check" to make trouble for Germany, in the hope that it would make everyone turn to a strong Russia to save them from the Germans.

Maybe he would use that blank check the way they wanted him to. And maybe he would find that it was better to cash it and use it to buy a "piece of the action" in the new Germany.

Meanwhile, there was Yuri Votolov. He had mishandled a mission, not led his men from in front and abandoned one of them wounded and the other dead. Such a man was useless for any purpose, except betrayal, and

Danilov intended to see that he wouldn't serve that purpose.

From the dugout, the colonel could hear grunting and cursing as Yuri struggled into his protective gear. The longer he took and the more he sweated, the better. He would come out of the cave in a fog of exhaustion, not likely to react quickly in an emergency.

Still, precautions were never wasted. Danilov reached into the pocket of his camouflage-pattern safari jacket and patted the PSM automatic pistol nestled in the bottom. The little gun could hardly kill a fly at more than ten meters, but if used as planned, the range would be more like ten centimeters.

"WHERE DO WE MEET?"

"My safehouse might not be the best place," Bolan replied.

"You—" Ben Shlomo began, then broke off. The Executioner had the strong sensation of something vitally important left unsaid.

He also suspected that it involved Willi Beck's little free-lance espionage ring, which made the safehouse totally unsafe for discussing it—the bugs that Bolan had already spotted could probably detect even quiet conversations.

"There's a drugstore across the street from the Tempelhof U-Bahn station. Know it?" Bolan asked.

"Yes."

"We can meet there and move out. I'll be at the station no later than eleven."

"The trains slow down by then."

"Who said I'd be taking the train?"

"I see."

"Good. I'll be wearing tan slacks and a black sweater."

Which he would pack in the suitcase and change into somewhere along the way. If the safehouse wasn't under surveillance by now, it was because Bolan was imagining threats, and he didn't think his imagination was that rampant.

"I will see you."

The line went dead.

DANILOV LOOKED at the luminous dial of his watch. Yuri had been underground for more than an hour after putting on the gear. Now he was taking his time about getting out of it.

Anton should have all the time he needed to get into position. Danilov reached into his pocket again, chambered a round in the PSM, then snapped on the safety.

An airliner flew by overhead, probably on its way to Dresden. An interesting place, that old Saxon capital. Now they were talking about restoring it to the baroque splendor from before the great fire raid of 1945.

Danilov doubted that even the capitalists could come up with the money for such an ambitious project.

A faint whistle sounded from the trees in front. It was so quiet that Yuri, thirty meters behind in the dugout, couldn't possibly hear it. Danilov not only heard it, he knew what it meant.

Anton had reached his planned position. Now to see that Yuri did the same.

The colonel hurried back to the dugout, doing a good imitation of a chair-bound colonel needing help from a field-wise junior officer. "Lieutenant, Lieutenant!" he whispered urgently. "Intruder to the front. No visual yet, but I need a second man."

Yuri lurched up the dugout stairs, his face slack and hair damp with sweat. But he had his AKR unslung.

Danilov suddenly felt caution. An automatic weapon could make even a fool seem wise if he fired first.

The surge of caution must have made him look even more foolish. Yuri's grin was almost smug. "All right, Colonel. Let's both get down, then we'll cover the approach from both sides. Oh, I forgot. You don't have anything but that PSM, do you?"

"No."

"There's another AKR in the dugout. Get it and the other pouch of magazines, and we can hold our front until daylight. I don't think anybody's going to want to be sneaking around here with a weapon after dawn."

Danilov's caution grew stronger. To go down into the dugout would mean turning his back on Yuri. Worse, he would be doing it while Anton might not have a clear shot at the lieutenant. The same story that he planned to tell about Yuri might serve the lieutenant for explaining his colonel's death.

Not for the first time, Danilov wished he could have found some way of executing Project Gamma and its relatives without all these young Spetsnaz stallions. He was a good soldier, but they were better and they knew it.

Danilov tried not to hunch his shoulders in anticipation of a bullet. He almost cried out with relief when the dugout door closed behind him, and his hands closed on the AKR. He slipped in a magazine, slung on the pouch, but didn't bother to sling the weapon itself. He was coming up with it in his hands, and the devil carry off Yuri if he so much as sneezed—

The shot cracked out as Danilov kicked the door open. The lieutenant fell backward, drilled straight through the forehead by the rifle bullet. The entry hole was neat; the hole in the back of his skull wasn't. In fact, his skull no longer had a back.

Danilov kept his head below the ground level and called out the agreed-on code word. A moment later he heard Anton's reply. Then he waited—it seemed like an hour—until the technician approached. He hardly heard the man. Anton was a very good field soldier, for someone so good with electronics as well.

Anton held his AK-74 in one hand as he looked down at the dead lieutenant. "That settles him, Colonel."

"Yes, it does." Danilov had the uneasy feeling that other things weren't settled.

"I don't want to do this again."

"I hadn't planned to ask you—"

"Colonel, I don't think you planned this one, either. But he's dead all the same. Next time you won't plan it, but you'll say you'll expose me if I don't do it anyway."

"You have my word—"

"Of a Soviet officer? There is no such thing anymore, remember, Colonel?"

"Officer or Soviet?"

"Don't play games, Colonel. I want out, or I go out and talk."

"The Germans would never—"

"Who said anything about the Germans? What about Major Bytkin?"

Danilov felt rooted to the spot. Oleg was a fanatic. He might approve of Yuri's execution. He would also feel that a mere suspicion of Danilov's loyalty justified his executing the colonel and taking over the mission. He would make a mess of it, but that wouldn't bring Nikolai Feodorovich Danilov back to life.

"What do you want?"

Anton relaxed. His hand held the rifle slackly. "Hard currency, the equivalent of a hundred thousand American dollars. And a Polish identity. I speak enough to fool most Germans or Americans."

"The Americans could bring up a native Pole. Many of them live in America."

"What I can't do with my tongue, I'll do with the money. So make it two hundred thousand doll—"

Anton's extortion came to an end as Danilov lifted the PSM and squeezed the trigger. Three of the rounds from the miniature side arm struck Anton in the throat and mouth. He made a gobbling noise, tried to raise his rifle, then clawed at his face and toppled.

Danilov scrambled back into the dugout and snatched his own protective gear from its rack. His fingers trembled as he snapped, zipped and otherwise fastened himself into the cocoon that allowed a man to live in the hell below.

He had to dispose of the bodies, and he knew where. There was a side tunnel with a pit at the end. The Germans had dumped the bodies of slave laborers down there. Danilov had seen the bones and knew that a few fresh ones would be hard to pick out. As for anyone smelling them—the gas didn't kill all bacteria, but the protective gear would shut out the reek of a sewage farm.

He had underestimated Anton badly, and even to some degree foolish Yuri. As he picked up Anton's body, Colonel Danilov began making a mental list of the people under him it would be dangerous to underestimate.

By the time he finished disposing of the bodies, it was near dawn and he had concluded that there were no fools under his command.

THE SIGN on the door read Adolf's. The proprietor was nearly Bolan's height, about half again as broad through the chest and belly, totally bald on top and gray-bearded below.

He was also totally uncurious about what Zev Ben Shlomo and Mack Bolan might be talking about in one of his back booths. The man ignored them completely and went about his own business.

"No data on other people—"

"Mossad people?" Bolan asked.

"What else do you think?"

"You weren't clear." He no longer doubted that Ben Shlomo spoke adequate English. The problem was his reluctance to speak at all.

"I think you should give me the data on your other people—" Bolan began, then held up a hand as Ben Shlomo started to get up. "No. Sit down, please.

"I mean only the people who might be close to one of my targets. Otherwise I might take them for enemies, and they'd be in danger. If I know who they are, I could warn them."

This was pretty basic fieldcraft, but for teams. Ben Shlomo had either worked all his career as a solo, or else forgotten what he'd learned in his days as a junior team member. Either way, he was as likely to give Bolan a headache as a helping hand.

"Okay. But you get only the names. They do not go to your office, if security is bad. And never to Beck."

"Never?"

"If Beck learns one name, we cannot work together. Or worse."

"Don't waste your breath on threats," Bolan said evenly. He was beginning to wonder if the encounter with Zev Ben Shlomo really had been such good luck after all.

"It would not be me deciding against you," Ben Shlomo said with a shrug. "My chiefs do not like losing agents because someone else talks too much."

"I've had my suspicions about Beck myself," Bolan admitted cautiously. "What about you?"

"Sloppy, and worse. I think—I say I *know*, but my chiefs are not sure—Beck is doubled."

"Beck himself?"

Ben Shlomo shook his head. "No. Someone close to him, which leaves maybe four, five people. He either does not know or maybe ignores it. But Beck does not keep secrets."

Which made him a likely candidate for the leak. Bolan's first sensation was one of enormous relief, that Hal Brognola had been spared a long and dismal manhunt.

Then the relief faded. Even if he and Brognola were satisfied that Beck was the source of the trouble, they would have to prove it to other people before Beck would be cut off. People like the CIA and the BND, not to mention the French DGSE. They all owed Ludwig for high-grade intelligence over many years, and none of them would pull the plug on him without hard evidence.

Even if they all did it eventually, they wouldn't do it fast enough to take Beck out of the field while Bolan was in Berlin. The Executioner sipped the last of his beer and smiled grimly down into the brew. It was going to be interesting, facing Mafia-hired rogue Spetsnaz soldiers without being sure his own people wouldn't shoot him in the back.

CHAPTER NINE

Bolan had picked his first target in Berlin carefully.

He wanted property rather than people. The German police would pay much less attention to a burned warehouse than to a sniped victim, even if the victim was a known criminal.

The Executioner knew that one or two raids on enemy supplies was becoming his most common way of opening a campaign. Was it becoming a predictable pattern? Patterns and predictability could kill. Especially when dealing with an old enemy such as the Mafia.

The American Mafia could have handed over their files on the Executioner to their European counterparts. Of course, even legal intelligence agencies didn't usually cooperate that much. Criminals were even less likely to do so—except for the Japanese Yakuza, and Bolan sincerely hoped that they weren't a factor in Europe yet.

The warehouse raid had another big advantage, which along with not annoying the police outweighed anything else. The local mafiosi were less likely to be using their tame Spetsnaz and other elite soldiers to guard warehouses.

Bolan crouched in the shadows outside the first of four warehouses on his prospective target list. The building had started life during the Third Reich as an SS training facility, and was built accordingly—reinforced concrete, steel beams and, during the war, a couple of bomb shelters.

It would take a small tactical nuclear weapon to demolish it and a truckload of thermite to burn it out completely. Bolan hoped for some help from the building's contents.

If his intelligence was correct, the building was a dump for Volkswehr weapons that arms dealers hoped to peddle to anybody with a convincing amount of money. This category usually included the Basques. Tonight's raid could also be one more favor to those friendly agencies. If you could call somebody friendly who used a security leak in your organization to make an embarrassing request . . .

He'd passed on Ben Shlomo's suspicions about Beck's group, in another mission-specific cryptic telegram to Brognola. That ensured that the intelligence wouldn't die with him or the Israeli.

Bolan wore his blacksuit, and carried the 93-R, the Desert Eagle, climbing and night-vision gear and a light pack of explosives. Hooded and gloved, he was almost invisible in the shadows. A thorough recon of the site confirmed the absence of electronic sensors.

No surprise, either. Heavy protection signaled that you had something worth protecting. The kind of armed-guard and attack-dog security common in the States skirted the edge of the law in Germany, besides telling everybody that you had some reason to be afraid of intruders.

Which these people did. A woman scorned had no fury compared to a terrorist who thought he'd paid good money for bad weapons. Bolan expected that tonight's work would be put down as the revenge hit of a dissatisfied customer.

The building was built into the side of a low rise in the ground. On the south side, away from the loading area, Bolan could almost have climbed the roof bare-handed.

He used the hook and line for greater speed, then used the cover of the roof's high cornice to do a final eyeball reconnaissance. Maps were useful; the evidence of his own senses was indispensable.

If the place had ever had skylights, they hadn't survived the postwar rebuilding. The same rebuilding had, however, driven two man-size ventilation shafts through the concrete slabs of the roof. The warrior noted that the fans in one were on, but the other seemed clear at least through the roof.

His pack held half a dozen prepackaged charges of C-4. Tying one to the climbing line with a slipknot, he set the fuse for five minutes. Then, searching the landscape for any sign of movement, he lowered the charge to the top of the junction box where the main power line entered the building.

Five minutes should give him plenty of time to get inside and locate any security measures that depended on electricity. When there wasn't any more electricity, he'd be ready to move.

Bolan slid down the ventilation shaft and found himself in such a cramped space that he barely had room to get out his wire cutters. Once free, they made quick work of the mesh screen on the shaft. He pushed out the free corner and dropped silently to the dusty floor.

The second floor looked not only unsecured, but unused and deserted. A few footprints suggested somebody had been there recently, as did randomly scrawled graffiti. One of the graffiti, although badly faded, was unmistakably a swastika.

The door to the stairs was locked, but an open elevator shaft had been run up through the floor in one corner. There was no elevator car, but a glimmer of light below indicated activity down there.

Bolan wasn't surprised. The most secure place in the building was probably the old bomb shelter. He'd work his way down there by stages. He checked the Beretta and his IR goggles and flashlight, the critical gear for the next stage, and started to climb down the elevator shaft.

It was a rough improvisation that had never been improved since it was built, with no luxuries like a safety ladder. There was also no place on the second floor to securely hook the climbing rope. The descent would have to be done the hard way.

Bolan climbed down from beam to beam, sometimes using more precarious foot- and handholds. Once his hand slipped on a patch of ancient grease. To keep from falling, he had to brace himself without worrying about the noise.

He froze for a moment and listened. Somebody was definitely at work on the first floor. He heard the voices of at least two men speaking in German, the sound of a file and the clink of small metal parts.

He resumed his descent as soon as the men resumed working, with no sign that they'd heard anything. One minute to go for the charge, and he wanted to be at the level of the first floor before it went off.

Bolan made it with seconds to spare. He had just time to spot an improvised workshop, with two men standing by a tool-covered bench. He thought they were working on an assault rifle, and on top of a pile of crates behind their bench lay something that looked suspiciously like an RPG-7 antitank launcher.

Then the C-4 on the junction box went off with a boom that was muffled by the thick walls of the building. As the lights died, the warrior saw the two men spring back from the bench, moving fast in spite of their heavy build.

Bolan hurled himself across the shaft, hitting the floor as he went into a paratrooper's roll. He came up with the 93-R in his hands, just as one of the men snapped on a flashlight. The yellow glare half dazzled him, but he could see the other man drawing an automatic.

It was a small one, probably a Walther PPK, but quite lethal at that range. It proved that the man was no innocent.

In the next moment he proved that he was certainly a fool. He ignored Bolan's order in German to "freeze," as well as the Beretta in the warrior's hand. He simply let fly with the PPK, hardly bothering to aim.

The next moment, he paid the price of shooting at a man who already had the drop on him. Bolan caressed the trigger of the 93-R and a 3-round burst drilled into the man's chest. The hardman knocked the bench over as he fell to the floor. His friend dived behind the bench for cover, drawing his gun and firing on the run.

The shots missed, as Bolan sprinted to a new position. By the time the Executioner was in place, the hardman was behind the overturned bench. He seemed to reckon that the heavy wood could protect him from 9 mm rounds. That, Bolan knew, was optimistic. The man also didn't know about the capabilities of the Desert Eagle.

He learned in the next moment, as he bobbed up to fire at Bolan, his bullet gouging paint chips from the battered concrete floor. Bolan's return shot punched a .44 Magnum slug through the bench as if it were cardboard and through the torso of the man behind it. He slammed against the wall, hung there for a moment, then slid down out of sight.

Bolan moved as fast as reasonable caution allowed to get around the table. As he approached the floor, another bullet ripped up from the floor, missing his thigh. He sprang back to flatten himself against the wall, staring at the man he'd shot.

The man had to be dead or unconscious, with a .44 round in his chest. He didn't even have a gun in his hand. The Makarov he'd been carrying lay amid the parts of the disassembled assault rifle.

As the third man raised the trapdoor to take another poorly aimed shot, Bolan spotted him. Instead of returning fire, he let himself fall with a convincing crash.

He lay still until he heard footsteps approaching. Through half-closed eyes he saw the gunner loom over him, a Czech CZ 85 in one hand. The man had good taste in guns, but that didn't save him as Bolan rolled, snatched up the Beretta and got off a head shot.

The gunner had barely hit the floor when the Executioner was up, pulling out a grenade, yanking the pin and bowling the bomb along the floor toward the open trapdoor. Bolan hoped he could discourage any further hardmen from coming up, without hurting any innocents who might be below in the bomb shelter—if there were any innocents in this building tonight, which he was beginning to doubt.

When the grenade went off, it touched off a major secondary explosion, with the eye-searing white glare of thermite. Then high explosives started cooking off. The trapdoor flew into the air, landing halfway across the floor, followed by bits and pieces of flaming thermite.

In the intervals between explosions, Bolan heard the almost comic popcorn sound of small-arms ammunition igniting, anything from a few rounds to a whole box at a time. He now had ample evidence that the place was in fact a major depot for illegal arms merchants, evidence that was busily destroying itself as he listened.

It was time to get out of there, before the flames set off enough explosive power to bring the whole place down on his head. Not to mention that this mission had turned out to be anything but a silent recon-and-demolition. Every police agency in Berlin and the CID from the American Berlin Brigade would have men there within minutes.

Getting out took longer than the warrior had anticipated. There was plenty of light from the blaze downstairs, but the smoke was getting thick. Thermite fumes clawed at Bolan's lungs and made his eyes water enough to blur his vision even more.

The main loading door was electrically operated, and with a lack of the usual German thoroughness the warehouse owners hadn't provided a hand crank as a backup. This left the two personnel doors, one of which turned out to have been bricked up. The other had a complicated security system, also electrically operated and out of commission.

Bolan searched in the thickening smoke for a manual release and finally gave up. Instead he pulled out one of the charges of C-4, set the fuse for one minute, slapped it onto the doorknob and dived for the nearest cover.

The warrior's night activities hadn't done the partly healed bullet crease across his back any good. He could feel blood oozing from the wound as he crouched, waiting for the C-4 to blow and hoping the concussion in the enclosed warehouse wouldn't damage him.

The door cooperated. It blew outward, nearly coming off its hinges. Bolan sprinted across the floor, glanced out to locate the nearest bit of cover and leapt to the ground without touching the stairs.

He'd just reached the cover of a drainage ditch when the final explosion went off. The bomb shelter must have held enough explosives to arm an active terrorist organization for years. Flames spewed from the door and ventilation shafts of the warehouse. Even the loading door buckled, allowing Bolan a glimpse of the inferno raging inside.

The warrior waited for the last burning fragments to fall before he stood and flexed his shoulders. His back was sore, but not damaged again, at least not to the point where he couldn't fight or shoot.

As he climbed out of the ditch, he heard a swelling rumble from the warehouse. The wall facing him was sagging inward, and as it sagged the weight of the roof pressed it down even harder. Then steel beams twisted with shrieks like damned souls, and half the warehouse collapsed on itself in a tumult of crashing and splitting concrete and swirling smoke and dust.

Bolan had covered at least half a mile before he heard the police sirens. The damp night air cleared his eyes and throat, and his back was no longer hurting. One thought, however, wouldn't leave his mind.

Instead of a low-profile first raid, he'd struck a major blow at an illegal operation. A major blow, but one that wouldn't affect the manpower his enemies had available, and would make the ubiquitous German police even more alert.

"GOOD DAY. This is Helmut Kuhn's residence. Who may I say is calling?"

"Ilse, it's me."

"Ah, Trudl. I assume you want to talk to your grand-father."

"I do."

The line was quiet for a moment, as Ilse switched the call upstairs. She could handle a switchboard better than Trudl herself, but then she had been a plotter at a Luft-waffe radar station during the war.

"Trudl, you took your time about calling. I hope you have not been pestering the people I told you to leave alone."

Trudl Kuhn started to bristle at her grandfather's lec-ture-hall tone. Then she realized that something was different. He sounded less concerned about her behav-ior than about something more serious.

Her safety? Perhaps.

She decided that while she had her grandfather on the line she would ask *him* the questions, and guess only about the ones he wouldn't answer.

"No, but I am about ready to file a missing-persons report on him with the police unless you give me some good reason not to. Then the people I have been leaving alone will be bothered by the police, whatever I do or say."

"I will give you a telephone number to call. You talk to the man who answers to the name of Siegfried. He will talk freely, because I have asked him to."

Trudl didn't doubt her grandfather. She had known for some years that he could ask many people, right up to the level of senators and ministers, all sorts of ques-tions, and they would very often answer. Some of it was undoubtedly his money and his reputation for honesty, but some of it had to come from somewhere else.

Did that "somewhere else" have anything to do with her father's disappearance? Was her grandfather doing all this out of guilt?

Those were questions she certainly couldn't ask him. Or anybody else, for that matter, including Siegfried.

She would call Siegfried, however. He might answer some of the other questions.

"I'll call, Grandfather."

"Good. And make that call from a public telephone, too."

It had to be true. He thought her telephones were tapped, and that she would be in danger if anyone knew she was communicating with him.

What had her father been doing, besides spending money on orgies that somebody else got on film?

"Thank you, Grandfather."

"Thank *you*, Trudl. You have taken a weight off my mind."

BOLAN RETURNED to the safehouse before dawn. He cleaned and secured his weapons, showered, put a fresh dressing on his wound, ate, then slept until early afternoon.

By the time he awoke, a cryptic telegram from Hal Brognola had arrived. It directed him to call one of the numbers for the BND and arrange a meeting with someone code-named Parsifal at the earliest convenience. It also suggested that he use a public telephone.

Bolan made the call, although he didn't like the implications of the last suggestion. It sounded as if Brognola thought the leak in Beck's organization was high enough so that he would have access to the bugs at the safehouse. Had the Mossad offered some more convincing evidence that the big Fed wasn't passing along?

Make that *couldn't* pass along because of the lack of secure communications. This was one of those situations where the safest solution was to scrub the whole mission. Or at least defer it until Bolan had a new base and secure communications.

That was the safest course for the Executioner. For the people who might in the meantime die at the hands of those Bolan hunted, it would be the most dangerous. So there was no choice, unless Bolan was to turn his back on his most deeply held principles.

He called and arranged the meeting for the next day, at the Tiergarten Zoo. The site was open enough to make it easy to detect a tail, but crowded enough so that anybody who wanted to keep a low profile would be reluctant to try a hit.

Bolan also had a couple of other assets that he didn't discuss. One was Zev Ben Shlomo. A call to him from the same telephone, and the warrior had his backup in place.

The other was the news report. The explosion in the warehouse was being called a tragic accident, the result of inadequate safety precautions. The Green Party was calling for the environmentally safe destruction of all former Volkswehr weapons, rather than trying to sell them to fascist regimes abroad.

For once, Bolan heartily agreed with the Green Party. The army of the former German Democratic Republic had simply left their weapons and gone home. Throw in everything the Soviet Group of Forces couldn't ship home or didn't have an offer for, and eastern Germany had to be absolutely awash with lethal hardware.

Some of the planes were staying in Germany, but much of the hardware was going to wind up in the hands of criminals.

"GOOD EVENING, Mr. Wegener."

Hans Wegener grunted something that might have been a polite reply, and something else that might have been a request for beer. The waiter in Schimmel's back room knew when one of his best customers had had a bad day, and took no offense.

Wegener's day had been worse than he would dare admit to his closest confidant. It had been bad for him, for the Beck organization and for his friends.

The volume of calls Helmut Kuhn was placing hadn't decreased. There had never been any safe way to put Kuhn's house under electronic surveillance, so much of what had been discussed had to be guessed. But there could be no doubt that Kuhn was on the trail of his missing son.

It had even reached the point where Wegener's man in the Berlin BND office had reported a call from Kuhn. Not to him, but he had overheard one of his colleagues planning a meeting on the basis of such a call. He didn't know who the man was meeting, but it was to be at the Tiergarten.

Wegener could do something about that—after dinner, for he wouldn't unsettle his digestion and waste one of Schimmel's fine meals. They had the Bockwurst tonight, and it was impossible to find a better version of that long sausage anywhere in Berlin.

The Bockwurst came, and half a bottle of wine with it. They improved Wegener's mood, in spite of the newspaper stories about the warehouse "accident."

A pity the Beck organization couldn't claim any credit for that. Sabotage was considered terrorism or American gangster tactics by too many Germans.

Also, some of those arms had been intended for the Basques. Their man in Berlin had already asked a few questions about the raids in Southern France. If he learned that the Beck organization had accidentally contributed to those raids, it would mean Wegener's having to go underground, with or without Dannemeier's help.

People talked about the "vengeance" of the big intelligence agencies. They didn't know what the word meant. The Basques did. It meant that if you harmed them, they came and killed you. Very simple.

Wegener almost ordered another half bottle of wine to calm his nerves. He changed his mind and had only a cordial. Then he paid and went out to the nearest public telephone.

It took him three tries to reach the man he wanted, but after that, business went as quickly as usual. Wegener had been Beck's specialist in hiring help on the streets of Berlin for five years. He knew most of the trustworthy men, and Carl Braun was about the best of them.

"We don't try a snatch?"

"No. Just find the meeting and get descriptions of everyone there."

"License numbers?"

"If they leave by car, all right. Don't push it."

"For what you're paying me, Wegener, I am barely willing to send my people out at all."

"Don't worry, Carl. If this leads where I suspect it will, there will be plenty of fun and money to go around."

Now came the call Wegener had been dreading. Carl was a street thug, but he was also a bully. Confront him with danger he couldn't handle, and he'd back down.

The tall fair man who called himself Schweiger and looked like he had stepped out of a Waffen-SS recruiting poster wouldn't back down from anything. He seemed to think there was no enemy he could not beat, and it was just possible that he was right.

Nonetheless, he and Dannemeier had to know. If Wegener told them soon enough and did what they asked, maybe they would answer a few of his questions. Such as had they killed Erich Kuhn, instead of relying on Wegener to mislay Kuhn's file on something called Project Gamma?

CHAPTER TEN

Zev Ben Shlomo called for Bolan the next morning in a battered Nissan. It was the sort of anonymous compact car that was found by the thousands along the streets of every major city. It looked as if it were carrying a small cosmetic firm's least successful salesman on his rounds, instead of two of the more dangerous men in Berlin to a crucial meeting.

As they drove around looking for a place to park, Ben Shlomo lit a cigarette and said, "I showed the ID and pictures to my chief. He took them to the BGS. They have no records of those men."

"Nice to have that confirmed. Did they ask any awkward questions about how you got the pictures?"

"If they did, my chief did not say. I am sure he answered them very politely if they were asked."

Bolan knew that was as much of an answer as he was going to get, and concentrated on finding a parking spot. Like any large city, Berlin had more cars than it had places to put them, and the search took a good twenty minutes. He also kept a lookout for tails, but didn't spot any and doubted anyone would be able to manage the job in this traffic.

They ended up a twenty-minute walk from the Tiergarten, left the car at different times and moved by different routes. Bolan was sure Ben Shlomo could keep his own rear safe, from what he had seen of the bald man.

Also, Ben Shlomo might not be in the Mafia files. They had very little to do with the Middle East, except for the Turkish opium business, and even that was largely in French and Corsican hands.

The Israeli probably was in the files of the GRU, the masters of Spetsnaz. But Bolan couldn't imagine what was left of the former Soviet military intelligence handing over vital files to random mafiosi. The kind of low-ranking Spetsnaz likely to go rogue wouldn't have access to the central files.

Bolan was the first to arrive at the meeting place, a circle of benches about two hundred yards inside the main gate of the zoo. A medium-size linden tree cast a welcome shadow, as the day was beginning to get hot.

Five minutes later, Bolan saw Ben Shlomo chatting with a sausage vendor and gave him the hand signal that asked whether he'd been tailed.

The Executioner got a thumbs-down, pulled out a newspaper and did his best to look like part of the scenery. He hoped it wouldn't get so hot that his sport jacket would look suspicious, since he had the Beretta in a shoulder holster and the Desert Eagle in a fiberglass attaché case.

Two minutes later a nondescript man sauntered past Ben Shlomo, then drifted toward Bolan. He tossed a crumpled paper bag at the trash can behind the Executioner's bench and missed. Bolan bent over, picked up the bag, uncrumpled it and read the note.

A jerk of his head, and the man sat down beside him.

"You Metzger?"

Bolan nodded. "You're . . . ?"

"Call me Dieter. I can't *stand* Wagner, so I never use the Parsifal name in person." Dieter's English was almost as accentless as Beck's.

"So, what do you have for me?"

Dieter jerked his head toward the entrance of the zoo. Bolan looked. Nothing stood out, nobody was acting suspiciously; he saw only a tall blond girl in a miniskirt and looking good in it.

"A problem," Dieter replied. "One of my colleagues—he uses the name Siegfried—had a call from Helmut Kuhn. Then he got a call from Trudl Kuhn, who said her grandfather had told her to call him about her father."

It took Bolan a moment to catch up, then he realized he had no idea who the Kuhn family was and said so.

"You haven't had a need-to-know?"

"Not for the Kuhns."

"It might be too late. Siegfried brought Trudl along. That's her over there in the miniskirt."

The woman was now brushing crumbs off her hands and looking toward the bench. Dieter made a small hand signal, and the blonde wrinkled her nose. It was a remarkably good imitation of a woman who was running out of patience with her boyfriend's gabbing with old buddies.

"I see. Not very professional of your friend. Or does Kuhn have something on him?"

"Probably. Or he might be something like you—willing to use irregular methods if the regular ones will let a real criminal get away. I do know that *I* owe him a few favors. So when he learned of this meeting and said that Herr Kuhn was interested in our helping his granddaughter..."

Bolan thought that Helmut Kuhn seemed to be a pretty good man for calling in markers. Unfortunately for Mr. Kuhn, the Executioner and Stony Man Farm didn't owe him anything. He had no markers to call in from them.

"I'll keep quiet about your part in this, Dieter, but the answer—"

"Should wait until I've finished."

"I thought you had."

Dieter took the hint. He ran Bolan quickly through a history of Helmut Kuhn, the wealthy industrialist, his son, Erich, and Erich's daughter, Trudl, who apparently had more to her than looking good in a miniskirt.

What really got Bolan's interest was the fact that Erich Kuhn had been working for the Beck organization, investigating a rumor of a Russian intelligence operation in Thuringia and a Russian intelligence operation working with German neo-Nazis and other right-wing nationalists.

"And one using undercover Spetsnaz agents?"

"How did you guess?"

"You've got me interested. Has something happened to Erich Kuhn?"

"When somebody doing that sort of work disappears, it's likely. He had some personal problems, and we think Beck or one of his people was blackmailing him."

"All right. I'll talk to Trudl Kuhn, if your backup and mine both think we're clear."

Both German and Israeli observers gave the all-clear sign, so Trudl Kuhn joined them. She was even more striking close up than from a distance, and those legs definitely belonged in a miniskirt. The rest of her was also well dressed, in a summer-weight tan blouse and a dark red jacket.

"Trudl Kuhn, this is Peter Metzger. Mr. Metzger is an American who might be able to help you find your father."

"Is he in the same work as you, Dieter?" Her English was smooth, with a noticeable but charming accent.

"I'm not CIA, if that's what you mean," Bolan said.

"I wasn't asking you."

"Well, I was telling you, and it's the truth. If you're going to assume I'm a liar from the start, I can't be of much help. And you'll be embarrassing Dieter and his friend, who are friends of your grandfather, and have put their careers on the line to help you."

If meeting Trudl Kuhn really gave him a handle on what Spetsnaz troopers might be doing wandering around Berlin, it was unlikely that anybody's career would suffer. At least not the careers of anybody on Bolan's side. But he had to knock that chip off the young woman's shoulder.

"All right," Trudl replied. "I suppose I deserved that. And my father... I really have no idea where to turn, to learn what happened to him. The police will make a mess and probably learn nothing. If you will not talk to the police..."

"I'll only talk to the police if I think they can help, and I'll keep your name out of it. I can't bind my German friends, but I think they'll at least be discreet."

"I suppose that is fair enough." Trudl took out a handkerchief and blotted sweat from her forehead.

"Where to begin?" she said, and seemed about to answer her own question when Bolan saw Ben Shlomo signaling.

"Excuse me a minute," Bolan said.

"Of course."

Bolan took a five-minute break to get in thirty seconds of conversation with Ben Shlomo.

"We are made. I have spotted three of Carl Braun's men that I know." He explained that Braun was a gang boss with a finger in several pies. One of them was working for Beck's organization. Ben Shlomo didn't know who used Braun's men, but that the organization used them at all was one reason he distrusted Beck.

Bolan scanned the zoo. "All right. I've had it with Beck and his games. We'll take advantage of Trudl Kuhn. I'll go home with her and help her pack for a trip to her grandfather's. Where does he live?"

"A huge house outside Frankfurt am Main."

"Okay. You and Dieter go to the safehouse and clean out my gear. If anybody objects, tell them it's a code-ten emergency. Then rent a car and meet me at— Where does Trudl live?"

Bolan memorized the address. "Meet me at the nearest U-Bahn station. Then we can ditch any tail, drop off Dieter to explain things to the BND and head for Frankfurt."

"You, Mr. Metzger, are an optimist."

"If we stay ahead of the bad guys, we'll have the edge."

"And if we don't?"

"Then we'll have a fight."

"I apologize. You are a realist."

THE BIGGEST DELAY in getting out of the zoo turned out to be persuading Trudl Kuhn to let Bolan go home with her.

"I had heard Americans worked fast, but this is ridiculous," she said, laughing but also wary. "You want me to take you home five minutes after we met?"

"Five minutes can be a lifetime." It would also be about as long as she would live, if she returned home alone and found that Braun's men had staked out her apartment. "Besides, I wasn't going to stay any longer than it took you to pack."

"Pack?"

This demanded more explanation. The idea of a trip to her grandfather's on a moment's notice took a while to sink in. Even then, she was stubborn.

"I am not so feeble that I cannot pack my own suitcases. Besides, Mr. Metzger, I would not trust you to pick out clothes for me. You would probably pick nothing but my bikinis and lingerie."

"I'm sure you'd look fine in either, but I wasn't expecting that kind of trip."

At this point Dieter picked up his own partner's signals that the opposition was on the scene, and took a firm hand. He switched the conversation to German, too fast for Bolan to follow in detail, but clearly getting across to Trudl that she had damned well better do what Bolan told her and nothing more or less. There were people watching them who might think she could lead them to her father, or who wanted to send her to join him.

Trudl was blinking hard when Dieter finished. "I am sorry. I called because my grandfather told me, no, he *made* me think that there could be danger. But when it actually happens it's hard to believe."

"I know. But wasting time not believing in what's happening can get people killed. I don't want that to happen to you, and I hope you won't call that being overprotective."

Trudl looked up at Bolan. She didn't have to look very far, even in low-heeled pumps. She had to be close to five foot eleven. "I call that being a gentleman. Very well, Mr. Metzger. You may come home with me."

HOME WAS AN APARTMENT no more than three-quarters of a mile away. Bolan could have walked it faster than it took to return to the street, find a taxi and guide it on a zigzag route that covered nearly three miles.

He was determined to throw off tails, however. The Germans in their own cars and Ben Shlomo in the Nissan should also help split the opposition. It was now a race, between getting Trudl Kuhn home and away and the enemy calling in the clans.

It was also a race that Bolan expected to win, unless there'd been a leak earlier than today. A BND man who was working for Beck, for example, with anything he knew going to Beck's mole ...

They reached Trudl's apartment just short of half an hour from the zoo. The concierge gave Bolan a thorough looking-over as he let them in. "Oh, by the way," he said to Trudl. "Your friend Hedwig came by about an hour ago. She had the key you gave her, so she should have got in all right. But I have not seen her come down."

Bolan didn't say anything until they were in the elevator, then whispered, "Who's Hedwig?"

"A friend of mine who sings in a cabaret over by the Europa Center. She was just going to drop off some tapes, so I wonder what happened. If she's had another lovers' quarrel, she is *not* going to stay with me."

The warrior punched the elevator button to take them three floors higher than Trudl's apartment. When they got out, he pulled her into an alcove.

"I think you ought to stay up here until I find out what's going on in your apartment. You'll be out of the line of fire—"

"Mr. Metzger, I appreciate your concern. But if Hedwig is in danger—she is an old friend from school. Also, if there are intruders in my apartment, they will be less alert if they hear me."

Bolan nodded. He wasn't surprised. Trudl seemed to have a lot of common sense, and half of combat craft was nothing more.

"Okay. But stay well behind me until we reach your apartment. Then be ready to hit the floor if I tell you to."

The stairs were bare concrete with rubber safety strips in a yellow concrete tube. It was impossible to walk down them silently, but no one confronted them. On the last landing before Trudl's floor, they stopped and the woman gave him a whispered orientation—which way the door opened, which way to the elevator and her apartment, was the hall floor carpeted and so on.

Trudl had an answer for all Bolan's questions, including, "Can you handle a gun?"

"No," she replied. "At least not a pistol. A shotgun, yes."

"Too bad. I was thinking of giving you the Beretta."

"Teach me, so I won't shoot you in the back, and I will take it the next time."

"Let's hope there won't be a next time, or even a this time. But you've got yourself a teacher."

They slipped down the last few steps almost on tiptoe, then Trudl flattened herself against the wall while Bolan opened the door a crack and peered out. It gave a view down the hall, past the woman's apartment to the elevator. Everything looked perfectly normal.

Trudl joined Bolan at the crack, then nodded, and bent to take off her shoes. She padded down the hall in her stocking feet while Bolan slipped along the far wall. When she reached her own door, he joined her, flat against the wall with the Desert Eagle held up near his temple. This could be a hostage situation, and that meant giving himself the maximum chance of a first-round kill.

His companion pulled out her key and slipped it into the lock. Then they heard a voice.

"Trudl?"

It was low-pitched, almost masculine. The woman shook her head. Bolan nodded and pointed at the keys. She turned them, the lock clicked open—and she threw herself back and to the side as the door opened.

A man stood there, tall, fair-haired, wearing a sport coat and flannel slacks. His left hand was at waist level, half-concealed.

"If you value your girlfriend's life—" the man began, in fluent German.

Bolan sprang into view. "Freeze," he barked in the same language. This man was no innocent, but he might be a valuable prisoner. He also might not understand Bolan's German, but he ought to understand the power of the Desert Eagle pointed at his chest.

Instead the man flung himself down and clear of the door. He moved so fast and vigorously he nearly turned a somersault. If Bolan hadn't moved just as fast, the bullet that tore out of the apartment would have hit him in the chest.

But he was clear, with the big .44 Magnum ready to strike back. His opponent was another man, also fair-haired but shorter, sitting on a chocolate-covered couch. He had his foot on the back of a bound and gagged woman lying on the floor, and a silenced Makarov in his hand.

The Magnum round blasted into his neck, and he flew halfway over the back of the couch, nearly decapitated. Bolan followed the bullet into the apartment, landing almost on top of his victim.

The first man had recovered his balance and drawn his automatic, but hesitated for a second. He couldn't shoot without risk of hitting either his partner—although that didn't matter anymore—or his hostage, his ticket out of there.

Bolan canceled all the man's options permanently with a chest shot.

"Hedwig! Are you hurt?" Trudl dashed into the room and knelt by the woman on the floor, ignoring the grisly corpse of Bolan's first victim. Then she started jerking at the gag.

When that came off, Hedwig's comments on the men left no doubt that she was more frightened than hurt. Apparently she'd been given a few samples of what was in store for her, if she didn't cooperate in trapping her friend. Since she knew they would kill her anyway, she pretended to go along, and they stopped quickly.

Hedwig's description of her treatment confirmed Bolan's suspicions. Trudl's would-be kidnappers weren't Carl Braun's street soldiers. They were professionals, probably, if not certainly more Spetsnaz.

Bolan used a kitchen knife to cut Hedwig's bonds and pulled her to her feet. She kissed him soundly in gratitude, then grinned.

"Best kiss I've had in years."

"Hedwig, you can stay here—" Trudl began.

"And be found with the bodies?" Bolan put in. Both women looked at the corpses, then gaped as if seeing them for the first time.

Trudl was the first one to speak. "I suppose I don't have time to pack?"

"You don't."

Bolan slipped the Desert Eagle back into the attaché case, checked the spare magazines for the Beretta and led the way toward the stairs, while Trudl locked the door behind them.

LUCK WAS WITH THEM. Trudl was the only one home that day on her floor, the apartment above was vacant and the tenant in the one below elderly and hard of hearing. Bolan's two noisy kills didn't sound quite suspicious enough to make anyone farther away call the concierge or the police.

Bolan and the two women left the building via the rear door, past the trash bins and down an alley that led to a small park. They crouched in the cover provided by a stand of trees until they were sure that the police weren't going to immediately cordon off the whole area and start a house-to-house search.

After fifteen minutes they hadn't heard a siren. Hedwig borrowed Bolan's jacket, since her dress was much the worse for wear, and he slipped the Beretta into the attaché case alongside the Desert Eagle.

His draw would certainly be slower but at the moment that was not important. Nine chances out of ten, if they were stopped now it would be by the police. Bolan's principles as well as common sense ruled out shooting at them.

They weren't stopped, and when they reached the U-Bahn station they found friends already there. The two

BND men had teamed up in Dieter's car, and had the corner under surveillance before Bolan reached Trudl's building.

"Our Israeli friend thought somebody else besides Braun's people might take a hand," Dieter explained. "So he said he would go solo to the safehouse and send us here. We agreed on a rendezvous."

Bolan described the shoot-out at Trudl's building.

"This is not the sort of day that wins promotions," he said finally. "Oh well, at least any police who stop us will have a hard choice—let us all go, or arrest two BND agents along with the suspects."

"The faster we're out of the area, the less chance of meeting the police at all," Bolan pointed out. "Where was that new rendezvous Zev proposed, in case we get separated?"

THEY WERE ON THEIR WAY out of Berlin before the evening newspapers appeared. Bolan tried to get the news on the radio, but the rented BMW's radio produced static, jazz and talk shows in about equal proportions, and no news.

As they passed Erfurt on the E40 Autobahn, it started to rain. Bolan stopped worrying about the pursuit and concentrated on his driving. Hedwig had fallen asleep in the back seat, her head on Ben Shlomo's shoulder. The Mossad agent sat with his Makarov in his lap, as silent as the grave and not looking much more friendly.

"He doesn't say much, does he?" Trudl said from beside Bolan.

"Today might not be any better for his career than for Dieter's," Bolan replied. "Israel needs to maintain good relations with the Commonwealth of Independent States to keep free emigration for the Jews there."

The two BND men had worked effectively as a team, hiding the trail of Bolan and his companions and arranging for a car that would be harder-than-average to trace. Then they'd vanished into the uproar of a Berlin evening rush hour, no doubt to report back to their chiefs with a plausible version of the day's events.

Bolan doubted such a thing was possible. He hoped they would at least be able to come up with something that kept them out of jail, or even on the BND payroll. Stony Man Farm needed Dieter, Helmut Kuhn needed his friend and right now Mack Bolan needed Helmut Kuhn and all of the man's assets.

With the shoot-out, he had burned his bridges, and at the same time launched himself on what could be a brand-new mission with no assured support.

The rain slackened about the same time they reached the former West German border. With the road conditions better on the western autobahns, Bolan kept the gas pedal floored all the way to the Rhine.

They got off the highway several exits short of the one for Königstein. Trudl navigated them through the neighboring suburbs, down residential streets, up commercial side roads and over what seemed to be a cattle track.

Bolan was sure of one thing. Without Trudl's navigating, he would have ended up thoroughly lost. Nobody who hadn't been raised in the area would have a chance of tailing them. Finally they climbed the hill to the parking apron in front of Helmut Kuhn's house.

CHAPTER ELEVEN

Bolan woke up after what seemed to have been a full night's sleep, to discover that it was just after eight. He'd barely slept four hours.

The bed probably helped. It had a polished walnut headboard with a digital clock, stereo, coffeemaker and color television. Its mattress was the latest in comfort, the blankets were virgin wool except for the electric one, the sheets and pillowcases were Irish linen and the pillows were stuffed with goose down.

The bedroom was as large as the whole suite of the safehouse and furnished with the same luxury as the bed. Bolan's feet nearly disappeared into the pile of the maroon rug when he swung them out of bed, the woodwork was generous without being too dark and heavy, and there was good modern stained glass in the transom window over the door to the bathroom.

The bathroom's tiles and fixtures were in various shades of green, except for stainless-steel faucet handles. The towels were thick enough to turn combat knives, snow white or cream with the monogram *K* on them.

Helmut Kuhn had set his mark on this house—or rather, the mark of his money and taste. He seemed to have plenty of both.

Bolan took a leisurely shower, then located the rest of his weapons and clothing. Except for the Beretta, which had spent the night under his pillow, the rest of the arsenal was in a cedar chest at the back of the walk-in closet. Someone had lightly oiled the Weatherby, but Bolan was glad to see that no one had tried to rearrange the demolitions pack.

The Desert Eagle hadn't been maintained since the previous day's shoot-out. Bolan spread a glossy German picture magazine on the light-oak desk in the alcove by the window and laid the automatic on it. He checked the magazines, tossed a round that seemed to have developed a bit of corrosion, then started field-stripping the Desert Eagle.

He almost had it back together when he heard a knock on the door. He hastily finished the reassembly, slipped the gun into the drawer and called, "Come in."

Trudl Kuhn walked into the room, wearing a faded blue flannel bathrobe at least two sizes too large for her, and no makeup. Her hair was done in two rough braids tied with rubber bands, and her feet were bare.

"Good morning," he said. "I'll have to thank your grandfather for his hospitality."

"That will have to wait. He is in the exercise room, along with your Israeli friend. Grandfather always does half an hour of isometric exercises and weights after breakfast. But come down anyway. I am sure Ilse can serve you in the breakfast room. We are painting the dining room, and I do not think Grandfather would want you in the library until he can show off the books. The really good ones, of course, are in his study."

"Just how big is this house, anyway?"

"Sixteen rooms, I think, if you don't count the bathrooms and the basement. I never can remember how many rooms are in the basement. It seemed that the builders were always in there, taking out a wall here and putting one in there."

Bolan sat down. "I'm more curious to meet your grandfather every minute. Now, if you wouldn't mind letting me get dressed . . ."

"Oh, go right ahead."

Bolan grinned. "You into nudism?"

"Only at the beach."

"Oh."

"You sound as if you doubt me." She put a hand on the belt of her robe. "I can prove it."

"I'm sure you can. But what about your grandfather?"

"He is not God. He does not see everything."

"Is that an invitation?"

"I suppose not. When I give the invitation, I will come through the door naked."

She caught sight of herself in the mirror. "*Du lieber Gott!* I had better at least go brush my hair. Grandfather will say nothing, but if I come down like this to a meeting Ilse will not let me hear the end of it."

She ran her fingers lightly over Bolan's back. Her touch was almost soothing, even on the battered skin of the bullet crease.

He held her hand for a moment, then let it go and watched her dart out the door.

HAL BROGNOLA'S REPORT from Parsifal indicated that the situation in Berlin had apparently gone from bad to worse. Bolan had left Berlin, heading for a destination Parsifal clearly knew but wasn't going to put into any communication originating in the Berlin BND office.

The implications were ominous. Clearly the Beck organization had gone from being useless to Striker, to being a potential danger. Only potential, because it wasn't clear yet if there was a real traitor in the organization, or just somebody who occasionally talked too much. If there was a traitor, his assets and contacts were still anybody's guess.

Bolan was clearly planning for the worst case. He was simply disappearing from Berlin and staying out of sight until he had secure communications with Stony Man Farm, directly or indirectly. That was fine with Brognola. Striker was the man on the spot, the one with the facts and also the greatest chance of ending up in somebody's cross hairs. His judgment was sound.

The big Fed's doubts were about his own judgment. The Beck organization had been so useful for so long to so many people that it was hard to believe it had sprung a leak. But the record of cowboys like Beck told a different story.

"We should have had more cutouts in our dealings with Beck for the past five years," Brognola said aloud to the wall calendar. The calendar was from a wildlife-protection organization and showed a grizzly bear in a bad mood. Right now, Hal Brognola knew pretty much how the bear must have felt.

IF KUHN'S breakfast room was any guide, his dining room had to be as large as a small airplane hangar. Bolan ate heartily, washing down the food with several cups of the best coffee he'd ever tasted. Trudl kept him company.

By mostly listening and throwing in the odd word here and there, Bolan learned a good deal more about Helmut Kuhn. He'd had a doctorate in molecular chemistry even before the war, during which he'd served with the army as a technical representative of his firm. He had a nominal commission as a captain, but after the war the denazification courts gave him a clean bill of health.

That clearance hadn't meant as much as the fact that he had already held several valuable patents. When German industry started up again, they became more valuable still. Moving from the laboratory to the management side, Kuhn parlayed those patents into his own chemical firm, and the chemical firm into an international conglomerate. Along the way, he also accumulated a tidy fortune, somewhere around sixty million dollars the last time Trudl heard an accurate figure.

"I don't know what will happen to it now," she said. "He has been unhappy for years about my father. But he thinks I am too young to have all that money, and maybe I do not want it. I would be plagued with fortune hunters."

She emptied her cup of coffee. "Oh well. Maybe some of Grandfather's friends will have some ideas that he will listen to. The special friends, anyway."

The phrase clearly was some sort of family code. "How special?" Bolan asked.

"Some more than others," Trudl said cryptically. "But I think he will be ready to meet us in a few minutes. When he does, you can ask him yourself. Now I am going to get dressed."

The woman practically danced out of the breakfast room before Bolan could ask her anything else.

HANS WEGENER WAS a widower—his wife had been killed in a multicar highway collision seven years before. He usually ate breakfast on his way to his office.

This morning, fortunately or unfortunately, he ate at home, so was there to answer when Carl Braun phoned.

The gang boss was unhappy. He made it clear how unhappy he was in a few well-chosen words. At least they started off being a few. By the time he finished, Wegener was almost too nervous to reply.

He had to say something, though. His connection with Braun was essential for his role in the Beck organization. Without the man's street boys, he would have less to offer Beck, and he would soon be out on the streets himself.

What would happen after that wasn't pleasant to think about. If they discovered any of his undercover dealings, it would be dreadful. If they discovered all of them, he would be dead. Never mind that Germany didn't have the death penalty. It wouldn't be the German government that killed him.

"Look, Carl, none of your boys were anywhere near the apartment, were they?"

"Twenty minutes away at most. That's how close a carload came to being in that shoot-out. That's how close you came to losing me for good, Hansel. I don't like losing my boys. Lose too many of them, and the ones who are left might suspect I don't care. Then *I* can lose."

"I promise—"

"You can take your promises and dump them in the Havel."

"Carl, we need each other."

"Maybe we do. But I don't need this kind of grief, with my boys coming so close to getting shot. Understand that?"

"Perfectly. I'm willing to let you off any more involvement in this particular project I'm working on. That's the one that led to the shooting. Everything else should be safe."

"Or so you say. Maybe I should learn a little more about this project before I take your word."

"Carl, it's not my secret to keep."

"I understand. You understand, too, that my boys aren't yours to get shot up."

Wegener cursed under his breath. He was being offered a trade: information about Project Gamma for cooperation in other areas.

If he let Braun know too much about Project Gamma, his own life would be in jeopardy. On the other hand, if Braun simply pulled his men off all Beck cases, Wegener would be out of a job in days.

Maybe he could find a middle ground—enough information to win Braun's support, but not compromise the project. Or at least not compromise it in any way that Schweiger would know about. When all was said and done, there was nothing he feared quite as much as Schweiger.

"All right, Carl. You can meet me for a little discussion on this business. I won't talk about it over the telephone. But I won't ask you for any more work, either, until we've talked. Fair enough?"

"Couldn't be better. Schimmel's tonight?"

Wegener fought back more curses. Braun wasn't the sort of man you wanted to be seen with at Schimmel's. If anything got into the media about this business, he would never be able to show his face there again.

But if Schweiger put a bullet in his stomach, he would be even worse off.

HELMUT KUHN MADE no effort to dominate the meeting from behind the antique oak desk in his study. He did it without trying.

Part of it was his physical presence. He was well over six feet tall, and still had most of his silvery hair. Although he stooped slightly, it was easy to believe that he worked out every morning.

The rest was his self-assurance. Without being arrogant, he seemed unable to doubt that anyone in his presence wouldn't listen to him. Since what he said was mostly worth hearing, he was usually right.

Bolan certainly wasn't going to miss a word. Neither was Zev Ben Shlomo, although he was trying hard not to fidget. Hedwig was still asleep.

"I helped her with that," Trudl said. "I gave her a sleeping pill." They were using English, out of courtesy to Bolan.

"Good," Kuhn replied. "I would not have let her sit with us anyway, but you have saved me from being rude. It would be to keep her out of danger, but if she is at all like you she would not care for that reason."

"You have that right."

"Of course, you know that you are also in more danger, the more you know about this," Kuhn went on. He sipped at a cup of herbal tea. "You can still leave, and let me and these gentlemen get on with our business."

"Is this 'business' going to tell what happened to my father?"

"Was he such a good father that you really need to know?"

"I did not choose him for a father, any more than you chose him for a son. But he was both, and we owe him that much loyalty. Besides, there are already enough people who want to kill me over this 'business' so that a few more will not matter."

Kuhn looked appealingly at Bolan who said, "I think Trudl has made up her mind on this. It would waste time to try to persuade her to change it."

That got the first real reaction from Ben Shlomo. His head jerked in a nod. "Yes. It would make sense to discuss what we came here for."

"And what is that, sir?" Kuhn asked.

"I do not know," Ben Shlomo said brusquely. "You do. So does your daughter. Otherwise I think she would not have brought us here."

Bolan thought the Israeli could have been more tactful, but agreed about the need to move along. Spetsnaz troopers hadn't earned their reputation by sitting around swilling vodka after their comrades were shot. They moved out fast, ready to hit hard.

"Trudl knows a little, and has guessed much. If she has referred to my 'special friends'—"

"Was my room bugged?" Bolan asked sharply.

"Mr. Metzger, I said 'if.'" Kuhn's tone chilled the air in the study for a moment. "There are no eavesdropping devices in this house. Not mine, or anybody else's. I have an expert from a reliable source sweep the place every week.

"Also, if someone did plant such devices in my house, they might indeed learn something. But the price for their knowledge would be such a public scandal as few can afford."

"Good," Ben Shlomo said. "So now that we know it is safe to talk, shall we begin? Mr. Metzger and I will be glad to listen as long as you like."

"Good. It will be quite a long tale. It is also one that is, I think, overdue for telling."

He set his teacup on the silver tray in one corner of his desk and folded his hands in his lap. "It begins almost when I went to work for my wartime employers...."

"SCHWEIGER HERE."

"Good," Danilov said. "I understand we are having trouble with one of our contractors."

"We are. He interpreted the contract to let him use his own people. They weren't properly trained before and they weren't properly trained now. We used two of our own, but both of them had accidents because our contractor had allowed unsafe conditions to develop."

"Was this deliberate, do you think?" Danilov asked. Which meant, had their men in the Beck organization been turned again, and set up a trap for Bytkin's two men at Trudl Kuhn's apartment?

"I do not know. It might be hard to find out without a long interview." That meant kidnapping the man and interrogating him without much regard for whether he survived after he talked. Bytkin executed such missions with cold-blooded professionalism, although it was obvious that he liked the actual interrogations. That was one of a number of things about Bytkin that made Danilov shiver when he thought of them.

Some of the skinhead neo-Nazis Bytkin recruited called him the Trained Wolf. It was an apt name. Bytkin was trained. He was not and never would be tame.

"We don't have the time. See that the contractor knows that we're not satisfied with his performance. We expect some compensation for the accidents to our people and will void the contract if there are any more problems like this one."

"I think he will not refuse."

Danilov hung up. No one tapping the phone could have concluded anything but what he'd been meant to conclude: two partners in a construction firm—one of

Danilov's fronts—weren't happy with one of their sub-contractors.

Which was quite true. Their man in the Beck organization hadn't performed adequately. Fortunately he would no longer be indispensable after the completion of Project Gamma. As part of tying up the loose ends, Bytkin could have him.

Bytkin himself might not last much longer, but Colonel Danilov saw no reason why the major shouldn't die happy.

BOLAN HAD LISTENED to the tale of events in Thuringia in 1945 and of Kuhn's postwar career with total attention. He could almost hear the click of pieces falling into place.

Kuhn's career explained, among other things, much of the effectiveness of the Beck organization. Also the real story behind a few episodes of ex-Nazis that should have turned into major scandals but somehow didn't.

Kuhn had made a habit of quietly letting any old colleagues with a questionable past go about their business, on two conditions. One was that they stayed out of politics. The other was that they provided him with intelligence, of whatever kind and in whatever quantity he thought they could provide.

Willi Beck was the darling of several Western intelligence agencies. But in Bolan's opinion, Kuhn made Beck look like a rank amateur. If he survived this mission, Bolan thought, he would suggest that Brognola consider proposing a formal relationship with Kuhn. He wouldn't be entirely sure about that until he'd discussed with Kuhn just what kind of ex-Nazi he'd allowed to go free.

That label covered a lot of territory. It could mean a man who'd carried a Nazi party membership card in order to keep his job and support his family. It could also mean somebody who'd laughed as he bayoneted Polish babies before their mother's eyes.

If Kuhn had been letting the second kind go, *he* might not be alive at the end of this mission. But the Executioner would give the man the benefit of the doubt—for now.

Ben Shlomo was clearly going to have more of a problem with that. In fact, his temper seemed ready to get the better of him. His face was red, and his nostrils looked pinched. He finally surprised Bolan by speaking quietly.

"What do you propose that will make us forget your letting war criminals escape?"

Trudl glared. Helmut Kuhn merely looked sober. "There are various kinds of crimes in war. I think all three men here are guilty of some of them."

"That's an argument against war, not against letting war criminals go free," Bolan pointed out.

"It certainly is, and one of many," Kuhn replied. "But there is one argument in favor of war, and that is, if someone else wants to fight, what alternative do you have?"

In the silence that followed, Kuhn continued to describe the present situation. His son, Erich, had fallen into the hands of blackmailers, apparently working for the Beck organization. Using his father's contacts, he had obtained information on something big and dangerous. He had sent one copy of the file to his father, and had been about to give the other file to the Beck organization when he disappeared.

"I suspect that he would have disappeared afterward anyway," Kuhn said. "But I think someone else had learned what he knew and acted first."

"Spetsnaz," Bolan suggested.

"On the basis of the file, I would not say that was impossible. But read this for yourself," Kuhn added. "It is not long. I am sorry I could not have it translated, but whom should I have trusted with the work?"

Bolan's ability to read German was adequate for most of the file, and Ben Shlomo was fluent in the language. The picture they both had fifteen minutes later was appalling.

"You are certain this is the same mine?" Ben Shlomo asked.

"The description so closely matches the mine and its location that I cannot believe otherwise."

"I do have one problem," Bolan said. "Blowing the mine and releasing the gas on the day of the ceremony would guarantee a big death toll of VIPs. But some of those VIPs are going to be Russians. I won't say the Russians have never sacrificed their own troops, but their own generals?"

Kuhn nodded. "That problem has occurred to me also. But the generals could be replaced by aides a few days before the ceremony. Or possibly they are all supporters of the Commonwealth, and the old hard-liners don't mind killing a few of them."

"It could even be that the man behind this is quite unofficial," Trudl added. "You Americans have trouble with CIA agents working for Libya. Why not a Russian intelligence agent doing the same?"

It certainly made as much sense to Bolan as renegade Spetsnaz working for the Mafia. More, perhaps, if the men they were dealing with thought their superior had some sort of official charter.

"We have a week," Kuhn told them. "I hope in that time we can find a way of dealing with this situation that does not put you people in more danger. If it is true that the leader of the project is working with the neo-Nazis, the area will be well defended."

"By gangsters and street fighters," Ben Shlomo said.

"I wish that were true. Nor does it please me to admit this to an Israeli whose family died in the Holocaust. But there are technically trained people and even BND veterans turning up in the ranks of the right-wing nationalists. They are not people who will fall over their own feet while you are shooting at them."

"All right," Ben Shlomo said. "But in that case we don't have anything like a week." He pulled out a copy of a newspaper and opened it to an inside page.

There was that photogenic couple who seemed to be permanent press agents for the Green Party. This time they were saying that the Greens were going to demonstrate at the cave, to protest environmentally unsafe methods of disposing of war relics.

The demonstration would take place in two days.

"Mr. Kuhn, I hope you will find it possible to help us make a quick trip to Thuringia," Ben Shlomo said. "For two reasons. One, the neo-Nazis hate the Greens. If they both turn up—as I am sure they will—there will be a bloody confrontation whether the gas is released or not.

"The second reason, I hope, need not go beyond this room. The woman in the picture is—well, you might need to know her name someday. For now, believe me when I say she is one of the Mossad's best female agents."

CHAPTER TWELVE

Bolan locked the Mercedes's trunk on the Weatherby and the rest of his gear, along with Ben Shlomo's baggage and Trudl's suitcase. She watched the lid close, then turned to her grandfather.

"You still want to go?" he asked. In the twilight it was hard to read his face, but Bolan knew he wasn't smiling.

"I have not changed my mind," she replied. Her words were aimed as much at the two agents as at Helmut Kuhn. "I have some friends in the Greens. If they are at the demonstration, I can talk to them."

"That is a better excuse than you gave me the last time," Kuhn said with a smile. "The last time you said you would drive them in your Porsche."

"I could have, too. The Carrera is almost as fast as a helicopter."

"Yes, and you would have had to fit Mr. Ben Shlomo into the luggage space behind the passenger seat. I do not think he would have cared to ride like that."

The Israeli agent managed a thin smile. As far as he was concerned, every second of delay was a new danger for his colleague with the Greens. That meant danger for Israel, too.

"The Germans will not thank us for infiltrating one of their political movements," he said. "The Left does not like intelligence agents and the Right does not like

Jews. My associate turning up with the Greens will give both of them ammunition.''

That reminded Bolan to go check his own ammunition supply.

Helmut Kuhn had turned up enough 9 mm rounds to fight a small war, without saying any more about where he got it than he had about where he arranged for the Mercedes. The car was in top condition except for the exterior, which was battered and faded enough to be inconspicuous.

It would take them as far as Butzbach, where they would transfer to a no-questions-asked chartered helicopter. It would lift them to Eisfeld in the Thüringer Wald, where another car would be waiting. This one would be an all-wheel drive BND vehicle, completely outfitted including chemical protective gear and a first-aid kit with atropine injectors.

''I don't know the formulas for the modern nerve gases, of course,'' Kuhn had said, ''but they are mostly descendants of our old Tabun. Compound 58 was intended to be a skin-permeable but nonpersistent improvement on that. The atropine is also the latest formula. So I would be surprised if it did not work.''

If it didn't work, Bolan and his companions might be worse than surprised, they might be dead. But the Executioner gave Kuhn full credit nonetheless for what he'd arranged on very short notice. They would be hard to tail on the way and ready for almost anything they could face when they arrived, thanks to him.

Hedwig came out and hugged everybody impartially. She had wanted to act as a decoy, driving the BMW back to Berlin. Trudl and Bolan convinced her that would be more dangerous than exciting, so she was returning to Berlin by way of a visit to her aunt in Munich.

"Goodbye, Trudl," she said, blinking back tears. "We *are* going to survive this."

"Who says otherwise?" Trudl said. She slipped into the back seat. The two agents climbed in front, Ben Shlomo in the driver's seat, and the Mercedes rolled out of the driveway and down the hill.

Looking back, Bolan saw that Hedwig kept on waving until a turn in the road cut off his view of her. Helmut Kuhn stood blank-faced, hands at his sides. For the first time since Bolan had met him, he actually looked his age.

THE AUDI HAD NO HOPE of keeping up with the big Mercedes if the man at the wheel was both good and fast. They also hadn't much hope of tailing it all the way across Germany, unless the men inside were much less professional than they were supposed to be.

However, orders were orders. That old German attitude still held good, even if the orders were coming from someone who, the driver suspected, might not be a German.

Schweiger had a German soul, at least, and for now that was enough for the Greater Germany party. The driver turned to his companion and pointed at his jacket.

His companion pulled out his H&K P-9 S from one pocket of his jacket, and the silencer from the other. A few twists, and the two were mated. With the subsonic .45 ammunition in the P-9 S and the silencer, they should make at least the first kill before the enemy knew they were close.

Schweiger hadn't actually ordered them to make a kill. But he had given no orders against it, either, and both men were professionals as well as members of the

Greater Germany party. They didn't carry their weapons to improve the cut of their clothes.

"SORRY WE DIDN'T GET a chance to give you that handgun orientation," Bolan said over his shoulder.

He didn't want to look back, and not only because the healing bullet crease still smarted when he turned his torso. The Audi behind them was doing a fairly professional job of tailing. It had taken him almost five minutes to recognize what it was.

That meant the people in the Audi would be sure he'd made them if he started looking back too often. They were just close enough to tell if he did, too.

"That is not quite such a problem as you thought," Trudl said. She opened her handbag, the only feminine item with her in the car. She wore a safari jacket over a bulky cable-knit sweater, baggy slacks and hiking boots.

When her hand came out, it was holding a Walther P-38.

Bolan not only turned his head, he stared. Trudl grinned. "What is the matter, Mr. Metzger? Haven't you ever seen one of these? My grandfather tells me the BND has been using them for years."

The Executioner knew perfectly well that Trudl's automatic had never been made for the BND. "That was your grandfather's, right?"

"Yes. It is the only pistol I know how to use, so he sent it along with me, it and a box of ammunition. It is safe."

"You said you didn't know handguns."

"I was not going to tell you about this one, not when we had just met. It is safe, but not quite legal to have around the house."

It would be considered still more illegal to shoot people with it, and Bolan hoped Trudl wouldn't freeze on the trigger if it came to that. She seemed too sensible to regard this expedition as an adventure, but that didn't mean she had all the skills necessary to survive it.

Bolan took a last look at the Audi and saw that it had dropped back. He turned around and kept his eyes firmly on the road or the rearview mirror until they reached the turnoff for the last stage to the rendezvous with the helicopter.

THE MAINZ CONTINGENT of the Green Party's demonstration was twenty-nine people in a chartered forty-five-passenger bus. That left plenty of room in the back, and after the lights were turned off Paul Allred seemed to think the back seat was private.

He put his arm around Suzanne Köbler and pulled her gently against him. So gently, in fact, that she was in his arms before she realized that she was on the way there.

He was also gentle enough that she couldn't really complain. Some of the other young men she'd met in the Green movement before she paired off with Paul seemed to have only one thing on their minds, and it wasn't the health of the Earth.

"Umm," she said.

"Sleepy?"

"Yes." She was telling the truth. The heavy reek of marijuana drifting back from where the smokers hung out wasn't helping. She thanked the Lord that the ventilation system was carrying the fumes back rather than forward. If the driver got half as high as some of the smokers already were, the bus might end up at the bottom of a river.

They crossed a bridge before Paul went on. "Too sleepy?"

"Well, now that you put it that way..."

"I will only put it ways that you like. You know that."

Curse the man, he was right. And she admitted that she was somewhat vain about her figure. Stripped, she looked a good ten years younger than her actual thirty-one.

It helped that she had no stretch marks. But then, Bren Zonis had been killed in Lebanon before their first anniversary, let alone their first child.

They had never found his body, so by Israeli law he was not dead and she wasn't a widow. That had not been so bad, as far as getting her into the Mossad, or helping persuade fellow agents to keep their hands off her. But it meant being lonely, in bed and out.

Paul seemed almost a boy, and he probably wouldn't like knowing that he was really bedding thirty-one-year-old Rachel Zonis, so she just wouldn't let him know. Very simple.

It was very simple to get undressed. She didn't wear a bra, so she was bare to the waist when she took off her sweater, and the rest of their clothes didn't take long.

HEADLIGHTS GLARED into the rearview mirror every time Bolan checked. Worse, they were the same headlights, their old friend the Audi.

He'd hoped the Audi would lose track when they stopped to change drivers, or else overtake them so that they could engage it. The men in the Audi were a little too good for that, however. They were hanging on, and if they had both radios and friends close at hand, things might get a bit hairy in the next few minutes.

The Audi didn't need to tail them all the way across Germany. If it followed them to the rendezvous with the helicopter, that could be enough. Helicopters were vulnerable to small arms, ready to turn into one big bonfire with a few well-placed bullets. Even reading the registration could give the opposition useful information.

Bolan realized that he was also getting useful information on the strength and efficiency of their enemies. Now all he had to do was survive to pass it on.

One thing at a time, though. He keyed the customized radio to one of the military frequencies. It was technically illegal, but he and the helicopter team would be done talking long before any BND listening station could get a fix on them.

"Nike One to Apricot. Come in, Apricot."

"Apricot here. ETA, Nike One?"

"Five minutes, but we have guests."

"You want advice on hospitality?"

"That's affirmative, Apricot."

"Wait, two, Nike One."

It felt like a lot more than two minutes, with the miles rolling on and the road getting rougher. Bolan decided to give Apricot, the helicopter team, about another thirty seconds before he pulled off the road and set up an ambush. They didn't need a hard kill, only a few minutes' delay. If by any chance the tailers were from the police, he didn't want a kill at all.

"Apricot to Nike One. We have some extra hospitality supplies. What's your speed?"

Bolan looked at the speedometer. "Forty."

"All right. There's a concrete flak tower coming up on your left. Take a seven count past that, then hard right. We'll take care of the rest."

"Somebody else taking care of the ambush?" Ben Shlomo grunted.

"Looks that way." Bolan peered into the darkness ahead, looking for the squat concrete shape of one of the old World War II antiaircraft towers that dotted the countryside.

He found it and started the countdown.

At "seven" he yanked the wheel over. The Mercedes was no sports car. It slewed, fishtailed and nearly went up on two wheels as it made a hairpin turn into what looked like a deserted farmyard.

The next moment, something bright flashed across the rearview mirror, squarely into the headlights. Flames and bits of metal scoured the road, and Bolan saw the Audi flip nearly onto its front, then fall back. The windshield was missing. So, it seemed, was the driver's head.

Trudl Kuhn stared back at the burning wreck. "Is...are they...?"

"Our ground support will make sure," Ben Shlomo said. "And please do not vomit in your grandfather's Mercedes. It will ruin the upholstery."

Bolan was about to back out onto the road when he saw a light blinking ahead, apparently from the middle of the forest. The headlights on low showed a narrow logging road, just negotiable by the Mercedes if somebody got out and walked.

"Zev, we need a man on foot. You're elected."

Ben Shlomo scrambled out and slammed the door.

In five minutes Bolan and his companions were climbing out of the Mercedes, almost under the rotors of a Bell JetRanger. He didn't recognize the corporate logo on the door, but assumed that enough money had changed hands to keep the crew's mouths shut.

Trudl Kuhn dashed toward the trees and threw up. Ben Shlomo looked at her skeptically, then at Bolan. "You really think we should take her?"

"What did you do in your first fight?"

Ben Shlomo looked at Bolan, then at Trudl, now efficiently wiping her mouth, and nodded.

Two minutes later the ambush team appeared—a man who introduced himself as Siegfried and another man with the unmistakable air of a special-operations trooper. They were carrying the sights and empty launch tube of a Milan antitank missile.

"For a car, that was overkill," Kuhn's BND friend said. "But it turned out to be easier to get one than to get an RPG."

"If you really want an RPG, I'm sure we can get you one," Bolan said. "We owe you."

"Just stay alive to pay it," the agent replied. He kissed Trudl's hand with old-fashioned elegance, stepped back and clicked his heels. *"Hals und beinbruch!"*

Bolan hoped that the traditional good-luck wish applied to secret agents as well as parachutists and skiers. He expected to find out within twenty-four hours.

In another minute the JetRanger was loaded, and the pilot lifted off even before the Executioner was fully inside the cabin.

THE HELICOPTER CLIMBED directly over the Audi's passenger. He lay, bloody and burned, on his back in the scrub.

Not all of the blood was his, or he would have been as dead as his companion. He not only had the portable radio, he had the strength to use it.

"To all Rheingold stations," he gasped. "All Rheingold stations. This is Weapon Eight. Weapon Eight reporting the helicopter. The helicopter is D6543L. I repeat, D6543L. It has the Jew and . . .''

His voice trailed off, partly because internal bleeding was beginning to choke him, partly because he thought he heard feet crunching through the forest. He needed his last strength to throw the radio into the trees, so that the enemies of Greater Germany might not find it.

The silenced P-9 S was gone in the explosion. He struggled to find his backup weapon, a Walther P-5. As light as it was, his arm didn't have the strength to lift it. He managed to thumb off the safety, rest the butt on the ground and point the barrel roughly in the direction of the noise.

When voices joined the crashing, he tried to squeeze the trigger. He managed to get off two rounds, but they hit nothing and only provoked a blast of return fire. Weapon Eight's stubborn passenger finally died.

THE GERMAN COUNTRYSIDE unrolled below—the tiny sparks of car headlights and warning lights on power poles, the larger glows of towns, the distant glare of Würzburg. A jet crossed their flight path, from right to left and slightly above them. Glowing twin tailpipes said military, probably a Luftwaffe Tornado on a night exercise.

Bolan crawled forward and asked the pilot about the registration of the flight.

"We're registered as a medical flight through to Dresden," he said. "We're supposed to be carrying whole blood and antibiotics. They had a lot of traffic accidents in the fog a few days ago.

"The real flight is leaving Sisters of Mercy Hospital in Würzburg about now. They'll overtake us and fly formation with us all the way to our destination. That will fool the radars. We'll go down together, then they'll pop up and we'll land.''

''You're staying?''

''Herr Kuhn's paying enough, and he likes things done thoroughly. Don't you?''

''You could say that.''

''I do. Don't worry about the formation flying, either. I did four years with antitank helicopters in the army. I spent most of my time down where you could look into a third-floor window, even if you didn't see anything as nice as the lady back there.''

''I heard that.''

''I meant it.''

Bolan hoped the pilot would keep his mind on flying instead of flirting and crawled back to where the cargo was tied down. The helicopter was well equipped for carrying fragile cargo, with tie-downs, racks and straps. Nothing would come loose in the air, and in a crash the danger was fire. For that the best remedy was running as fast as you could away from the crash, before the ammo cooked off.

Helmut Kuhn did indeed like things done thoroughly. Bolan wondered if the old man would approve of how thoroughly he was going to check out Kuhn's special friends for their war-crimes records.

NINE GREEN PARTY BUSES rolled through the hills toward the demonstration site. Rachel and Paul were much too busy in the rear seat to notice the convoy.

They were also too busy to notice a few bad-tempered or drunken night owls, who shook their fists from the roadside or passing cars. Some shouted obscenities. One threw a rotten apple, which left a fast-drying smear on the side of one of the two buses from Cologne.

By the time the two slept in each other's arms, the buses were crossing the bridge over the Fränkische Saale. A man in Bundesgrenschutz uniform counted them as they crossed, then walked to his unmarked car. A strictly nonregulation Beretta automatic banged against his hip as he walked.

"Weapon Twelve to Leader Station. Weapon Twelve to Leader Station. I have a nine-count at Point Ten. Repeat, a nine-count at Point Ten."

The radio was as nonregulation as the pistol. Fortunately it was German-made. The disguised Greater Germany party activist remembered the tales his grandfather told him about the uselessness of Italian soldiers. He was not happy at being sent to a critical post of duty armed with an Italian weapon.

CHAPTER THIRTEEN

The JetRanger landed the team in a clearing north of Eisfeld as the eastern sky began to turn pale. The lights of their companion crept overhead, then circled, as Bolan and Ben Shlomo unloaded their equipment. Trudl lent a hand, while the crew of the helicopter stayed at the controls, the rotors still whirling, ready for a quick takeoff.

The moment Bolan led Trudl clear of the rotors, both ducking for safety, the JetRanger lifted off. Moments later it joined its companion, which swung out of its circle and into formation. Then both helicopters vanished among the fading stars.

"Come on," Bolan said, picking up his pack. He'd rearranged it for better balance during the flight. Helmut Kuhn's staff might have a lot of skills, but packing a combat load wasn't one of them.

Trudl shouldered her pack, then struggled with the straps. They got tangled in the belt for her pistol, which she now wore openly on her hip. If the forest patrol came by, it was going to be hard to explain their equipment as that of a hunting party, not to mention that it wasn't hunting season in the Thüringer Wald.

The directions Bolan had memorized told him to set a compass course NNW, and he did this as well as the going allowed. Trudl's long legs and sense of balance carried her easily over the ground, but Ben Shlomo seemed to be having a rough time.

"The Lord did not make me an infantryman." Ben Shlomo grunted as he bent to pull his foot out of a badger hole. With both hands and Trudl's help, he succeeded, although he nearly left his boot behind.

After that the going eased, and about half a mile into the forest they came to a logging road. They took standard formation then, with Bolan leading, Trudl on one side, and Ben Shlomo on the other. Another half mile was supposed to bring them to their ground transportation.

The half mile was more like three-quarters, and they had to cross a small bridge that left Bolan feeling unpleasantly exposed. They crossed it leapfrog style, however, and just around a curve on the other side they came to a brown Auto-Union Munga field car.

At least it seemed the brown was paint, not mud or dirt. At some point in its career the field car had been dropped off a cliff, then dragged back to the shop upside down and repaired in the dark. It went beyond being nondescript to being memorably ugly.

But it had four-wheel drive, cargo racks, heavy-duty suspension designed for the road they were traveling and a driver who handed Bolan the right codes. He carried himself and his H&K MP-5 K with the upright but casual alertness of the seasoned special-operations trooper.

Bolan was beginning to wonder how many of Germany's unpublicized but proficient elite units his allies had called on. He hoped for quite a few. This mission was still facing long odds, not likely to get shorter any time soon.

The man spoke English and had a radio that received both police and military frequencies. He gave Bolan an update on the progress of the Green demonstration.

"The buses are still rolling into a parking site by the old village at the foot of the mountain," he said.

"Which way is the wind blowing?" Ben Shlomo asked.

"Fluky and light," the man said. "It could be worse."

"Any sign of counterdemonstrations, or intruders on the mountain itself?" Bolan asked.

"We don't really have heavy surveillance anywhere except the camp and its approach roads," the man replied. "Every so often we have one of the helicopters swing a little toward the mountain, but we can't do too much of that. We can't even have too many helicopters in the air at the same time. The Greens would think we were going to dump riot gas on them from the air, or something."

If the Greens were downwind of the cave and something blew, they might have much worse than riot gas dumped on them. It looked as if Helmut Kuhn's influence in high places didn't go far enough to make them believe his guess about what was going on inside the mountain. The police forces were neither briefed nor equipped for dealing with a large-scale poison gas attack.

The situation was a classic prescription for trouble. More than one group in the field, each with its own mission, and no coordination between them.

Since the demonstration wasn't illegal, all the police were supposed to do was watch it in case any crimes were committed or anybody ended up endangering themselves or others.

Bolan and his people were supposed to break up the demonstration peacefully, then see that everybody kept on going until they were out of range of any gas released from the mountain. After that they were to do a recon of the mountain itself, undeterred by the Greens, police, neo-Nazis, Spetsnaz or local wildlife.

This, of course, assumed that neither the demonstration nor breaking it up would warn any bad guys on the mountain. Or that once warned, they wouldn't either run and live to make more trouble, or come down and massacre the demonstrators.

"Oh, by the way," their driver said. "We had to load the rest of your gear in a second Munga. It just wouldn't fit in one. My comrade drove it into the woods, as it was all in military crating."

"Into the woods" was a mercifully short walk, and the rest of the gear included not only all the chemical-warfare equipment but three folding-stock MP-5s with ten magazines apiece. Bolan showed Trudl how to get her suit on, then started pulling his own outfit together.

At least Helmut Kuhn's people continued to be more or less on the ball. They weren't going to have to decide in favor of one mission because it would be suicidal to carry out the other.

COLONEL DANILOV KNEW that all the work gangs there since yesterday had been vouched for. All had the proper papers for dedicated members of the Greater Germany party or sympathetic groups, with all the oaths properly sworn and all the initiation fees paid.

Danilov sometimes wondered about those initiation fees. Were the Germans, even the fascist ones, drifting away from old-style mystical rites? Or was somebody in the Greater Germany party thinking along the same lines as he was, that a Nazi revival could be profitable whether it succeeded or not?

However they'd come into the Greater Germany party, the eight men on the current crew were of a much higher standard than their predecessors. Most of the others had been middle-aged, flabby and no brighter than they had to be. These eight were younger, fitter, more intelligent and easier to keep at work.

No, one of them was approaching now. Danilov tried to put a name to the unsmiling young face before him, but failed. He was doing a larger share of his own clerical work now, and there was no less of it.

At least the cover story about an accident to Yuri and the desertion of Anton was passing, for now. In fact, the risk of Anton's betraying them might have frightened the Greater Germans into sending up some of their better people.

"Mr. Dannemeier, we have heard a rumor that there will be a Green Party demonstration near the mountain today."

That was no rumor, but a plain fact. It was also something that Danilov intended to ignore if possible. The Greens had no good reason to actually endanger the project's security.

"As long as they keep their distance, we will not reveal our presence."

"How great a distance do you consider safe? Remember that there will be police watching them. The Greens are not trained observers, but the police and any spies they have among the demonstrators—"

Danilov held up a hand. "I understand. I do not think that we will have any problem if we leave no evidence on the surface. Nobody will follow us down this hidden entrance, even if they discover it."

"So we should abandon normal working routine and move all compromising equipment below ground?"

"Yes." He hated to lose a working day, with so few left before the ceremony and the real chance to do damage. But they did have a small margin for error, maybe a large one if these new people continued to work the way they had.

"We are at your service, Mr. Dannemeier."

Danilov hoped the man and his comrades were at his service for a few more days. Otherwise, those whom *he* served would not be pleased.

RACHEL ZONIS THOUGHT she saw some of the bus drivers slipping off into the trees. She told herself that she was being paranoid. Even if it wasn't her imagination, she was certainly paranoid to imagine that this necessarily meant trouble.

Some of them probably just wanted to stretch their legs. Others might not be Green sympathizers, although the bus companies had been fairly good about sending drivers who were at least polite. They might not want to be around, though, if some hothead started trouble and the police used that as an excuse to wade in.

There were a lot of reasons why Rachel didn't want the police involved, and the fact that her cover might not survive arrest was only one of them. These were kids, some of them no older than her baby brother, Yigal. The idea of German police wading into *anybody* ate at her nerves and stomach, even though she'd been luckier than people like Zev Ben Shlomo. Her grandparents had money; they'd been able to buy passage for themselves and their relatives to Israel or America before the doors slammed shut on Europe's Jews.

These demonstrators were also German, a voice told her. Did she care what Germans did to one another?

Yes. If you didn't care, you wound up like all the people who stood by during the Holocaust.

Out loud, she asked Paul, "Is everybody here?"

"I think we ought to wait for the Earth Brotherhood convoy," he said. "They had some real old teakettles with them, and I'm sure they've had to stop for breakdowns."

"All right. Why don't we have each group send ten people up to the mine entrance, with enough posters and vidcams to get started? Everybody else can pitch tents, dig latrines and so on."

"Hey, Suzanne. Remember we're officially leading only the Mainz team. I have to consult with the other chiefs."

"Do that, then." She knew that this was true, but also that he might use "the other chiefs" as an excuse for not letting her lead. German men were—well, they were German men.

"If they agree, toss you for who leads our ten?" he asked, as he turned to go.

She made the gesture for "perfect." She would have liked to be sure of going first. The cave had been a military site. With her background she had a better chance of detecting things like old booby traps, possibly still lethal after two generations. But Paul wasn't stupid, just inexperienced. It said much in his favor that he was willing to toss for leadership.

Rachel looked up at the sky and saw clouds drifting in from the west on the erratic wind. It would be chilly this high in the uplands, if the sun went. She zipped up her jacket and told herself that the shiver was only from the wind.

THE MUNGA FIELD CAR wasn't exactly a mountain-rally vehicle, but four-wheel drive and a light load made the difference. The two Mungas groaned and wheezed, rattled and squeaked, but made it to the last stretch of road.

Bolan sat in the lead, the Weatherby across his lap and his mask pulled aside. All three of them wore ponchos that concealed most of their protective gear from a casual observer.

The ponchos wouldn't help if they were stopped, of course, but they had IDs as a BND combat engineer recon team, with Trudl as their civilian consultant. The IDs wouldn't stand up to a check all the way back to Bonn, but would probably pass muster at the nearest corps or police headquarters.

They were an impressive job, on this kind of notice. Once again, Bolan had the feeling that Helmut Kuhn made people very unwillling to disappoint him, and that if he couldn't make them unwilling, he might make them afraid.

On the last stretch, they went to the lowest gear and the lowest speed, as quiet as possible and ready for a quick stop. They were taking a slight risk, riding this close, but there was plenty of cover between the road and the slopes of the mountain.

A greater risk would be walking too far and arriving exhausted. It was growing cooler the higher they climbed, but the best protective gear was infernally hot and uncomfortable. Even a man as fit as Bolan could wear himself out, doing too much too fast while wearing it.

With less than a mile to go, Bolan looked back again. He went to full alert as he saw something on the road behind them. He put his mouth next to the driver's ear and said, "Drop back to the rear position. I think we're being followed."

He used hand signals to pass the news to Ben Shlomo, as the lead Munga slowed to let the Israeli's vehicle pass. The reply was an interrogative. Bolan shook his head.

He didn't know who they were, and if they were police it might be embarrassing at worst.

They might also be people who had no business here, or reinforcements for the same kind already on the mountain. He intended to find out.

Ben Schlomo's driver stepped on the gas as Bolan's Munga took the rear. It fell into position, just as a big Hanomag field car lurched around the bend. It was having difficulty navigating the narrow, steep road, so the warrior had plenty of time to study it.

Civilian paint job and marking. Civilian fittings, toolboxes and so on. Probably army surplus, like the Mungas. An unmarked police vehicle? Bolan didn't want to use binoculars, to avoid tipping off the driver behind, but the driver didn't look like a policeman.

"Hey!" came the shout in German from behind. "Get out of the way!"

"You take your turn," Bolan's driver shouted back, doing a good imitation of a man angry at somebody else's bad road manners. "We can't stay stuck all day behind that elephant you're driving!"

"It won't be all day," somebody shouted from the back. "I think we're on the way to the same—"

The speaker was abruptly silenced. On the way to the same— What? Place? And what was that place?

"We're from the special weapons group," Bolan called. "Who are you?"

"Weapon—" the loudmouth began, and again was silenced.

Bolan patted Trudl on the shoulder and pointed to the floor. She didn't need the message repeated. She crawled down, fitting herself in between the seats as well as someone her size could do. Then the Executioner tapped the driver on the shoulder.

"Get ready to hit the gas if they start shooting." The driver nodded.

Bolan cupped his hands and mustered up his best German. "We are from the special weapons group of the office of the chief of engineers! You are entering a potentially contaminated area. Stop and let us inspect your equipment before we allow you to proceed!"

That would be putting his credentials, not to mention his German, to a harsh test. But if they submitted, it was a point in their favor.

What happened next was ten points the other way. The Hanomag stopped, slewing as the brakes caught unevenly. If it had been going much faster, the high-sided, heavily loaded vehicle might have rolled over.

But it stopped safely, doors popped on the sides and rear and a crew of skinheads poured out. Most of them were carrying weapons, a motley collection that Bolan mostly couldn't identify from such a distance.

He didn't get any closer, because at least two of the skinheads started shooting immediately. That settled the question of innocence. The Munga driver had his foot on the accelerator before the first bullet flew past his ear.

Bolan dropped one man with the MP-5, then shifted to the Weatherby as the group scattered. A moving vehicle made a poor platform for a scope-sighted rifle, and at that range Bolan could have done better with iron sights. He still managed to drop two more men before the others were under cover, shooting randomly but only wasting ammunition.

Then to Bolan's surprise the Hanomag started off again. He couldn't see anybody in the cab, but the big van was definitely coming after him. Lightly loaded now, and with an obviously skilled driver, it was actually gaining on the Munga.

The tactics were obvious, and a credit to whoever thought them up. Chase the two Mungas, and that would buy time for the men on foot to reach the mountaintop and their friends. The Hanomag crew wasn't short of guts or skill. What did they have for weapons?

One of them at least had a subgun, probably another MP-5. Bolan saw the man hang out of the cab, sighted the Weatherby as the man fired, heard bullets drill into the Munga, and Trudl squeal, then got off his own shot. The Magnum round took the subgunner in the chest and sent him cartwheeling out of the van into the ditch beside the road.

The warrior chambered a fresh round and bent to check Trudl. Before he could tell if she was hurt, his instincts warned him of new danger. The Weatherby came up, just as somebody leaned out of a roof hatch in the Hanomag with an RPG-7 leveled at the Munga.

The Weatherby shot and hit first, but the shooter's dying reflex squeezed the trigger of the RPG. The Magnum's impact threw off his aim, though. Instead of slamming into the Munga and spreading it in pieces all over the road, the rocket-propelled grenade flashed past and punched into a small stone bridge.

The Munga bounced, all four wheels in the air, as it hit the smoking cavity. It bounced again as it hit scattered blackened stones. A tire pierced by a fragment blew, and the driver fought the car back to a straight line.

Then the Hanomag struck the damaged bridge just as Bolan slammed the Weatherby's third round into the driver's side of the windshield. The dead RPG gunner flipped out of his hatch as the Hanomag went up on its nose. Stone crumbled under the vehicle and sprayed out into the creekbed on either side. The Hanomag slammed back on its wheels, with both front tires blown and both front wheels splayed out as if the axle was broken. There was no sign of the driver, but pieces of windshield were mixed with blood on his seat.

"Go back and finish them off?" the driver asked.

Bolan shook his head. "Their passengers might come up and give them fire support. Get on the radio police frequencies. Say we have signs of a terrorist attack on the site and give the vehicle's position. Warn them that other armed terrorists might be in the area."

"Very good," the driver replied. "But they might bring in helicopters and start gassing everything that moves, including us."

"We've got protective gear," Bolan pointed out. "You and your friend don't, but you aren't staying around here. Haul out and report."

"But—"

"My friend, we don't want heroes today. We need you and your buddy, alive, out of here and reporting to headquarters."

The driver managed to salute sarcastically. Bolan ignored him, to see if Trudl Kuhn was all right.

She was, by a narrow margin. At least one 9 mm round had punched through the side of the Munga within inches of her ear. When she shook her head, strands of clipped hair floated loose.

She picked up one of the strands and stared at it with frightening intensity. "My grandfather always said that anyone who harmed a hair of my head would pay for it. But they already have, haven't they?"

"I expect so."

"Do you want me to go back with the drivers? If you ask, I will."

"You won't be a passenger, Trudl. You can come if you want to. Just don't vomit when your gear's buttoned up. That will force you to take it off."

"Oh. I think I will come along. Having come this far—" Then she did throw up, but not much, not in her mask, and in fact very neatly over the side of the racing Munga. She'd straightened up and wiped her mouth off by the time they pulled up behind Ben Shlomo's car, parked on the side of the road with both its crew under cover with drawn weapons.

"Heavy opposition?" the Israeli asked. Bolan nodded. "Think we should turn it over to the police?" the Mossad agent added.

Bolan swallowed a biting reply. He was being tested, and this was the wrong time and place for that. "No. The police aren't set up for a full-scale firefight. We can buy them some time to get ready. There's also the Greens."

"You mean the police won't protect them?"

"They might protect them if the Greens will listen. If they won't, we might have to imitate a terrorist band to get the Greens moving."

"I fear Mr. Metzger is right," Trudl said. "Some of the Green leaders are very stubborn."

Ben Shlomo said something, but since it was in Hebrew neither she nor Bolan could tell what it was, except that it probably wasn't complimentary to Germans.

COLONEL DANILOV HEARD the distant gunfire, ending with what sounded horribly like an explosion. He cursed. Some of those fascist sons of bitches were getting trigger happy and then into a fight with the police, no doubt! Preserving security would be difficult now, even if the police didn't make a connection between the fascist militia and the mountain.

One of the Spetsnaz hurried up. "Mr. Dannemeier, we have heard on the radio reports of terrorists in the area."

"Police reports, or merely somebody jumping at shadows?" It took all of Danilov's training to maintain his cover identity. He hoped the Spetsnaz weren't going to start breaking theirs without orders.

"Somebody is talking to the police, anyway. The German police take reports of terrorists very seriously."

The man clearly wanted to ask "Do we fight or run?" but didn't dare put it that way to a superior officer.

Danilov silently thanked the man for his discipline. His own answer would have been "Neither," because either meant the end of Project Gamma. But doing nothing was beginning to seem like wishful thinking, and also might make even Spetsnaz troopers nervous.

"The security detail is to draw its weapons and double up the guard on all key installations," Danilov said. Even to himself, his voice sounded like a tape recording. "Nobody is to fire unless attacked by an identifiable terrorist, or on my orders."

"Very good."

The code name "security detail" meant that the troopers were to draw only pistols and shotguns, weapons that a corporation's antiterrorist unit might have. If he'd said "the operational forces," it would have meant breaking out the concealed infantry weapons for an all-out fight.

The messenger had just left when Danilov's telephone rang. It was the guard at the cave. His voice was muffled by his protective gear, but the colonel could tell he was nervous about something.

"Mr. Dannemeier, the whole work team has sealed the door into the caves behind them. I cannot open it."

"What? Who authorized this? I did not."

"No one. They just did it."

"Who is on the detail?"

It took a moment for the man to find the list, a moment that for Danilov seemed to stretch into the next century. Then the man began reading off names, and Danilov's stomach turned over.

Most of the men were the younger ones, but two were technical experts from the old team. One of them, Muller, was an electronics expert who had designed the firing circuits for the explosives that would blow the cave and release the gas.

If he was in there, the German fascists now had complete control over Project Gamma. Unless the exterior override controls had been hooked up—and Danilov remembered that he'd deliberately put off doing that for security reasons.

His discipline couldn't keep him from cursing in Russian. He only hoped no Germans heard.

IT HAD SOUNDED like gunfire to Rachel Zonis and to a few of the Greens who were veterans. They looked at one another, then at the mountain.

They didn't learn anything at first. Then a big woman Rachel knew only as Louisa pointed at the sky.

"Look! The police helicopters are on the move!"

There were four of them, and they were all heading toward the demonstrators.

"They're going to gas us!" someone screamed.

Rachel swore under her breath. Always and forever, there was someone who lost his head and started a panic.

Paul was as fast as Rachel, and more direct. A fist slammed onto somebody's skin, and a lanky youth sprawled on the rocky ground, holding his jaw.

Rachel threw herself into the brief silence. "Listen, people!" she shouted. "We need observers at the cave mouth. Enough to bear witness to the accident they're trying to cover up! Ten will do. I want volunteers with gas masks. Everybody else, stay here, stay in the open, and if the police tell you to move, don't argue—"

"Traitor!"

This time it was a woman who had shouted. Louisa slapped her. Louisa was big enough to follow up with a punch if necessary, and the woman knew it.

"I'm going up there now," Rachel continued. "I need nine more, and remember, with gas masks!"

"I'm with our sister," Louisa shouted. She ran after Rachel, as the Israeli started up the mountain.

Rachel slowed down to let her catch up. She wished Louisa had stayed below to help Paul keep the hotheads under control. Rachel's bad feeling about this day was getting worse every moment.

But that was Louisa, always volunteering for everything that let her prove women were as tough as men. In Louisa's case at least, that was true.

CHAPTER FOURTEEN

Bolan's team was making a final check on its gear when they heard the Mungas start up and rattle off down the mountain. The Executioner let out a pent-up breath. This mountain could suddenly get very unhealthy for anybody not in a protective suit. Helmut Kuhn didn't have unlimited funds for supporting the widows and orphans of people who'd got themselves killed being brave in the wrong place at the wrong time.

"I was afraid we were going to have to start those fools moving with a shot," Ben Shlomo said, hefting his MP-5. He wore his gear more easily than Trudl, as easily as Bolan. But then the Israelis had trained more seriously than most other countries in coping with chemical warfare.

Bolan unfolded a map of the mountain on the ground and knelt beside it. "The main entrance was over here. That's where the Greens are and the ceremony will be. So anything illegal won't be there, or if it is the police can watch for it while they're watching the Greens."

"That leaves quite a lot of mountain to hide secret entrances," Ben Shlomo observed.

"I do not think the Mossad honors you so highly for pointing out the obvious," Trudl said. He shot her as poisonous a look as he could through the mask.

"Kuhn said there were only two places where the mine and the caves beyond came close to the surface, on this side of the mountain. Here and here." He tapped the map, ignored Ben Shlomo's mutter about an old man's memory and went on.

"The first one's away from the road, and there's a mile of open ground between it and any heavy cover. The second one has a logging road to within half a mile, and from the road, tree cover almost all the way to the crest."

He didn't need to tell them which one he was choosing, but he was surprised when it was Trudl who pointed out the problem. "The skinheads might be on the way to the second one, or at least guarding it."

That got her a different kind of look from Ben Shlomo.

Bolan nodded. "Right. So when we climb the hill, we climb carefully."

The Executioner took point, and the little patrol moved out.

COLONEL DANILOV was speaking on the telephone that linked the cave with the command post. He wasn't happy.

Neither, to do them justice, were the men he talked to. Having sealed the cave behind them, they knew they might have sealed themselves in their own tomb. All of them had gas masks, but the kind of gas in the cave might still be able to kill on contact. It was supposed to be nonpersistent, but if you were in the same underground tunnel with it that wouldn't save you.

"This is not the right moment," Danilov said for perhaps the fifth time.

For the fifth time, the same reply came back. It was rude gutter German, and it implied that Danilov and the Greens were both capable of amazing sexual perversities.

Danilov let the insults pass. "Can you put somebody on who knows something about politics?"

The comment drew more obscenities, followed by silence, and then by a more cultured voice.

"What politics do you want to talk about, Mr. Dannemeier? The politics of letting those cursed Greens preen and prance, when we can destroy them by flicking a switch? Or the politics of cowards who want to let them go?"

Danilov took a firm grip on what remained of his temper and said, "The politics of people who would use a powerful weapon on a mouse."

"The Greens are not mice."

"All right, rats, possibly. But the men we have been preparing for are lions. Why waste our big gun on rats?"

"Because the rats are here now, when we have the gun. The lions might not come at all if they are warned. And can you be sure that they have not been warned?"

That German, Danilov reflected, was too sensible. He had put his finger on the weak point in the colonel's argument. Not using the gas today meant, very likely, never using it at all. The Greens had focused too much public attention on the mountain a week too soon.

For that reason alone Danilov didn't really mind the idea of slaughtering them wholesale. It would be a thoroughly nasty incident, with a high death toll, and accomplish some of his objectives.

Not all, though. It would kill rank-and-file members of a bourgeois romantic rabble, not high civil and military officials of a dozen governments. It would make the Germans vigilant without creating a crisis.

It would, in fact, very likely put Danilov out of business permanently. That was not desirable, for several reasons besides the probable displeasure of his superiors.

"If you will unseal the cave and come out—"

"Why should we? Do you really think we trust you, Mr. Dannemeier—if that is really your name?"

Danilov went cold, and for one of the few times in his life, he was at a loss for words. If he had been in control of the charges at that moment, he might have fired them simply to bring the cave down on top of those loud-mouthed Germans. His secret would then be buried with them.

But no override meant no control from Danilov's post. He was cursing that oversight again when the line went dead.

As it did, a messenger thrust his head into the command post. Danilov cursed the man even before he could open his mouth. Then he took a deep breath. "If you are bringing bad news..."

"Ah, the skinheads have come up the hill. They say they were attacked on the road by the terrorists. They also want to know where their comrades are."

Danilov groaned. He had been right to curse the man, although truly the bad news wasn't his fault. He picked up his AKR and rose.

"Secure the radio and have a concealed squad of the operational forces ready for action."

"I serve the Soviet Union."

That was breaking cover with a vengeance, but Danilov doubted that it really mattered anymore.

RACHEL ZONIS WAS in the embarrassing position of a leader who had to run to keep ahead of her followers. Most of the people flocking uphill after her seemed to be like Louisa, sound of mind and limb. Her jogging shoes also weren't really made for the terrain, and many of the others wore boots, which were.

She still wanted to get there first. She knew what kind of death was waiting in that cave, or at least Zev Ben Shlomo had told her what Helmut Kuhn said. Kuhn had never made the ranks of the "righteous Christians" in Israel, but short of that he was about as trustworthy as a German of his generation could be.

Somebody behind her was cursing. A girl, one of Louisa's friends, had turned her ankle on the rock. Louisa stopped to let her catch up, then knelt to look at the ankle.

The rest stopped and gathered around. Rachel called Louisa out of the circle, while someone with a first-aid kit examined the ankle.

"Louisa, she'll need help getting back down."

"Meaning that I should go?"

"Why not?"

Louisa looked hard at Rachel. "Suzanne, is there danger up here? More than you've been telling us about?"

"Yes." She looked up the slope, then at the helicopters that seemed to be circling lower each minute. "But it's not from them."

"Then what is it?"

Rachel cursed herself for arousing Louisa's curiosity in an effort to save her. Louisa was the only one of her friends from the movement in danger. Paul and the others were all down below; they would have a chance to run.

"I know something about chemistry. Those old explosives could be unstable. Spontaneous detonation, that sort of thing."

"So you think we should bear witness from a safe distance?"

"I don't know what would really be a safe distance." With nerve gas, it would be at least ten kilometers, preferably upwind.

"Then we'll go on as we planned. We have to be there, don't you see? They might think again, if they see they can't hide their crimes."

That hadn't prevented the Holocaust. Bearing witness to the crime was fine, as far as it went. Shooting the criminal so that he wouldn't do it again went further.

IT WAS EASY for Bolan's team to stay clear of the skinheads. They straggled, kept poor security and were noisy. The only thing the warrior feared was stumbling over one of the stragglers. He kept Ben Shlomo's gift, the silenced "clean" Makarov, drawn for that situation.

It didn't happen. The team reached the edge of the woods right on the trail of the skinheads. There were eight or nine of them, and they seemed to be arguing with somebody's security detail. With the pistols and shotguns, Bolan was willing to believe they might be a security detail—until he spotted the machine gun in the trees.

Binoculars brought it close. It was an RPK, with a crew of two, and a sniper and observer just visible beyond it. All four looked more like Spetsnaz than security guards, and they had a perfect enfilade position on the skinheads.

If the shooting started, it was going to be a massacre. The skinheads might do some damage before they went down—they were packing plenty of firepower. They wouldn't get the machine-gun team; they might get some genuine innocents.

The obvious solution was for Bolan and his team to simply skate around the whole confrontation and go warn the Greens. Unfortunately the quickest way to the other side of the mountain lay right past the clearing.

The Executioner noticed that Ben Shlomo had disappeared. Beating the bush for him would be a waste of time. He only hoped the Mossad agent hadn't decided to take matters into his own hands.

A minute later Ben Shlomo moved back into sight. His gear was dirty but not torn. He crawled up to Bolan, lifted his mask and whispered in the Executioner's ear.

"The skinheads are who we know they are. I think those guards are Spetsnaz. The problem is, the skinheads say they're looking for some friends. The security chief is saying their friends are down in the mine already. He looks unhappy."

Friends of the skinheads. More neo-Nazis, down in the mine.

To release the gas. What other reason could they have?

Bolan raised the Weatherby. "I'm going to wing one of the skinheads. That should start a firefight. While they're hitting each other, we get across the crest fast. I think somebody's about to release the gas."

THE SHOT THAT STRUCK the skinhead was a heavy rifle bullet. The man knocked down two of his comrades as he crashed to the ground, and spattered others with blood.

Colonel Danilov didn't wait to see what the skinheads' reaction would be. He dived for the nearest cover, rolled, raised his AKR and simultaneously fired off a burst and shouted to his men in German, "Commence operations!"

The ambiguous command held the skinheads in the open for a critical few seconds. They would have been more critical if one of the skinheads hadn't pulled out a grenade. It soared into the trees, bounced off a trunk and exploded in front of the RPK.

Danilov could see that it was a blind, almost lucky throw. The machine-gun team thought that their position was compromised. Firing on the move, they shifted to a new location. For a whole thirty seconds, they were either blocked by trees or inaccurate.

This left the firefight in the hands of the lighter weapons, where neither side had a clear edge in firepower. The skinheads had more submachine guns than Danilov cared for, and bullets kicked up dust and rock chips all around him for a moment. He heard someone cry out in Russian, popped up, squeezed the trigger on the AKR and only stopped firing when the magazine ran empty.

As it did, the RPK opened fire. The skinheads who hadn't run or gone down were in its sights. They died where they stood, scythed by a withering burst. One of them threw a grenade as he went down; the throw was feeble and it fell among his comrades. If any of them were shamming death, the grenade put an end to their act.

Danilov carefully inserted a fresh magazine in his AKR before standing. "Count off," he shouted.

The troopers did so in Russian. Even if there were any Germans alive within hearing, it didn't matter. Project Gamma was dead, along with four troopers, with two more wounded.

The only victory left for Danilov was to get enough of his men off the mountain to start over again. He gave the signal for escape and evasion, and heard a pistol shot as one man carried out the first step—killing a comrade too badly hurt to travel.

THE MEN BELOW GROUND didn't hear the Russian voices. That would have told them nothing they didn't know, anyway. They knew they were betrayed, and they looked at Muller.

Muller nodded and muttered under his breath, like a prayer, "For the Fatherland." He wouldn't say "Führer and Fatherland." No one would bear that sacred name again.

Then his sweaty hands closed the firing circuits, and the explosives erupted, opening the mine entrance on the far side of the crest and hurling three-quarters of a ton of Compound 58 through the gap.

WHEN SHE HEARD automatic-weapons' fire, Rachel Zonis knew that bearing witness had suddenly become irrelevant. What the Americans called hauling ass was now much more important.

Fortunately she didn't have to argue with anybody. Even Louisa was looking down the hill, and several people were already edging backward.

Then the explosion seemed to tear out the whole hillside. It took Rachel a moment to realize that most of the rocks were going to fall short of them.

"Masks!" she shouted. They started jerking on their stolen police masks. Against what was in the cave, the filters were probably not very effective, but if they got only a light dose and the symptoms were recognized in time...

One rock fell short but rolled, and Louisa was right in its path. Rachel screamed, then Louisa screamed much louder—and briefly—as the rock rolled over her, crushing her from the waist down. She thrashed her arms wildly, gagging with the pain, rapidly going into shock.

Before anyone could move to her aid, the second explosion erupted. This one was smaller, curiously muffled and seemed to throw out smoking barrels rather than rocks.

The gas was supposed to be nonpersistent but skin permeable. Rachel had her mask on when the first of the barrels rolled past her, venting its contents as a sickening yellow vapor.

Louisa was past showing any reactions to the gas. Rachel felt a tingling, and a sudden nausea as the cloud swept over her. Then the nausea twisted her in the middle, and she dropped to her hands and knees. A moment later she was in convulsions.

BOLAN AND HIS TEAM were over the crest when the gas was released. They all wanted to sprint, and all knew that they could manage at best a clumsy shuffle.

Once they reached the point of the Green demonstration, however, they went immediately to work. The antidote injectors were spring-loaded, strong enough to push through heavier clothing than most of the demonstrators wore.

Bolan had for the moment left his Executioner self behind. He might have never carried a weapon, so completely was he absorbed now in saving lives. He knelt, pulled out injectors, used them and tossed them away with the precision and speed of a high-powered machine.

Trudl worked beside him with almost the same skill, even if her face was white under the mask. Ben Shlomo was doing his share, too, and Bolan wondered briefly what his thoughts were, about saving German victims of gas.

In less than ten minutes, the Green demonstration had divided itself into two groups. There were the ones caught by the gas and injected with antidote, and there were the rest, who'd started running at the explosions.

One of the dead was the female Mossad agent. Bolan knew when Ben Shlomo found her. He knelt beside her briefly, then stripped the windbreaker off another body and covered his late colleague's face with it.

There were injectors left over. Bolan put most of them in a bag, then wound up and tossed the bag downhill.

"Gas antidote!" he shouted. He called three times, and the third time someone heard him.

"Will they be able to use it?" he asked Trudl.

"They should have some people who learned first aid in the army."

"Good." Bolan was beginning to sweat in his gear, in spite of the wind. That wind was a blessing, though. For now it was blowing from downhill up toward the crest, and sending most of the remaining gas away from the Greens. The gas would blow along the crest, dissipating before it reached anyone, or over it, to reach only those dead or deserving to die.

"It seems that Mr. Kuhn's work was mostly successful," Ben Shlomo said. "The gas was lethal and skin permeable. It remains to be seen how persistent it was, and of course, how much it had deteriorated."

"I think my grandfather would be quite happy if it had deteriorated into uselessness," Trudl said coldly. "As would I."

Bolan headed off the quarrel. "People, save it. We need to be out of here before somebody gets too curious. Being in gas gear makes us hard to recognize and for awhile makes us look official. But I don't want to wear out our welcome."

They were over the crest of the hill before the first police helicopter landed in front of the demonstration. Bolan listened briefly on the police frequencies for any sign of pursuit, heard nothing and took point again on the downhill leg of their exfiltration.

CHAPTER FIFTEEN

Bolan and his team ended up with nearly an hour's lead over any possible pursuit.

They listened to the police radios for nearly half that time before they heard any mention of people in chemical protective suits. It was another half hour before the police radios started suggesting that inquiries be made about these mysterious people.

"Knowing police bureaucracies, it'll have to be shot all the way up to the top in Bonn for debate. After they talk it over, it'll have to be signed and countersigned five ways before they'll put it on the air." Bolan looked at his watch. "I guess we can afford to stop and take a break."

His companions looked as if they needed one. It would have helped if they could take off the gear, which now made them more rather than less identifiable. But the warrior wasn't quite ready to gamble on the nonpersistence of the gas. Even a mild dose, with the antidote quickly injected, could leave them helpless for hours, maybe days.

Then hypothermia might finish them off at night, if none of the fleeing Spetsnaz soldiers stumbled on them to do the job by daylight.

DANILOV LOST ONLY one man to the gas. He was the rear guard, and he was farther behind than he was supposed to be anyway. When Danilov saw the man lagging, he fell back himself, raised his AKR and waited.

When the man's face turned white and he vomited, Danilov pulled the trigger.

That made seven men down of the twenty at the Project Gamma site. He had only eight of the remaining thirteen with him, although he hoped the others would turn up before long.

It wasn't pleasant to think that the balance of power within his group had now shifted in favor of the fanatical Major Bytkin. Bytkin, and Wegener, the man he had recruited in the Beck organization.

Of course, Wegener wasn't necessarily loyal to Bytkin. Indeed, from his past history, he seemed unlikely to be loyal to anyone for very long.

But perhaps it was time to remind Wegener that he, Danilov, held the keys to larger rewards than Bytkin ever could offer. It was an advantage that the criminal had always had over the honest man, and Bytkin was nothing if not honest.

"BREAK'S OVER." Bolan looked at his watch. "I allowed ten minutes, and we've been here twice that long. On your feet, everybody."

"Yes, Sergeant Major," Trudl said, sketching a salute and nearly poking herself in the eyepiece with one gloved hand. She rose, as gracefully as anyone could in chemical-protective gear.

Ben Shlomo got to his feet more slowly. Inside the mask, his eyes seemed to be brooding.

"I think I have a question," he said. "Was there any chance that the evidence of Project Gamma was deliberately not placed in the right hands?"

Bolan didn't like either the tone of the question or the look on Trudl Kuhn's face. "What would have been the right hands?"

"The German police, of course. If GSG-9 had raided that site, how many of the Greens now dead would be alive?"

"We don't know how many are dead," Trudl Kuhn replied. "Remember, the gas deteriorated, and we gave the antidotes." She spoke more politely than Bolan had expected.

The Executioner nodded. "Also remember that we had more freedom to use deadly force than GSG-9 could have. They could never have provoked that firefight between the skinheads and the guards I'm nearly certain are Spetsnaz. If you're worrying about Nazis, Zev, remember how many real ones we've accounted for."

"And just what is that supposed to mean?" Ben Shlomo asked. His voice was raspy. Bolan hoped heat exhaustion wasn't hitting him. They were down out of the breeze, the sun was high and the suits were turning into sweat baths.

"It means that you seem to suspect my grandfather's reasons for sending you and Peter against Project Gamma," Trudl snapped. "Peter's argument should have occurred to you, as well! I think you and he are better than GSG-9, too!"

"Normally I would be grateful for such a compliment from a lady," Ben Shlomo said. In the chemical gear, his courtly bow was a grisly parody. "But when she asks me to praise a German of her grandfather's generation—"

Bolan decided to intervene. This was getting out of hand.

"Zev, Trudl, both of you knock it off!" He managed quite a blast even through the mask, and got both their attention.

"I don't want any more sniping. Trudl, Zev lost more relatives in the camps than you have fingers. He's had to live with that every minute he's around Germans, and that's been five years.

"You can live with him for a few more days, or I take a break in this mission to dump you back on your grandfather. You're not a passenger, but you are a guest. Your invitation can be withdrawn. Understand?"

"Y-yes." She sounded desperately determined not to let Bolan get to her. She wasn't succeeding.

"Zev, she's not asking you to praise her grandfather or anybody else. She's asking you not to jump to conclusions, and I'm asking you to watch your mouth. I don't want to have to take this up with your chiefs or mine. Keep it zipped, and it stays among the three of us."

The Mossad agent shrugged. "You are more right than not. I still want to inquire if there was any legal avenue that the evidence allowed us to pursue. If there was not, then—" he glanced at Trudl "—your grandfather did very well indeed to bring us in."

"As long as you're discreet, you can inquire all you want," Bolan said. "In fact, we owe you one. I'll talk to my liaison about what he can do to help."

"What is the world coming to, when secret agents talk like lawyers?" Trudl said. She arched her eyebrows in mock amazement.

"Better agents who talk like lawyers than cowboys like Willi Beck," Ben Shlomo said.

Bolan nodded. He didn't want to get into a discussion of Beck in front of Trudl. She was cleared only for the fact that the Beck organization wasn't trustworthy, not any of the background.

He was sure there was a lot more in Beck's background than met the eye, and that it deserved some careful study.

That was one reason he suspected it would be a while before he went back to chasing mafiosi or their German partners. Another was the Spetsnaz. It would be nice to think the firefight and the gas had accounted for most of them, and that the German police would round up the rest.

Nice, but overoptimistic. The German police lacked firepower, training and coordination to tackle this kind of job on a nationwide basis. The fear of a centralized police force like the Gestapo made German police jurisdictions as big a tangle as American ones. The fear of looking bad abroad made them reluctant to set up special task forces.

Also, in this case too much publicity would make people ask embarrassing questions. Bolan had never heard of a government that encouraged that. It was one of the reasons for his war. Governments afraid of being embarrassed had let too many predators get away, to kill again.

The undercover Spetsnaz team was likely to escape, if it was up to the Germans to stop them. This mission that had come out of nowhere was going to keep the Executioner busy for a while.

COLONEL DANILOV'S MEN lived up to one part of the Spetsnaz reputation—they spoke German so fluently that they could pass for Germans. A couple of talented ones could even manage Berlin, Rhineland and Bavarian accents, depending on which was best for their current cover identity.

Safely into the Thüringer Wald, they broke up into small parties, changed their clothes to look like hikers and started hiking. They all had papers that would pass muster as long as they weren't stopped until they'd put a good many miles between themselves and the death caves.

If they were stopped, they all had the usual poison capsules. Danilov could only hope that they also had the discipline and motivation to use them.

It was possible, in fact, that there would be some advantage to working directly with Oleg Bytkin again. The major had a powerful motivator for any undisciplined team members: he shot them.

Eventually, of course, this would bring about his own death. Possibly Danilov wouldn't lift a finger, let alone a weapon, to cause it. "Fragging," as the Americans called it, was a fate that Oleg had been courting ever since he was commissioned. If it overtook him here in Germany, few would be suspicious and no one would be willing or indeed able to inquire too closely. Danilov would have a free hand.

Meanwhile, there was a great deal of work to be extracted from Major Bytkin, starting with a new network of safehouses, going on to exploiting the partial failure of Project Gamma with his tame neo-Nazis, and ending who could tell where?

Danilov wouldn't have said that he was optimistic, as he shouldered the kind of stout pack a middle-aged businessman might have carried for a few days' hiking in the Thüringer Wald. He would have said that there was still reason to hope that with his remaining assets, he could sow much confusion in Germany, to the advantage of either himself or his friends in the Commonwealth. Or possibly both.

Not being an optimist, however, he was well equipped to deal with suspicious people in his path. He carried his AKR rolled up inside his sleeping bag, and one of the two canteens on his hip was false, with grenades inside it. The PSM automatic, being so compact, rode in a leg pocket of his trousers.

BOLAN'S TEAM MANAGED to actually run the last hundred yards to the rendezvous with the Mungas. Trudl set the pace, her eyes positively blazing with desire to get out of their miserable sweatboxes. Even Ben Shlomo managed to keep up with her, and Bolan brought up the rear, eyes flicking back and forth across the landscape, examining every tree and boulder that might hide an enemy.

It was an easy mistake and a common one, coming in from patrol, to think that you could let down your guard because you were in friendly territory. It was a mistake that could kill. Bolan wasn't afraid of the neo-Nazis, if any were left in fighting condition. But with the Spetsnaz still on the loose...

Nobody sent bullets flying or grenades arcing at them. Bolan's team reached level ground, and one of the drivers tossed them a packet of chemical-detection paper. Bolan unwrapped it and handed a piece to each of his companions.

"Rub this all over your suits. If it changes color, that means there's persistent contamination."

The paper didn't change color on any of the suits except Bolan's, and even then the change was barely noticeable. The other two stepped back to pull off their gear, while one of the drivers sprayed Bolan with decontaminant from an ordinary fire extinguisher.

Five minutes later, Bolan's suit also tested clean. He stripped it off and inhaled great gulps of fresh air. The air around here was supposed to be heavily polluted, but after the air inside the suit, it tasted like a sea breeze.

The warrior stuffed his suit into a plastic bag. When all three suits were bagged and sealed, he hauled them into the woods and covered them with dead branches.

"That will keep them from contaminating the soil before they're found," he said. "They will be, but probably not until there's a thorough search. That should take a day or two even to organize, and we'll be home free by then."

Ben Shlomo's expression showed that he knew Bolan was talking for Trudl's ears. A look at the woman showed that she knew she was being lied to, and was about to explode.

"All right, we're not going to be home free until we've finished covering our trail and asked a few questions back in Berlin. But—have you ever heard the saying, 'The journey of a thousand miles begins with the first step'?"

They nodded.

"Good. Then let's take that first step, by getting out of here."

IN BERLIN, Hans Wegener watched the television news special bulletins and struggled to keep the horror off his face.

If half of what the announcers said had really happened, he would be lucky to escape with his life. The skinheads would be out for his blood, and Carl Braun and his people certainly wouldn't protect him.

He was still not without resources, however, and the man who called himself Schweiger was only one of them.

Braun's gang might be another—although even Braun couldn't control all his people. One of them, thinking his knowledge of how this disaster began was worth something, might also start looking for a buyer.

There was still another resource, even if it was for the moment far away and of uncertain strength. He hoped the two numbers he had would connect him fairly quickly, because he needed to move faster than his enemies, who weren't slow on their feet.

He also hoped that once he gave the Basques the name of the man who did them so much harm, they wouldn't be curious about how that man had come to be sent against them in the first place. Curious Basques turning into vengeful Basques, and vengeful Basques coming to Berlin to settle their account in blood had been one of Wegener's nightmares.

Now, perhaps he could bring the Basques to Berlin to be somebody else's nightmare. If so, the man who had ruined Project Gamma might not survive long enough to savor his victory.

CHAPTER SIXTEEN

The two Mungas kept to side roads all the way out of the Thüringer Wald, then stopped under tree cover three hundred yards from a gas station. It was the least risky course of action. They needed more gas to reach the rendezvous with the helicopter, and gas stations were still few and far between in what had been East Germany. But driving up to a station that might have police orders to report suspicious vehicles would be ill-advised.

"If they insist that we drive up to get the gasoline, we can suspect that the alert is out," one of the drivers said. He hefted an empty twenty-five-liter can. As the least memorable of the other faces, Ben Shlomo was carrying the second can.

The two men were back within ten minutes with the gasoline. "He didn't even ask for more than the standard price, although we woke him up after closing hours," the driver said.

"Yes, but I think he suspected something," Ben Shlomo added. "He said that if neo-Nazis—he called them conservative nationalists—were behind the incident, it proved they were much better organized than he had thought."

"So?" Trudl queried.

"He did not sound as if he disapproved."

"It's good news if they are organized," Bolan said. The others gaped, except for Ben Shlomo. He merely looked at the warrior as if he doubted either the big man's sanity or his sense of humor.

"The official line has been that the neo-Nazis are a fringe group, mostly skinheads and other people who can be counted on to trip over their own feet. They're supposed to be politically impotent and nothing to worry about.

"Now they've shown that they can recruit enough competent people to carry out a major act of terrorism. The government is going to be too embarrassed to do anything in public for a while. Long enough, probably, for us to settle with a few people the government won't be able to reach."

Ben Shlomo nodded. "Just as long as they move before something like this happens again. Remember what happened the first time Germans tried to ignore the Nazis as an embarrassment."

MAJOR BYTKIN LOOKED at the four men in front of him.

"Razor, Tiger—are you ready?" It came naturally to him now to use their Spetsnaz nicknames in German. This was what he liked most, next to going on a mission himself. The nicknames made him feel more like a Soviet soldier, and less like an impostor.

Until today, Danilov had taken the hog's share of such work. Now it was Bytkin's turn. If he had the chance, he could make such a record with the men left to him that the group might come to him if anything happened to Danilov.

After today's failure, that might come about naturally. It would certainly be easier to arrange.

The two men Bytkin addressed nodded. Both of them wore coveralls and carried toolboxes, which held all the equipment they would need to sabotage the truck park of Transportkunst, one of Helmut Kuhn's holdings.

"Any questions?"

"Yes," Tiger said. "Why not the old man himself?"

"Because that would be revealing in public our knowledge of his connection with the mine incident," Bytkin replied. "Then people would wonder how we knew, and start asking questions. They will ask them anyway, but the longer we put off that day, the more damage we can do."

The two men nodded again. They didn't quite salute, but they drew themselves up and were keeping step as they left.

Bytkin hoped they would remember to break step before they reached the street. He turned to the other two men. "Barbed Wire, Little Father. You have planned your mission?"

They had. Bytkin listened, keeping his face expressionless but occasionally nodding. The two men were among the best assassins in the Spetsnaz Fourth Group. Maybe among the best in the whole Spetsnaz.

"Why not hit her in her apartment?"

"Her building is for women only," Little Father explained. His name came from his being short and prematurely bald. In fact, he could lift the back end of a field car, and was nearly Bytkin's equal in unarmed combat. "We might not be allowed in. We would certainly attract notice."

"Of course, there is the alternative of setting the whole building on fire," Barbed Wire said. He didn't like women. He didn't really like anyone, but it seemed to Bytkin that the sergeant liked women less than others.

"No." There was a fine line between attracting no notice and attracting too much. One dead woman was on that line. Twenty dead women would be over it, particularly if the one they were after was lucky enough to escape.

"As you wish," Little Father replied. He flexed his fingers. "We shall try to make it look like an ordinary street crime, and let the reporters spread the panic."

They would do that very well, Bytkin knew. One of socialism's assets that had survived the collapse of the Soviet Union was the Western media. They might yet dig the grave of capitalism with only an occasional push from outside.

"THAT IS NOT a helicopter," Ben Shlomo whispered.

Bolan held up a hand for silence. It said something for the tension they all felt, that it was the professional Ben Shlomo stating the obvious.

It certainly wasn't a helicopter parked in the clearing. It was a large truck, with a canvas top and toolboxes on the side. Bolan couldn't tell the color or markings, but thought he recognized a G-5, once the all-purpose heavy truck of the East German army.

Then a man in coveralls with a submachine gun dropped out of the rear gate.

"Narcissus," the subgunner called. Bolan noticed movement in the back of the truck. If they didn't get the right call sign, the rest of the team was ready to open fire. Once again, Helmut Kuhn or one of his friends had put professionals on the job.

"Oak leaf," Trudl called back.

"Orchid," the man replied.

They quickly went through the eight-word recognition sequence. When they were done, the man hurried over. Bolan recognized Dieter.

"Sorry about the change in plans. Parsifal had intelligence that the helicopter was compromised."

"Reliability?" Ben Shlomo asked.

"B-2."

That meant an above-average source almost certain of his information. Enough to act on, with lives at stake.

"So we shifted over to the backup. It's a G-5 with a false bottom to the cargo bed. Kuhn took it over a few years ago when one of the professional refugee smugglers died."

"What happened to him?" Trudl asked.

"He promised to bring somebody's wife out, took his money, then took more from the Stasi for selling her back. The husband found out and shot him."

Trudl applauded. Bolan had to agree with her sentiment. The business of getting East Germans across the border after the Wall went up had attracted both heroes and people in it for the money.

Some of the mercenaries at least delivered what you paid them for. Bolan had no quarrel with those. The former owner of the truck, on the other hand, would have been on his list of eligible targets any day, only someone else got there first.

"All right, people," Bolan said. "Let's load up and move out. How long to the next safe point?" he asked the BND man.

"A guess would be four hours. We'll try to make it shorter than that, for your sake. The suspension on this old cow is nothing to boast about, and the people who rode where you will ride did not expect comfort."

"GOOD NIGHT, Hedwig," the manager said.

Hedwig muttered something that she hoped sounded polite. It had been a long evening, with the audience either too drunk or too tired to applaud even her best numbers. About all the drunks did was shout for her to strip, until the waiters moved them out.

Otto did keep a respectable place, she had to admit. He paid well, kept the customers in line and kept his hands off her, which was more than could be said for the manager at Trudl's place.

Poor Trudl. Her father gone God only knew where, her grandfather a cold fish if there ever was one but with all the money in the world except ten marks, and not a reasonable man in all the world to hold her when she wanted to cry.

"Heddie, you sound like you're coming down with a cold," Otto said. "Let me get you some of my mother's homemade pastilles. They're not too heavy with sugar, and they've cured my sore throats for thirty years."

It was meant as kindness, so Hedwig didn't tell Otto what to do with the pastilles.

The two Spetsnaz soldiers waited outside in the darkness. "You told me she always leaves promptly after her last act," Little Father grumbled.

"She is a woman, and what is 'prompt' to a woman is not the same as it is to us," Barbed Wire replied. Then he stiffened. "There! She came out of another door."

The woman who was down in the Berlin police records as Ilse Herter never knew that her latest wig made her a near-twin of Hedwig. Particularly at night, to a couple of tired Spetsnaz assassins who had been trying to hide in an alley for longer than even their trained muscles could endure in comfort.

She did not know what the soft pad of footsteps behind her meant. She turned, snatching out of her handbag a nail file sharpened to a needle point and a razor edge. As the shadow turned into a man, she lashed out with her secret weapon.

Barbed Wire had many problems with women, but one in particular turned out to be fatal that night. He expected them to be too frightened of him to resist.

So he didn't guard against Ilse's weapon with the skill he would have used against such a weapon in a man's hand. The point opened the flesh of his neck, and the edge opened his jugular vein.

Then Ilse made her first mistake. She screamed. Little Father didn't know that his comrade was dying on his feet, trying to stop the mad rush of blood from his neck. He only knew that Hedwig was giving the alarm.

His massive hand swung like an ax against Ilse Herter's neck. It snapped like a twig, and there was no life in her eyes by the time she slammed down on the pavement.

But her scream had alerted the few people remaining in the cabaret, including Hedwig. Armed only with Otto's pastilles, she was about to dash out into the night, when the last of the waiters on duty stopped her.

"Forgive me, but I was an Alpine trooper, and I am bigger and tougher than you are. Well, maybe only bigger," he added, at Hedwig's glare. Then he pushed past her, lunged at the side door and was out into the street and into the sights of Little Father's Makarov. It had a silencer and a full magazine of special subsonic ammunition, which made it inaccurate at more than fifteen meters.

The distance to the waiter was less than ten, so Little Father had no trouble hitting him in the eye, mouth, neck and chest. Like Ilse, he was dead before he hit the ground.

Then it was Hedwig's turn to scream. She didn't follow the waiter, however, and so avoided his fate. Instead she slammed the door and screamed again, this time for Otto to call the police.

Then she threw her arms around the nearest human being, who happened to be Otto. She didn't realize this until he gently pried himself out of her embrace, saying that he couldn't call the police and hold her at the same time.

ONE BY ONE, Bolan's team slid out of the cramped secret compartment in the old truck. They waited, the Executioner and Ben Shlomo with drawn weapons, until the all-clear signal came from the cab. Then they darted across the damp grass to the back door of a guest house. One of the BND men followed with their gear.

The man tossed the bags in, but a frown from Bolan kept him from doing the same with the Weatherby. He handed it to the Executioner snug in its now-greasy case, saluted and headed back to the truck. Bolan closed the door, and as he locked it heard the truck start off.

Trudl leaned against the whitewashed wall of the stairs and let out a long breath. Then she pushed her hair back from her eyes—until she noticed the grease on her hands.

"Ugh. What did they carry in that compartment besides refugees? Pigs? I must look like a witch."

Bolan thought she looked fine, if a bit tired, but his rule against arguing with teammates applied here, too.

"I do not remember anyone briefing us on this place," Ben Shlomo commented.

"Neither do I," Bolan said. He didn't add that people got killed over this sort of slipup, but with Ben Shlomo he didn't need to.

"Let me sneak upstairs to see if there is anyone there," Trudl said. "Then if we have the place to ourselves, I can look out a couple of windows and see if I recognize any landmarks."

"How will that—" Ben Shlomo began, then stopped before Bolan needed to say anything. "Go on, Trudl."

The young woman managed a weary smile at Ben Shlomo's thawing. "My grandfather bought an old guest house a year ago. The owner spent a great deal of money rebuilding it, but did not know how to attract customers. Grandfather thought it would be a good weekend retreat for senior executives who needed to get away from their desks. If I can look out the window, maybe I can tell if this is the same one."

"Fine," Bolan said. "Only let me go first."

The warrior went up the stairs cautiously, but found nothing but empty halls and well-furnished if dusty bedrooms. Four of the five bedrooms had private baths.

Meanwhile, Ben Shlomo had checked out the ground floor, and came up to report that it was clear, too. "I suggest that we keep the lights off," he added. "It is close to dawn, and the fewer signs of life this place shows, the better."

"It *is* the place," Trudl called from the largest bedroom. "I can see the Fulda River from here, and there is a red-tiled church tower by the railroad bridge."

"Very good," Ben Shlomo said. "Then I suppose we can accept your grandfather's hospitality until someone tells us what to do next. I hope they have left us some food, at least."

Ben Shlomo went downstairs, and they heard banging pots, doors opening and closing and mutterings in Hebrew. Trudl sat on the huge bed, then lay back on the heavy quilted bedspread with its pattern of gold and green diamonds, and kicked off her shoes.

"If the water is running, may I take a shower?"

"Go ahead."

Trudl vanished into the bathroom, carrying her case. Bolan unzipped the Weatherby's case, pulled out the sight and tested the mounting and alignment. Then he worked the bolt a few times, pulled out the cleaning rod and patches and started basic maintenance. About then he heard the water start to run in the bathroom, and a moment later steam crept out from under the dark oak door.

Nothing wrong with the water supply, either. He pulled out the ammunition pouches and began counting rounds. There was plenty for the Weatherby, not so much 9 mm. But it would be easier to fire 9 mm ammo than Weatherby Magnum rounds.

He was putting the magazines back in the pouches when the bathroom door opened and Trudl Kuhn walked out. She wore nothing except a few drops of water. As Bolan watched, one of them trickled between her breasts.

"Do you remember what I said, in my grandfather's house?" she asked.

Bolan stood and took her in his arms. "I accept the invitation."

CHAPTER SEVENTEEN

The kitchen was well stocked with canned, bottled and freeze-dried foods. Clearly nobody had been there for a while, and it was obvious that the place had been set up more as a safehouse than as a weekend retreat for stressed-out German businessmen.

A satellite dish antenna rose from the roof, as well as several other carefully disguised antennas. At least one telephone had a scrambler, as did the fax machine. The computer was state-of-the-art.

No weapons, though. Either Helmut Kuhn didn't want anyone stumbling on proof that he was operating on the edge of the law, or he assumed that all the people who used the safehouse would be carrying their own weapons.

In the case of Bolan's team, he was right. They could cope with anything short of a full-scale attack on the house.

On the radio, they heard that deaths in the mine incident now totaled seven Green demonstrators, twelve persons known to have neo-Nazi associations and an estimated thirteen others who hadn't been identified. There were guesses about the number of injured and the number of those who would be permanently affected. Also broadcast were numerous details concerning the gas, the explosives, silver mining—both medieval and modern—much of it highly technical and provided by experts.

There were no police bulletins to be on the lookout for suspicious persons connected with the incident.

"If the government has any sense, it'll turn the job over to GSG-9 and the BND," Bolan said. "But that won't keep questions from being asked in the Bundestag in a few days. By then we have to be tied in with somebody else and know how to complete this mission, or scrub it."

Bolan didn't add that he was going to complete his own mission, whatever Helmut Kuhn, the Bundestag, the Beck organization or the Mossad might have to say about it. They could read that in his face.

"I can ask—" Ben Shlomo began.

"Hush," Trudl said.

"—explosion and fire at the truck park of Transport-kunst last night. Reports indicate that the explosion might have been a terrorist bomb.

"Two murders were reported in a single incident in Berlin last night, outside the Cabaret Ausbruch. A prostitute was killed by a barehanded blow to the neck, and a waiter who attempted to rescue her was shot four times with a silenced 9 mm automatic.

"Police are refusing to comment on whether either of these incidents is connected with the poison gas incident. An unidentified source said similar techniques were used, but this could be coincidence."

Ben Shlomo muttered something particularly sulphurous in Hebrew, but Trudl was staring at the radio and blinking.

"The Ausbruch! That's where Hedwig sings. Oh, God, they must have been after her!"

"I wonder that your grandfather could not protect her," Ben Shlomo said.

"She probably told him what he could do with his protection," Trudl replied with the ghost of a smile. Then she stumbled to her feet and up the stairs.

Bolan waited a decent interval, then went up and knocked on the closed bedroom door.

"It's not locked." Her voice sounded steadier.

The Executioner went in. Trudl was sitting on the still-rumpled bed, staring at the drawn curtains over the window.

"This is—what is the American phrase—'getting out of hand.'"

Bolan could offer no reassurance. "Do you think we fooled you about what you were getting into?"

"No. But—the others who are being dragged into it...Hedwig, only because she was my friend. My father. My grandfather."

"Your father might have been trying to cheat one of the major intelligence agencies," Bolan said. That was almost true and gave away no secrets. "Your grandfather, I would say, is having the time of his life."

"I believe that part, yes. But the ones like Hedwig, I feel so guilty."

"I'm not a philosopher, Trudl. I try not to put anybody in danger who doesn't expect it. So did you. I can kill, when the person is trying to kill me or somebody innocent. You haven't had to do that yet, but I don't advise feeling guilty. All guilt does is make you an easier target for the next person who comes after you. And that's a stupid thing to do."

She stood up and kissed him. "Very well, Peter. I will try not to be stupid."

"DANNEMEIER HERE. Our cooperative project was not completely successful, I am sorry to say. The usual problems with suppliers of subcomponents."

"These things happen," Major Bytkin replied. His tone was bland and corporate. It helped that he was able to imagine himself as sitting at a fumed-oak desk, wearing a suit and discussing another man's business successes and failures with calm detachment. "Is your team returning to the head office, or do you have other prospects that would justify your staying where you are?"

"I think any opportunities here will not need the full team. At least not for several days. Do you need my people at your office, or working with our partners?"

That meant, did Bytkin plan to operate with the rest of the team under his direct control? Or was he planning on using them to stiffen the surviving neo-Nazis, Carl Braun's gang and any other miscellaneous soldiers he might pick up off the streets of Germany's cities?

"We will need some extra people in the head office, I think." The sabotage at Transportkunst had gone very well, with several million marks' worth of trucks destroyed but nobody killed. The attempt on Hedwig, on the other hand... If Barbed Wire hadn't died in the effort, Bytkin would have killed the man himself.

"We don't want any of these transfers to get into the business press, you realize."

"I think our operations will be on such a small scale that the press is hardly likely to find them worth covering. Inflation raises the cost of paper and reporters along with everything else."

Bytkin had too much firsthand knowledge on that point. Certain well-placed GRU accountants had been able to transfer large sums in hard currency and gold to several foreign accounts. One of those accounts had supplied this operation in Germany over the past year.

Now the account was running low, foreign intelligence agencies were on the track of some of the other accounts, the Russian government was asking where the money was and general chaos threatened. Oleg Bytkin suspected that he was living in a world where ultimately the accountant was mightier than the Spetsnaz trooper, and he didn't like the idea.

He knew for a fact that he didn't like that world.

"I think the first transfers can begin immediately. But a meeting should not be delayed too long."

Bytkin agreed. He also knew that one might be delayed indefinitely by police surveillance—or permanently, by a GSG-9 trooper putting a 9 mm slug through Danilov's head.

"Certainly. After the first transfers arrive, we can agree on a date and place."

Cryptic telephone conversations and watching the television news could pass only so much information. The first troopers Danilov was able to send to Berlin would have to hand-carry a quantity of coded intelligence.

"I see no problems. Goodbye."

THE DAY IN THE SAFEHOUSE passed so quietly that Trudl said she felt as if they were on a raft in the middle of the ocean.

"That is a less pleasant feeling than you might think," Ben Shlomo said. "I remember being mostly aware that when daylight came I would still be in range of Arab air patrols. When one wishes to be rescued, it is fine to be conspicuous. When one wishes not to be bombed, on the other hand..."

That was more than Ben Shlomo had ever said about his career. Field agents were a pretty closemouthed lot, and Mossad agents even more so than most.

At dinner Trudl produced a corkscrew and what she said was the only bottle of wine in the house.

"I shall speak severely to my grandfather about his hospitality. A safehouse ought to have at least a small wine cellar."

She opened the bottle, a standard-brand Rhine white, and poured three glasses. "Mr. Metzger, do you want to propose a toast?"

Bolan was saved from being at a loss for words by the unmistakable sound of a helicopter descending nearby. The wineglasses remained forgotten on the kitchen table as they sprinted for their defense positions.

Using the Starlite scope, Bolan was able to see that the helicopter had landed on the far side of a patch of woodland. He shifted windows, cranked one pane open and rested the Weatherby on the windowsill. From the edge of the woodland to the house, anybody coming at them would be as exposed as a mouse on a pool table.

Instead of shadowy figures slipping out of the woods and scattering to flank the house, Bolan saw a light flashing. After he'd read the message, he was tempted to use his own flashlight to ask for a repeat. Helmut Kuhn, here?

But it was the old man himself who came striding up to the house a few minutes later. He wore baggy English tweeds that might have been forty years old, a Tyrolean hat and walking boots. His only concession to age was a walking stick, which Bolan noticed was heavy enough to be a good club.

Another of those ubiquitous special-operations veterans came with him. The man had no weapons in sight, but suggestive bulges in his windbreaker and pants hinted at a sizable arsenal.

"Did you come in the compromised helicopter?" Ben Shlomo asked.

Helmut Kuhn seemed to look down at the Israeli from even more than his considerable height. It was the first time Bolan remembered seeing the Mossad man embarrassed.

"Yes. Remember that because it is compromised, it is the last thing our enemies will expect me to use. They will expect me to sneak around in trucks with secret compartments. I am too old to go sneaking, and if I can ride in comfort *and* confuse our enemies, why not?"

Since nobody had an answer to that question, they all went inside. Trudl poured two more glasses of wine, but the bodyguard refused.

"I should refuse, too," Kuhn said. "The doctors have begun to worry abut my liver, or is it my kidneys? I tell them that if my organs are wearing out after seventy-eight years of hard use, why should I worry? They seem determined to save me, however, whether I wish them to or not."

He lifted his glass. "To our coming success."

Bolan and Ben Shlomo sipped. Trudl emptied her glass at one gulp. Her grandfather's eyebrows rose, then he laughed.

"Trudl, I will not argue with you. Not when I bring both good and bad news. The bad news is that they have found your father's body."

Trudl looked at the table for a minute, then nodded. "How did he die?"

"The official story is suicide. The BND is sending in a forensic expert who knows Russian assassination poisons, but that is a secret. Act as if it were suicide until I tell you otherwise.''

''Poor Father,'' Trudl said. ''It will make my mother happy to have her bad opinion of him confirmed, but somehow I am not glad of that.''

''The good news—'' now he looked at Bolan ''—is that you have, oh, call it a hunting license. I will not list the people who confirmed it, on the basis of what we learned about you. I merely say that it will not be revoked until the people responsible for the mine horror are dealt with.''

He went on to describe what was in fact Bolan's original mission, with different targets. Instead of mafiosi, he would be gunning for neo-Nazis and undercover Spetsnaz. He would also have a partner in Zev Ben Shlomo.

''Has this been approved by our contacts?'' Bolan asked.

''Gentlemen, I believe both of you have a generous— is the intelligence term 'charter'? If you, Mr. Metzger, are who I think you are, you do not really need a charter. But the answer to both of you is yes.''

Bolan might not need a charter. The Mossad certainly didn't need the embarrassment of having one of its top agents caught terminating Germans, even ones who deserved it.

But apparently they'd bitten that bullet, and so had the German authorities. Bolan's opinion of them went up a bit. Not much, because he and his companion would still be deniable and expendable if anything went wrong. But this much he could say: some Germans had learned some lessons from the past. In fact, one of them was sitting at this table.

Ben Shlomo poured the last of the wine into his glass and drank it quickly. "Mr. Kuhn, forgive me if this is another insult, but why are you doing this?"

Kuhn's hard blue eyes seemed to go blank, staring across years and miles. "Because I stood by once, thinking I could do nothing. Perhaps I was right, then. This time I would be wrong.

"Also, gentlemen, would you like your only monument to be a footnote in some volume of military history? 'The first nonpersistent nerve gas is believed to have been developed during the final years of the Third Reich, under the name Compound 58.'"

"I'M NOT ASKING for a formal disband order on Beck," Hal Brognola said to the well-connected government official on the other end of the telephone line. "I know we couldn't do it, and anyway, I don't think it's necessary."

The other man sounded approving. The approval chilled swiftly when Brognola went on. "I am asking for a complete cutoff for about thirty days. We don't hear them, they don't hear us. For those thirty days, I *do* want us to act as if there were no such person as Ludwig or Willi Beck, or anybody else listed as part of his organization."

The disapproval hung in the air as Brognola continued. "This has German approval. If it has our approval, Beck's two biggest customers are out of the picture. If word gets around, it will certainly influence all the other major agencies and services. Beck can't do much with what he picks up from the Czechs or the Kurdish exiles."

Brognola held the telephone away from his face until he could control the urge to snarl at the other man. The official was usually more of a gentleman than this. It looked as if the German government wasn't the only one getting antsy over the incident in the Thüringer Wald.

"I can certainly arrange a confidential briefing for any reasonable number of people with a need-to-know for this evening. Fair enough?"

It seemed that it was.

CHAPTER EIGHTEEN

Bolan's team agreed with Kuhn to operate out of the guest house until further notice. It was in fact set up to serve as a safehouse. As far as Kuhn knew, no one who might inform their assorted enemies knew about its real status.

"Also, even if they know about that, they are not likely to know certain of its features," Kuhn added. "I suppose you have wondered about the wine cabinet having so little wine in it?"

Trudl was the only one who had the nerve to nod. Her grandfather grinned. "Follow me, please."

The liquor cabinet was large enough to hold a complete fold-out bar and sixty assorted bottles. Instead it held nothing but a lot of dust.

The dust puffed up, making Trudl sneeze, as Kuhn ran his fingers up and down the hinge side of the door. "Ah, here it is," he said at last. "Now, to be sure it works..."

He twisted between thumb and forefinger something Bolan couldn't see. The top half of the cabinet's rear wall unfolded outward. Behind it was a control panel, with enough buttons and readouts to control a submarine.

"These—" he pointed at the left side of the panel "—seal all the windows and doors with armored shutters. They were sunk into the walls, so I am not surprised you overlooked them. There are also a few internal doors, not quite as rugged but certainly needing some time for an enemy to open.

"These on the right, set assorted booby traps. Not lethal ones, but various kinds of riot gas will annoy and confuse an enemy."

"They will also annoy and confuse you if you are in the same room with them," Ben Shlomo pointed out. "In fact, you are showing us how easy it is to seal yourself in your own tomb in this house."

"On the contrary, I am showing you how to delay pursuit while you evade," Kuhn said. He pressed a small blue button in the upper right-hand corner.

Now it was the bottom half of the wall that swung, this time inward. It swung all the way down to form a flight of steps leading onto a steel slide that ran off into darkness.

"At the bottom of the slide is a tunnel nearly four hundred meters long. It comes out in the woods where I landed my helicopter. There are several doors that can be closed on the way, and a few more booby traps."

"Grandfather, I knew you were generous when you took this place over, but how much did this cost?"

"A few hundred thousand marks for cleaning and reinforcing," Kuhn said. "This building goes back to the fifteenth century, remember that. The tunnel, I suppose, was built between then and the Thirty Years' War. It would be handy to avoid marauding bands of soldiers, as you can imagine.

"I also suspect there is more down there than the tunnel. I have noticed a few side passages that were bricked up centuries ago. One day when I can dabble in archaeology instead of counterespionage, I might see about opening them."

"May that day be soon," Ben Shlomo muttered.

"Still not trusting an old German?" Kuhn asked, but they could tell he was joking.

"I trust few men more," Ben Shlomo said. "No, I mean only that when you can come down here and knock out the bricks, our fight will be over."

Bolan nodded. Unfortunately he had the disagreeable feeling that Helmut Kuhn might be acting as a spymaster for quite a while. He wouldn't call work as good as Kuhn's "dabbling."

"There is one more thing," Kuhn added. "As the last thing you do before using the slide, turn the button that opens it hard to the left." He tapped it gently.

"That activates a timer. It will close and lock the door automatically in thirty seconds. The mechanism has its own power supply. Even if the house supply is disconnected, the door will still close. So try to have thirty seconds' lead over your enemies.

"It does something else, and for that reason I call it the Samson Button. You have seen the spare oil tank in the middle of the furnace room, I trust?"

They nodded.

"It contains very little oil, but something in the range of a ton of explosives. Four minutes after the door closes, the charge goes off. It should not bring down the tunnel, but it will certainly bring down the house, if you will pardon the jest."

Ben Shlomo frowned. "As I recall, Samson was still inside the temple when he brought it down on the Philistines."

"That also is an option that you might find useful," Kuhn said in a level voice. "I know enough about what our enemies can do to prisoners that I can assure you I would gladly use it. I would prefer that you were luckier than Samson, of course."

"He had no choice," Ben Shlomo pointed out. "He had been blinded, after losing his strength when Delilah cut his hair."

Trudl contemplated Ben Shlomo's bald crown. "You are in no danger of that fate, at least."

THE NATIONAL COMRADESHIP Party was a conservative nationalist organization, claiming chapters in fifteen major cities and forty smaller ones. Its more realistic leaders counted about twenty-five permanent chapters and twenty or thirty that came and went.

Few of its two thousand members were old enough to have been Nazis, and none of those old enough had been. Its meetings produced more dirty beer steins than anything else, plus an occasional pamphlet on how Germany had a unique opportunity to be truly united at last, and history would not forgive failure, and so on.

One of those realistic leaders in the Berlin chapter was a man named Klaus Berger. It was his good luck and his friends' as well that he was on security watch the night the meeting hall was raided.

He saw the Greens at twilight marching openly up the Ernst Mach Strasse toward the meeting hall, and heard their chanting. Being a veteran and a forestry helicopter pilot, he also looked for less obvious enemies.

He found them, although Little Father had concealed his nine men well enough that a civilian would have overlooked them. As it was, he spotted four of them almost at once.

That was enough to send him racing inside, locking the door after him.

"Don't panic, people," he called. "There are Greens on the way. But I think they have paramilitary support. They might not be the real thing."

"Why not?" one of the hard-line members snapped. "We've always known that the Greens are paid by the Communists. Why shouldn't their masters lend them storm troops?"

There wasn't time for Berger to point out that Greens and Communists weren't the same thing.

"I've locked the front door. Somebody see to the back door and shutter the windows. Stay away from both the doors and windows.

"I want the women and children up on the second floor now. We join them if the marchers do break in. Then we barricade the stairs with furniture."

Berger looked around the room. He had the attention of all eighty people in it. He raised his voice to be heard above the swelling chants outside and shouted, "If anybody has a weapon, don't tell me about it. Don't use it, either, unless they come in shooting. We're not those pigs of the Greater Germany party. We don't want blood."

"If they want ours—" somebody shouted.

A stone crashed through a window, and a woman cut by flying glass screamed. The incident could have started a general rush for the stairs, but Berger was there first. He punched one panic-stricken man in the stomach, saw him topple backward and clear three or four more of his comrades off the stairs. Berger held open a gap for the women and children.

They streamed past Berger to safety, while more level-headed men started heaving furniture in front of the doors and slamming the shutters. One window had no shutters, so a couple of hefty steelworkers lifted an antique china cabinet and slammed it down in front of the window. That should stop bullets, Berger knew, but guns might not be the most potent weapon out there.

The chanting increased in volume. The skinheads disguised as Greens didn't know their efforts were serving to mask the noise of the Spetsnaz teams moving into position.

Nothing could mask the noise of an RPG-7 round blowing in one of the windows, or a demolition charge hurling the back door off its hinges. Berger saw weapons sprout in more hands than he'd expected, mostly pistols, knives and clubs. He doubted most of them would be useful against these professionals backing up the Greens.

He still wished he had something in his own hand. He hadn't felt so helpless since the day a Luftwaffe F-104 sliced the tail rotor off his training helicopter. His pilot managed to get it down without killing anybody, but the wild ride down to earth was the longest moment of Berger's life.

Another RPG round smashed into the china cabinet. It absorbed most of the explosion, but erupted into flying splinters of wood. More screams rose as people clapped their hands to torn cheeks and pierced eyes.

By good luck, half the casualties were to invaders climbing in the first broken window. They hesitated, nervous like all unseasoned troops over casualties from friendly fire. Berger yelled at the men with guns to face both front and back, in case the Greens hit the open back door.

Somewhere outside, a sniper heard Berger's orders over the din, shifted position and put cross hairs on the dangerously able leader. All that saved Berger was jumping down from the chair where he'd been standing, as the sniper's finger closed on the trigger.

A bullet meant for his chest seared across his cheek and one ear. He yelled in both surprise and pain, and lifted his hand to the ragged flesh and oozing blood. At the same moment he smelled smoke and heard a helicopter approaching.

Another explosion roared, drowning out the helicopter. Fragments chewed the flesh of Greens and National Comradeship members impartially.

Fortunately the last RPG round scattered the thermite thrown in the back door. Some of the pieces were too small to go on burning and guttered out. Others died on fireproof surfaces. Some found flammable material, upholstery, rugs, or piled pamphlets and paper napkins. The rear door was suddenly blocked by half a dozen fires and a wall of smoke that kept each side from attacking or even seeing the other.

Then half a dozen police sirens howled in the distance, getting rapidly closer, with fire engines chasing the police. The helicopter's engine changed note as it began to hover. A voice blared through a loudspeaker.

"Halt! This is an illegal terrorist attack. You are ordered to halt and submit to arrest. Repeat, this is an order to halt and submit to arrest. Any person leaving the area—"

Berger didn't see what happened, but the sequence of noises told him enough. First a ripping noise, as the shoulder-fired AA missile climbed into the sky. Then a bang, as its heat-seeking head guided it into the helicopter's exhaust. An explosion, as the engine flew apart, shredding the helicopter's crew at the same time as it ignited the fuel tanks.

Then screams as the crowd outside broke and ran, and more screams as those who hadn't run fast enough were caught under the crashing helicopter. Berger swayed, gripping the stair railing to keep from falling. He didn't know whether he should faint, vomit or run for his life.

He found a fourth course, giving first aid to the wounded of both sides. Seeing him in action drew others after him, to tear up clean clothes for improvised bandages and compresses. Meanwhile someone had dug out the chemical fire extinguishers and was working on the fires in back.

Berger didn't even lift his head, until the front door crashed open and a squad of riot police stormed through. One of them lifted the Lexan face plate of his riot helmet and put his hand on the butt of his P-9.

"What in the devil's name is going on here?" the policeman shouted.

Berger stood, tried to wipe the blood off his hands on his best trousers, then gave up. "The devil's work, yes, but who helped him I don't know."

"If you're lying—"

Then Berger had to wrestle one of his own people to keep him from shooting the policeman. The policeman's comrades surrounded Berger and his opponent, and the billy clubs went to work.

One cracked sharply across Berger's temple, and he crumpled to the floor.

A HELICOPTER REACHED the safehouse two hours after the news report on the Green–Comradeship Party clash. The Executioner and Ben Shlomo were already armed, suited up and ready to go. They raced to the helicopter, with Trudl close behind them. All three ducked under the still-whirling rotors and scrambled aboard. They were five hundred feet up before they could get strapped in.

The pilots were different and so was the color scheme and registration number. But the helicopter was a JetRanger, and Bolan recognized some of the interior features of the one that had taken him to the Thüringer Wald.

Flying under false colors was a serious offense in most well-regulated countries, and Germany was nothing if not well regulated. The fact that Kuhn expected to get away with disguising one of his choppers said a lot about the tolerance the authorities were extending to Bolan and his team.

Not that Bolan was surprised. The civilian casualties in the fight had been much lighter than expected, mostly minor wounds and only five dead. But four policemen were dead, two federal ones from the helicopter and two Berlin officers sniped, no doubt as the Spetsnaz disengaged.

All four had died in six minutes, and in Germany that many policemen didn't usually get killed on duty in six months. The authorities had to be asking the same question Bolan was asking himself, in the vibrating cabin of the JetRanger as it raced low toward Berlin.

Which would come first? The authorities finding the guilty parties, Greens or reds, or a policeman who'd lost a friend drawing down on some more or less innocent Green, and creating a nationwide uproar?

Without approving of them, Bolan understood policemen who stepped over the line and settled scores. He also understood that if that happened now, his mission would be in major-caliber trouble.

Ben Shlomo returned from forward. "They have no briefing for us," he said, then shook his head in mock sorrow. "When I was younger, I remember once we had our briefing in the air, on the way to the objective. We had just finished when the jump light went on."

Somehow it didn't surprise Bolan that Ben Shlomo was a veteran of the legendary Israeli paracommandos.

It would have surprised him if anybody had been able to pull together the briefing on this occasion.

"Let's brainstorm it," he suggested.

They batted ideas back and forth, with Trudl mostly silent, as the JetRanger went down to the treetops. Now the landscape outside was less well lit. They had crossed the former East German border. It was even less likely now that someone would be able to see a helicopter hurtling past at treetop height.

The banners at the confrontation said Earth Brotherhood. Apparently some of those arrested were actually members of the faction. Others were hangers-on of any political cause that offered excitement, sex or the chance of a good fight. There were some with neo-Nazi records, but the official story was that they'd joined the demonstration to protest the moderation of the National Comradeship Party.

"If a lot of Germans do not die laughing at that one," Ben Shlomo said, "I will have a very low opinion of the German sense of humor. Even lower than the one I already have," he added.

"If it keeps everybody and his uncle out of our hair long enough for a few polite questions—"

"Where?"

"The Earth Brotherhood. Their headquarters are near the Free University. That area is more or less off-limits to the police. We, on the other hand..."

"If we are not forbidden to do it."

"We can't be denied permission if we don't ask for it," the Executioner replied, which drew a stifled giggle from Trudl.

"You *do* think they are up to something."

"They didn't keep their members in line. That's what you expect from organizations like that. It's not a crime, usually. This time, people got killed."

"Also, they were too late for the mine incident—"

"Lucky Earth Brotherhood," Trudl put in.

"They might not see it that way. They might think they missed out on one of the great moments in the history of the Green Party. So they have to prove their faith somehow."

"They certainly picked a stupid way of showing it."

"Let's arrange it so that you can tell them that yourself."

They turned from objective to tactics, as the lights of Berlin began to glow on the horizon ahead.

THE FIRST MAN Hans Wegener met when he reached the office the morning after the confrontation was Willi Beck. This by itself was no surprise. Beck didn't boast about getting up earlier than the opposition or his staff. He merely did it, and had done it for as long as Wegener could remember.

What did surprise him was Beck's appearance. He looked as if his liver had betrayed him during the night. He was pale, sweating and totally unconvincing as he tried to keep a light note in his voice.

"Just some sort of virus," he said. "Probably the first case of the Berlin flu, as they will no doubt call it. Besides, you are the pot calling the kettle black. Have you been sleeping at all these past few nights?"

"The world has not been very helpful in that matter, Willi."

Which was true, but it was also true that Wegener had been losing sleep. The requests from Schweiger, the Trained Wolf and his chief, Dannemeier, were becoming more peremptory. So far Wegener had met them all without involving Carl Braun or raising anyone's suspicions. It was a race between his being discovered and his providing his masters with something that would buy him a way out of Germany.

This kind of race, Wegener was discovering, didn't make for restful nights. But regardless of how tired he was, there was his desk to subdue. No doubt it was loaded with material that had come in overnight. He pushed open the door of his office and confronted two square meters of glass-topped white particleboard with nothing on it that hadn't been there the night before.

He dismissed the unease that surged in him. No doubt the secretaries were as slow as usual. Even being cleared for secure data couldn't make a woman as responsible as a man!

Wegener made himself a cup of coffee and was sipping it when he heard voices in the corridor.

"Not a damned thing in all night."

"I don't have it quite so bad. A little bit of commercial data from Sweden."

"Who cares about quality-control problems on Volvos? That's not our main business."

Wegener listened with his unease growing, until it turned into fear. Somebody somewhere had turned off or at least turned down the flow of data into the Beck organization. Data they lived by, data they needed to survive. Data Wegener needed to have available for his own select circle of customers.

He didn't want to think why this might have happened. That it had happened at all was frightening enough.

THE BRIEFING OF THE TEAM in Berlin took five minutes at most. Long enough to hand over a map of the Earth Brotherhood's headquarters and a few rules of engagement. Long enough for Bolan and Zev Ben Shlomo to each ask a couple of questions and get them answered.

That was it. Then they were alone, in a garage on the northern edge of Pankow, with their equipment and a Trabant, the former East German standard passenger sedan.

At least it was new, from the last run at the factory before it shut down after reunification. A quick inspection showed a large engine and a heavy-duty suspension, as well as weapons racks in the trunk, back seat and under the dashboard. It also had a radio equipped for military and police frequencies.

"Why do I have the feeling that we are driving around in a former Stasi car?" Bolan asked no one in particular as he fitted their weapons and gear into the vehicle. He could see two different sets of fittings, and suspected that this was another vehicle Kuhn's operations had acquired covertly.

He considered again the implications of the briefing being so precisely aimed at the Earth Brotherhood. Had someone working for Kuhn or the BND come to the same conclusions that he and Ben Shlomo had?

Or was there a chance they were being set up to make trouble for the Greens? The party wasn't popular with a wide range of Germans, not all of them conservative but including a good many industrialists.

Helmut Kuhn was an industrialist.

And Mack Bolan, the Executioner, was a man who knew perfectly well that worrying about unanswerable questions could get you killed.

Correction. This wasn't an unanswerable question. The answer probably lay at the Earth Brotherhood headquarters. The only problem was how to get it—quietly.

A MAN IN A CHEAP blue suit with a slightly more expensive Italian vinyl suitcase got off the 4:00 p.m. train from Munich at the Bahnhof Zoo in central Berlin. It was actually 4:20, because the tracks between the old border and Berlin weren't as well maintained as the ones in the former federal republic.

However, his reception was still waiting for him by a tobacco stand. The reception put down his magazine and lit a pipe, his recognition signal. The newcomer put down his suitcase and knelt to check the cuffs of his trousers, his reply.

They walked off together to a battered Renault that the third member of the team had brought all the way from Bordeaux. It was actually as battered as it looked, but under the rear seat was secure storage space for what they would need in Berlin.

Not that many of the men expected much difficulty in killing one man, if they could find him. They were, after all, three of the best assassins the Basque resistance movement possessed, and even operating in strange territory they had seldom failed.

But before they moved against their prime target, they needed to make the territory a little less strange. That suggested a meeting with their informant, whose name appeared to be Hans Wegener. *He* appeared to be curiously reluctant to commit himself to such a meeting, but that wasn't a problem for the Basques.

They were also experts in persuading reluctant informants to meet them.

BEN SHLOMO SWUNG the Trabant out of traffic with the deftness of a Grand Prix driver. Several horns blatted behind, brakes squealed and rude words in German flew their way.

Trudl sprinted across the stretch of grass between the sidewalk and the curb, leapt into the rear seat and slammed the door behind her. Ben Shlomo made a racing start, and Bolan heard more rude German as Trudl sprawled across the seat.

"I also brought some suitable clothes," she said, "in case you want me to go in with you. Or I can be there when you burst in. I knew you could not tell me in advance about your plans. So I was prepared for either eventuality."

It seemed that Helmut Kuhn's gift of thoroughness had been passed along to his granddaughter. Probably to his son, too, although Erich had got precious little good out of it.

"Right now, stay in what you have on," Bolan said. That was black slacks and a plain red sweater, both well made without being obviously expensive.

"Very good," she said. "I can always see if one of the Brotherhood would like to take me out for a drink. That will give me an in to their headquarters."

"If they do not, they have poor taste even for Germans," Ben Shlomo said, taking his eyes off the road to wink at Trudl. Since he didn't slow down, for a moment Bolan thought he was closer to death than he had been at the mine.

Fortunately the ten-wheeler's driver had good reflexes and his truck's brakes had just been overhauled. They screamed as his hood nearly nudged the Trabant into a traffic island. Ben Shlomo waved jauntily at the contorted face of the driver, then accelerated away.

"Zev, it would be a good idea not to attract the attention of the police," Bolan said. "Understood?"

Apparently it was. Ben Shlomo at least kept his eyes on the road and his foot wasn't quite so heavy on the accelerator as they made their way across Berlin toward the headquarters of the Earth Brotherhood.

IT HAD TAKEN quite a while, and when the connection finally went through it was well after working hours in Berlin and lunchtime at Stony Man Farm. And Hal Brognola wasted no words once he had Willi Beck on the line. He told him about the shutdown and cutout and waited for the reply. One of the advantages of secure lines was the ability to yell at the bearers of bad news. Brognola expected Beck to use the opportunity to the full.

Instead Beck gave a sort of deflated half sigh, half groan.

"How long is this going to last?"

"Thirty days, minimum."

"I might have some trouble returning to business after such an interval."

"Willi, you can retire with a clear conscience and our blessing. Also our money."

"Buying me out?"

"No, just letting you down more easily."

"What about my people? Or are they the problem?"

"One or maybe more of them is."

"I see." Brognola began to wonder if Beck had gone off the line when the German American spoke again.

"I would like a favor from you. I will fax you a couple of photographs. Have them run through your computer for matching. They might give me an idea of where to look."

"You don't want to say any more?"

"Mr. Brognola, I am sending it to you because I do not want anyone in Germany dealing with the matter. I did not want that at the time I hired ... the man in question. A false accusation..."

There was a mystery here, one that could put Striker in danger. Brognola didn't like that kind of mystery, and Willi Beck was stonewalling him on the answer. Unfortunately it was kind of hard to break down a stone wall from across the Atlantic and half of Europe.

"All right, Willi. Hustle on those faxes, and we'll see what we can do."

Which meant what Aaron Kurtzman could do, basically, because Brognola didn't need any more favors from the CIA. The DDI had barely been polite at the briefing, and when he went along with the cutoff of Beck's organization it was with a dirty look at Brognola. The Justice Department man knew that dirty looks from that DDI were promises of future trouble.

Striker was just going to have to do his usual job of broken-field running between uncertain friends and known enemies. Meanwhile, Brognola would try to at least keep the spectators from rushing onto the field.

CHAPTER NINETEEN

Two black-clad figures slipped out of an alley, across a narrow street and up to the back door of Earth Brotherhood headquarters. They squatted in the shadows under the back stairs while they compared their observations.

"Two windows lit up, both on the same side," Bolan said. He wore his blacksuit and a ski mask.

Zev Ben Shlomo was also in black, togged out in slacks, sweater and tennis shoes. His ski cap was perched on top of his head. He'd smeared camouflage cream all over his face and neck.

"This is the side away from the skylight," the Israeli said. He used a pencil flashlight on their map. "How are you at picking locks?"

"How are you at cutting glass?"

Ben Shlomo grinned and pulled down his mask. Staying in the shadows, the men slipped around the corner to the south side of the building. It faced onto another alley, and across from that was a medium-rise apartment building. The alley was lit only by the apartment windows, but there were quite a few of those with people at home. Bolan hoped they were all too busy watching television to notice black-clad intruders climbing onto their neighbors' roof.

The Executioner hooked the roof coping on his second try, and Ben Shlomo climbed up the rope. At his all-clear signal, Bolan joined him. They retrieved the rope and crept over to the skylight.

Glass cutters and suction cups made quick work of two panes. Unfortunately the frame left the opening too small for Bolan. Ben Shlomo slipped through, and working from underneath with a small saw cut through one end of the frame section. The screech of the saw set Bolan's senses on maximum alert, in case anybody heard.

Nobody seemed to. The building had thick walls and a well-insulated roof.

Bolan swung around to make sure they weren't being watched from the apartment building, then joined Ben Shlomo below.

The Earth Brotherhood seemed to share its building with several other small firms. Bolan landed between the drinking fountain and a door labeled Nadia Rohrbach, Instructor in Cosmetician Training. He and Ben Shlomo stalked down the side hall to the main corridor without needing to pick any locks. There they saw the lighted window in the door with the stenciled sign, Earth Brotherhood.

Bolan looked at his companion, who nodded. The Executioner stepped back, then rammed his foot hard against the door just below the lock. The door flew open with a crash that cracked the glass, and the two men bounded into the room.

About twenty people stood there, one of them Trudl. She did a convincing act of surprise and fear as the two black-clad figures entered. The rest weren't acting.

The gun somebody pulled out from under his sweater wasn't a prop, either. Ben Shlomo's eye was faster than the man's draw, his foot faster still. The man and his chair flew over backward. The weapon was jarred from his hand as he hit the floor, and it bounced almost to Bolan's feet. The Executioner promptly put one large shoe on it, then picked it up and stuck it in a pocket of his blacksuit.

"Very good." The warrior couldn't pass as a native German, but a good loud voice would help him play tough cop to Ben Shlomo's nice cop. "This is an unofficial investigation into the Earth Brotherhood's actions in the past few days."

"You mean illegal," a young man sitting beside Trudl said.

"We have all the authority we need," Bolan replied. He pulled out the Beretta. He also had the Desert Eagle, but that was too distinctive a weapon to use for anything but serious shooting.

"Put that away," Ben Shlomo said sharply. "These are misguided children, not criminals."

"I've had my friends killed by children," Bolan said. That this was perfectly true gave an edge to his voice, which came through even in German.

"It wasn't the children who shot up the Comradeship headquarters," Ben Shlomo pointed out. "It was cowards hiding behind them and using their bodies as shields. We've come to find out who those cowards were."

Two men and a woman made a dash for the back door of the room. Several others jumped in surprise, blocking both the Executioner and Ben Shlomo.

Trudl saved the moment. She also jumped up, but onto her chair, and jerked the Walther P-38 from the waistband of her slacks.

"Halt!" she shouted. Two of the fugitives did. The third grabbed the doorknob. But the ones who'd jumped up were by now scrambling to get clear of Trudl's weapon.

This gave Bolan and the 93-R a clear shot. To reduce the danger of ricochets in a closed room, the warrior fired into the door. Three rounds gouged a neat pattern of splintery holes a foot to the right of the fugitive.

He reached the correct conclusion: he wouldn't leave the room alive. He turned back and sat down, just as somebody Bolan didn't see whipped Trudl's chair out from under her.

She went down with a scream, and Bolan now saw that her attacker was the man who'd been acting possessive.

The Executioner swung with his left without dropping the Beretta. The punch crashed through the man's guard and into his cheek. He toppled sideways, knocking over several chairs as he went down. Bolan pushed the chairs out of the way and knelt with the Beretta about an inch from the man's nose.

"You can't shoot me! That's murder!"

"It would be pest control, but no, I wasn't thinking of that. I'll just let the lady take you outside and bring you back when she's done."

Trudl sat up, rubbing a few strategic spots and looking like a Valkyrie in a bad mood. A ripple of laughter began at the back of the room and worked its way toward Bolan.

Ben Shlomo grinned. "That is more the spirit. Now, I have to say that my friend and I both knew some of those killed in the mine incident. We both knew some of those who died at the Comradeship headquarters."

The grin faded, and Ben Shlomo's dark eyes burned into those of everyone facing him. Even Trudl took a step backward.

"You know where this led, two generations ago. Help us stop it now. My friend and I, if worse comes to worst, we can take some of the bastards with us. You will be sheep and the people behind this the wolves.

"We are the sheepdogs. Help us, now!"

The nightmare of the Holocaust was in every word and gesture, and Bolan saw that the Mossad agent was reaching his audience. They started to sit down. It was the woman who had made a break for the door who was the first to speak.

"What precisely do you want to know?" She was a plump young woman, who sounded as if she believed that everything should be precise.

Ben Shlomo looked at Bolan. The Executioner stepped forward and holstered the Beretta.

"I'll start off by asking, was the demonstration against the Comradeship people official or spontaneous? If it was official, whose idea was it? If it was spontaneous..."

By the time Bolan reached his fifth question, he was already getting answers to his first.

HANS WEGENER finally left the office at ten o'clock, the last man to leave, other than the security guards on night duty. He had spent the day tidying up everything he was responsible for, including scrubbing his wastebasket.

He stopped on his way out to check his personnel file. He had been too busy for several weeks to touch it, and he was beginning to feel it would be well to have it completely updated. The cold breath of unemployment was blowing on the back of his thick neck, and turning up his collar would be no use against this wind.

Discovery and arrest had a certain dignity. Losing his job because the firm went out of business made him no better than a Ruhr steelworker.

He leafed through the folders, a document at a time, mentally noting which ones needed updating or discarding. Then he came to the photographs and stopped abruptly.

His photograph as a young man of twenty-five was turned on its side. It had been straight up when he last saw it, and he hadn't touched it since then.

Someone else who had the two-key authority and the electronic codes had been in the personnel files. His file, looking at a picture.

Looking, or more?

An iron fist seemed to squeeze tight around Wegener's heart. He leaned against the drawer, so hard that it slammed shut. It pinched a finger, and in his rage and fear he let out a yell.

The guard was on hand in much less time than Wegener wished. He seemed more sympathetic than suspicious, but he firmly led Wegener out of the secure room and made him sit down with his head between his knees while the guard locked up.

"Shall I call you a taxi, Mr. Wegener? I will call the parking management and warn them about your—"

"No, no. I really am fit to drive. I—I think I am catching the same thing that Mr. Beck seemed to have this morning. Some kind of flu. Do not be surprised if I do not come in tomorrow."

The guard let him out, and he drove home without any trouble. But he couldn't get to sleep. He kept imagining coming to a meeting at the offices, and there was Beck up at the podium of the briefing room, flanked by two GSG-9 men with pistols, and pointing at him.

THE TRABANT WHINED into sluggish life, Ben Shlomo let in the clutch and they swung out into the sparse traffic.

Bolan looked behind, as the headquarters of the Earth Brotherhood vanished. Half a dozen of the members were standing on the front steps. He couldn't tell if they were grateful, angry or just stunned at learning how far they'd been out of their depth.

They were innocents, and for that reason he was sworn to protect them. But there were innocents who didn't have a chance to learn the truth, and those who shut their eyes to it. He would defend both kinds, but he would talk plainly to the second kind.

He'd done that tonight, as much as his German would let him, and Ben Shlomo and Trudl had done more than their share to help him. The Earth Brotherhood might have fewer members after tonight. It would certainly have fewer naive ones.

"You know these types, Trudl," Ben Shlomo said. He was driving so sedately that Bolan knew he had to be tired. "Will they be sensible after this?"

"What do you mean by 'sensible'?" she asked. "If you mean will they do exactly what you want them to do—"

"Aha, your notions about Germans are showing, I think," Ben Shlomo said. He smiled, though, to show that he was joking.

Trudl said something in German that Bolan thought it was probably just as well he didn't understand, but it made Ben Shlomo's smile wider. Then she shrugged.

"If you mean will they do their best to keep their hotheads from running wild, yes. They will also keep their promise to tell their members to call the police if there is danger, not to take the law into their own hands.

"How many members will do this, I think, depends on how fast the police come the next time."

Bolan nodded. It was a problem as old as society, or at least as old as police forces. If the police couldn't or wouldn't prevent crimes, how much could you ask people to bear before they acted themselves?

He hoped that the German police knew they had to move fast on any more confrontations like the past two. Police forces who sat on their rears and then complained about vigilante justice weren't his favorite kind of people.

The headquarters was now a couple of miles behind them. Ben Shlomo swung the Trabant on to the autobahn for a few miles. They were all silent for a while as he dodged in and out among the trucks rolling into Berlin with the next morning's groceries.

"Where to?" he asked finally.

"Back to the garage," Bolan replied. "It has a couple of roughed-in rooms on the second floor."

"Is it secure?" Trudl asked.

"The most secure place is one nobody knows you are in," Ben Shlomo said.

"In that case, a hotel would do as well—" Trudl began.

"I will compromise," Ben Shlomo told her. "No hotel, but we can find an all-night restaurant and get something to eat. I do not remember seeing a kitchen in that garage. There are places that feed truck drivers, if nothing else."

"But I brought enough cash for a hotel, I assure you," Trudl said, making one more attempt.

"Back to the garage," Ben Shlomo insisted. "After all, Trudl, Peter did say it had two rooms."

Bolan didn't need to look at Ben Shlomo's face to see that he was trying not to grin. He also didn't need to look in the rearview mirror to tell that Trudl Kuhn was blushing.

"YOU ARE FREE TO GO," the Berlin police lieutenant told Klaus Berger. "No charges will be filed against you."

"What about the others?"

"That is not up to me, of course. But I will say that most of you behaved with honorable restraint, and made our work easier. Also, many of you have been hurt. I think it likely that the prosecutors will consider that sufficient punishment in nearly all cases.

"In fact, unofficially, I commend your leadership and courage. I also ask you, unofficially, to keep your people from asking about the investigation. There is much to it that must remain secret for now. Justice will be done, but one cannot always chase rats without going down into the sewers with them."

"You are a poet, Lieutenant."

"If you think that is poetry, it must be the late hour affecting your brain, as it has certainly affected mine. Go home, Mr. Berger, and get a good night's sleep. In fact, a friend of yours is outside in his Mercedes, waiting to give you a ride."

"A friend?" Klaus Berger couldn't recall many friends who drove a Mercedes, or any who would come to pick him up at a police station at this godless hour of the night—morning, rather. Consoling himself with the thought that nobody was likely to try kidnapping or assassinating him under the eyes of the police, he picked up his bag and followed the lieutenant outside.

It wasn't only a Mercedes, it was a cream-yellow Mercedes 520 with smoked-glass windows. When the door opened, all Berger could see was a shadowy interior and a long arm beckoning. He thought the seats had custom leather upholstery, but couldn't be sure.

He was sure that the voice greeting him was that of an older man, but one still in good health—and still accustomed to getting his own way.

"Please climb in, Mr. Berger. I think we have matters to discuss."

As helpless as a bird charmed by a snake, Berger obeyed. The upholstery *was* leather, and the car had a good many other luxuries, including a small bar and as many controls and electronic displays as his helicopter. It also had a chauffeur—or was it a bodyguard?

None of this was as remarkable as the man sitting beside Berger, taller than Berger even though age had stooped him somewhat. His hair was silver but abundant and his blue eyes as clear as a boy's.

"If you wish to smoke, please feel free. I do not smoke myself, but the air-conditioning is excellent. Also, my driver is discreet."

Berger didn't smoke, and anyway his hands were shaking. He forced them to stay in his lap as the Mercedes rolled away from the station.

"If I may introduce myself, I am Helmut Kuhn. I see that I am not entirely unknown to you. I hope it is unknown that I am unofficially but quite legally helping to find the people responsible for various bloody incidents in the past few days."

"Including the attack on the Comradeship meeting?"

"Very much including it. You see, Mr. Berger, I think you have gained more influence in your own organization from that event. You might even be listened to with more respect in other nationalist organizations."

Kuhn leaned back against the upholstery, as the Mercedes swept past a block of department stores. Berger saw a few night workers silhouetted in the front windows, changing displays for the morning's customers.

"I am old enough to know where many of the slogans your organization and those like it led. I am therefore not very sympathetic to them. Yet it is also true that many of those slogans would have led nowhere without Hitler. There are no Hitlers now. Or at least I hope not.

"There are many men like you, decent conservatives. I can talk to them, and I hope they will listen to you."

Berger wasn't so tired and sore that he couldn't add two and two. "You want me to talk to the other nationalist leaders?"

"Yes. I can give you a list of the people I think you should start with, but I am sure you can add to it."

"I make no promises, Mr. Kuhn, unless you tell me what you want to say. To lie down before the Greens—that I will not."

"You will not be asked to lie down before anybody, I think," Kuhn replied. "In fact, this very night friends of mine are investigating some of the Greens and taking a message to *their* leaders. We wish to learn just who it was who attacked your headquarters."

"If you learn, will you tell me? And let me pass it on to my comrades?"

"Yes." Helmut Kuhn was clearly no politician. He said yes or no in a moment, without reservations or trying to confuse the issue. Berger found himself warming to the man. A fine leader for the new Germany, if he had believed in it.

Berger listened as Kuhn outlined his plans. Berger was to make the rounds of the nationalist organizations and speak to their leaders. They shouldn't retaliate against the Greens, and should keep their extremist members under control or at least out of the streets, avoid demonstrations and large meetings for a while and generally not only look but *be* innocent.

"Reasonable people will not mistake you for the skinheads and other neo-Nazis if you do these things," Kuhn concluded. "There are always unreasonable ones, but they are also fewer. Meanwhile, the police and other agencies can be on the trail of those really trying to set you and the Greens at each other's throats. We think some of them might have foreign connections."

That left a great deal unsaid, but Berger knew he wasn't going to learn any more. Kuhn's next question was a surprise.

"In what helicopters do you have ratings?"

Since Berger had done nothing for a living but fly helicopters since he was nineteen, and was now thirty-three, he had ratings in just about every type of helicopter seen in German skies. He began to list them.

Kuhn smiled when Berger was done. "I can arrange, I think, one of those for your use. You will be on leave of absence from your forestry-patrol job. Instead, you will be testing the rapid deployment of pollution-control teams for toxic accidents. Even the Greens will applaud."

Klaus Berger didn't at the moment care much who applauded him. He was almost too tired to care about anything, and in fact fell asleep before Kuhn's Mercedes reached his apartment building.

Kuhn and the chauffeur-bodyguard didn't actually carry Berger up the stairs and tuck him into bed. But he was sure one of them at least guided his footsteps, till he was safely inside his apartment.

THE GARAGE'S TWO ROOMS had beds, although the one in Bolan's room was rather crowded with Trudl in it as well. He had offered to sleep on the floor, but she wouldn't listen to him.

"Tonight, that would not be the act of a gentleman," she said firmly, as she pulled off her sweater. "Tonight the act of a gentleman will be to take this lady to bed and make love to her for as long as he can."

"What about the lady?" Bolan asked, smiling.

"The lady will do the same." She pushed her slacks down her long legs, then gripped his hands and pulled him down so that she could kiss him.

Afterward they lay in each other's arms. Trudl didn't seem interested in Bolan's scars or their history. Instead, she propped herself up on one elbow and stared at him until the Executioner began to feel like a specimen on a scientist's microscope slide.

"You do not look dangerous now," she said finally.

"Oh? When did I?"

"Several times, but I was thinking of tonight. You were playing the 'bad cop' and Zev the 'good cop,' correct?"

Bolan nodded.

"I thought of how it would have worked if you did it the other way around. Then I laughed, because it would not have worked at all. You cannot look nice. A gentleman, yes, but always someone it would be dangerous to have angry with you.

"Zev, on the other hand, looks like—oh, an uncle who makes a living as a salesman. A nice man, but not very successful, so everybody feels a little sorry for him."

"Actually Zev's looks are better for fieldwork than mine. The best field man is somebody who is completely invisible in any group of more than five people. I'm afraid I stand out. So would you.''

''What? There is no place for beautiful blondes in intelligence work?''

''Not as much as the novels would make you believe. There's always a place for people who can think on their feet, though, and you certainly qualify there.''

''Thank you.'' She laid her head on his chest and ran her fingers down his body. ''But now I am not on my feet, and I do not want to think.''

of any division in any group of more than five people. I'm afraid I must cut. So would you."

"What? I am—is he mad that should say that?" The cigarette wobbled.

"I told as much to the mayor, much later, when I saw him. I have a sharp tongue for people who can drink on their own money, and you certainly must a drink."

"I thank you."

CHAPTER TWENTY

Another morning came to Berlin.

Carl Braun sat having breakfast with one of his principal soldiers. They had both heard rumors of men inquiring about Hans Wegener. Now Braun had solid information about at least one of the men making inquiries, as well as a decision to make.

"What about Wegener himself?" the soldier asked.

Braun dipped a slice of toasted black bread in the last of his coffee and shook his head. "Not yet. He might still be useful, or at least harmless, if he takes warnings. Also, there is the Beck organization. If anything happens to one of its people, the police will give it more attention than usual. The police are very nervous right now."

"That is God's own truth," the soldier replied. "I have told most of my men to walk softly for a few days."

"Good. But can you find two or three for a meeting with this man who is so curious about Wegener?"

"Certainly. What message should I send?"

"Wegener is our territory. Discourage further interest in him."

It was an order for killing. The soldier was very good at it, and could come up with several men equally good. Braun didn't expect to be bothered with what he called "tourists"—criminals from out of town—asking about Wegener again.

On the East Coast of the United Sates, it was ten o'clock in the evening. When the telephone rang in Hal Brognola's office, no one heard it. His answering machine recorded a coded message, acknowledging receipt of the faxed photographs from Berlin at a certain highly secret installation in the suburbs of Washington. It also promised to honor the priority given to identification of those photographs.

IN CASE POLICE were looking for an unmarked Trabant, Ben Shlomo had painted company logos on the doors of the vehicle. The paint was dry by the time Bolan and his team finished breakfast. They had no duties until eleven o'clock, when they were supposed to check in at one of the BND numbers for messages.

That gave them three hours. They decided to spend the time making their temporary refuge a little more habitable. Ben Shlomo, the least conspicuous, volunteered to do the shopping.

"Of course, the moment we assume we will be staying here, we will be ordered to be in Munich for lunch," he added.

He came back ten minutes later, with a bemused expression and a newspaper. Bolan took the paper and frowned. It held an announcement of a large Green Party demonstration, to be held at a place called Marisplatz the next morning.

The Israeli muttered something about people who were green between the ears, they used their brains so little. Bolan read the article over again.

"We'll ask about it when we call in, but you notice the Earth Brotherhood isn't listed as a sponsor. I think we should also call back our friends of last night, and remind them of their promise. It might be too late to cancel the demostration—"

"Knowing the Greens, I think it is," Trudl put in.

"But if they all keep an eye out for trouble, it'll help. Zev and I can do a better job with security if we don't have to fight the people we're trying to protect."

"Yes, and it will help even more if Helmut Kuhn can talk to the conservative clubs," Ben Shlomo said. "It will also make our work easier, if we know we are shooting only neo-Nazis and Spetsnaz storm troopers."

Bolan knew that was critical. The danger of some well-intentioned German conservative getting killed might lead the police to pull them back. He also knew that this might lose their best chance of hitting the real bad guys.

He would use that argument with Kuhn and the BND. But if they thought the risk was too great, he would have to accept their judgment. Anything else wouldn't only scrub his role in this mission, it would wreck cooperation on his original one.

The Mob would be on the top of the heap after the neo-Nazis and undercover Spetsnaz were dead, in prison or back in Russia—if there was any place there for them. The Russian government might be as eager as the Germans to hunt down the Spetsnaz. Half of the power brokers wouldn't forgive the Spetsnaz for trying at all. The other half wouldn't forgive them for failing.

"I WANT YOU TO BE in personal command of our men at this demonstration," Colonel Danilov said.

Major Bytkin looked meaningfully at the walls. He had electronically swept the cellar for listening devices the previous night, but capitalist technology in that area was highly sophisticated. The sweeping devices remaining to the Berlin Spetsnaz group, on the other hand, were the remnants of what they had brought initially. Like the hard currency, the spare parts were shrinking.

"I have complete confidence in Little Father."

"You had complete confidence in him the night he did not kill Hedwig, but instead an honest whore and a waiter. Two dead, and for what except to make the police already more nervous than they were!"

"Barbed Wire killed the whore, as you know. And if the police are already nervous, what does it matter how many we kill?"

"Bytkin, I am not in a mood to listen to jokes, if that was a joke, which I doubt. You have never had much sense of humor."

"I have never lacked a sense of duty, either."

"I was not accusing you of that. I merely wish that you be there to watch Little Father while he is watching our other men, and they are watching our supposed allies." The Project Gamma group—Danilov still called it that, even if the project was as dead as the traitorous German technicians—was calling out everybody it thought would listen. Even if barely half responded, there would still be several hundred people making a counterdemonstration at the Green rally.

Even without help, incidents were certain, violence probable. With the kind of help that nine Spetsnaz experts could provide, violence was certain and a bloody day more than likely.

It still seemed to Bytkin that Colonel Danilov wasn't the same man he had been before the incident in the Thüringer Wald. Was he losing confidence in his men? Or was sending Bytkin into the field personally meant to keep him from watching Danilov?

Bytkin couldn't encode a mere suspicion and send it to the man who had asked to be informed of any questionable behavior by Danilov. He had been strictly ordered to communicate with him as little as possible, to avoid compromising the link.

The Group of Forces in Germany was a shadow of its former self, with only a few bases left and only caretaker parties of troops left on each one.

The total fighting capability of all the Russian forces left in Germany was perhaps the equivalent of one motor rifle regiment. But there were advantages as well as disadvantages to this. There were few traitors and weaklings to sabotage those still loyal to socialism.

Bytkin's contact was one of those loyalists. He was not Spetsnaz, but the next best thing, a colonel in the Parachute Troops. Ryazan made good men—a pity more of them hadn't remained good in the face of the criminal betrayal of socialism.

Bytkin knew his contact would. If that colonel more than two hundred kilometers away was true to his oath, it was less important if the colonel across the cellar table wasn't.

"WE HAVE A PROBLEM," Bolan said. Trudl looked at him, and he shook his head. "No, I don't think you need to leave. The 'we' includes you."

Ben Shlomo frowned. "Peter, are you sure this is—"

"Are you sure you want to go back to discussing me as if I were not here?" Trudl asked. She looked daggers at the Mossad agent. He subsided.

"Okay, Trudl," the Executioner said. "You are about to be awarded a one-time clearance for anything vital to our job tomorrow. If you don't want to be part of it, we can arrange a trip back to the safehouse before dinner."

Trudl Kuhn's blue eyes seemed to be fixed on something beyond the scabbed, peeling walls of the second-floor room. Then she sighed.

"I suppose I would be in danger of being kidnapped and tortured for the information?"

"Yes," Ben Shlomo said, in a tone like a brick dropping down an empty well. Bolan could almost hear the echoes. Trudl's expression didn't change.

"My grandfather could have let the SS sergeant kill the mine laborers. He didn't. My father could have paid off the blackmailers in cash, instead of doing work that cost him his life. He didn't. I could run away from this whole business, whether I can help you or not. I won't. So what is the problem?"

"They don't want us on the roof as snipers," Bolan told her.

"Who are 'they'?" Trudl asked.

"The guy on the telephone sounded like a very senior police or military special-operations expert. I don't suppose he would have been talking to me without authorization from even higher up."

"What did he sound like?" Ben Shlomo asked.

"I got the impression of a large man whose vocal cords had been damaged at some point many years ago."

"That would be Major Beppo Ullmer," the Israeli said. "He's third in command of GSG-9."

A major in Germany's elite counterterrorist force certainly matched Bolan's description. He was also someone whose judgment the Executioner could trust. GSG-9 had in fact been trained by the Israelis after the Munich Olympics murders in 1972. They weren't at the level of the British SAS, the world's most elite counterterrorist force, but they were in a tie for second place with the U.S. Army's Delta Force.

In Major Ullmer's judgment, having Bolan and Ben Shlomo on roofs as snipers would create identification problems. "We want to make sure that there are only two kinds of people up on the rooftops tomorrow," he said. "Our people and targets. If you are up there, you could become a casualty of friendly fire."

"He doesn't sound very friendly to me," Trudl said.

"I think he's concerned for a couple of things besides what he told me," Bolan said. "One is what happens if one of us gets killed. The other is what happens if we're blown by some Spetsnaz observer or even a free-lance journalist."

"Did he say anything about our staying away from the whole situation?" Ben Shlomo asked.

"No. He did give us the colors of the day, so we can dress for recognition by friendlies."

"Good. I think he wants us there more than some of his superiors do, and is trying to say so. At least, that is how I would do it in his position."

"Assuming you're right—"

"Let us assume that and go ahead. I have an idea that depends on Trudl's cooperation, but with it I think we can do well.

"There is on the square a skiers' shop. Now suppose you, Trudl, be a skier who is returning some rented skis to the shop and has been caught in the crowd. You will be carrying a ski case. In that ski case will be Peter's Weatherby."

"You would trust the granddaughter of Helmut Kuhn that much?" Trudl said.

"The granddaughter of Helmut Kuhn has proved herself worthy of trust. So has Helmut Kuhn." This left Trudl nothing to say, and Bolan was too curious about Ben Shlomo's plan to interrupt, so the Israeli went on.

"Now, I look young enough that I can pass as a Green, with a cap to cover my bald head, and a change of clothes. As a Green, it will make sense for me to carry a backpack. You can put many things in a backpack."

"What particular thing were you suggesting?"

"A backpack will hold an MP-5 K very nicely. So will an attaché case, such as the one Peter might carry if he is willing to dress as a businessman."

The MP-5 K was the German answer to the American Ingram. Bolan had fired it a few times, preferred the Ingram but knew that Heckler & Koch had built a very good second-best if you needed a concealable subgun. It was more than likely that tomorrow they would.

"All right," Bolan said. "I think we have a way of tackling this now. Let's get together our shopping list."

The list was quite long, but part of their equipment now included a generous wad of Barclay's and American Express travelers' checks, matching the cover identities of Bolan and Ben Shlomo. Trudl Kuhn would use cash, in stores where she was not a regular customer.

"Which is more than you might think. I usually do not forget that I have only one back to put clothes on, and only two feet to wear shoes."

"They are both excellent, too," Ben Shlomo said.

"What?"

"Your back and your feet. Also other parts of you, I would imagine—but I am a gentleman."

Trudl kissed Ben Shlomo on both cheeks and then on top of his bald head. They both broke up. The Executioner stretched his long legs and smiled.

The granddaughter of one of the Third Reich's servants—a reluctant one, but a servant nonetheless—and the grandson of Holocaust victims had made their peace.

THE ANALYST at the secret center in Virginia was already at work when his supervisor joined him. In fact, he'd finished the assignment, except for the last detail, which he didn't have the clearances to obtain.

He was sitting, staring at an UNAUTHORIZED ACCESS PROHIBITED on his terminal, when the supervisor walked up behind him.

"Got it?" the older man said.

"Except for this." He jerked a thumb at the screen.

"Maybe I can help you. Let's see what you've already done."

The supervisor pulled up a chair and spread the printout and folder across his lap. He looked at it, or so it seemed to the junior analyst, until coffee break time.

The junior analyst wanted coffee, but knew there was no rushing the older man. Legend had it that he had been in intelligence since the Spanish-American War. He had certainly been in the OSS and the Air Force in World War II. He had retired some years ago, but been called back for the Gulf War and showed no signs of returning to his condo in Reston. Death now seemed the only way of getting him off the backs of the junior analysts.

"You've done a good job, and I'll put that in writing," the older man said. "I'm satisfied that our friend and Ludwig's, Hans Wegener, is in fact the same person as the boy in our picture."

"Okay, so we know who the boy is. Who's the guy in uniform?"

"His father."

"But that's an SS uniform. How could Wegener be his son?"

"So, who says that SS men didn't have balls?"

"I didn't say that. I wanted to find out more, got the name Manfred Scheel, then went after that file and got this." He pointed at the terminal.

"Um," the supervisor said. "I can't give you a need-to-know, but will you settle for a background briefing?"

"How far back?"

"In 1946 there was this SS lieutenant general who was going to be tried as a war criminal. Somehow he wound up in Argentina, where he died sometime in the seventies."

"So?"

"The hard part is, there were rumors about his buying his way out with about ten million dollars in looted jewels. A couple of recognizable stones did turn up, in places you don't want to know about.

"Also, the man talked about 'his son' a few times. The official file said his wife was killed in the bombing of Dresden and his son in Normandy. So who was he talking about?"

"An illegitimate kid, by somebody he didn't want to talk about?"

"Right the first. I don't know about the second. But I do know one thing." He tapped the photographs of Wegener. "If General Scheel had a bastard, we're looking at him right now."

CHAPTER TWENTY-ONE

Carl Braun's chief soldier was nicknamed the Pirate, because he had a tattoo of an old-fashioned sailing ship on his left arm. That and memories were the only things left from his days as a merchant seaman, the last time he had made an honest living.

Not that it wasn't a good piece of work, for a man from Bremen to rise to first soldier of a Berlin gang. But there were times when the soldier thought that dealing with a first mate hadn't been as bad as dealing with Carl Braun.

The man he and his two companions were supposed to kill was late. This was neither surprising nor as yet alarming. The man might not know the schedules of any of Berlin's public transportation systems, and lack the money to take a cab. It wasn't impossible that to keep a low profile he was walking.

Certainly when he appeared, the man was on foot. A slim dark-haired figure in dark brown slacks and a gray sweater, he sauntered around the corner where the drugstore was just closing. For a moment he was silhouetted against the lights. Then the lights died, and the Pirate tapped his driver on the shoulder.

The Audi rolled forward out of the alley, turning as it crossed the street. It pulled up beside the man.

He didn't seem surprised. Instead he smiled, showing very white teeth. The Berliner noted that the man didn't appear to have shaved today, but then he was from the south, where they had dirty habits.

"You were asking about Mr. Wegener?" the Pirate asked.

"I might have been." His German was correct, but heavily accented. Not a French accent after all. Spanish?

"I think you were," the Pirate said in Spanish. Something flickered in the man's eyes, and the soldier knew that he had guessed something important.

"If I was?"

"I can answer your questions, if you come into the car with us. This is not a good place to stand and talk."

"I think it is a very good place."

The Pirate realized that the negotiating part was over. He slid out of the car, with his H&K P-9 held behind his back.

In that moment, the Pirate blocked his companion in the rear seat. In that moment also, the man on the sidewalk shot the man in front of him, smoothly drawing a Browning Hi-Power and sending three rounds into his opponent's chest. And at the same time, another man came around the corner with a Llama .45 Compact and shot the driver. The stubby automatic held only seven rounds, but two of the big bullets were enough to shatter the windshield and the driver's head.

The third man was still alive. He jerked out his own Walther PPK and fired wildly. His bullets left starred holes in the drugstore window but did no harm to his opponent. Then the first man tossed a grenade into the car and both he and his companion dived to the ground.

The grenade blast blew out the Audi's windows and shredded the third soldier. He was still alive but not yet in pain when the gas tank exploded. Then he screamed once, before the flames consumed him.

A third man joined the pair. "You could not have left some for me?" He spoke in Basque.

The leader felt so good about the successful execution of some of Wegener's men that he didn't reproach the man for breaking cover. He merely slapped him on the shoulder.

"You know I am greedy, my friend. For women, for fine guns, for stupid people to kill...."

"I forgive you this time, Paedo."

Then all three Basques faded into the shadows, to continue their hunt for Hans Wegener.

THE CONNECTION WAS GOOD, but the line wasn't secure, so the Executioner and Brognola were using the mission-specific cryptic. It wasn't really designed for telephone use, but it was better than no communication or leaking intelligence.

"The local staff seems to have all the technical experts it needs," Bolan concluded. "We've been asked to maintain observer status unless the competition becomes really serious."

"Knowing the competition, they will," Brognola said.

"That was my feeling. Any developments at your end?"

"One. We have a confirmation that one of the associates of our local office had a previous connection with the predecessor firm."

That particular phrase wasn't mission specific. It meant one thing—the Third Reich. And "local office" meant the Beck organization.

"Do you know which associate?" Beck's internal security had impressed Bolan less each time he learned more about it. The secretaries and security guards couldn't have been the leak, but they might have helped the man who was.

"The chief of operations."

Bolan frowned. That meant Hans Wegener, and he had a growing suspicion that Wegener had some sort of a hold over Beck. This didn't make him any the less a suspect. In fact it made him a more likely one. But it narrowed the Executioner's choices—confront Beck and risk being stonewalled while tipping off Wegener, or go directly to Wegener and undercut Beck.

The warrior had a feeling that maybe undercutting Beck or putting him out of business permanently wasn't a bad idea. But it wasn't his decision to make. Anyway, tomorrow he was going to be too busy to worry about side issues.

"We aren't working enough with the local office for their chief's associations to affect us," Bolan said. "What about my getting back to you after tomorrow's meeting?"

"Fine. We should be able to go over the whole thing in detail by then." Which meant a secure link that didn't go through the Beck office, or else the leaks stopped so that Bolan could use Beck's line.

The Executioner was willing to let Brognola run with this particular ball. For Bolan, the big game was tomorrow.

THE VOICE ON THE LINE mixed obscenities and gagging sounds. Wegener recognized Carl Braun, but in such a rage as he had never heard the man. There were rumors of Braun's ferocious temper, but until tonight they had been only rumors.

No more. Wegener listened in silence without even trying to speak until Braun had vented his rage. Then he asked, trying to keep his voice steady, "What happened?"

"What happened?" he shouted. "You are trying to make me believe that you don't know what happened, when you are responsible for it?"

"If I do not know what it is, how can I know—"

"Shut up!" Braun said, in the coldest voice Wegener had ever heard. He obeyed, listened and in moments he also wanted to vomit from sheer terror.

Three of Braun's best men had gone to deal with someone who was inquiring about Wegener. Braun made this sound like a favor to Wegener, proof that he still supported the man. Wegener didn't dare call the gang leader a liar, but knew he was one. This had been a turf fight, no more.

But all three of Braun's men were dead, in what seemed to have been an ambush. An ambush that could only have been possible with advance warning, such as Wegener might have given.

"You thought you could declare war on me, dispose of me, without my finding out until it was too late!" the gang chief raged. Wegener had to hold the phone away from his ear to avoid pain.

"You had better think again. Think very carefully in whatever time remains to you. It will not be long."

The line clicked into silence.

Wegener sat in that silence for some time. He wished he could wrap it around him like a cloak of invisibility, and not take it off until Braun lost interest in vengeance for his men.

Reason slowly returned. He couldn't become invisible. Braun wouldn't abandon his hunt. Wegener had only one choice. Flee, to the men he had been serving. He knew where to find them, or at least someone who would take him to them.

But that would only solve his problem for a short time. His friends would have to want to remain friends, and to protect him from those who would come after him. Braun, the police, the man called Peter Metzger, even Beck himself—all would be on his trail.

There was only one way to buy his way out of this, and that was with intelligence his friends didn't have and couldn't hope to get once he left the Beck organization. And there was only one way to get that intelligence.

Wegener hadn't carried a gun on a regular basis for some years, but when he had, he paid good money for his weapons. He also didn't worry much about whether they were legal in Germany. He knew the Beck organization would protect him in most cases.

So now that he needed to strike at Beck, he had his choice of several weapons. He finally picked the Browning Hi-Power. It wasn't absolutely the best of his guns, but it would be the hardest to trace. The Korth Combat Magnum was more powerful, but it had been an indulgence, bought with nearly the last of the money left by his shadowy father, and Korth kept detailed records.

Wegener intended to fade away into the night, like those who had killed Braun's men and left Wegener to face the gangster's rage.

FROM THE NEXT ROOM, Ben Shlomo's snores floated into the hall. Bolan gently shut the door on the Israeli's noisemaking and knocked on the door of his own room.

"Come in."

Trudl Kuhn stood by the shuttered window, breathing the trickle of fresh air that crept between the shutters. She wore a jumpsuit several sizes too large for her. Her hair was roughly tied into a messy ponytail. She wore dangling earrings, loafers that clashed horribly with the jumpsuit, and rings of grease were visible under closely trimmed fingernails.

"How do I look?" she said.

"Interesting. Like a factory worker who spent all her money on that skiing vacation."

"But not like myself?"

"No."

"Good. I listened to what you said about Ben Shlomo and you, the way you look. I decided that I could not hide my height and I did not have time to dye my hair. But the rest... Would anyone who knows the Trudl Kuhn who always dresses well think that I am she?"

"Not unless they were a trained observer."

Her face twisted. "Some of those Spetsnaz will be."

"Yes, but they might not have a file on you. Maybe your grandfather, and almost certainly Zev and I. Probably not you."

She looked ready to pout. "You think I am frightened?"

"No. I'm telling you the truth. You've done a fine job of disguise for the conditions we'll face tomorrow."

"Thank you, Peter," she said. "I was afraid that you were trying to keep me from being frightened by lying. That would spoil our— No, I will only say, what could be our last night together."

She slipped off her shoes, then unzipped the jumpsuit and tossed it on the floor. "I bought something silly while I was shopping," she said. "One of those flimsy nightgowns that is hardly there at all."

Bolan grinned. "Why take the time to put it on, when we'll just be taking it right off again?"

"GOOD...DAY?" the guard said, obviously bewildered, as Wegener flashed his identification at the door of the Beck offices.

"I could not sleep, so I thought I would turn night into day by doing some work," Wegener said.

The guard frowned. "There is still nothing coming in, Mr. Wegener."

"That does not matter. My interest is in data already received." That statement would have passed any lie-detector test. "Sometimes you can gain new insights by looking over old facts. That might help when we start receiving data again."

"Of course, Mr. Wegener."

As he hurried down the hall toward the archives, Wegener thought that the guard had been almost too cooperative, considering the time of night. But that could be his own imagination, which between fear and fatigue was certainly working hard.

Wegener had long since learned his way around the internal security of the Beck organization. The job had taken Wegener nearly two years, but he had done it, thought he had remained undetected so far and intended to reap the harvest tonight.

It would be the last thing he would ever reap in the Beck organization, or possibly even in Germany. But the alternative was being a standing target, doomed to reap nothing but a burst of lead whenever Braun overtook him.

Wegener ransacked the files with almost gleeful abandon. As he stuffed his briefcase, he realized that Beck's long-standing refusal to computerize had been a backhanded piece of good luck. The man had been threatened with lack of cooperation from several of the large agencies for not doing so, but he always gave them something too valuable to ignore. That bought their acquiescence, Beck's freedom to go on as he had and now Hans Wegener's chance for a new life somewhere away from Berlin.

The attaché case was beginning to bulge at the seams when Wegener heard footsteps outside the door to the archives. He slipped quickly into the corner where he would be hidden behind the open door. He shifted the attaché case to his left hand and drew the Browning with the other.

Locks and keys rattled, electronic security devices peeped like hungry birds and hissed like snakes. The door swung open, and Willi Beck entered.

For a moment, Wegener thought he might explain his presence, then remembered that he'd heard two sets of footsteps. Their source entered the room—the Turk Mustafa, with a Beretta 82 already drawn.

The decision was now out of Wegener's hands. He shot Mustafa in the neck and the head, so that his blood sprayed over Beck. The German American clawed at his eyes with his left hand and at his pocket with the right.

He put a round straight through Beck's left hand. It entered his skull through the bridge of his nose and blew the back out of his skull as it exited. He slammed backward against an open file drawer, his blood oozing onto the papers.

Wegener ran out of the archives, gun in hand, to meet the guard running in. He also heard alarms sounding, but no sirens as yet. If this had been a trap, they had been too slow to spring it. He waved his gun toward the archives room, as the guard drew his.

"Don't shoot! It was Mustafa. He went mad and shot Beck. I shot him. Go see for yourself."

It had been lucky that Beck brought Mustafa. He had a bad reputation among the rest of the staff. If any of those cursed Turks was more likely than another to go berserk, it was Mustafa.

That knowledge slowed the guard's draw. His own pistol was still pointed toward the rug when Wegener shot him. It was another head shot, in case the guard was wearing a bulletproof vest.

Then Wegener sprinted for the stairs. The rest of the building would almost certainly be deserted at this time of night. He had been lucky so far. He wouldn't need much more luck to get out of the building without anyone seeing him.

Then the police would have a mystery on their hands, even if they were already on the way. Who had littered the Beck offices with bodies? They would have to inquire about who and what was missing, and that would take time.

Time the police might not have. They had the Green rally, which might turn into a riot. They wouldn't want to take men off that tomorrow, even for a triple murder.

That would give Wegener a day's head start, and he doubted that he would need more. Not with the help of his friends. And what he had in his attaché case guaranteed that help.

Wegener was out of the building and several hundred meters from the building before the first police car swung around the corner on two wheels, siren howling. He was careful to make a perfectly normal start when the light turned, as much as he wanted to roar off into the night at top speed.

Instead he held the car to the speed limit and discovered that his breathing was normal and his hands weren't shaking on the wheel anymore. He felt the weight of the Browning in his jacket pocket and patted it briefly.

All those who had said he was a fat scholar who knew books but had no fieldcraft would have to think again. Tonight he had acted, fought, killed and escaped.

Tonight his father would have been proud of him.

WEGENER FOUND A REFUGE within an hour, made contact with his friends within two and was at one of their safehouses before dawn.

Danilov didn't change any of the plans for the Green rally. He did, however, detail two of the best men not assigned to the rally to guard Wegener, and his best surviving intelligence analyst to go over the contents of the man's attaché case.

As dawn reached Berlin, the Greens began converging on the Marisplatz by bus, car, U-Bahn, motorcycle, bicycle and foot.

At the same time, a middle-aged Trabant rolled out of a garage in northeast Berlin, heading for the same destination. And in threes, by three different routes, nine hard-eyed men were also on their way to the Marisplatz.

CHAPTER TWENTY-TWO

Major Bytkin was trying by sheer force of will not to sweat. It was going to be a hotter day than usual for Berlin in the spring, and he was dressed for normal temperatures. His respectable bourgeois topcoat and three-piece suit were a disguise that would pass muster in the most respectable parts of the city.

In fact, they had. He had been given almost obsequious service at breakfast, he and his similarly dressed team. They had no difficulty finding a taxi. The class system of capitalism, he decided, had certain advantages—at least for socialists who could use it as a weapon against the capitalists themselves.

The taxi stopped and let out Bytkin and his team. He didn't bother to check the rest of the square to see if the second team was in position. He trusted its leader, as he trusted Little Father, who was leading the team actually marching with the counterdemonstration. Also, he didn't want anyone to have too good a look at his features.

With his hat pulled down over his face, Bytkin led his men toward cover.

THE FIRST PART of the rally was listed as a silent vigil, though three thousand people made a certain amount of noise just breathing. Add a few hundred who were whispering to each other, listening to headphones or guzzling soft drinks, and there was plenty of background noise.

It would have been easier for Bolan to spot ringers without all three thousand people singing environmental songs, chanting environmental slogans or cheering at pointed remarks from speakers with large bullhorns and not much to say into them. It would also have been easier to keep a lookout for the rest of his team.

Trudl was easy to spot, if you knew what you were looking for. Even in a German crowd, she was one of the taller women, and even in a baggy jumpsuit nobody could mistake her for a man.

Ben Shlomo, on the other hand, had done his famous disappearing act for the first twenty minutes. Bolan finally spotted him by the large handkerchief in the recognition colors that hung out of the top of his backpack. The handkerchief was so filthy that the colors were barely recognizable, and no one would be tempted to grab it and see what lay underneath it.

Bolan's sport coat was now unbuttoned. He wouldn't look like a German businessman if he took off his tie, tempted though he was. He also moved carefully so the swing of the jacket wouldn't give anyone a view of the shoulder holster with the Makarov. With the MP-5 Ks, the Beretta wasn't needed, and the attaché case had plenty of room for the Desert Eagle.

The warrior studied the crowd. He was fairly sure about two ringers, but one of them was a woman, which meant she was probably a German undercover police officer. The other was a hard-faced man who didn't look particularly at home in the crowd, but he also wasn't studying it carefully, as Bolan would have expected from one of the Spetsnaz troopers.

That was all he'd found in the part of the crowd closest to him. Three thousand people covered quite a bit of pavement. Bolan knew that for a while longer the initiative was with the enemy. The only possible response was not to worry until something happened, then react fast enough to block the other man's move.

Five minutes dragged by, then ten more.

Bolan was as patient as a cat at a mousehole, but he was also beginning to think that maybe a silent vigil could go on too long.

His watch showed twenty mintues gone when he saw a young man leap up onto the portable podium the Greens had brought with them. He turned on the microphone, instantly producing a hideous squeal of feedback that seemed to go on forever.

Then the Executioner recognized the man. It was the leader of the Earth Brotherhood, who had somehow managed to slip into first place on the speakers' list. Fine. As long as he had the mike, that vital asset would be in the hands of the good guys.

Listening to political speeches wasn't one of Bolan's favorite activities. If he had to listen, he liked them short. Today was different. As far as the Executioner was concerned, that young man could still be talking at sunset, if his voice lasted that long.

IN THE ALLEY, Major Bytkin finished dumping his suit into a trash container. The suits of his comrades already lay in the bottom, among the fruit rinds, old newspapers and other refuse. Those clothes represented long hours of work for some German laborer, and now he was tossing them away like so much garbage. Nor would this be his last change of clothes today.

Capitalism, Major Bytkin decided, offended his sense of order. The garbage it left was offending other senses, as the sun rose higher. And the puerile bleatings of that gelded ram at the microphone were offending his ears. Bytkin decided that the fool wasn't going to survive the day, whatever else happened.

He pulled on his cargo pants, dropped the silenced PSM revolver into one pocket, pulled on the shoulder holster with the Skorpion machine pistol and held out his hand for the jacket. The man known as Lightning handed it to his commander. Its pockets sagged with ammunition and grenades, both explosive and riot gas.

Bytkin was ready for either selective or mass killing. He was determined to have mass killing by the end of the day, but would be as happy if the Germans could see their way to killing one another. That had been the whole purpose of the team since the earliest days of its conception, even before it was infiltrated into Germany and made contact with Colonel Danilov.

Danilov might have other purposes in mind. Bytkin had none.

A new sound rose to compete with the speaker. For the first time, Bytkin smiled. The sound was the chanting of many voices, distant, distorted by the alley, but growing louder and clearer as the chanters approached.

"Greens out! Greens out! Greens out!"

Little Father's team and the unwitting allies of socialism were on their way.

BOLAN COULDN'T USE binoculars without risking his cover. So the German riot police were already deploying across the entrance to the Marisplatz before he got a good look at the new arrivals.

They seemed to be a mixture of skinheads, street people and the miscellaneous types ready to join a riot that you found in any large city. No ordinary conservative nationalists, as far as Bolan could tell, or at least none of their banners. Helmut Kuhn and maybe a sudden attack of common sense had done their work.

Whoever they were, there were certainly at least five hundred of them. Not enough to overwhelm anybody, Greens or police, but enough to make trouble and cover the tracks of a whole platoon of Spetsnaz.

Bolan started edging around the Marisplatz, listening with half an ear to the speaker's platitudes, giving the rest of his attention to Trudl. He tried to look like a businessman who'd stopped by the rally out of curiosity, but now that it was getting nasty had remembered a meeting on the other side of Berlin.

That act took him halfway around the crowd. Then the counterdemonstration got close enough for their chanting to drown out the speaker. He turned up the volume. They turned up theirs. Somebody among the Greens got a bullhorn and called on everybody to sing "Love the Earth."

Three thousand Greens all doing what they thought was singing drowned out the counterdemonstrators. It also drowned the orders Bolan could see the police trying to give through *their* bullhorns. He hoped they were relying on secure radios for tactical coordination.

Right now, though, they didn't need much tactics or coordination. They'd put a solid mass of riot-equipped policemen between the two groups. One double line faced the Greens. Another faced their opponents. Both presented an imposing barrier of Lexan-visored helmets, Kevlar vests, riot guns and clubs, all carried by large and well-trained Berliners. Theoretically the two groups could now stay in this harmless confrontation until they shouted themselves hoarse.

If it stayed harmless. Apart from Spetsnaz, Bolan had a couple of worries. The Earth Brotherhood leader couldn't make himself heard to cool down any Green hotheads. Also, the counterdemonstrators wouldn't attack the police, but might try to slip around through alleys and outflank them.

Bolan cotinued to head for Trudl, through a steadily thickening mass of Greens. He also tried to keep an eye on the three or four alleys and streets closest to the counterdemonstration.

MAJOR BYTKIN HAD SENT Little Father with the counterdemonstration for a reason. It would put the best man in the most critical place.

But the Spetsnaz major could see his own role expanding, as he watched the big man make his way through the crowd. He would have stood out to Bytkin's trained eyes, from his military grace of movement, his purposeful searching of the crowd with eyes that missed nothing and the attaché case gripped in his hand.

Bytkin, however, recognized the man. The major's memory hadn't failed him in spite of the reverses of the past few days. This was the same man who had been at Gunther Wissmann's death scene. A professional, an enemy—and someone on the spot who might recognize Bytkin.

In one of his rare moments of humility, Oleg Bytkin conceded that he might have made a mistake at the time of Wissmann's death. He had allowed the big man too good a look at him, not allowing for his being active on the other side.

Well, too much activity on the part of any man could always be brought to an end. Nine ounces—the old Russian slang for a 9 mm round to the back of the head—would do it quite thoroughly.

"Carp," he said. The young-looking senior sergeant stepped forward. "That big man with the attaché case."

The round mouth that had given the sergeant his name opened wider. He fingered his pockets.

"I'll drop a couple of gas grenades right after I shoot," he said. "Hide me, make them think the police have opened fire."

"Good thinking."

Then Carp headed out of the alley. In a moment he was hard to pick out of the mass of Greens. In another moment he was impossible.

It was only after Carp was gone beyond recall that Bytkin saw the big man studying the alley and street entrances. It seemed that he suspected the direction of his opponent's next move. But then, Bytkin had never doubted that the man was a good professional.

He would have to be better than good to pick out Carp before the sergeant was in position for a shot. Nobody was professional enough to be a danger with a hole blown in his skull.

CARP PASSED within ten feet of Trudl Kuhn without her recognizing him as a danger. The failure was mutual, her act as a frustrated working girl completely convincing.

Zev Ben Shlomo had seen that the Executioner was watching the streets and alleys. He concentrated on watching Trudl, to see how people reacted to her. That would be, if not a dead giveaway, at least a highly suspicious circumstance.

Besides, Trudl Kuhn was pleasant to look at, even dressed as she was. Zev Ben Shlomo had hardly believed he would ever think that about a German woman, but then there was more to Trudl than hair, height and figure.

He remembered that many of the Germans who had formed the ill-fated White Rose resistance group under the Nazis had been children of the privileged who rejected those privileges and died miserably at the hands of the Gestapo. Trudl Kuhn was one of them in spirit.

It was during his watching Trudl Kuhn that Ben Shlomo noticed the Spetsnaz. He could tell from the first that the man was moving in a particular direction, or at least with a particular goal. He was trying to pretend otherwise, but he couldn't deceive the Mossad agent's trained eye.

Carp's eyes gave him away. Unseen by the Spetsnaz sergeant, Ben Shlomo saw which way the man was looking. No matter which way he moved, he never took his eyes off Peter Metzger for more than a few seconds.

Ben Shlomo began his own drift through the crowd. He was just out of reach of Carp when the man pulled out a PSM automatic. There were too many people around to use his own Makarov, let alone the MP-5 K, and the man was within easy range of Peter Metzger.

So Ben Shlomo let out a yell of raw agony, sounding like a man who'd had a red-hot sword rammed into his belly. It startled everybody around him. Some moved back, others moved toward him. Nobody who had room to move stood still.

Before everybody started to move, Carp had positioned himself perfectly for a clear shot. Now his target was blocked half the time, and his orders were strict—hit the big man first. Without those orders, he could have killed half a dozen people in the few seconds after Ben Shlomo's cry.

The Spetsnaz sergeant was a quick thinker. He couldn't calm things down, so why not make them more confused? He reached into his pocket for one of the grenades.

Doing that took his attention off the people around him for a few critical seconds. That was just long enough for Ben Shlomo to close the distance, kick Carp in the belly and wrestle the PSM out of his hand. The grenade fell to the ground and a moment later popped off.

CS gas rose in a swelling cloud. It might have knocked out dozens of people or caused a panic in which dozens more were trampled. But people were already moving back from the two fighting men. There was just enough room for them to keep on moving.

Then Ben Shlomo heard the distant flat crack of a shot and prayed as he hadn't in years that no one else recognized the sound.

THE SHOT CAME from Little Father's Walther P-5, firing a 9 mm tumbler at the skull of a skinhead less than ten feet away. The Walther was his favorite gun, and it should have been impossible for him to miss with it.

Unfortunately he fired at the exact moment his target shifted on his feet, trying to see over the heads of the police lines into the Green crowd. The scuffle and rising gas cloud had all his attention.

He didn't hear the bullet miss his shaved scalp by inches, but he saw and heard what happened when it drilled into the face of a policeman ten feet beyond him.

The policeman's visor was Lexan, resistant to rocks, bricks and fists, but not to bullets. It shattered. So did the man's face. He reeled, trying to fire his riot gun, but lost strength too fast. When the rubber bullet exploded from the barrel, the weapon pointed almost straight up. The bullet soared over the counterdemonstrators' heads and eventually landed on a roof.

Little Father had intended to shoot a counterdemonstrator and provoke a police attack. Instead he'd shot a policeman. The police weren't at first aware of what he'd done. Several of the people around him thought they were.

Two men next to Little Father made a grab for him, which turned out to be a fatal mistake. They thought they'd immobilized his gun hand, which they hadn't. He shot one of them in the chest, then kicked the other in the knee and shot him in the head as he fell to the ground.

Many more people witnessed these two deaths than the death of the policeman, including both policemen and counterdemonstrators, as well as a police sniper on a rooftop nearby.

The sniper didn't have a clear shot, because men from both sides swarmed all over Little Father. The Spetsnaz assassin went down under the weight of his attackers, so that he died from a cracked skull and a crushed chest.

One of his Spetsnaz comrades tried to shoot into the mob, no longer thinking of the mission but only of saving his comrade. Unfortunately he was in an open space when he drew his weapon, and the sniper on the roof was one of the best in Germany. He got a perfect head shot on the second Spetsnaz soldier at a range of eighty meters.

The third member of the Spetsnaz team was toward the rear, in case of trouble or opportunity there. He saw just enough to realize that the trouble wasn't the kind he'd expected, and the opportunity was gone. The only thing left to him was to use his cover identity to get clear of this shambles, and try to make his way to the rendez-vous.

LIKE SO MANY OTHERS that day, Major Bytkin saw only part of what was going on and understood only part of what he saw. However, he both saw and understood enough of the fight between Carp and Zev Ben Shlomo to know that he would have to change his plans.

He signaled his sniper to come forward. The man was as good with the Steyr-Mannlicher SSG rifle he was carrying as with the Dragunov he had trained on when there was still a Soviet Union. At the range to the podium, he didn't even plan to use his telescopic sights.

Bytkin insisted, however, and when the major insisted, the idea of disobeying him didn't occur to most people. So the sniper locked his sight in place and adjusted it quickly.

Not quickly enough. By the time he was ready to shoot, the cloud of gas was rising across his line of sight. Also, to his fury as much as to Major Bytkin's, the podium was empty.

THE PODIUM WAS EMPTY because the Earth Brotherhood leader was hiding under it, with Trudl Kuhn beside him holding the old Walther P-38. She wasn't quite aiming it at him, but he had no doubt that she would if he tried to run.

The Executioner crouched just outside the support structure, the Weatherby in his hands, shielding it from the Greens with his body. The podium in turn shielded him from Major Bytkin and the sniper.

When she'd seen the fight and recognized Peter Metzger's hand signals, Trudl Kuhn plunged through the crowd. She used elbows, knees, feet and the butt end of the Weatherby in the ski case to clear a path. Fortunately nobody recognized a concealed rifle butt when it hit them.

She tossed the ski case to the Executioner, then followed him as he weaved through the crowd toward the podium. The speaker was just suggesting another song, when he saw Bolan waving to him and holding up the still-cased Weatherby. Trudl was beside the man who'd raided the Earth Brotherhood headquarters, and the total effect convinced the leader that he should yield the platform.

Bolan waited behind the podium just long enough to be sure that the danger wasn't indiscriminate shooting. Then he removed a ski mask from the attaché case, pulled it over his face and vaulted onto the podium.

His appearance nearly started a panic. It also gave the sniper a target. The sniper got his cross hairs on Bolan—and in doing so, revealed himself to a sniper almost as good as the one who had killed Little Father's teammate.

The police sniper aimed his PSG rifle at the other sniper's head. It was a long shot with his target partly in shadow, so hitting the man in the chest was good shooting.

The Spetsnaz sniper collapsed, thrashed about on the ground and rolled over on his fallen weapon. Major Bytkin slipped out of cover just far enough to retrieve the weapon. He also drew his PSM. Nothing but the mercy shot was left for the sniper.

His movement drew him far enough into the light to be visible to the Executioner. The first kill had drawn Bolan's attention to the alley. By the time Major Bytkin appeared, he had the opening in the Weatherby's sights.

Through those sights, he saw a face he remembered as well as Major Bytkin remembered his. For both Mack Bolan and Oleg Bytkin, remembering faces was part of their profession.

Then Bolan made sure that Bytkin remembered nothing at all, by slamming a Magnum round from the Weatherby into his left cheek and out the back of his skull.

The remaining Spetsnaz team had plenty of evidence of heavy, organized resistance. They had no evidence that any of their comrades had succeeded in forcing the situation out of control. From the amount of shooting they'd heard, it seemed likely that not all of their comrades were still alive.

Those who were had to be left to proceed undercover to the planned rendezvous, and thereafter follow the orders of their senior surviving officer. They weren't totally unhappy that this officer might not be Major Bytkin.

Four of the nine Spetsnaz soldiers sent to the Marisplatz made a clean escape. Four were dead, and Ben Shlomo had Carp unconscious and ready for the police by the time they had any attention to spare for anything but the counterdemonstrators.

Trudl Kuhn helped the Earth Brotherhood leader get the Greens out of the square in an orderly manner, which made the job of the police easier.

Mack Bolan made everybody's job easier by simply disappearing for a few minutes, until Greens and counterdemonstrators were moving in opposite directions, firmly urged on by the police.

CHAPTER TWENTY-THREE

The Executioner's hope that the rest of this mission could be left to the German police didn't last long.

It wasn't that they had delayed informing him of Willi Beck's murder and the ransacking of the Beck organization's files. That was inevitable. The local police were slow to realize that this was a terrorist or security case and toss it upstairs. The people higher up who caught it had their minds almost entirely on the Green rally and its potential for trouble.

What bothered him was that they hadn't been able to find which of Beck's key people were missing. Nor had they insisted that office staff be brought in to go through the archives and find out what had been lost.

In a small-town sheriff's department in the rural U.S., Bolan would have suspected this was sheer incompetence. In the case of the various German police organizations, he suspected other things, likely to be almost as serious.

One was jurisdictional jealousy. The other was the law-enforcement professionals' dislike of amateurs. That meant the Beck organization, but also to some extent Bolan—"Peter Metzger"—and above all, Trudl Kuhn.

"I don't think you realize how dangerous this situation could become," Bolan told the police captain who seemed to have been assigned to keep an eye on him. "If nothing else, Helmut Kuhn and his granddaughter could both be in danger."

"They will hardly be in more danger than they were already," the captain replied. He seemed to be unsure whether he should play tough cop or nice cop. By personality he seemed more suited to playing nice cop, and under other circumstances Bolan would have felt sorry for the man. He was a professional reduced to the status of errand boy.

"Can you be sure? The BND—"

"The BND, Mr. Metzger, has much to do over this case and all the others of the past few days. I am sure they will do as much as they can as quickly as they can, without you or me shouting in their ears."

Trudl Kuhn didn't shout, but if glares could kill, the captain would have been dead. "Meanwhile, you will not even see if Beck had any of the BND's secrets, and where they have gone now?"

"Miss, I think this is a matter where you are out of your depth. Mr. Metzger, I have reason to believe, is a professional intelligence man. You are none of those things."

The "go home and have babies" message couldn't have been clearer. Bolan stepped between her and the captain, just in case she lost her temper completely. They didn't need her hauled off to jail for assaulting a police officer.

"As you say, I'm a professional," the Executioner said evenly. "And I think you're making a mistake. I hope, however, that it isn't a serious one. I don't wish to be proved right through any more people being killed."

"That wish does you honor, Mr. Metzger," the captain said. It was a dismissal, and not a moment too soon. Bolan took Trudl's arm and walked her out of hearing.

"Call your grandfather. Now."

"What shall I tell him?"

"Arrange a meeting."

"A guarded one?"

"Yes. Ben Shlomo and I will both be there."

"Good. What about you?"

"I also have some calls to make." A little prodding of the BND might save time, which in turn might save lives. Hal Brognola could do that prodding more effectively than Bolan. The BND would be reluctant to back up "Peter Metzger" now that the other police agencies were unhappy with him. There would be other cases, and they needed cooperation all the way down the line.

Everywhere it was the same. Create a monolithic central police force, and you got tyranny. Divide authority, and cracks opened, big enough to let criminals slip through.

Either way, people died, and the Executioner couldn't save them all. But as far as Trudl Kuhn and her grandfather were concerned, he was going to make a damned good try.

COLONEL DANILOV continued to think highly of Hans Wegener and his intelligence from the Beck archives, even if they did arrive in the middle of the night.

Like Wegener, he was grateful that Beck had resisted computerizing his files. By lunchtime, when the news of the violence at the Green rally reached him, he was even more grateful.

By midafternoon, he had extracted some critical data from the Beck material. He also had a clearer notion of just how much more Wegener might know.

It wasn't as much as Danilov had hoped. Wegener's connection in the BND, for example, hadn't supplied him with much intelligence of value. Had the man been poorly chosen, underpaid or turned?

Danilov didn't expect ever to learn. He was glad enough of what he had, which promised to help him salvage something from the disaster of Bytkin's operation.

He knew more or less accurately the dimensions of that disaster by midafternoon. Two telephone calls had given him that intelligence. He trusted they had revealed nothing to the German authorities.

If that was an inaccurate assumption, he feared that any further operations might mean walking into a trap at the head of his men. Based on the Beck material, however, there was one further operation that held considerable promise. If he could wait until dark before leaving Berlin, all the men who were likely to escape and evade would have done so. He could pick them up at the rendezvous and bring his strength up to twelve men plus Wegener. Three more would be needed for the helicopter.

He placed a call to Twenty-First Century Helicopters, ready to cut the connection if anyone sounded suspicious. No one did. "Mr. Dannemeier's" cover was still good, and so was his credit. The company would have one of its Mi-8s at the agreed point, at the agreed time.

Danilov hung up, nearly dropping the telephone in the process. He realized that his hands were sweating. He wiped them off on a towel. He had to appear completely in control of both himself and the situation if he was to secure Wegener's cooperation.

The analyst stuck his head into the office. "I am done with these," Danilov said, pulling the folders into a pile. "Find secure portable storage for them."

"Portable?" the man asked, then pulled his face straight as he remembered the penalty for questioning orders in the field.

Danilov nodded. "Portable. Also, have our medical technician start waking up Mr. Wegener, and somebody prepare a meal for him. I wish to talk with him again."

BOLAN SAT IN A BOOTH in a restaurant called the Eisbär—Polar Bear. Most of the walls were mirrors, and he couldn't help thinking what an appalling toll a bomb here would take, as the mirrors shattered and mowed down the customers.

One of his companions was Dieter, Hal Brognola's man in the BND. He had two more of his people on guard at the door, along with Ben Shlomo. Any bomb thrower was going to have to get past them.

The police might not be cooperating, but the BND seemed to think it owed Stony Man Farm or the Americans enough to put soldiers in the field. Not many, and they had orders to keep a low profile, but probably enough to help.

Much of the rest was up to the Kuhns.

"I think your suggestion of hiding under police protection is not a bad one, Mr. Metzger," Helmut Kuhn said. "It would be better if I was sure who the police were protecting, us or themselves."

"What do you mean by that, Grandfather?" Trudl asked.

Her grandfather's answer was delayed by the arrival of the waiter with a platter of veal, a bowl of red cabbage, a basket of bread and a bottle of chilled Piesporter wine. When the waiter had gone, Kuhn poured the wine before going on.

"I mean they might wish to prevent any more... amateur law-enforcement efforts. Not only by us, but by

Peter here. Do you think he would not listen if the police said that he should lie quiet or you would be charged with something?"

"What?"

"Illegal transport of weapons, for one thing. That can be tried under the terrorism laws, and it is a very serious matter. You would probably not be found guilty, but how long would it take? Would not Peter most likely obey the police, rather than subject you to such an ordeal?"

Bolan had the feeling that in some areas the "amateur" Helmut Kuhn was thinking ahead of the "professional" Executioner. It didn't bother him. He wasn't equally good at everything, and in fact had owed his life many times to people who knew things he didn't.

"It would certainly affect me," he said. "But your being in danger from roving Spetsnaz would do the same. Will do the same." He sipped his wine, with long-practiced skill in making one drink last a whole evening.

"The safehouse is an alternative," he added. "But how safe is it?"

"What do you mean?" Trudl asked.

"I mean that we don't know what Beck learned about your business, and what our missing mole has taken with him. At the rate the police are going at it, we might not learn for a while."

"All the more reason, then, for the safehouse," Kuhn said. "If the police think we are quietly under their control, they might not be so eager to investigate the Beck affair. I grant you, there were three murders. But one was a Turk, another a guard, and Beck himself was a 'cowboy' as you put it. If it does not get on the evening news that the police are dragging their feet—"

Bolan held up a hand. "All right. I can take a hint. You could even be right. But I think you and Trudl should be out of Berlin by tonight."

Over the rest of dinner they divided up their forces. Bolan would remain in Berlin, working with Dieter and the other BND men if he didn't need to go solo. The BND men had to stay closer to their offices and not disappear for days at a time, otherwise the low profile their agency was trying to keep would be blown.

Zev Ben Shlomo would go with the Kuhns, acting as security at the safehouse. Most of the security would depend on no one knowing they were there, however.

DANILOV HAD TWELVE MEN with him by the time he decided he couldn't afford to wait any longer. With the three in the helicopter, that made fifteen. They should certainly be enough, if they moved against Kuhn's refuge before it could be turned into a trap. Afterward they should be enough to guard both Wegener and Kuhn until they could be turned over to the men waiting at Raubenheim.

It was a pity that they had to crawl out of Berlin by truck. But Magirus-Deutz three-tonners roamed the roads around Berlin by the hundreds. Mi-8 helicopters were much less common and much more conspicuous.

Security was worth guarding, however. So far they seemed to be ahead of the enemy, or three of Bytkin's men wouldn't have made their way to the truck. Germans had both manpower and organization enough to do better. Either they were slow, or something was holding them back.

Perhaps the fear of scandal? Quite likely. But if they thought they had scandal to fear before, they should wait for Wegener's revelations. Even if he was making up half of it, as Danilov suspected he was, his fantasies would fill the evening news for months.

It wouldn't be as complete a victory as the success of Project Gamma would have been. But it would be enough to let Danilov return to his superiors with some of his mission accomplished. Perhaps even enough that they would send him out again, this time without the Trained Wolf to keep watch over his superior.

SCHÖNEFELD INTERNATIONAL Airport had been East Berlin's main field before unification. Now it served a limited number of flights, plus assorted air charter, air taxi and air cargo firms. It also virtually shut down at night, which made it an ideal departure point for the Kuhns.

Bolan stood on the ramp, watching Trudl climb gracefully into the JetRanger. Helmut Kuhn faced him, raising his voice to be heard over the whirling rotors and whining engine.

"You might need to get out of Berlin yourself in a hurry," he told the Executioner, handing him a business card. "If you do, call this number and ask for Barbarossa."

"As in Operation Barbarossa?" Bolan asked.

"The man prefers to think of Frederick Barbarossa, the medieval German emperor."

"The one who will rise if Germany ever needs a champion? He reminds me of King Arthur."

"You are a man with a broad base of knowledge, Mr. Metzger, in spite of pretending to be only a soldier. The man who will call you back is a helicopter pilot working for me."

The associations of the name *Barbarossa* made Bolan frown. "Not one of your 'special friends'?"

"An honest conservative, although I think he is a better helicopter pilot than he is a politician. But he knows that my friendship is worth much to him, and helping you ensures that friendship. You can trust him."

"Thank you, Mr. Kuhn."

"I'll see you again, Mr. Metzger. We have things to talk about, you and I."

Bolan didn't know what they could be, but he had a hunch that Kuhn was right. He also expected that Barbarossa would turn out to be reliable. Kuhn was a good picker, and got results out of the most unlikely kinds of people.

He waited until the JetRanger's lights vanished in the hazy night sky, then walked back to where Dieter and a companion stood guard over their car.

CHAPTER TWENTY-FOUR

The Mi-8 had started off life in a Polish factory. It had then served in the air force of the German Democratic Republic. When that service ceased to exist, the helicopter wasn't as state-of-the-art as the MiG-29 Fulcrums. The new united Germany put the Fulcrums into service as fighters and put the Mi-8 out to pasture with Twenty-First Century Helicopters.

Colonel Danilov established a relationship with the firm shortly after his emergence as Dannemeier, and pushed a good deal of business their way. There was no problem with chartering the Mi-8, with enough fuel to take it anywhere in Germany—fuselage tanks optional.

There was one problem, and right now the problem was sitting across the cabin from the Spetsnaz known as Sasha the Walrus. He was a junior accountant with the firm, who had to be in his hometown quickly because his mother was dying. The charter manager had insisted that they give him a lift, offering a discount if they did and threatening to refuse the charter if they didn't.

Since there was no time for Danilov to find another helicopter, the accountant went along. Sasha knew that the young man had probably signed his death warrant. He also knew it would be his own job to carry out the execution. The other two men in his team were both busy flying the noisy old helicopter.

The young man stretched and looked out the open door. It was hard to read his face in the dim cabin light, but the Walrus thought the man looked confused.

Then he crawled over to Sasha and put his mouth close to the Walrus's ear. "We should be over the Rhine by now. What's wrong?"

Sasha muttered something about head winds. The young man looked no less confused but less unhappy. Sasha used the time he'd bought to crawl forward and talk into the pilot's ear.

"Our passenger is nervous."

"You know what to do."

"Out?"

"No. The body might be found too soon."

"All right."

Sasha crawled back. He had to wait a few minutes, because the accountant was sitting too close to the door. If a struggle developed, one or both of them might fall out.

"Excuse me," the man said, "but I didn't think head winds were a problem this low."

"You've got your altitudes confused," the Walrus said. "It's up high that the winds are light. Down below—"

"What about the jet stream?" the man asked.

Sasha didn't know the jet stream from the Volga River, but he did know a man getting suspicious when he saw one. There was nothing to throw, and gunplay inside a helicopter was always a bad idea, so Sasha suddenly leaned back, rested his weight on his hands and kicked out with both feet.

His boots slammed into the accountant's chest. The Walrus heard ribs crunch and saw the man's expression change from annoyance to fear.

Before it could change any more, Sasha was across the cabin, chopping the man across the throat with the side of his left hand. The larynx shattered, the man's eyes bulged as he choked on fragments of larynx, then a tip of a shattered rib pierced his heart and his eyes rolled up in his head.

The Walrus waited until the man was still before hauling him feetfirst to the rear of the cabin and stuffing him into a corner under a tarpaulin. He'd turn up if the helicopter was thoroughly searched, but if that happened the mission was down the drain no matter what. If they won through to Raubenheim, one dead German more or less wasn't going to give anybody a fever.

From the cockpit, the pilot nodded approval. Sasha pulled out a length of sausage and began to carve off pieces with his knife, sticking them in his mouth on the point of the blade.

TRUDL KUHN LET her grandfather and Ben Shlomo into the safehouse, then followed. The Israeli was already beginning a security walkabout.

"Let me come with you," Helmut Kuhn said. "I am familiar with the place. I will notice if anything has been changed." To Trudl, her grandfather looked ready to drop in his tracks, but she knew that any hint of this would insult him. "Trudl can go to bed," he added.

"I think I had better come with both of you," Trudl said with as much dignity as she could manage. She actually was as tired as her grandfather seemed to be, but it seemed they both had too much pride to admit it. "I need to be familiar with all the security controls."

"In case you have to 'get the hell out of Dodge'?" Ben Shlomo asked with a weary grin.

"Where did you pick up that phrase?" she asked.

"Once, in—never mind where—the only movie theater in town was playing nothing but American Westerns for a week. American Westerns, with Arabic subtitles."

That didn't narrow the location too much. It also didn't surprise Trudl Kuhn. She was past being surprised at anything about either Zev Ben Shlomo or the man who called himself Peter Metzger.

WHEN COLONEL DANILOV boarded the Mi-8 at the rendezvous, the first thing he saw was Sasha the Walrus, munching on the heel of a sausage. The second thing was a tarpaulin-wrapped shape in the rear corner.

The pilot explained, and Danilov shrugged. "We had better bury him. There is soft ground between here and the truck."

"Do we have time?"

"Yes. I do not want the men aboard until just before we lift off. They will hide until then. A helicopter and a truck separately might not attract so much notice. A helicopter full of men is something to be remembered."

"When do we want to arrive?"

"Just after dawn. Our informant has poor night vision, and we can detect ambushes better."

"They can detect us better, as well."

"Then we take what we already have and fly it to Raubenheim," Danilov snapped. He hadn't realized until he spoke how close he was to drawing his PSM and shooting the cautious pilot.

He clasped his hands one over the other until they stopped quivering and his breath came normally. Nobody seemed to notice how close he had been to the edge of control.

It would have been foolish to shoot the pilot. They had only one other man able to fly the helicopter. If anything happened to him, they would be stranded in the middle of Germany.

"What about our friend?" Sasha asked. It took Danilov a moment to realize that the man was talking about Wegener.

Danilov made a gesture indicating that Wegener was sleeping. He wasn't only sedated, he was also in handcuffs. The colonel had assured the German that this was for his own protection, so that none of the nervous Spetsnaz men would think he was trying to escape and kill him.

It seemed to Danilov that Wegener hadn't taken much comfort from this fact. Indeed, it seemed that it was beginning to dawn on Wegener exactly what kind of situation he had put himself in, through working with "Herr Dannemeier."

IN BERLIN, Mack Bolan went to bed in what seemed a cold and empty bed over the garage.

He trusted Dieter and the other BND men to provide security, at least for the night. As for his mission—dealing with the Spetsnaz was no longer part of it until relations with the police eased. Moving against the mafiosi would be acceptable, but most of his targets were probably on the move themselves.

It would be days before Berlin settled down and was no longer a city looking suspiciously over its shoulder, ready to call the police—and with policemen on call at every corner. During that time, it probably was best for the Executioner to play the Invisible Man.

He'd be less likely to compromise his friends in the BND, essential for either mission. And he'd be much more likely to surprise his enemies, when he came out shooting at the end of that time.

IN VIRGINIA, Hal Brognola was working late.

Setting up things with the BND so that Striker didn't have to simply hop a plane out of Tegel back to the United States had used up a few favors. The BND was probably going to want all the data in the Beck files, or maybe even close down the organization entirely.

The big Fed realized that the first was inevitable and the second was going to happen anyway, no matter what German intelligence said. After the thirty-day cutoff, only a miracle could restore the credibility of a free-lance intelligence operation. Willi Beck was a man known for that kind of miracle, but he was dead.

By the time Brognola had finished on the phones and faxes to Germany, it was midafternoon and he had a deskful of routine business. It was amazing how little time was really spent in intelligence dealing with world-shaking matters. A lot of time was devoted to soothing the ruffled nerves of informants, information brokers and agents of other intel organizations.

After four hours of such glamorous work, Hal Brognola put on his suit coat and went home. It was a fine spring evening, but that didn't improve his mood.

What would really improve it, he decided, was to have Striker either home and out of that mess in Germany, or turned loose on those rogue Spetsnaz thugs. Right now Bolan could neither shift to another mission nor finish either of his German ones.

THE END of Hal Brognola's working day in Virginia saw a faint gray light in the eastern sky over Germany. As it strengthened, Trudl Kuhn woke from a dream of Peter

Metzger's embraces to find her pillow damp. It wasn't sweat, either—if anything, the room was chilly.

She was going to miss Peter when he returned to America—if that was where he came from. He was American by birth, she was sure, but she doubted that he had what other men would call a home, anywhere on earth.

She padded barefoot across the room and looked out into the half light between darkness and dawn. A faint breeze blew through the windows. Nobody could see her or any other sign that the house was inhabited now. She threw off her nightgown and did aerobic exercises naked in front of the window.

Ninety miles away, thirteen shadowy figures carrying long packages slipped from a Magirus-Deutz truck, across two fields and into a patch of woods. There they boarded a Mi-8 helicopter. The last man out of the truck wired a grenade to the ignition key. Anyone curious enough to try moving the truck would pay for that curiosity by destroying himself, the truck and the trail of the survivors of the Project Gamma Spetsnaz team.

As the sky turned pink, the whine of turbines split the air and the helicopter lifted into the sky.

CHAPTER TWENTY-FIVE

Hans Wegener awoke to find the floor and walls rattling and shaking under and around him. He also heard a hideous din that sounded like a helicopter low overhead, and the voices of several men. He thought they were speaking Russian, but it was difficult to tell over the rotor noise.

He was vaguely aware of somebody in coveralls squatting beside him, jerking up the sleeve of his shirt and jabbing a needle into his arm. Hard, too—the doctor who gave him his shots when he did his military service had been gentle by comparison.

The needle must have injected some sort of stimulant. Wegener felt the sleepiness, fatigue and confusion leave him. Fear promptly replaced it. He knew now that he was not under a helicopter but aboard one. Something big and military, judging from the size of the cabin, the austere furnishings and the abundant stenciling everywhere he could see.

And it *was* Russian that the men around him were speaking. At least a dozen of them, too, every one with a weapon in sight—submachine gun, assault rifle, pistol, as well as grenades and pouches that might hold things Wegener didn't want to think about.

He felt like a rabbit who had fled from the hunters only to fall among a pack of wolves. Indeed, where was that grim-looking man whom he had heard called the

Trained Wolf? He could see the man he had known as Dannemeier on a fold-down seat at the forward end of the cabin.

As if Wegener's look had called him, Dannemeier rose and came over to the German. Wegener tried to shift to a more comfortable position, and for the first time realized that he was handcuffed to a tie-down ring on the floor. Abandoning hope of comfort, he tried to at least sit up, to maintain some dignity.

Dannemeier looked down at Wegener's struggles for a moment, as he might have looked at the last writhings of a landed fish.

"Awake, I see."

"Uh," Wegener said.

"If you pretend to be asleep, we have other ways of waking you up. They won't be as gentle as the injection, believe me."

"I am awake."

"Good," Dannemeier said, then kicked Wegener in the stomach. The kick was hard enough to be horribly painful and make the German fight for breath. He was vaguely aware that it wasn't hard enough to knock him out. Dannemeier could go on kicking him like that for a long time, and he would be awake for all of it, until he was screaming for mercy with whatever breath he had left.

"That was just a sample of what you will get if you lie to us, or do anything else we consider uncooperative. I am an amateur at this. If it turns out you need more, I will turn you over to those of my men who are professionals. There is one, for example, who can use a file on a man's teeth to reduce him to a shrieking hulk in minutes. He learned in Afghanistan."

Wegener knew with dreadful certainty that he had jus been told that these men were indeed Russians, proba bly Spetsnaz. He also suspected that he was a dead man or they wouldn't have told him as much as they had.

He still tried to maintain some dignity. "I thought had cooperated very well, Mr.—"

"Refer to me as Colonel Danilov, if you please." The polite phrasing was balanced by another kick, this time to Wegener's groin. He would have screamed if he coul have found the breath.

"Yes, Colonel," Wegener finally managed to gasp. " have cooperated. I brought all the files. I will go on co operating. I—"

"Enough. The files are useful, of course. But you wil interpret everything in them for us. You will also tell us everything that you learned in the Beck organization that is not written down. If you do that, we might help you escape the penalty for treason."

The penalty for treason in Germany was life in prison. It didn't include either death or torture. Wegener had thought that life in prison was a fate worse than death. But then he hadn't known what kind of death he migh be facing.

"I will cooperate," Wegener said.

"I hope that is a promise you intend to keep. Now, the first question I must ask you is, have you warned Hel mut Kuhn about our planned attack on his little ref uge?"

Wegener looked blank. "I did not—"

The kick this time was to the side of his knee. Dani lov also waved one of his men over. The man knelt be side Wegener, drew a long sharp knife and held it with the point barely touching Wegener's right eyeball.

"You can interpret documents without one eye, testicles, fingers or quite a few other things," Danilov said. "It will be harder to live afterward without these things, of course, but the choice is yours."

"No," Wegener screamed. "I have not told him or anyone else. I did not know that data was in the files!"

"Somehow, I believe you," Danilov said.

Then the colonel turned away. "The son of a bitch has fainted again," he announced.

"I am sure we can detect any trap the fools set for us," Danilov told his men. "But I remind you, we want prisoners. Helmut Kuhn is the most valuable, but we might be able to bring him in if we find his granddaughter there. So she is to be left alone until she has done her work."

Afterward would be a different matter, as Danilov could tell from the faces of the men. Most of them had been picked for this mission because of their knowledge of German and their experience at covert operations and "wet work."

Some of them had gained that experience in Afghanistan. Trudl Kuhn would be begging for death long before her wish was granted.

"GRANDFATHER," Trudl called from upstairs. "I hear a helicopter. Did we ask for pickup? We just got here."

"I did not," Kuhn shouted back. As if by magic, Zev Ben Shlomo appeared at his side, hand hovering close to his holster.

"Trudl," Kuhn called again, "get your clothes on, something not too colorful, and good strong shoes. Then get down into the basement. If you hear anything at all suspicious, get into the tunnel and keep going."

The two men stood at the front door of the house, listening to the approaching helicopter. "Too big for most civilian types," Ben Shlomo said judiciously. "Could be American."

The Americans still had several bases in this area, but Kuhn shook his head. "It is too early for the day missions and too late for the night ones."

"An emergency mission?"

"Perhaps. Let us hope it is not an emergency for us."

That hope diminished every second. The helicopter was coming low, fast and straight for the house.

"Zev," Kuhn said, raising his voice now to be heard, "get out of sight. Secure the house, then see that Trudl reaches the tunnel and *keeps going!*" He put a hand on the Mossad agent's shoulder. "*Shalom,* my friend."

"*Auf wiedersehen,* old man," Ben Shlomo said. His grin was a trifle lopsided. He seemed to know, as did Kuhn, that talking of seeing each other again was more than optimistic, if this helicopter was what they both suspected.

Then Ben Shlomo vanished inside. He must have run down the stairs and opened the security panel without stopping to breathe. Doors started to slam and shutters slid closed almost at once. The house was completely buttoned up before the helicopter shot up over the trees between the house and the road.

It was an Mi-8, and it had barely room to land on the front lawn. Kuhn held on to his hat with both hands to keep it from being blown over the rooftop. For no particular reason, he felt that he would lose dignity if he faced kidnappers without his hat on.

He would lose almost as much dignity if he had sealed the house and frightened Trudl for no reason at all. Then he doors of the helicopter sprang open, and Helmut Kuhn stopped worrying about that.

They were well trained, these kidnappers. Not one of them pointed a weapon at him when they saw him standing unarmed and clearly visible. They deployed from around the helicopter, until their weapons covered all sides of the house and every approach to it.

Only then did the man who appeared to be their leader approach Kuhn. He was of medium height, stocky in a fashion that said "Russian" to the German, with blue eyes and a face that seemed made for intimidating people. He carried a submachine gun—one of those cut-down assault rifles, the AKR—and an automatic pistol was holstered at his hip.

"Good morning, Mr. Kuhn." His German was flawless. Kuhn decided to conceal his knowledge of Russian. "Taking air a bit earlier than usual?"

"If you are here, you know my schedule," Kuhn said. 'I am an early riser. If you live to my age, you will be one, too."

The blue eyes flickered. This man, Kuhn decided, was not as calm as he was pretending to be. He couldn't be pushed into major errors of judgment, and if Kuhn tried he would doubtless end up sedated or bound. But if polite remarks could push the man into the kind of small mistake that added up...

"Since you are awake and dressed for traveling, I suppose it would not be an imposition for you to join us in the helicopter?" Danilov asked. He managed not to be too sarcastic.

"Certainly." Kuhn stepped forward so briskly that he passed right between the two guards intended for him.

They had to hurry to take their assigned positions on either flank.

"Wait!" Danilov called. Kuhn stopped and turned around. This time his guards went on several steps ahead of him. The look their commander gave them would have curdled fresh milk.

"We need to search your house," Danilov said. "I would appreciate it if you would lend me your keys."

"You may have anything on me," Kuhn said, trying not to sound smug. "Unfortunately the security devices cannot be opened from the outside once they have been set."

"They can certainly be opened from the inside!" Danilov snapped.

"Of course, but we are outside, a fact that I am sure has not escaped your notice."

For a moment Kuhn thought Danilov was going to pistol-whip him, which would end this charade. He decided that he had gone too far, at least for now.

"Forgive me. I did not mean to imply that you lack judgment. I merely indicated that I cannot help you."

"You can help us very easily," Danilov said. He signaled to one of his men, who came forward with a large knife. "Whoever is in there will hardly like hearing you scream, as we carve pieces off you."

Kuhn kept a grin off his face with an effort. Every minute these people wasted in the hope of getting into the house was a minute more for the Samson Button to do its work. He raised his voice, to be sure that everyone around the house—and inside it as well—would hear him.

"You can do as you please. But there is no one inside to be moved by my screams. Also, I am an old man. You

might want to have a doctor examine me, before you
begin the kind of interrogation for which you are famous. He will tell you that I am likely to die under it,
and everything I know will die with me."

And if that didn't spur them into action inside the
house, he had badly misjudged both the Israeli and his
granddaughter.

Danilov cupped his hands and shouted in Russian.
Kuhn kept his face immobile as he realized the officer
was calling for his demolition experts. He hoped the
charges wouldn't go off too soon.

Then the helicopter's turbines whined into life, and
the rotors' tidal wave of churning air made Kuhn grip his
hat again. The Mi-8 lifted off, flew in a circle low over
the house and landed a hundred yards away, toward the
grove of trees that hid the exit from the tunnel.

Kuhn again forced his face to remain a mask. It was a
pity that they had moved the helicopter out of range. It
would be even more of a pity if it collapsed the tunnel,
but that was unlikely. The tunnel was solidly built, and
in places nearly twenty feet underground. Besides, if it
did collapse after Trudl and Ben Shlomo passed through
it, it might damage the helicopter.

Then Kuhn's guards were practically dragging him
away, as four men started unloading green canvas
pouches from their backpacks and placing them against
the front door.

"ARE YOU CARRYING your Walther?" Ben Shlomo
asked. There was a suspicious bulge in the waistband of
Trudl's slacks.

"Yes."

"I hope you are not—"

"I hope *you* are not going to waste our time arguing with me," Trudl snapped. "I am not going to take on a squad of Spetsnaz with a pistol. I am also not going out of here unarmed and helpless."

With the argument put that way, Ben Shlomo saw the sense in it. He and Trudl might have to split up in order to evade the assault team successfully. The Spetsnaz would be short of time; they might not be able to manage a serious pursuit. But the last-ditch effort of the Spetsnaz wasn't the only possible danger.

"Very good," he said. He knelt and twisted the Samson Button. "Now let us run! The tunnel may be strong but it is old and that will be a powerful blast. I do not want to be any closer to it then I have to."

Trudl sat down and put her feet on the steps, then clapped a hand to her mouth. "Good God! Did you send the distress signal?"

"It went out automatically when the doors and shutters slammed, and I keyed the radio to the special frequency Peter Metzger gave us, too. Help will be on the way. Now move, or I will kick you down the steps!"

Trudl stuck out her tongue at him, then vanished into the shadows. A moment later Ben Shlomo followed. Twenty-two seconds later, the timer swung the cupboard shut and started the fuse on the explosive charge in the dummy oil tank.

At Schönefeld Airport, the ringing of a telephone awoke Klaus Berger, dozing on a bench in one corner of a hangar.

"Barbarossa here," he said.

"Barbarossa, this is Siegfried." Berger recognized the voice. He had dealt with the BND man who called himself Siegfried.

"Shall I start up?" He looked across the hangar to the Bell 206 parked in a dimly lit corner. It looked down for maintenance, but in fact it was fully fueled. It would take one man two minutes to have it ready for takeoff.

"Make all preparations except start-up," Siegfried directed. "Parsifal will come with two men, and you will pick up a fourth at a location to be designated."

"At your service," Berger said.

The prospect of actually flying a helicopter into something like a combat situation made him feel like a teenager. He decided that politics would never again hold the attraction they had. He would fly until he got too old, then settle down with some nice girl and raise children to be anything but politicians.

THE RINGING TELEPHONE didn't wake up the Executioner. He was already awake, dressed and fully equippped.

"Metzger here."

"Parsifal. Barbarossa is alerted. We will make pickup at your location."

"Condition Five?"

"As far as we can tell."

That meant an armed assault on the safehouse was actually in progress. Bolan frowned. Had Helmut Kuhn only ended up playing bait for the Spetsnaz holdouts?

Maybe, and if so that was his right. But it didn't help matters that he might have involved Trudl, as well.

TRUDL AND BEN SHLOMO beat the explosion out of the tunnel by less than thirty seconds. They saved that margin by shutting only every second door they encountered.

From inside the grove, they watched the old guest house hurl smoke, chunks of stone and steel, and gouts of flame in all directions. A secondary explosion followed, as the shock wave touched off the newly rigged detonators on the Spetsnaz demolition charges.

They saw one Spetsnaz man fly into the air, and thought they saw pieces of others joining the rain of debris.

They didn't see what both of them hoped for, the helicopter crumpling under the weight of falling wreckage or bursting into flame. It rocked on its landing gear, its rotors flapped, and Trudl thought she saw windows breaking and rivets popping. But as the blast died away, the helicopter was still there.

The guest house, however, was sinking into a pile of smoking rubble. One wall and parts of two others still stood, but the rest had collapsed on itself.

Through his binoculars, Ben Shlomo studied the remaining men moving around the house. "I see two, three, four—ah, there's your grandfather—and another who looks like he's giving orders..." He was silent a moment, then continued, "Six left, I think, plus whoever is in the helicopter. Samson did better when he pulled the temple down."

"Yes, but there was no one coming to chase off the rest of the Philistines, and we are not buried under the temple ourselves."

"Are you sure you have *no* Jewish ancestors? Arguing about the holy books that way is one of our bad habits."

"As you say, it is a bad habit. No, I am only a woman who has been living with fear and that damned Samson Button for a week!"

Ben Shlomo put his hand on hers, and she didn't pull it away. With any luck, her time of fear and his time in Berlin were about over, and the change would be a relief to both of them.

CHAPTER TWENTY-SIX

Bolan hadn't expected his pickup to land on the roof of the garage. There had to be a dozen local and German laws against it, not to mention power lines, telephone poles and other problems for low-flying helicopters.

But there it was, a Bell 206 LongRanger, the younger, heftier brother of the JetRanger. Somebody with red hair and a grim look was sitting in the pilot's seat, and Dieter was waving from the door. Bolan scrambled up the rusty ladder to the roof, dashed across it and barely got inside the door before the aircraft lifted off.

He slid into the copilot's seat, turned to thank Dieter, then nearly went for his Beretta. Two dark mustached men were sitting in the cabin, wearing stocking caps and dark coveralls. One had an MP-5 in his lap, the other held a full-size G-3 assault rifle upright beside his seat and both wore holsters.

They were two of Beck's Turks, from the shoot-out at the construction site. In fact, the one with the G-3 was the one Bolan had knocked to the ground.

Dieter needed only a look at Bolan's face to realize that explanations were badly needed. "These are men from the Beck organization—"

"I recognize them," Bolan said evenly. He knew enough Turkish to say, "And how are you and your friend?"

The man with the G-3 said, in English and in the same tone, "My brother Mustafa was murdered by Beck's traitor. Bora and I will be much better when we have avenged him."

Dieter nodded. "I was looking for some—backup?— for you. Trained, reliable men, not associated with the BND. We could not take the field unless the police requested, but Bora and Ismail could."

They certainly looked tough and competent, and Ismail at least had the best of reasons for being loyal as well. Bolan decided that last-minute recruits were better than no recruits at all, if one was going to shoot it out with a squad of Spetsnaz.

By now the helicopter was over the Köpenick area of southeastern Berlin. As the built-up area vanished behind, the pilot began to gain altitude and speed.

"We need to hurry," Dieter said. "Not just because of what might be happening at the safehouse, either. Somehow the alarm went to the chartered helicopter. Those pilots took off also, and are on their way to rescue Helmut Kuhn."

"Why didn't—" Bolan began, then answered his own question. Security. The less the pilots knew, the less they could reveal.

Which was fine, except that security had left them not knowing enough to stay out of a firefight or an ambush. The number of innocents who needed the Executioner's help had just increased by two.

TRUDL WAS RIGHT to suspect that the Mi-8 was damaged in the blast. If it hadn't been moved, in fact, it would undoubtedly have caught fire and been totally destroyed.

Colonel Danilov was painfully aware of this as he stood up. The pain in his ears, in most of his joints and in his stomach as he surveyed the ruins of the house and the bloody fragments that were all that remained of four of his men.

He whirled on Helmut Kuhn, his hand on the butt of his PSM. If that fascist bastard so much as twitched an eyebrow...

But he didn't speak or change expression. Kuhn only rose slowly to his feet, brushing the dirt and bits of debris off his clothes. Their fine gray wool was charred in a few places and dirty in more, Danilov noted with savage satisfaction.

Danilov pulled his hand away from his weapon. Like Wegener's intelligence value, Kuhn's hostage value was too great to ignore. Losing his temper would merely end the mission when it was on the verge of as much success as he could now hope for.

Or was it? Danilov told Sasha the Walrus to guard the prisoner and make a brief search of the rubble, then hurried to the helicopter. There he found popped rivets and cracked windows, as well as bent frames, wrinkled plates and a burst hydraulic line. The last was the most serious.

"I can fix the aircraft so it will make one more flight, if we do not have to go too fast or too high," the pilot said.

"That is all we need. How long will it take?"

"Maybe half an hour."

"If you can do it in less—oh, the devil's grandmother! If you can do it at all, you'll get the Order of the Red Banner, or whatever they call it these days."

The pilot saluted. "I serve the Soviet Union."

He climbed back into his helicopter, while Colonel Danilov walked around it again. This time he noticed something odd on the ground.

No, *in* the ground. A shallow trench ran across the field, from the direction of the house on one side of the helicopter, toward a grove of trees on the other side. It looked very much as if something underground had collapsed, making the earth above sink down.

Something underground. Such as a tunnel, running from the house to the grove? A tunnel, which had served as an escape route for the others in the house, the others Kuhn had lied about?

The others who had murdered four of Danilov's soldiers?

For a moment the colonel wrestled with a fiercely compelling impulse to go back to the house and shoot Helmut Kuhn in the stomach, simply for the pleasure of watching him die slowly. In the next moment he pulled out his command radio and called up the Walrus.

The orders were simple, coded and quickly obeyed. In five minutes four men besides Danilov were moving in open formation toward the grove.

FROM INSIDE THE GROVE, Zev Ben Shlomo and Trudl Kuhn watched the Spetsnaz approach. Trudl knew now exactly how a bird being stalked by a cat had to feel.

Except that she was a bird with broken wings, who couldn't fly away before the claws and teeth sank into her flesh.

Her stomach twisted and she swallowed bile.

"Do not panic now, Trudl," Ben Shlomo said. "I would not blame you if you did, but it will not help.

They do not have us surrounded, so you had better run while you can.''

He rolled so that she could reach into his backpack. She pulled out an MP-5 K and stared at it.

"That is yours, and the ammunition pouch, too. Five more 30-round magazines, as I remember it.''

"You said—''

"I was wrong. Do you know how to work that?''

"Peter taught me to use the regular one, with the folding stock.''

Ben Shlomo had been among other things a firearms instructor for the Mossad, with a specialty in foreign weapons. He now gave the quickest weapons course of his life—how to load, hold, aim, fire and reload the supercompact MP-5 K, by preference shooting your enemy but above all not shooting yourself.

It took him one minute. He reflected that this was probably the last course he'd ever teach.

At the end of the minute Trudl slung the subgun and almost but not quite saluted. Ben Shlomo kissed her hand, then half rose and kissed her on the cheek.

"Now *shalom,* Trudl." Then he added a phrase in Arabic.

"What does that mean?''

"It means may the fleas of a thousand camels infest your—hair—if you do not run like the wind!''

Apparently Trudl didn't wish such an infestation. She vanished into the trees. Ben Shlomo waited for the rattle of automatic-weapons fire that would mean she had been spotted, or the scream that would mean she had been hit.

He heard neither. After another minute or two, he crept forward and unfolded the stock of his own MP-5.

He would have liked something on the order of a Galil, or even one of those overweight German G-3s. With that he might have even taken out the helicopter.

But the cards were dealt, and his hand could have been a lot worse. Anyway it was the only game he had left to play.

He jacked a round into the chamber, snapped off the safety, shifted a pine cone out from under his left thigh and settled down to wait.

THEY WERE OVER A STRETCH of forest that Bolan couldn't put a name to, when the pilot called Dieter forward. The Executioner slipped out of the seat so that the BND man could have access to the radio.

The conversation was entirely in German, and half of it was in code. Bolan relaxed, trusting Dieter and saving adrenaline for later. He was going to need it.

"That was a report from our office in Fulda," he said. "A MiG-29 on a training flight reported an explosion approximately where the safehouse is located. It made a second pass, and identified a red-and-white Mi-8 at or near the site of the explosion. It has the fuel to remain on station."

The phrase "MiG-29" made Bolan start, until he remembered that the Luftwaffe had taken over a whole squadron of the high-performance jet fighters from the defunct GDR air force. It made perfectly good sense for one to be flying over the Fulda Valley.

It would make even more sense to have a few more in the air. Bolan grabbed Dieter's shoulder. "See if they can scramble a few more jets. Tell them not to go too low, or they could spook the bad guys. Also tell them to look out for us and for the charter JetRanger."

The conversation this time dragged out, thanks to poor radio reception. When Dieter finally pulled off the headset, he was frowning. "I think I got through. They cannot go too low anyway, because of the hills. The pilot who made the original sighting said he will try to home friends in on the Mi-8 if it takes off. I don't know if I reached them about the JetRanger."

Bolan gripped the back of the seat and let out a deep breath. About all they could hope for now was that the crew of the JetRanger knew a firefight *before* they flew into it. That, and Trudl Kuhn's not being bound hand and foot aboard the Mi-8.

COLONEL DANILOV'S first sign of an enemy in the grove was a bullet kicking up dust inches from his right arm. He rolled by sheer reflex away from the point of impact, and three more bullets missed by a wider margin.

Not a safe one, though. The bastard in the grove had nearly hit him on the first burst. Danilov lay behind a mound of earth and studied the grove. No smoke, no trail, nothing moving. The range was about right for a submachine gun, though he wished they had a grenade launcher....

From inside the grove, an automatic weapon rattled. It sounded like a submachine gun, too, and this time the burst was on. A Spetsnaz trooper rolled into view to Danilov's left, thrashing wildly, clawing at a bloody chest and belly, actually biting at the sod in his agony.

The enemy's weapon fired another burst. The Spetsnaz trooper's agony ended.

So did the mystery of the enemy's location. Danilov saw a bush move in a way that no breeze could explain. He pointed, then signaled.

From right and left, AK-74s fired into the bush. Their green tracers were almost invisible in the morning light, but dust and leaves flew from where the rounds hit.

While the AK-74s fired, Danilov rolled again, pulling out a grenade. The enemy was pinned down; now to finish him off. If it was somebody with hostage or intelligence value, too bad, but it had been the other man's choice to fight.

The grenade hit a tree above the bush, bounced into the top of it and rolled away before it exploded. Danilov cursed in both German and Russian. They didn't have enough ammunition to let the AK-74s pour in another continuous stream of covering fire.

It would still be a while before the helicopter was fixed. Danilov and his men weren't going anywhere until it was. So they had time—plenty of time to outwait one opponent they'd already fixed in position, then finish him off.

ZEV BEN SHLOMO had planned to hold the Russians in play as long as possible. Trudl was clear of the grove, but needed time to get farther if possible. Also, the longer he tied up the Spetsnaz, the better chance of somebody coming along to at least take out their transportation.

That Mi-8 was the key to the whole situation, and once again Ben Shlomo would have sold his soul for a G-3 with a grenade launcher. One grenade through the cockpit window, or even a few tracer rounds into the fuel tank, and the Mi-8 would be history.

His plans fell apart, because the Spetsnaz turned out to be almost as good as the stories about them said. He engaged only two and killed one before the others pinned him down, then another threw a grenade.

The Russian probably didn't realize what a good jo[ ]
he'd done, Ben Shlomo thought. That grenade burs[ ]
high, and a lot of the fragments went into the bushes o[ ]
the trees.

Quite a few went into him. His arm hurt, his nec[ ]
hurt, there was blood in his mouth, and from the way hi[ ]
breathing felt he was damned sure one lung was punc[ ]
tured. There was an awful pain in his back that coul[ ]
have been a big fragment going through from behind.

He wasn't going to last long enough to do more dam[ ]
age, unless he could get those bastards close. How?

They knew about Trudl. She'd be one of their mai[ ]
targets. If they thought they had her at their mercy...

He tried calling softly, pitching his voice high. It didn'[ ]
sound like a natural woman's voice, but it would help i[ ]
they thought she was wounded. They'd fall all ove[ ]
themselves to patch her up so they could torture her t[ ]
death afterward.

"Grandfather..." Ben Shlomo moaned in German
"Grandfather, help me. It hurts."

Even to his own ears, Zev Ben Shlomo sounded con[ ]
vincingly pathetic. But then he had been a fairly goo[ ]
amateur actor in school, and what was a field agent bu[ ]
another kind of actor?

DANILOV COULD BARELY understand the words, the[ ]
were so broken by pain and despair. But it was a woman[ ]
and the only woman around here who would be callin[ ]
for her grandfather was Trudl Kuhn. The next bes[ ]
prize—and the best way of making Helmut Kuhn co[ ]
operative and talkative.

Danilov wasn't quite such a fool as to lead a mad dash into the grove. He sent all the spare AK-74 magazines to one man, who was to hold his position. The colonel and the remaining men were to make a wide sweep around the enemy's flank. If Trudl Kuhn did have it in her to shoot again, she would be cut down with no danger to her attackers.

The maneuver was simple enough that even Danilov had no trouble knowing what came next. In ten minutes he and the other men were approaching the bush from the left rear.

BEN SHLOMO WAS HANGING on to consciousness by the grace of God and some leaves he'd stuffed into the wound in his back. That had partly reinflated the lung, even if the leaves hurt like the devil. They would also leave the wound horribly dirty, but Ben Shlomo didn't really expect to live long enough for an infection to develop.

The bushes were crackling now. He shifted, cautiously in case the Spetsnaz had left somebody watching from in front. They probably had. They weren't stupid.

He saw three figures looming behind a curtain of leaves. Another few steps and he'd have a clear shot.

Another few steps and they'd see he wasn't Trudl Kuhn, and just let fly.

A good target was no use to a dead man.

He found the strength to lift and swing the MP-5. He couldn't recite the whole "Hear, oh Israel..." prayer, but what he was able to mutter as the submachine gun bucked in his hands would have to do.

He lost consciousness even as the return fire slammed into him. Pain and his life left him at almost the same moment.

DANILOV CRAWLED out of the grove, dragging a dying man behind him. The other was already dead. The colonel shot the dying man, then stood and stepped into the clearing, hands raised so that he wouldn't be shot by his own man.

He thought he wouldn't care who was waiting, after the stupidity of falling into the trap that little bald Jew had laid for him. But he was relieved to see a friendly face behind the AK. He was even more relieved when the rifleman took the lead as they walked back toward the helicopter.

Danilov wasn't just afraid of more traps. He was beginning to be afraid to have any of his own men behind him.

In a muddy ditch under the roots of a poplar tree, Trudl Kuhn wept silently for Zev Ben Shlomo. Tears cut tracks in the mud on her face. But there was no mud on her hands, or on her weapons. They were ready, and so was she.

Ten minutes north of the safehouse, the JetRanger rocketed along, skids only feet above the hillcrests and treetops.

Three minutes behind it was Klaus Berger's Long-Ranger. Bolan had made every adjustment he could think of to his weapons and was now watching the Turks work on theirs. Klaus Berger flew the helicopter as if he was part of it, and Dieter now occupied the copilot seat permanently as he tried to raise the JetRanger.

All he could reach was the MiG-29, and the fighter was encountering scattered clouds that affected the pilot's ability to observe the ground. Bolan hoped that the weather wasn't about to deteriorate. A helicopter chase was quite enough of a challenge without that.

CHAPTER TWENTY-SEVEN

Danilov returned to the Mi-8 to find the repairs almost completed. Or at least that was what the crew said.

"What do you mean 'almost'?" he snarled. "Will the aircraft fly or not?"

The pilot looked at his watch. "Right now, it could get off the ground, then come straight back down. If you want more, let me strengthen the connection on the broken line."

"How long will that take?"

"Five to ten minutes, if I don't have anyone bothering me while I'm working." The pilot turned away, unaware of how close he'd come to being shot.

Danilov let out a stream of obscenities, then climbed into the cabin to check on the prisoners.

Both were conscious. Hans Wegener was clearly in pain from his taste of Spetsnaz interrogation techniques, and scared nearly out of whatever wits he'd had.

Helmut Kuhn was sitting cross-legged on the floor, his cuffed hands in his lap. Danilov couldn't look at the man without envying both his serenity and his being so limber at nearly eighty.

"Is there anything you wish, Mr. Kuhn?" Danilov asked. He decided that Kuhn would get the soft treatment for as long as possible, and not only because of his age. It might impress Wegener with what he could hope for if he really cooperated.

Danilov had no objection to subjecting Beck's man to a full interrogation, but there might not be a chance for that. The more intelligence Wegener yielded voluntarily, the more expendable he became—and Danilov was staring in the face a situation where he might not be able to get everyone back to base.

Hundreds of kilometers of potentially hostile country lay between him and Raubenheim. Potentially, because having two German hostages might disarm resistance. Even one might be enough, and if he had to choose, Danilov would prefer to be able to choose Kuhn.

Kuhn replied to Danilov with a thin smile, then held up his hands. "I would prefer to either have a seat or to have these removed. I have arthritis in the knees that makes sitting on the floor this way highly uncomfortable. I might faint."

And if he did, reviving a man of his age could be a tricky business. The team had a good field medic, with the latest in German medicines and equipment. Still, he was trained more for the wounds of healthy young soldiers than for emergency geriatric medicine.

"You will be safer with your hands cuffed," Danilov replied. "My men would prefer not to have to guard their backs even from you. But you may certainly have a seat."

Danilov personally helped Kuhn to one of the fold-down seats and lowered him into it. He thought of strapping the old man in, but decided against it. With arthritis in his knees and nearly eighty years in his bones, could Kuhn really move fast enough to do any harm, when he had no use of his hands?

Then the Walrus thrust his head into the cabin. "I hear helicopters, Colonel."

"Two?"

"One close, and I think another farther off."

Danilov jumped to the ground and stared at the tree-tops and the sky above them. He could hear the rotors of one helicopter, certainly, and the sky was clouding over, so that accursed MiG-29 was nowhere in sight.

If the oncoming helicopter was armed and alert, they would have to try evading it on foot, which meant the end of the hostages. But if it was some civilian blundering into the area...

"Everyone get inside the helicopter," he shouted. "Quick. We want everything to look normal."

Then he jumped back in and dragged Hans Wegener to his feet.

"You can be useful sooner than you thought. I want you to come with me to call that helicopter down. We are going to try to capture it."

Wegener gagged with the pain as the colonel hauled him to his feet. He stumbled as he climbed down from the helicopter, but he kept going. He knew what would happen if he didn't, even without seeing the automatic in the colonel's hand.

TRUDL KUHN NOW realized that creeping back to the house wasn't the wisest thing she could have done. She would have been hidden from any search the Russians could make if she'd stayed in the ditch. Now it was only luck that was hiding her.

But she had to see for herself what had happened to her grandfather. She had just enough sanity to know she couldn't rescue him herself. But she knew, however, that anything she learned would help Peter Metzger do the work.

So she was barely a hundred yards from the house when the JetRanger came into view. She could see the two men waiting for it, and that one of them was clearly not feeling well. A prisoner, a wounded Spetsnaz?

Whoever the cripple was, the other was definitely in charge. She was almost certain that he was the same man she'd seen leading the surviving Spetsnaz back to the helicopter after Ben Shlomo's death. It had been a brief look at long distance, but what Trudl had been through the past few days had improved her memory for faces.

She was certain the men were setting a trap for the incoming helicopter. If it was Peter Metzger, he might shoot his way out of it. If it was someone else—an "innocent" as he called them—they were in trouble unless someone warned them.

Unless she warned them, at the risk of revealing her position and joining her grandfather in death or as a hostage.

Death held surprisingly little terror for her. She had settled that in her mind when she heard Ben Shlomo's last fight. But capture by the Spetsnaz... Her stomach turned over, and she felt cold sweat prickle all over her.

Or could she force them to kill her? The H&K might be good for that, at least, and there was always the old business of saving the last bullet for yourself.

She had laughed at such scenes in adventure movies. She decided she would never laugh at them again—if she ever got a chance to see another one.

Now the helicopter was above the trees, slowing as it approached the rubble of the house. It was the chartered JetRanger, and she could see the two civilian pilots in the cockpit. Peter could hardly be riding in that one. Trudl thought she saw a second speck in the sky behind it, but couldn't be sure. It was too far off to affect the outcome of this trap, anyway.

Rolling over on her back, she pointed the little submachine gun toward a patch of sky just to the left of the helicopter, and squeezed the trigger. Then she swung the gun toward the right, to make sure that a few bullets would hit—enough to notice, but not enough to bring the helicopter down.

She could hardly have achieved better results if she'd set off a bomb. The JetRanger reared back like a startled horse as the pilot yanked on the controls. A few more bullets, from the helicopter on the ground, stitched its belly. Then it was climbing rapidly out of range to join what definitely was a second helicopter, swinging in a wide circle around the battlefield.

Trudl hadn't risen to her feet, but her movement on nearly bare ground had revealed her location. Men began to climb out of the helicopter, guns in hand.

Then suddenly one of the men she'd seen headed toward her at a lumbering run. She was no longer so sure that he was injured or a prisoner, not the way he was coming on. She thought she heard him calling for help, but could that be a trick?

Yes. The man was trying to trick her into letting him get close, thinking he was hurt or afraid to shoot. There was an easy response to that trick, and she gave it by rolling over and drilling a 10-round burst at Hans Wegener.

Only three bullets hit him, as Trudl wasn't a complete master of her new weapon. But three 9 mm rounds were quite enough to stretch Hans Wegener lifeless on the trampled ground.

Trudl Kuhn would have died in the next moment, if Danilov hadn't been between her and his men. Before they could move to gain a clear field of fire, he shouted, "Take her alive, you fools."

Nobody fired, but nobody moved, either. Danilov realized that he had asked more of his men than even Spetsnaz were willing to give. In a rare moment of understanding, he knew that he also wouldn't be ready to charge across open ground in the face of a submachine gun, even in a woman's hands.

It tasted foul to see a woman who was less afraid of dying than Spetsnaz troops, but he had seen it and there was no changing it. The only thing left to do was return to the Mi-8, contact one of those helicopters and warn them that Helmut Kuhn was aboard.

That should at least allow a dignified retreat to Raubenheim—and Helmut Kuhn wasn't without intelligence value himself, once he was where he could be interrogated without interference.

BOLAN WAS ABOUT to order Klaus Berger to land, then lead Dieter and the Turks into action on the ground, when the Mi-8 came on the radio.

The message was short. They had Helmut Kuhn aboard, and his safety depended on their safe departure. If anyone didn't believe them . . .

A tall, silver-haired figure appeared and jumped down from the right door of the helicopter.

The man made the two Spetsnaz flanking him look like servants rather than guards. But it was unmistakably Helmut Kuhn, handcuffed and looking rather tired, but alive and in one piece.

For once Bolan agreed with a Spetsnaz officer—the voice on the radio certainly had a field-grade bark to it. Keeping Kuhn in one piece was a good idea. He wouldn't stay that way in the middle of a firefight, still less in a crashed helicopter.

Besides, Bolan had seen something or someone moving on the ground about a hundred yards from the helicopter, about where the JetRanger crew had reported taking fire. They'd said it looked like a woman shooting at them, which meant Trudl, unless the world had gone completely crazy in the past few minutes.

Bolan promised safe conduct as long as Helmut Kuhn was alive and well, and the Spetsnaz officer acknowledged. Two minutes later, the Mi-8's rotors swung slowly, then blurred into full rotation, and the battered machine clumsily lifted off.

The two Bell machines landed, to secure Trudl and check for damage to the JetRanger. Klaus Berger gave as his professional pilot's opinion that they had time for this.

"That Mi-8 is damaged," he said. "If it can reach a Russian base in the East, that is about all it is good for."

That could still be enough. The Russians had a handful of bases in what had been East Germany. Some of these were virtually joint operations with the Germans. Others were closed to everybody except official NATO observers under strict conditions.

If the Mi-8 reached one of those bases, the Spetsnaz men would probably never come to trial. They would be smuggled home, to reappear with new identities in Germany a few years later, or strengthen the ranks of the hard-liners' storm troops.

As for Helmut Kuhn, the German authorities would certainly ask for his return. They might get him back. Or they might receive his body, after his death from a "heart attack." Or they might receive nothing, except a claim that he had suffered delusions of imprisonment, escaped and vanished.

Communism might be dead. Russians capable of ruthlessly playing the old kind of games were alive and numerous.

TRUDL KUHN'S NERVES finally got the better of her when the Russian helicopter lifted off with her grandfather aboard. She curled up on the ground, and was nearly in the fetal position when she heard another helicopter landing.

That had to be Peter. She forced her arms and legs to uncurl, and shakily got to her feet. It would never do to have him see her frightened out of her wits.

Then he was there, big, dark and comforting as he put his arms around her and let her shake and sob against his chest and shoulder. When she was cried out, she stepped back and stared at him.

"What about my grandfather?"

"The Russians have him on the way to one of their remaining bases over to the East. We're trailing them. Our BND connections are arranging for refueling for us, and for air surveillance of all the Russian bases."

"What good will that do?" Trudl snapped. With half her mind, she felt that if she just became angry enough, a solution would pop out of thin air. The other half knew this was ridiculous.

"We'll know where he goes," he said. "Those Russian bases are ultimately under German law. If they harbor murderers and kidnappers, the Russians could lose German economic assistance. They need machinery and management experts a lot more than they do a bunch of rogue Spetsnaz.

"Now, we've got a police helicopter on the way. We'll stay here until they arrive, then they can take you—"

"The police will take me nowhere," Trudl said firmly. "I am coming with you"

For once Bolan seemed to be at a loss for words. Trudl pressed her advantage. "I agree that it might not be safe for me to stay here alone. But you will lose time waiting for the police helicopter. The fastest solution is for me to come with you."

"She is right, Mr. Metzger," one of the helicopter pilots said. "Her weight will not affect our range or speed, once we have refueled."

"Okay, Trudl. Welcome aboard."

Five minutes later, they were flying along the Fulda Valley. From the rear seat of the JetRanger Trudl Kuhn looked out at German land where, for nearly two generations, the Americans had expected to fight Russians. Now, instead of Russians marching east through the Fulda Gap, Germans were flying west to put their united country in order.

Trudl looked down. The country passing below looked too peaceful for such scenes. Even the smoke from the ruins of the safehouse was invisible behind them.

CHAPTER TWENTY-EIGHT

The Fulda Gap and the old border were far behind the Mi-8 now. Colonel Danilov kept looking out the window, which always showed the same thing—blue sky overhead, with only a low ground haze to mar the visibility. The clouds farther west were staying there.

Low ground haze wouldn't hide them from much of anything, least of all interceptors with look-down radar. If the shield named Helmut Kuhn failed to block those interceptors, Danilov and his men were dead.

Sunlight sparkled off a canopy high up in the blueness. It was a MiG-29, maybe the same one refueled or another one called up while the first of the pack landed. Danilov was less concerned about the insult of having a Russian-built plane chasing him than about the MiG-29's potential.

In the hands of a good pilot—and the Luftwaffe was good, no doubt about it—the sinister-looking fighter was one of the few in the world that could stay with a helicopter without stalling in. The pilot would need not only skill but luck, and orders that he be willing to risk a low-altitude ejection, but the MiG was equipped for that, too.

Danilov went forward, sparing a glance for Kuhn. The old man seemed to be asleep. Should the medic examine him? Perhaps the stress of the day's events were finally taking its toll.

The colonel entered the cockpit. The control panel showed a large number of gauges either not registering at all or registering past the danger line.

"I have sent out the signal you gave me, and the base has acknowledged," the pilot said. "I do not know what you expect anyone at Raubenheim to do, when we're still forty kilometers out."

"I expect you to fly this helicopter, instead of spouting defeatist talk."

"Comrade Colonel, this helicopter should not be flying at all. If it reaches Raubenheim safely, I will begin to believe in God, or at least in angels holding up lucky aviators."

Danilov couldn't even take the satisfaction of cursing the pilot. He needed the man with a clear head and both hands on the controls too badly. The copilot was almost as good, but "almost" could kill them all.

The copilot was now looking out his window. When he turned back to the pilot and tapped him on the shoulder, there was something in his face that Danilov didn't care for.

The two pilots looked at each other, and Danilov became even more nervous.

"What is it?"

"I think we have more than those fighters to worry about," the pilot replied. He couldn't take his hands off the controls, but the copilot pointed.

Danilov needed his binoculars to see what the copilot was pointing at. Then he knew that his own face could hardly be one to inspire confidence.

Three helicopters were paralleling the Mi-8's course just above the treetops. One of them looked like that damned JetRanger, with civilian markings but obviously some sort of elite commandos aboard.

The other two were unmistakably late-model Hueys. They were the transport model rather than those lethal HueyCobra attack helicopters, but that hardly mattered. They could outmaneuver even a healthy Mi-8. They could probably close on this cripple until someone in the door could hit it with a pistol or even a rock, let alone a machine gun.

"I'm going to open the doors and post men with AKs at all of them," Danilov said.

"Are you sure that is wise, Comrade Colonel?" the pilot asked.

"Of course it is very foolish," Danilov snapped. "As anyone can see, I was dropped on my head as a child. You, on the other hand, were dropped on your balls, and so have none!"

The pilot looked as if he would give ten years off his life to leave the controls and punch Danilov in the face.

"Comrade Colonel, the open doors will increase the drag still further. This will reduce our speed and increase our fuel consumption and possibly create control problems. Also, our legal status is—"

"Take our legal status and shove it!" Danilov yelled. "I am not going to let us be a helpless target. If they think we *might* fire back, it will make them cautious. They will take time to close. They might even have to consult with their headquarters, which will take more time. But they do not have that much time. We are approaching Raubenheim!"

"Very well, Comrade Colonel. I suggest that we wait as long as possible before opening the doors. I really do not like our fuel state."

"SOMEBODY SHOULD TELL that pilot to— Is the phrase 'check his six'?"

"Look behind him?" Klaus Berger said.

Dieter nodded.

"He should, but he might not be able to maneuver. Or he might fear giving our friends a chance to close on him."

Not that the three helicopters flying loose formation on the Russians could do anything if they did. Bolan knew that one of them was the JetRanger with no weapons aboard except Trudl's. The two Hueys had been hastily scrambled out of a German army base, and had nothing aboard except the crews' side arms.

For psychological warfare, the three helicopters were fine. Any actual shooting would fall to the LongRanger following the Russian at treetop height, directly behind it.

They were coming over a range of hills, and Berger lifted the machine just enough to clear the crest. They flew over it along a logging road, with trees rising above them on either side. Bolan estimated that they had no more than ten feet of clearance on either side.

In spite of his level voice, Dieter's face was greenish-white. Even the Turks were trying hard to pretend that the idea of slamming into a tree at 120 miles per hour was all in a day's vengeance for Mustafa's brother.

Now they were over the crest, the last in this range of hills, the last high ground before Raubenheim. The haze and brown coal smoke kept the base itself from being visible at that distance and altitude, but Bolan knew it would show up soon.

Once it had held an entire Soviet tank division and supporting units, including a helicopter base with a swarm of Mi-24 Hind gunships. The tanks and Hinds were all gone now, but more than a caretaker party of Commonwealth military personnel remained behind.

Among them, Bolan was sure, had to be at least one man who could answer important questions about the events of the past few days. He might not answer them without a gun pointed at him, but the warrior could supply that.

"How far to Raubenheim now?" Dieter asked. It sounded as if he had a choice between talking or passing out.

"Fifteen kilometers," Berger replied, then added, "they're opening the doors on that wounded bird ahead!"

THE OPENING of the Mi-8's doors filled the cabin with a hideous din of engine, rotors, wind and tormented metal.

Helmut Kuhn didn't worry about the noise level. He wasn't going to be subjected to it long enough to damage his hearing, after all. Also, he had learned everything he needed to know, thanks to the Russians talking freely in his presence. He had expected that they wouldn't treat him harshly, for fear of injuring him. They would certainly ignore him as a physical threat—a man of nearly eighty years.

And their not knowing how much he had learned would give him the final margin he needed.

A pity that he couldn't live to pass on what he learned. But he had to give Peter Metzger or whoever was following him a clear shot. Wegener, Beck's traitor, was dead, apparently at Trudl's hands—asking her about that was another thing Kuhn would miss—and he himself was the last hostage.

Then the Spetsnaz troopers scrambled to the doors and slid them open. In each door a trooper crouched, pointing his assault rifle out into the sky.

Kuhn's face twisted. The doors were blocked—or were they? None of the troopers, he noted, had safety harnesses on. One of them was kneeling in rather an unbalanced position, and now the two men at the front of the cabin were looking forward into the cockpit. Colonel Danilov apparently had some orders.

If they were for the treatment of his guest, they were about to become superfluous.

Helmut Kuhn moved much faster than most men of his age. The Spetsnaz trooper's balance still might have survived an effort to grapple and throw him out. Kuhn didn't bother with that.

He simply lunged into the man, knocking him forward. Kuhn still weighed nearly 180 pounds, and that generated a solid impact. The Spetsnaz soldier held on to his rifle a moment too long, and when he did let go his torso was already outside the helicopter in the slipstream.

The slipstream and rotor wash did the rest. The man had time for one scream that Kuhn heard. Then Kuhn himself was outside, in the churning air along the helicopter's fuselage.

He dropped out of it swiftly into near-silence except for the air rushing past him. He had never realized how quiet the sky could be, when you were alone in it, with nothing between it and you. He was annoyed when the Spetsnaz soldier screamed one more time, and relieved when the scream was suddenly cut off.

The earth rushed up at Helmut Kuhn. He stopped worrying about goodbyes he hadn't said. Then a stone wall smashed his skull and broke his back in a single flare of light and darkness mixed together, and he stopped worrying about anything.

TRUDL KUHN'S BREATH turned solid in her throat as she saw the two men falling from the helicopter. One was Spetsnaz, but the other—

"Turn back!" she shouted at the pilot. "See who those men were!"

The pilot looked at her. She put a hand on the MP-5 K. It was an unnecessary gesture. He was already manipulating cyclic and collective to drop the JetRanger out of formation with the two Hueys and examine the bodies. Meanwhile, his copilot was on the radio.

Static crackled, making Peter Metzger's voice barely recognizable.

"You confirm two jumpers?"

"Roger. We are making a visual ID check."

"Confirm IDs if possible and signal us. Don't take off again without orders."

Trudl glared at the radio.

The pilot searched for a clear space near the bodies. They were fairly well separated, so he picked the one Trudl said looked like her grandfather and landed close to it.

"Miss Kuhn, I am sorry to have to ask you, but—"

Trudl swallowed. "I know. I am the only one who can be sure. I will be back when I am sure. Then, please leave me alone."

"Of course."

She felt the pilot's eyes on her all the way to the body, so she didn't cry until she had identified it and made her report. Then she sat down, holding her grandfather's hand the way she remembered him holding hers when she was a little girl. The sun-warmed stone wall was comfortable under her, and there was nobody to see her cry.

"CONFIRMATION," Dieter said. He was still pale, but now his voice held cold rage. "The identified jumper was Helmut Kuhn. He is dead. The second jumper has not been identified. The JetRanger will remain with the Kuhns for security."

"May God receive him into Paradise," Bora said. He counted his magazines. "Perhaps we can even give him an escort there, if Mr. Berger can make this machine go faster."

"If nobody minds walking home, we can overtake them very nicely," Berger said. "Only hang on. This might be a little bit rough."

Bolan, an experienced helicopter passenger, knew that Berger was making a considerable understatement.

"HE WHAT?" Danilov screamed. The pilot winced at such raw fury so close to his ears.

"The prisoner jumped—" the Walrus said. His normally florid face was several shades paler than usual, and he was twisting one end of a sweat-sodden mustache.

"How?"

"The man assigned to watch him was on duty at the door. The old German . . . we did not think . . ."

"You certainly did not think!" Danilov screamed. The PSM suddenly filled his fist and he fired two bullets into his subordinate's chest. He put a hand to the holes as they started to bleed, then looked at Danilov with more curiosity than anger.

A hand gripped Danilov's wrist. It twisted as he swung around to grapple with the hand's owner, but something sharp suddenly slipped into his thigh. He looked down.

The copilot was holding a combat knife, the point several centimeters into Danilov's left leg. Then he twisted again, and pain and surprise made Danilov drop the automatic. The copilot scooped it up and dropped it into a pocket of his flight jacket.

"Comrade Colonel, the next time you draw a weapon aboard this helicopter, one of us will shoot *you*," the pilot said. He might have been saying that he preferred beet borscht to cabbage borscht, for all the expression in his voice.

It was that which convinced Danilov that he should hold on to what was left of his sanity.

THE LONGRANGER MIGHT not have caught the Mi-8 in time if the two Hueys hadn't maneuvered between the Russian machine and its goal of Raubenheim. Making alternate passes across its nose, they forced the pilot to turn in slow circles just outside the secured area. He didn't dare hover, and he was reluctant to land.

That might push Danilov over the edge. The pilot knew he wouldn't be doing his duty to the others aboard if he allowed that to happen. A fight between him and Danilov would doom them all.

Also, those Hueys might have enough paratroops or whatever the Germans used on this kind of mission to cordon off the landing zone. The pilot wouldn't drop men he had carried so far into enemy hands at the last moment.

So he also maneuvered, using all his skill and flying the battered Mi-8 right at the outermost edge of its envelope. The unarmed dogfight was still going on when the LongRanger caught up, with the Executioner crouched in the door. He and Klaus Berger were the only two men aboard who hadn't become slightly airsick during the past wild minutes of chasing the Russian at treetop height or below.

The Weatherby was made for precision shooting from a fixed position at a fixed target. Air-to-air gunnery wasn't part of its design specifications.

But design specifications go out the window when a good man holds a gun, and the Executioner was the best. Aptitude, training and long familiarity with the rifle added up to more than design.

His first hit only punched metal, but the clang of the impact told everyone aboard the helicopter that they'd been caught. The pilot looked inquiringly at Danilov. The colonel looked longingly at the base perimeter, no more than two kilometers away.

"Start him down," Danilov said, then turned to the copilot. "I suppose you will trust me with my pistol now?"

"Of course, Comrade Colonel."

Danilov had just holstered his weapon when the LongRanger maneuvered to give Bolan a head-on shot.

Even a pebble sucked into a turbine engine could be fatal. The second round had many times the kinetic enrgy of a pebble. Turbine blades didn't just crack, they shattered. The damaged engine died on the spot, and flying debris started the other one winding down.

The pilot managed to put the helicopter into autorotation. That and the low altitude brought the aircraft down on top of a low hill, bare except for a few stone walls. One of the walls snapped off the tail rotor, but that was the total extent of the damage.

Flying bits of turbine blade and molten lead had pierced fuel tanks and fuel lines. The helicopter should have come down as a fireball. But too much fuel had been used or leaked out. There was nothing left to explode, hardly much left to burn.

The pilot pushed Danilov after the copilot, then fumbled for his straps. Danilov bent to help him, but the pilot pushed him away, then handed the colonel his own Makarov.

"You need it—" the pilot began. Any more words were lost in a spray of blood. The pilot coughed to clear his throat, then his eyes glazed over and he fell back into his blood-smeared seat.

Danilov looked from the dead pilot to the dead Sasha, to his handful of live men scrambling out the door. The pilot had bought him a last chance, one he probably really didn't deserve but that he would take anyway.

Slinging his AKR, Danilov hurried after his men.

IT TOOK ONLY a couple of passes for Danilov to realize which helicopter was dangerous. It was that civilian Bell, the one that they hadn't seen until after Helmut Kuhn's death. That was the one with the GSG-9 sniper or whomever they had aboard.

With that knowledge, Danilov's training and that of his men gave them a chance. Moving when the other helicopters were overhead, going down when the sniper's mount swept overhead, they leapfrogged most of a kilometer toward the base fence.

One more kilometer. A thousand meters, and they would be safe. They were expected, and Danilov had brought a lightweight radio and confirmed this.

Eight hundred meters. Five hundred. One of the troopers went down, his thigh drilled by a heavy-caliber bullet. Blood gushed, and Danilov could see white shattered bone in the wound. He shot the man in the head and took his AK-74.

He shot a full magazine into the sky. Was the sniper's helicopter taking evasive action? It was getting cloudy now. In the dimmer light Danilov could see the green lines of tracer from his men's weapons, the red lines reaching down from the automatic weapon in the helicopter.

Only two magazines left, but only two hundred meters to go. Danilov signaled to his men, and the copilot waved a reply.

The men jumped up and raced toward the fence that marked the perimeter, while Danilov jumped up and ran the other way. His rifle blazed green into the sky, and this time the helicopter flew across one of those lines. He saw holes appear, saw smoke from the engine, but didn't see the grim-faced figure aiming the heavy rifle from the left-side door.

So Nikolai Feodorovich Danilov died without knowing how, as the Executioner's shot smashed into his forehead and ripped off the top of his skull.

BOLAN SAW HIS MAN go down, then heard Klaus Berger shout to hang on, they had to land. A moment later the LongRanger came down in what was more crash than landing, but stayed upright. Berger cut the power before anything could catch fire, and the rotor blades only chewed their ends off slicing up stony turf.

They climbed out, Bora helping Ismail, who had taken a bullet in the foot from the last desperate Spetsnaz trooper. Then they all scurried for cover, or at least rocks large enough to make them difficult targets. There were four Spetsnaz men left, all of them carrying weapons, and they were still fifty meters short of the wire. If they thought they were still in danger...

They were, but not from Bolan's men. From guard towers to the left and right, machine-gun barrels suddenly thrust out. Yellow-white flame winked, and green tracers swept along the fence.

Like puppets with their strings cut, the last Spetsnaz survivors collapsed. Bolan thought he saw one actually touch the wire before he died. Then there were only four sprawled shapes to add to all the others, as the machine guns fell silent.

"What the devil was that all about?" Dieter asked. He looked as if he was finally out of his depth.

"I think it's known as 'eliminating embarrassing witnesses,' " Bolan replied. He had to translate that into German for Ismail, and Ismail translated it into Turkish for Bora, but nobody disagreed.

BY THE TIME Bolan climbed out of one of the Hueys, Trudl Kuhn was cried out. She sat beside a rosebush, leaning against the wall, looking at the abandoned garden plot where the bodies were being laid out. A Stal-

lion helicopter had brought in a mob of paratroopers
policemen and other efficient well-armed people, an
they were hard at work.

She still needed an arm braced on the wall to get to he
feet. It didn't hurt that Bolan gripped her other han
and gave her even more help. After a moment, she eve
felt steady enough on her feet to lean against him.

"I'm not going to cry again, Peter."

"Never?"

"Not today, anyway."

She kept that promise, even when she stood in th
circle of his arms, looking down at her grandfather'
body. But her grandfather made that easy.

Those who die violent deaths do not look peaceful
and an old man who has fallen five hundred feet is no
a pretty sight. But Helmut Kuhn was in death what h
had been in life, a man who looked very hard to stop.

Some of the Spetsnaz looked the same way. Trud
suspected that after a few years she wouldn't be angr
with them. She might even recognize them as brave me
who had died for a bad reason, very much like the sol
diers of the Third Reich.

But there was one man, with Peter's bullet through hi
mouth, who was different. Trudl knew without bein
told that he was the one behind all this.

"That's the leader," she said.

"We think so. How did you guess?"

"Look at his face," Trudl said. "Do you remembe
the *Totenkopf* badge of the Waffen-SS, the white death'
head?"

"Yes."

"He looks just like that."

EPILOGUE

Bolan indulged himself in a few luxuries during his last few days in Berlin.

One was a secure telephone call to Hal Brognola, using a new line laid into the office of the now-defunct Beck organization. It was being taken over by the BND, with Dieter as project officer, and Bolan had the run of the place.

"To put it as briefly as possible, Hans Wegener was able to lay hands on about five million dollars of his father's Nazi loot. That was the initial stake for Willi Beck, when he went free-lance."

"Didn't Beck ever get curious about the source of the money?" Brognola asked.

"If he did, we'll never know. I think Beck was having too much fun to worry about little details like that."

"Fun." Brognola didn't raise his voice, but he made the word sound like an obscenity. "His fun certainly got a lot of people killed."

"He probably never thought it would end that way. Meanwhile, though, he certainly wasn't going to alienate the man to whom he owed so much."

The Executioner heard Brognola grunt. "Is that all?"

"The BND has a team trying to fill in the details, but right now they're trying to find out who Wegener was running in their service. They want to clean their own house first.

"Even when they're done with that, they'll have their work cut out for them. Most of the people who knew the details are dead.

"You understand that most of them deserve it. But the fact remains, the only living man who knows the real secrets is some GRU officer at Raubenheim, and guess what our chances are of talking to him?" Bolan didn't mention his own suspicion that there might be a second man—or else the one GRU man had been playing the two senior Spetsnaz officers off against each other.

"You sound like you want to track him down."

"If I knew who he was, he'd be history. But I can't just barge in and start shooting, so the loose ends are going to stay loose."

"Including our Basques?" Brognola asked.

"Keep in mind that the men they killed were all suspects in two or three murders apiece, and the usual assortment of gang activities. The Germans aren't shedding too many tears for them, and neither am I."

"That makes three of us," Brognola said. "But keep a low profile in Berlin, Striker. It would be embarrassing for you to be popped by some two-bit Basque after fighting a whole platoon of Spetsnaz."

"Embarrassing isn't the word I would use, Hal, but I take your point."

The other luxury was a long weekend with Trudl Kuhn.

They checked into the Hotel Egwe, and Trudl showed Bolan *her* Berlin, as much of it as they could manage in three days. He was there to talk her through nightmares.

They both knew it was all they would have of each other, but they were grateful to have that much.

It was the last evening before Bolan flew out of Tegel for Dulles, and they were eating a late-evening snack in a Kurfürstendamm coffeehouse. Trudl stirred cream into her coffee and frowned.

"Problems, Trudl?"

She shook her head. "No. It has just begun to sink in that I am a millionaire at twenty-two. Oh, Ilse and many of my grandfather's old friends will get a good deal. But I am a very rich woman."

"So think of something to do with it."

"I have been. Do you know that I actually thought of going on with Beck's work, and my grandfather's?"

"You have the right instincts for it."

"Yes, but there is more than instinct. There is not being a beautiful young woman whom no one will take seriously."

Bolan nodded.

"There is military knowledge. And there is not having nightmares about the people you kill."

"Hans Wegener isn't worth nightmares."

"No, and he doesn't get any. He killed my father even if not with his own hands. But there would be others, not so evil. Then the nightmares would come, and you would not be here to help me with them."

Bolan sipped his coffee in silence. Trudl probably had already made up her mind. She wanted an audience, more than she wanted advice.

"I think I will go back and finish at the Free University," she said. "That will give me time to think, and maybe teach me how. Or maybe I will find something that I can do well, with proper training.

"My grandfather was right. Germany will always need all the help she can get, to be what she ought to be. If

some of the help can come from me, my grandfather wil
sleep easier.''

Bolan didn't mention that Helmut Kuhn's grand
daughter could also sleep more easily. The word was ou
in the appropriate circles—any trouble for Trudl Kuhn
meant much worse for the people who caused it. Brog
nola had called in markers for that one, but the Execu
tioner would enforce the order on his own if necessary.

Trudl looked down at her coffee cup. "If I have an
more, I shall not sleep tonight." She grinned. "But then
I was not planning to." She raised her hand and sig
naled for the waiter.

A biochemical weapons conspiracy puts
America in the hot seat. Don't miss

With a desperate situation brewing in Europe, top-secret
STONY MAN defense teams target an unseen enemy.
America unleashes her warriors in an all-out counterstrike
against overwhelming odds!

A new warrior breed blazes a trail
to an uncertain future in

JAMES AXLER

DEATH LANDS®

Twilight Children

Ryan Cawdor and his band of warrior-survivalists are transported
from one Valley of the Shadow of Death to another, where they
find out that the quest for Paradise carries a steep price.

In the Deathlands, the future looks terminally brief.

BATTLE FOR THE FUTURE IN A WASTELAND OF DESPAIR

EARTHBLOOD

AURORA QUEST

by JAMES AXLER

The popular author of DEATHLANDS® brings you the gripping conclusion of the Earthblood trilogy with AURORA QUEST. The crew of the U.S. space vessel *Aquila* returns from a deep-space mission to find that a devastating plant blight has stripped away all civilization.

In what's left of the world, the astronauts grimly cling to a glimmer of promise for a new start.

Available in July at your favorite retail outlet.

Don't miss out on the action in these titles featuring
THE EXECUTIONER, ABLE TEAM and PHOENIX FORCE

The Freedom Trilogy

Features Mack Bolan along with ABLE TEAM and
PHOENIX FORCE as they face off against a communist
dictator who is trying to gain control of the troubled
Baltic State and whose ultimate goal is world supremacy.

The Executioner #61174	BATTLE PLAN	$3.50	☐
The Executioner #61175	BATTLE GROUND	$3.50	☐
SuperBolan #61432	BATTLE FORCE	$4.99	☐

The Executioner ®

With nonstop action, Mack Bolan represents ultimate
justice, within or beyond the law.

#61178	BLACK HAND	$3.50	☐
#61179	WAR HAMMER	$3.50	☐

(limited quantities available on certain titles)

TOTAL AMOUNT	$
POSTAGE & HANDLING	$
($1.00 for one book, 50¢ for each additional)	
APPLICABLE TAXES*	$ _____
TOTAL PAYABLE	$ _____
(check or money order—please do not send cash)	

To order, complete this form and send it, along with a check or money order for the
total above, payable to Gold Eagle Books, to: **In the U.S.:** 3010 Walden Avenue,
P.O. Box 9077, Buffalo, NY 14269-9077; **In Canada:** P.O. Box 636, Fort Erie, Ontario,
L2A 5X3.

Name: _____

Address: _____ City: _____

State/Prov.: _____ Zip/Postal Code: _____

*New York residents remit applicable sales taxes.
 Canadian residents remit applicable GST and provincial taxes.

GEBACK5